Star Ranger

Book 1

Andy Mac

Invoke Creations

First published by Invoke Creations, Canberra.

Star Ranger Book 1 of the Star Ranger Saga

Copyright © 2025 by Andy Mac

First edition.

ISBN: 978-0-6456235-2-9

This novel is entirely a work of fiction. The names, character and incidents portrayed in it are the work of the author's imagination. Any resemblance to actual persons, living or dead, events or localities is entirely coincidental.

Andy Mac asserts the moral right to be identified as the author of this work.

Requests to publish work from this book should be sent to:

info@invokecreations.com

Visit the author's website at www.andymaccreative.com

Cover art was created by Nicola Matthews © 2025

Typeset using Atticus

To my two beautiful children,

you are my everything.

Chapter 1

STORMS

God damn storms!

Rainstorms, sandstorms, ice storms, and even solar storms. Always storms. Always violent. Always a pain in my ass!

Hot red sand from the planet's surface beats against Seth's high-tech exploration suit, attempting to shred it to pieces. Sand has a knack for finding its ways into even the smallest of places and making things uncomfortable. Seth hopes he left nothing on his pack, his chest rig, or his suit open to give his adversary the opportunity it needs to make his life harder.

A powerful gust of wind stops Seth in his tracks as he attempts to push deeper into the storm. He has to lean forward so that he doesn't get pushed backwards or, even worse, knocked over. Aside from his son, tucked away safely in the dropship days away on foot, he's the only soul on this planet. And yet, he'd still be embarrassed if he fell over like some rookie. His pride and ego won't let that happen.

Taking advantage of the pause, the powerful gust of wind forces upon his march forward, he checks the heads-up display in his helmet. Suit integrity is at one hundred percent. "Good times." He jokes to himself as he laughs at the situation.

Seth shrugs off the planet's attempts to ruin his day. As annoying as the storm is, he doesn't care that much, it is part of the job. The main thing annoying him about the storm is that he will have to spend the next month removing sand from places he didn't know existed. And the dog. "That damn dog will have crap in its artificial hair, indefinitely. I'm still removing grass seeds from the dog's coat from a planet we scouted three contracts ago." Seth grumbles. These are all minor inconveniences for him and conversations to have with himself to help keep him sane.

Once the wind gives in a little, he pushes on. Seth is a Planet Scout and one of the best in the galaxy.

Since humanity left Ancient Earth and arrived in the Core system long ago, the Space Corp, the military arm of the Galactic Government, had done all scouting of new planets and systems outside of colonised space. But with recent advancements in faster than light travel, humanity has found so many planets suitable for mining or colonisation that it is cheaper and safer to get contractors to do the scouting. This frees up the military to deal with warring planets, pirates, and makeshift governments trying it on with the galactic hierarchy.

Once scouted, the contractor crews, via their current Corporation assignment, detail all information back to the government, who technically 'own' the planet. If they find the planet suitable for colonisation or high yield mining, the government will sell it off to one of the Mega Corporations. The Mega Corps, as most people refer to them as, will either mine the planet dry or start a new colony. Whichever option they choose, it is done with profit in mind. And they always make a profit, even with the high government taxes and payouts.

This is the last sector Seth needs to scout before he and the family can get off the planet and leave the system. He has been on the surface exploring this rock with his son and daughter for well over a month now. Personally, Seth prefers to stay on a planet for an entire scout, but he will let the kids go between the surface and their ship sitting in orbit. He runs a rotating roster depending on the surface conditions of the planet and the system conditions in orbit. This is their third contract back-to-back with no time off except for the travel between systems. They are all looking forward to a well-deserved break back within colonised space. Seth doesn't like too much downtime though, so their break will only be short. Only rest as little as needed, he always tells the kids.

The storm is increasing in its intensity again, as if the planet is trying to keep Seth around for a little longer. This planet is habitable, but it's also a shithole and on the decline. It's made of rock and sand and has no large bodies of water on the surface or underground, according to the scans they did from space upon entry. No oxygen or specialist suits are required to keep him alive on its surface, but it sure helps with the sandstorm. Regardless of where he scouts, Seth always wears his high-tech one-piece exploration suit under all his exploration gear. Not only does it keep him in a stable condition so that he doesn't die from the environmental extremities a new planet can throw at him, it also keeps him comfortable and clean.

Chaffing, blisters, ingrown hairs, infections, and other annoying minor issues like these are not the dangers people think a Planet Scout would face on a day-to-day basis. The average spacer and planet dweller thinks extreme climates, indigenous creatures that want to eat you alive, or falling down a giant crevasse to your death are a day-to-day occurrence. Civilians romanticise the life of a Planet Scout. They think it's all action and adventure. Maybe for some of the lucky few who get sent to scout out a cushy tier-one planet, but not Seth. Seth and his 'crew' have become the best at what they do because of their meticulous attention to detail, solid planning, and extreme levels of discipline, not risk taking and adventure seeking. It's the little things far outside of colonised space that can bring a mission to an abrupt and deadly end.

Over his high-tech suit, he wears a chest rig which carries some of his daily go to items. Lighting systems, comms units, ropes, and other scouting tools. He also carries a specialised medium-sized backpack that connects to his suit. It holds most of the things he will need to keep himself alive should he become stranded or stuck for a couple of days before the kids could come and get him. Even though not required on this planet, he wears his fully enclosed helmet and connects it to his suit for a complete seal, something he is glad to have done in the current sandstorm. The helmet not only protects him from the elements, but it filters out the sand, dust and any pathogens that may be in the planet's air. The heads-up display in the large glass visor shows all his nav points and environmental data that he wants displayed.

Strapped to his right leg is his sidearm. A specialised pistol good for rapid, powerful fire at ranges out to about one hundred metres. A farewell gift from his previous employment. The information he gathered from the recon they did from orbit before landing on the planet backed up the data provided to him by the Corp, that this rock was barren and void of life. Which after spending the last month plus on the ground he can confirm to be true. But he has learned the hard way from previous inaccurate Corp reports, so he always conducts his own orbital recon first and always carries his sidearm. Alien bats spawning out of caves or two-foot-long blood thirsty lizards trying to eat you while you sleep make for the opposite of a good time.

Moving out of a desolate open plain, although it's hard to tell in the storm, Seth pushes into a large rocky ravine. The red dust is playing tricks on his built-in optics and heads-up display, so he turns them off and looks through the glass of his visor to get a better view.

Suddenly, he sees something move against the flow of the storm. "Ray!" Seth calls out over the raging winds to his cyber-netic AI dog. The dog moves in by his side, ready and waiting for a command. "Can you see anything up ahead, boy?" The dog looks for a second, then stares back up at him blankly. "Ok, I guess I'm losing my mind then. Come on, stay close."

Seth heads deeper into the ravine, Ray in a heel at his left side. After several more minutes of walking through the storm, he sees something move again. He stops and stares to make sure it's not his eyes playing tricks on him. *That can't be.* He thinks to himself. In the distance, he sees what looks like a redheaded woman in a flowing red dress dancing in and out of the storm.

"Sara!" He screams out at the top of his lungs as his heart pounds. The woman fades back into the storm out of view, so he sprints forward, overwhelmed by emotions. As he reaches the spot where he saw the woman, he frantically begins searching for her. *Maybe she survived, maybe she got stranded on this shithole of a planet.* A myriad of thoughts run through his head, justifying how his wife could still be alive and on this planet. Even after her disappearance and assumed death ten years ago. In his frantic searching, he hears a soft voice come over the wind, or is it the wind itself?

Sssssssssssssseeeeeeeeeetttttttthhhhhhhhhhhhhhhhhhhhh

The voice calls his name. He frantically looks around and sees her again. This time near the base of the cliff wall. He rushes after her, Ray in tow, unsure what his master is searching for. As he gets closer, the image comes into focus. It is his lost wife. After all these years, he has found her. As he gets close to her, she smiles and disappears back into the red sand of the storm. He feels tears swelling in his eyes and a pain deep in his chest. Cursing, he looks around, searching for her in the storm. He sees her once more off in the distance. This time, he simply stares at her. *Why would she be wearing a dress, Seth? How would her hair move like that in the storm, Seth?* The critical thinking part of his brain starts to speak up. She smiles at him again before turning around and walking into the cliff face. He does not run to her this time, however. This time, he slows down to a walk as reality starts to take hold.

When will this stop my love?

He feels the pain in his chest grow as he realises this is just another vision.

Seth started having visions of his wife over a year ago, but they seem to be happening more frequently now. The more recent visions of Sara have become more lifelike. Until recently, what he saw was less like a vision and more like momentary glimpses of someone just out of sight. However, his most recent visions seem to be directing or leading him somehow. And that's what Seth feels is happening here.

The hot red sand of the storm continues to beat against his suit as he slowly drifts towards the cliff face, one foot in front of the other. When he reaches Sara's last location, he discovers that there is an entrance to a cave. *Is this what you wanted me to see? Are you trying to show me something?* Seth seems confused. Looking inside, he sees nothing but darkness and sighs. The weight of his lost wife bearing down on him. Seth stands there for a moment and takes a few more deep breaths to regain his composure. *Alright, if this is what you want from me.* He calls Ray to his side, then taps two fingers on the left side of his helmet under his ear. This activates the helmet's external light source and engages low light vision in his HUD. He takes one last deep breath, still fighting back tears, before advancing forward and getting swallowed by the darkness.

The interior of the cave is rocky and dry with a layer of red sand that has blown into the cave from a millennium of storms. Seth wouldn't usually explore a cave on his own, or at all, as the risks are too high. He would scan it from space with the Scout's high-tech data collection suite. But the vision of his wife seems to pull him in. Plus, he is glad to take a break from the storm for a moment. *That's one less week of cleaning the dog*. He thinks to himself once inside.

Seth follows the cave forward, having to duck in certain parts because of the low roof and the odd stalactite getting in his way. He feels like he is moving into the mouth of a colossal beast as he heads deeper inside the cave. Suddenly and without reason, Seth feels a warm sensation flood over him, as if the temperature has changed several degrees in the cave. He looks around, unable to identify a cause for the sensation. He feels something pull at him so looks down to see his foot begin to sink into the sand covered floor. Instinctively he attempts to pull it out, but looking down, he is no longer wearing his specialised boots or any shoes at all.

"Come on Sethy, keep up." A voice echoes from in front of him. Seth looks up and sees a young Sara standing right there. She is wearing a bikini top and some small swim shorts, her beautiful red hair flowing down her tan back. "Let me take you somewhere, you haven't been for once." She says with a mischievous grin on her face. Seth, without any thought, follows her through the sandy tunnel. There is a bright blue light up ahead and he can hear water bubbling beyond. Sara moves to the exit of the white sand tunnel "Ok Sethy, when you get here, close your eyes."

"Okay." Laughs Seth. Not only is she cute, but she is also the only one he lets call him Sethy. If any of his military brothers or fellow soldiers called him that, he'd punch them right there on the spot. But he lets her get away with it. As he reaches the exit of the cave, he puts both hands over his face to show that he isn't looking. She tells him to wait there and count to twenty. He does what he is told, counting out loud for Sara to hear.

When he removes his hands from his face and opens his eyes, he is almost blinded by the light. He stands near the edge of a large crystal-clear natural pool being fed by a waterfall from high off in the jungle above. High rocky cliffs covered in a variety of green jungle plants and moss surround the entire area, giving the place a dreamlike atmosphere. He looks around to find Sara. She is standing on a rock near the edge of the natural pool. When they lock eyes, she calls out. "Well, come get in, silly!" Before he can reply, she dives into the water. He watches her for a second, amazed at how one person can be so incredibly beautiful. He follows suit by running to the rock where she had just stood, before jumping in.

The pair are all alone in one of the most beautiful places he has ever seen. He catches up to her after she makes him chase her around for a short while. When he does, she spins around, putting her face right in front of his. She then gently places her hands behind his neck and pulls him in for a kiss.

Seth shakes off the memory from what seems like a lifetime ago and looks down to make sure he is still wearing his boot. Thankfully, he is. "Argh!" He growls before hitting himself in the centre of the chest several times to shake off the emotional pain. He then takes a hard breath out before pushing deeper into the cave.

Eve lounges in the pilot's chair of the Obsidian Scout as the ship floats in a geosynchronous orbit above the red planet. Her grey and orange flight suit sits unzipped and wrapped around her waist, and she has a simple black singlet on covering her athletic upper body. She runs her hand through her long dark blonde hair. One side is in plaits and the other is still out after brushing it. "Where is he?" She complains out loud. Frustrated, because her father should have checked in by now to let her know his location, and because she is over being out here and wants to get back to colonised space. The ship needs maintenance and supplies, but more importantly, she needs some decent fresh food and some real gravity.

Frustrated, Eve slaps the comms switch. "Fin, this is the Scout, over." A couple of seconds pass without a reply. Flicking through the controls on the console, she tries again. "Fin, this is the Scout, OVER." The annoyance obvious in her voice. But still no response. She visually checks all the controls on the console, looking for any red lights or errors.

"Rose!" She calls impatiently to the ship's AI.

"Yes Eve, how can I be of assistance?" Replies the robotic female voice of the ship's AI. Eve rolls her eyes. *Dad could have chosen any voice at all for the ship's AI, but no, he had to have a grating, robotic voice.* She thinks he did it just to annoy her.

"Rose, are all the comms systems on the ship working?" She asks, confidently knowing that she has checked her work and that they are, in fact, fully operational.

"Yes Eve, all communication systems and communication paths are operating at one hundred percent."

"Are all the comms systems on the drop ship working?" She folds her arms, staring at her screen, awaiting a response. Several seconds later, the artificial voice replies.

"Yes Eve, all communications systems and communications paths are operating at one hun—" Eve cuts off the ship's AI, smacking the comms switch.

"Fin! Answer the god damn comm!"

"Unidentified call sign. This is the Obsidian Scout, drop ship Alpha. Please identify yourself." Fin replies from the drop ship down on the planet's surface. Eve's face turns bright red.

"Identify! Identify! Who else do you think is out here, you idiot?" She knows her younger brother is baiting her, but she can't help but get angry. She really needs to get back to civilisation for a couple of days.

"Settle down big sis, I was finishing up a set of push-ups. What's up, everything good?" He says, trying to calm her back down, not wanting to deal with an angry older sister when he gets back to the Scout.

"Push ups! What are you, bored or something?" She asks angrily.

"Only boring people get bored." Fin answers, impersonating one of their father's favourite come back lines.

Two years after they lost their mother, their father started taking them with him on his contracting jobs. They were only twelve and fourteen years old at the time. As expected, the pair would always complain about being bored and Seth would always respond with the phrase. 'Only boring people get bored.' This made them angrier, and they would complain even more. One day, they must have pushed their father too far with their pre-teen nagging and whiny attitudes, so he decided to not allow them the opportunity to be bored anymore.

That's when the training started. They were either working out, doing schoolwork, or learning military and scouting skills from their father for fifteen hours a day. They dedicated the remaining time to eating, cleaning, and sleeping. At first, they hated all the work their father made them do and wished they were anywhere else but on the Obsidian Scout with him. Eve can still hear her father's voice barking at her to run faster, her legs burning as she struggled through another lap around the Scout's training bay. But now, at eighteen and twenty respectively, they appreciate what he did for them. They absolutely despise sitting around doing nothing and refuse to be bored. Eve believes it was some type of child abuse that happened to turn out right.

"Dad hasn't checked in yet and I'm worried." Eve has never known her father to be late, and she is worried.

"How late is he?" Asks Fin with zero concern in his voice.

"Are you not looking at the time?"

"Yeah, no, just tell me."

"Thirty minutes."

"Thirty minutes. Is that all! Give him at least another thirty before you freak out, sis."

"What are you talking about Fin? He is never late."

"Are you not looking at the video feeds on the Scout?"

"Don't be a smart-ass Fin!"

"Seriously though, Eve, there is a massive sandstorm. It's probably messing with his comms. His entire suit would be coated in sand. I would be surprised if he can even see his hand in front of his face."

Eve pauses for a second, then rolls her eyes. *Damn it! Fin is right.*

"Okay fine. Give him thirty more minutes, then I'm officially freaking out."

"Roger that, sis. Fin, out."

Eve slumps back into the pilot's chair, checks the console once more, folds her arms, and lets out an enormous sigh.

A hundred metres beyond the entrance, the cave begins to slope downwards. The further in Seth explores, the more the cave opens, allowing Seth to stand straight without fear of hitting his head. As he ventures deeper, the sand under Seth's feet gradually gives way to smooth stone. *Too smooth.* Seth thinks to himself. He stops, confused, and has a look around. *Is this some sort of natural rock? That shouldn't be.* He reaches down and runs his gloved hand over the floor. It feels smooth to where it may have even once been polished.

Seth takes off his helmet and places it next to him on the ground. His head enjoys the break from being trapped inside its perfect grip. He runs his hand over his shaved head and short beard, making sure there is nothing attached to his skin that snuck past his helmet. He reaches back and loosens the shoulder straps on his backpack. Pulling it off and swinging it around in front of him, he opens the pack and searches inside. Finding what he wants, he pulls out a small rod. He cracks it and it lights up, filling the entire tunnel with a warm yellow glow, as if a little sun was hiding inside the rod, waiting for its moment to shine.

Now, with an improved light source, he can properly inspect the floor. He determines it was once polished, and further ahead he sees there is some type of symbol carved into it. The symbol looks like two interconnecting triangles on their sides. Every line seems to have a sharp, almost perfect sixty degree bend. "What the hell is this?" Confused, he walks ahead, holding the rod by his side so as not to blind himself. Seth studies the symbol but can't recall seeing anything like it before. He reaches up and turns on his shoulder camera so he can show the kids when he gets back to the ship.

"Shit, the kids!"

He calls them kids, but they are both technically adults now. And both are more reliable and capable than many men and women twice their age. *What time is it? I was probably supposed to check in already.* Seth checks his forearm computer and sees that he is forty minutes late for his comms check. He knows Eve will be upset and worried, which makes him feel like a piece of crap. He doesn't like letting the kids down.

"Scout, Alpha. This is Sierra One, over."

Eve replies almost instantly. "Dad, this is Eve. Is everything Okay? Why are you late with your comms check? And send a LOCSTAT."

"Sorry Eve, I thought I saw something interesting in this ravine, so I had to have a look." He can't tell her about his visions of her deceased mother. It will make her to upset, that or she will think he is crazy. "I lost track of time, sorry." He isn't sure she will believe him, as it's out of character for him. That and he would tear them a new one for being late.

"Alright Dad. Is everything okay?"

He can hear the genuine concern in her voice over the comms. This makes him feel even worse, as she must have been worrying the whole time.

"Yeah, I'm fine. I have entered a cave system and found something interesting. Let me look around, then I will get back to you shortly."

"A cave system!" Eve knows something is up now. Being late for a comms check and exploring caves is very out of character for him. "Okay but send that LOCSTAT first, and stay safe alright Dad?"

He keys in the location status report on his forearm computer. His computer gathers relevant data on his location, temperature, air quality, toxicity, and multiple other environmental factors which will help Eve and Fin if they have to come save him for any reason. This information also adds to the overall planet data pack they give to the Corp at the end of the scout. "Roger that beautiful. LOCSTAT sent." Her father's relaxed tone helps to calm Eve's nerves.

He shouldn't call her beautiful. She is not a little girl anymore. Eve is a six foot three, strong, confident woman who could kick his ass if she really wanted to. She is a better mechanic and can fly the Scout better than him with her eyes closed. Although he would never admit that to her. But, at the end of the day, she will always be his little girl, no matter what.

Once he finishes the report, he returns to what he was doing and studies the symbol carved into the floor, but nothing jumps out at him. It doesn't look familiar in any way, it doesn't look like text from any spoken languages used in the galaxy, and it doesn't look like a logo or symbol from any Corporation that explores planets or does mining. To Seth, it doesn't look human. He spends several more minutes studying the symbol from different angles, heights, and distances. It still seems very foreign to him, unlike anything he has ever seen before. Even the way it's carved into the floor differs from what he would expect. Giving up trying to figure out its meaning, he follows a small line on the polished floor to a nearby wall. *Nope, a dead end.* Looking up at the wall, he suddenly realises that it has also been polished. He takes a couple of steps back and shines the light on the wall so he can see it more clearly. The wall is almost five metres high and five metres across.

As the light bounces off the wall, he notices several dark spots which look like small openings. *What in the actual hell is this place? Why has the Corp got me searching a planet where someone has already been? Did the government lose the records for this place or something? And who made all this?* Questions flood his mind. He moves closer to the opening, shining a light inside for a better look.

"Ray, are you seeing this?" A rhetorical question. The dog's AI programming makes it more intelligent and able to process data faster than humans, but Seth also installed the K9 programming so that Ray will act like a dog. Ray stares back at him, tongue hanging out of his mouth. "Sooo you don't know either then hey boy." Seth quips knowing he is really talking to himself. The opening is about a foot across and two feet deep. Seth is hesitant to approach but can't control his curiosity. On closer inspection, Seth sees what looks like a handle inside the opening. Seth pauses for a moment, confused by what he is seeing. The only other place he has seen a handle similar to this is on the outside of an airlock on modern ships.

Hesitantly, he reaches in and gets a firm grip on the handle and pulls. Nothing happens. He tries harder. Still nothing. *Try to give it a twist old man.* He thinks to himself. The handle slowly begins to twist, then Seth hears a small mechanical click. He lets go and jumps back, scanning the room behind him for any danger. He sees nothing but isn't satisfied. "Ray, check the caves to make sure we are alone." He whispers to the dog. All his senses now on high alert.

Who could have built this? It seems like old school human tech, but when would humans have been out here? Perhaps an ancient scouting party from the Great Journey? He finds the whole situation confusing. With all the wonders humans have discovered since leaving Earth, they have never found another intelligent civilisation. Some quadrupedal pack animals as smart as dogs and some very sophisticated old flora, but no creature smart enough to build doors or polish rocks.

Ray quickly turns and sprints off back down the tunnel towards the entrance, scanning its surroundings as it goes. The dog's optics allow it to see in multiple spectrums, so it needs no light to search the cave. It also has a variety of other sensors which collect data as it goes. Waiting, Seth listens intently for a bark. Nothing. Shortly after, Ray returns, doing a quick lap around him, rubbing against his leg, then going back to the position he was in before. Sitting and staring at Seth with his tongue hanging out. "Okay so I am going crazy. That is a door handle of some sort, right?" Ray tilts his head to the side in response.

Seth returns to the opening and reaches back in, grabbing the handle. This time he twists, then pulls and hears another louder click. Anticipating the noise, this time he pays more attention. He thinks the noise is coming from inside the wall. "Okay

Ray, let's try one of the other ones I guess." He goes to the next small opening and shines his light inside. He sees another handle. "Well, alright then boy, let's see what this one does." He repeats the process and hears another click. He pauses, waiting to see if anything happens. Nothing. He looks back at Ray for recognition and gives him a nod before moving on to the remaining openings and repeating the process. He completes all the handles he can see, but nothing happens when he twists the last one. Seth moves back to Ray and studies the wall.

"What do you reckon, boy?" Seth crosses his arms, staring at the wall. "Do you think there is an order to it or something?" Seth pauses for a moment. "Sorry master, what was that? Try looking around the rest of the cave to make sure you haven't missed anything. That's what a clever boy would do?" Seth says in a goofy voice, impersonating what he thinks Ray would sound like. "Good thinking dog. I will do what you have asked of me." He chuckles to himself. *Yep, I need to get off this planet and back to colonised space.*

Seth looks around methodically from left to right and bottom to top. Meticulously searching every inch of the surrounding area of the cave. Eventually Seth finds what looks like small carvings on a part of the cave near the start of the polished floors. Upon closer inspection, Seth notices that someone has carved the same symbol on the floor into a circle on the wall. It also looks like a large stone button. *This must be it.* He calls Ray to the ready position. Ray stands up and leans back, priming his legs and lowering his head to keep his profile smaller and more aerodynamic. Seth draws his sidearm from its holster and aims it at the door.

A wave of fear and anxiety comes over him as he is unsure of what will happen when he pushes the symbol. Anything from absolutely nothing happening, to blowing up the planet are all possibilities. Taking a deep breath in, he acknowledges the feeling, then simply lets it go as he takes a slow breath out. He takes two more deep breaths and gets on with it, counting down from three. As he counts one, he pushes hard against the symbol as he grits his teeth. A dull green light emanates around a large square section of the wall, followed by a loud cracking noise and a rush of air. Ray starts barking and spinning around in circles, visibly upset. One side of the green lit square then slides open, confirming Seth's guess that it is, in fact, a giant door.

"Ray heel!" He raises his voice loud enough for the dog to hear over its own aggressive barking. Without looking, Ray quickly spins back by his side. A low growl now filling the room. "Shh, it's okay Boy." Whispers Seth to calm Ray. Once Ray is settled, Seth waits silently in position, daring not to move. *This shouldn't be here. This planet should be uninhabited. What the hell is going on?* Seth thinks as he stares at the glowing green alien like door. He has to remind himself to breathe every now and again as the anticipation of what could be beyond the door overtakes his mind.

Around ten minutes pass and he can't see or hear anything coming from the doorway. Seth relaxes his posture and holsters his sidearm as he moves over to his backpack, Ray in tow. Taking a knee, he calls up Fin and Eve over the comms.

"Scout, Alpha. This is Sierra One, over."

"Scout over."

"Alpha over."

"Sitrep. After exploring the cave, I thought I had come to a dead end. However, upon closer inspection, I found some type of foreign symbol and a man-made structure of some sort." He pauses, contemplating his words. "Well, I don't know if it's man-made, but it definitely didn't occur naturally. Anyway, there is some sort of ancient looking mechanical door that required me to open several levers and push on a symbol of some sort before it would open."

"Wait What!" He can hear Eve's high-pitched voice come down the comms link accompanied by a load of static.

"I found a door emanating a dull green light leading deeper into the cave system. So I am going to search inside. I'll give updates through Ray, as I'll lose comms if I go any deeper." Seth states confidently.

"Are you sure Dad?" Fin asks, concerned. Seth thinks he may be underestimating the whole situation if Fin is questioning him. His son is possibly the most relaxed risk taker he has ever known.

"Yeah, I'm good. I will give you guys frequent updates as I go. Ray will act as the comms relay station. Eve bring the Scout into the atmosphere. I'm keen to wrap it up and bug out of the system after I check this cave. Oh, and grab your brother on the way, will you. I'll send coordinates for a LZ. Acknowledge, over."

"Alpha, acknowledge. Stay safe and see you soon, old man. Out." Replies Fin.

"Dad!" Eve's voice rises sharply through the comms.

"Scout, acknowledge. Over!" Seth states firmly.

"Scout, acknowledge." Eve's voice lowers to one of defeat.

"Make sure you report in every ten mikes. Out." She ends the conversation before he has a chance to argue. But it doesn't matter, he will report in every ten minutes anyway. Not to keep her happy, but because she is right in ordering him to do so. She is only enforcing his own rules upon him.

Seth pulls up the digital map on his forearm computer and designates the coordinates at the start of the ravine. This is the closest and most accessible place for the Obsidian Scout to land. He turns to Ray. "Ray." He orders in a serious tone. "I want you to set up a comms relay back to Eve and Fin. I want you to pull my bio's and location info every ten minutes and send it to both callsigns until Alpha has docked back in the Scout." Ray moves into a position in the centre of the room next to Seth so that he can best pass the comms. Seth waits, checking his forearm computer for the link to establish, then sends the LZ coordinates back to Eve via Ray.

"Ray, guard."

Seth grabs his helmet and places it back on, then un-hooks the axe attached to the side of his pack. Standing up, he heads to the door, gently leaning against it in an attempt to try to open it as quietly as possible. To Seth's surprise, the door opens easily, considering its size and weight. He grips the axe in both hands before silently slipping inside.

Heading down a small winding tunnel, Seth notices that the floor remains smooth and there are even several steps. After one hundred metres, the tunnel opens to a larger cavern. Seth pauses at the entrance and strains his eyes to look around. There are several dull light sources in the roof lighting up the cavern, but he can't quite figure out what the light is coming from. Seth taps the comms link on his forearm computer to report this back to Eve and Fin. He also turns off the lighting system on his suit to see if these mysterious lights are bright enough for him to see. They are, so he leaves his off in case there are any bugs or critters in here that are drawn to bright lights.

Seth scans the area, identifying a rocky outcrop that he thinks he can climb up. From there, he can hopefully get a good look at a light source and the surrounding area. Seth steps out from the safety of the tunnel and cautiously moves into the cavern. As he gets closer to the outcrop, the lights get brighter. He quickly lowers his profile and freezes in location. *Are these things god damn sensor lights!* After pausing for a moment to scan his surroundings, he continues to the outcrop stepping over medium-sized rocks and manoeuvring around the odd boulder. Once he arrives it's an easy climb up to inspect the mysterious light source. The light is coming from a large glowing orb several metres above his already elevated position. *It is a light of some sort and not some alien creature, but where the hell is the power coming from?* Seth looks around but cannot find anything. *Is it a natural light source maybe? No, it can't be. It got brighter when I approached.*

From the rocky outcrop he has a better view of the area. The entire cavern has a polished floor, but it looks like parts of the cave system have crumbled down over what could be thousands of years. The far end of the cavern is bathed in a heavy darkness. He can't see a far wall but can identify a large rectangular boulder at the mouth of the darkness. Doing his best to stay silent, he hops off the outcrop and moves toward the boulder. On closer inspection, he sees that the large rectangular boulder has carvings all along it. Looking around, he notices to his left another large rectangular pillar reaching from the floor to the roof. It also has carvings on it. *Very interesting.*

Discovering a broken area on the right side of the cavern wall, he realises the large stone in front of him once stood tall, echoing the left pillar. *Is it some type of entrance or gate way?* Seth looks around for a moment, taking in the environment. *Only one way to find out, I guess.*

Taking his time he climbs silently onto the fallen pillar. Ahead, there's nothing but a vast sea of darkness. The lights haven't turned on in this section of the cavern yet, if there even are any lights in there to turn on. Even though he can't see into the darkness before him, he gets a sense that whatever is in front of him is enormous. The pure weight of the darkness to his front feels like it could crush him.

Seth figures that if the lighting system is movement based, the only way to get the lights to turn on is to move forward. So he climbs down the other side of the fallen pillar using some of the carvings as holds. As his feet hit the floor, the lighting system instantly starts to turn on. Seth stands watching in awe as the lights come on one at a time, revealing what lies in front of him. As each light turns on its as if an explosion of space ignites in front of him. *You could comfortably fit an entire galactic class transport frigate inside this place!* Seth can't even see the other side of the cavern as the lights are still turning on. The giant expanse of the cavern sends a chill down his spine.

He quickly sends back another report to the kids.

Moving forward, Seth doesn't realise, because of the dull lighting, that he crosses over a large set of symbols on the floor. This set is four interlocking triangles as opposed to the two back at the entrance. As he crosses over the symbols, the floor of the giant cavern lights up in front of his eyes. A dull green glow, like the one that came from the entrance, emanates from tiny ruts carved all throughout the cavern's floor adding more light to the enormous area. "Holy crap! What the hell is this place?" Seth has never seen anything like this before in his life.

Before he takes another step forward, a loud crack resounds from the other end of the cavern. It sounds like stone breaking apart and crashing onto the cavern's floor. Freezing in place and lowering his profile, Seth looks around. His heart beats loudly in his chest. *Control your breathing and check your surrounds for danger old man.* Seth orders himself as he takes a couple of deep breaths to help calm himself down. Last thing he wants is to be stuck in a cave-in or killed by a giant boulder falling from the roof high above.

The sound of what Seth believes to be falling rocks ceases, and his shoulders ease as he senses no immediate danger nearby. Standing up, he feels a faint tremor ripple through his body, followed by an eerie, all-encompassing silence that swallows the cavern. Before he can fully process what's happening, a series of stronger vibrations surge through him like crashing waves, stealing the air from his lungs. Then, without warning, a deafening, earth-shattering roar reverberates through the cavern. The sheer force of the sound drives him to his knees.

Chapter 2

TRAINING

The powerful thundering roar reverberating throughout the cavern eventually stops. Seth shakes his head and tries to pop his ears as he stands back up and scans the area. There was something guttural and tortuous to the sound. But once his helmet's audible features kicked in and dulled the ear-splitting noise, he swore he could hear faint hints of feedback. The type you get from an old ship's analogue speaker system. In all of Seth's travels, he has never seen or heard of anything that can make a noise like that. Seth feels a cold sweat run down his back. *Switch on!* He commands himself as he remains in the present, breathing deeply and focusing on his surroundings. As much as his instinct is to run back to the ship, he must find out what that noise came from. It's his job. Reaching down, he makes sure his sidearm is secure in its holster, then he squeezes his axe tightly in both hands.

The Military Academy on Utopia is a buzz with activity as family members from all over the galaxy come to see their son's and daughter's graduation parade. Seth looks out the window of the small room he has lived in for the best part of a year.

The odd combination of starch, polished brass, and shoeshine fills the air. He watches as the families of the recruits walk past in their best formal outfits. Mothers wear funny hats and carry tissues, while the fathers wear ill-fitting suits. Seth knew in advance that his parents couldn't afford to travel to the Core system to see his graduation, but they would be watching the live broadcast that the Academy was filming. Which still gave him a sense of pride.

"Recruit McCallan." Calls out a stern voice. Seth spins around in an instant.

"Yes Sir." Seth answers back in a loud voice. The Drill Sergeant stands in the doorway of his room looking as mean and foreboding as he did on the first day Seth arrived at the Academy.

"How bout you stop gawking out the goddamn window recruit, and put your goddamn feet together when I'm talking to you… if you're not to fucking busy that is!" The Drill Sergeants voice gets louder as he fires up, and the more he fires up the more he curses. Seth knows that the Drill Sergeant is going to task him with something, so he stands at attention, waiting for a command.

"Better. Now how bout you grab the rest of this sorry arse platoon and get outside and form up so I can make sure you bunch of soft jawed weaklings aren't going to embarrass me today!"

"Yes Sir!" Seth replies loudly and confidently.

Seth moves from near the window to leave the room, but the Drill Sergeant doesn't budge. He stands in the doorway, staring daggers at the recruit. Seth has to duck around the Drill Sergeant doing his best not to mess up his dress uniform while daring not to touch the instructor. The Drill Sergeant grunts at the recruit as he slides by.

When he gets into the hallway, he stands to attention again and shouts out as loud as he can, using his diaphragm, just as they have taught him to do. "THIRD PLATOON! ON PARADE!" The hallway fills with recruits who rush outside to the small parade ground at the entrance to the recruit's accommodation. They move as quickly as they can, also doing their best not to mess up their dress uniforms. Seth makes his way down the corridor, checking each room while the Drill Sergeant marches behind him, stalking him like a predator stalks its prey.

Outside the accommodation block, the soldiers of Third Platoon form up in three ranks. Two ranks of ten and one of nine. The last spot being for Seth, who is the tallest recruit. Being the tallest means, he gets the pleasure of having to stand at the front, leading the platoon and setting the pace for the platoon. All things to get a beasting for if done incorrectly, or not to the good Drill Sergeants standards. Seth runs over to his position and stands at ease along with the rest of the recruits in the platoon.

The Drill Sergeant marches around to the front of the group and calls them to attention. All the recruits snap to attention, making one loud crack as all thirty pairs of boots slam into the ground simultaneously. The Drill Sergeant then moves down each rank, inspecting every recruit's dress and bearing. After re arranging several soldier's uniforms and dressing down several more for looking like 'bags of shit', the Drill Sergeant moves back to the front of the platoon.

"Right, listen in Third Platoon. The good Platoon Commander wants to say a few words. So, make sure you listen in hard, as I know your little pea brains can't retain information, even when your pathetic lives depended on it!" The Drill Sergeant marches to the rear of the platoon as the Platoon Commander, who was off to the opposite side, marches to the front.

The Platoon Commander is a fit, tall, good-looking man in his mid to late twenties who seems to slide into place with poise and grace. He is the complete opposite of the Drill Sergeant, who seems to punish the planet's surface with every step he makes.

"Third platoon. Stand at… Ease." The Platoon Commanders voice has a much softer and posh tone to it than the Drill Sergeants. The platoon snaps back to the at ease position, feet apart and hands clasped behind their backs.

"Third platoon." The Platoon Commander says to get their attention, as if he is about to give another command. "As you should all be aware, the military academies Commanding Officer will host today's parade. You have all rehearsed this multiple times, but there will be a little surprise. Today the Commanding Officer will award the Student of Merit." This is not a surprise to any of the recruits, but none dare mention that to the Platoon Commander.

"Having watched your performances over the past year, I can only assume that someone from Third Platoon will be named Student of Merit." There are some excited whispers amongst the group and Seth can feel the mood change to one of excitement.

"Shut up, keep your panties on, and listen in Third!" Yells the Drill Sergeant. Reminding the recruits that he is right behind them and watching their every move.

The Platoon Commander smiles. "If you are the deserving soldier and your name gets called out, answer the normal way by shouting Sir. From there, come to attention and fall out of formation and march to the front of the podium and come to a halt, being sure to stay at attention. Then the CO will call you up. March up, salute, then do as asked by the CO or his staff officer. If the CO gives you anything, hold it in your left hand, shake his hand with your right hand, then step back and salute. When the CO is finished with you, he will dismiss you and you can march back to your position. Do you understand Third Platoon?"

"Yes Sir!" The platoon answers in unison.

"Good. I believe the Regimental Sergeant Major and several other guests will be on the podium with the CO. So be sure not to embarrass me." The Platoon Commander pauses and looks over the platoon, making sure they are representing him to the highest standard. Satisfied, he calls the platoon back to attention, then summons the Drill Sergeant back into position before marching off.

"Well, it looks like the Platoon Commander thinks very highly of you. That or he knows something that I don't." States the Drill Sergeant in a sarcastic voice. "Like all the other platoons are filled with shit-eating, mouth breathers, and one of you turds somehow got Student of Merit by managing to not crap your panties for a whole day!" Even though the Drill Sergeant and all the other instructors constantly yell and scream abuse at the recruits Seth knows it's all part of the game. It's about making them excellent soldiers. Seth once saw the Drill Sergeant punch another instructor for bad-mouthing Third Platoon. The instructors care for their recruits and want every recruit to be the best soldier possible. For some weird reason, they find the best way to do that is by beasting them for eighteen hours a day.

Under the Drill Sergeant's instruction, the platoon marches off towards the large parade ground for their last parade as recruits.

Seth stands at ease behind the giant parade ground with all the other platoons lined up in ranks and files. He tries to catch a glimpse of the crowds out of the corner of his eyes, but he dares not turn his head to look around. The Drill Sergeant has installed a healthy fear in all the recruits, so the mere thought of even moving an inch while on parade sends an icy shiver down Seth's spine.

There are thirty-four platoons making up over one thousand military recruits. From the smell of perfume in the air and the loud hum of conversations, Seth guesses the crowd is at least ten times that. Filled with families, instructors, academy staff, high-ranking military officers, and government officials. Only one course a year graduates from the Utopian Military Academy, making it a big event for all the locals, soldiers, and veterans from the Core system. They all come out to watch the parade, remember good and bad times, and catch up with old friends for a drink or two. The Core system has always been very patriotic and proud of the Galactic Military and what it does for humanity.

The parade runs as they have practised. They all march on to the sound of the band, who play traditional military music, they form up, they come to attention for dignitaries as they arrive, and they stand at ease trying not to pass out when speeches take much longer than they should. Thankfully, the parade is only running slightly over time from what Seth can tell.

As the speeches drag on, Seth's mind drifts back to another parade, years ago, when he sat in awe of the soldiers marching before him. The soldiers looked so impressive. Strong looking men and women with a confidence he had not seen in a person before. Ever since that moment, he wanted to join the military. He too, wanted to be professional, strong, and proud of himself, just like the graduating recruits were. Plus, he never wanted an office job like his parents had, working for the Galactic Government back on their home planet. Seth craved action and adventure, even if he didn't actually know what that meant yet.

Finally, it comes time for the Commanding Officer to an-nounce the Student of Merit before giving his thanks and farewell speech. Seth wondered if someone from his platoon might actually get the Student of Merit award, or if the Platoon

Commander was talking himself and the platoon up. Recruit Zanilt got a perfect score on all his shoots, and Recruit Al-abreen smashed out all the medical training. Both her parents were surgeons on Elysia, and she was determined to become a military doctor. So, her performance in the medical training section of the course wasn't a surprise to anyone.

The Commanding Officer begins his speech by thanking all the VIP's and relevant officials whom Seth and most of the recruits have never heard of. He then gets to the part about the Student of Merit. The slight rustling of uniforms ceases, and the parade ground goes silent as the recruits hang off every word of the CO.

"Student of Merit." The Commanding Officer says a little louder than all his thank you speeches. He was once in their position, so he knows they were probably tuning out and this is the bit they are most keen to hear. The Commanding Officer addresses the crowd now. "Student of Merit, for those that don't know, is awarded to the top student of the entire course. The student that both the instructors and officers of the academy think has consistently performed to the highest of standards. In fact, not only have they performed to the highest of standards, the soldier has also out preformed all other students on the course." The Commanding Officer pauses for effect.

"Now securing the coveted title of Student of Merit is no simple task. Over the last year, the recruits have undergone some of the most arduous training in the galaxy. The beginning of the course starts with the recruits learning basic military skills like marching, and how to prepare a uniform. The recruits then progress to combat marksmanship, first aid, and navigation, where they learn the skills they will need to use during their military careers. After we deem them competent in these skills, we take them out of the classroom and begin exercising them. They start with quick exercises operating in multiple environ-ments, including space. They have to learn to deal with zero gravity... and zero sleep." The Commanding Officer pauses again. This time for the laugh he knows he will get from the crowd, who is filled with current and ex-serving men and women who have all enjoyed the same training.

"After this, we really put them to the test. We drop them on a planet where they must survive in small groups, then we do the same in harsher climates, like an asteroid field, and on a desolate moon. Then we work them up from small teams to operating as an entire company where they refine the skills they have already mastered and learn some new ones too. Once they have completed all these challenges, comes the biggest challenge of all. The Cauldron. A weeklong nonstop test where each individual soldier is pushed beyond their perceived limits." The Commanding officer pauses, scanning the crowd and the recruits. Giving them all the time to remember what, for some, was the hardest challenge they have ever faced.

"Once the soldiers have successfully completed the Cauldron, they are eligible to graduate and be chosen as the Student of Merit. Now, this is never an effortless task for the staff, but we have chosen an exceptional Student of Merit from the graduating class this year. So, without further ado, I will now announce this year's Student of Merit." All the recruits hold their breath in anticipation, hoping it is them or at least someone from their platoon, so they have bragging rights over the other recruits.

"Student of Merit for class seven four, eight one eight is… Recruit Seth McCallan!" The crowd erupts with cheers and a volley of claps as Seth stands there, stunned.

Over the loud applause of the crowd, Seth can hear one of his fellow recruits from the rank behind him aggressively whispers to him to get moving. Seth snaps attention as per the Platoon Commander's instructions. He falls out of the platoon ranks, before nervously marching off to the Commanding Officer in a daze.

This must be a mistake; I'm going to get halfway up and someone will realise they have the wrong person and I'll have to march back like a loser. Oh god!

Seth keeps marching forward while trying to control his breathing. He arrives at the podium where the Commanding Officer calls him straight up. The Regimental Sergeant Major who stands beside the Commanding Officer overtly looks at an X marked on the ground ushering Seth onto it with his eyes. Seth has never spoken to the Regimental Sergeant Major and has never wanted to.

You only talk to the RSM if you are in big trouble. Rumour has it you only see him if you are getting kicked off the course and out of the military. Seth notices another man of the same rank standing behind the Regimental Sergeant Major. One he hadn't noticed before. The man stands a good foot taller than the others. He is also a lot more relaxed in his posture, but his massive, powerful frame, and the look in his eyes, give him an air of authority greater than the rest. Including the Commanding Officer.

The man has on a black beret and almost more medals on his chest than he has a chest, which is a lot. He also has a well-kept, thick beard. *Wait, I didn't think you were allowed facial hair in the military?* Seth locks eyes with the man and a shiver runs down his spine. The bearded man gives Seth a warm smile, which he returns out of fear. The man looks as if he has seen a lot in his time. Instantly, Seth understands that this is a seriously dangerous person.

The Commanding Officer steps from behind the microphone as his staff officer appears on stage and hands him a long wooden box. Moving back to the microphone, he continues. "First, I would like to congratulate Recruit McCallan on his accomplishment. He has surpassed the expectations of his class-mates, his instructors and, by the look on his face, his own expectations." The Commanding Officer smiles at Seth as he says this. Making light of the situation helps Seth relax a little.

"For earning the title of Student of Merit Recruit McCallan receives not only the envy of his classmates and the respect of all the Academy staff, but most importantly, he receives the warrior's blade. The blade is made from extremely rare materials so that it never needs to be sharpened, and it will never chip, bend, or break. The reason the Student of Merit receives the warrior's blade is not just because of its roots as an ancient fighting weapon, but because the blade does so much more than serve as an instrument of war. It is a tool to aid in survival, exploration and the development of humanity. All things that we hope Recruit Seth McCallan will embody in his bright future career in the military." The Commanding Officer pauses, looking Seth in the eyes smiling, proud of the recruit in front of him.

"Congratulations and thank you… Private McCallan!" The Commanding Officer starts clapping and the entire audience joins in. A volley of claps from both the audience and the graduating class continues as the Commanding Officer steps over and shakes Seth's hand. At the Commanding Officer's request, Seth moves and poses for the military photographer. As soon as they take the photos, the Staff Officer takes the wooden box from Seth, shaking his hand and telling him it will be waiting for him back in his room. The Commanding Officer then steps back. Seth salutes, then marches off the podium and returns to the ranks of his platoon as the clapping slowly fades. The whole time, all Seth can think about is the bearded man who is watching him intensely.

The parade continues for another thirty minutes before wrapping up as per rehearsals. The last item being where the Commanding Officer promotes the entire class from the rank of Recruit to Private, signalling the end of their initial training.

As they march back to their accommodation block, Seth is in a daze. He wonders how he managed to get Student of Merit and can't believe it's real. His class mates whisper congratulations and joke under their breath about how they knew it would be him all along. Something Seth was obviously not aware of.

When they arrive back at the accommodation, the platoon comes to a halt. The Platoon Commander then hands the platoon back over to the Drill Sergeant, who assumes his position in front of the platoon on the small parade ground.

"Private McCallan, fall out and follow me! The rest of you stay there and don't move a god damn muscle!" The Sergeant screams angrily before marching into the accommodation block. Seth quickly falls out and marches after the Drill Sergeant, unsure of what he has done wrong.

When he enters the building, the Sergeant is leaning up against the wall waiting for Seth. "Good one Private McCallan, now the god damn Platoon Commander is going to strut around thinking he is shit hot because you busted your ass all year. Fuck my life McCallan!" The Drill Sergeant leans forward and shakes Seth's hand.

"Ummm yes Sir." Seth stands at attention, shaking the man's hand, confused by the situation.

The Drill Sergeant laughs. "You're a fucking Private now McCallan. It's not my job to yell at you every second of the day anymore. You earned yourself that blade. Well done!" The Drill Sergeant slaps Seth on the back before releasing his grip. "That been said, as soon as we head back out of here, I'm going to tear you a new one in front of the rest of the platoon so they don't think they are anything special."

Seth laughs with the Drill Sergeant. "Roger that Sir."

"Good man McCallan. Now go into your room. Someone wants to see you." The Drill Sergeant shoots Seth a wicked smile and points him to his room. Seth goes to duck around the man as he did this morning, but the Drill Sergeant politely moves out of his way. The complete opposite behaviour to earlier in the day and a show of respect.

Seth racks his brain, wondering who could be waiting in his room. He knows his parents could not make it, so he is sure it's not them. As he walks into the room, he sees a massive, powerful, bearded figure in combat fatigues with his back to him. Standing exactly where Seth stood this very morning before the March out parade. Seth snaps to attention.

"At ease, Private McCallan." Says a voice to his side. Seth turns his head to see the Regimental Sergeant Major standing next to him so moves into the at ease position. Feet apart, arms clasped behind his back, body straight and tall. "Private McCallan, I would like to introduce you to Warrant Officer Class One A." *A! His name can't be A, can it? That's ridiculous.* The beast of a man slowly turns around. He is holding the large box containing the Student of Merits Blade. Seth gulps, hoping that the giant man isn't about to take the blade out and murder him with it. The Regimental Sergeant Major chuckles out loud. "A, isn't his actual name in case you were wondering, Private." Says the RSM, somehow able to read the young soldier's mind. "A, wants to have a talk with you. I'll leave you two alone. But before I go, I just wanted to say good job on getting Student of Merit Private McCallan." The RSM turns and walks out. "All yours A."

"Thanks, RSM." The man says casually in a rough voice before turning his attention to Seth. "Thanks for your time today, Seth." A doesn't use his rank or surname, which Seth finds odd. "I wanted to have a few words with you before you get swooped on by all the Academy staff. Before they push you down a certain life path that suits their agenda more than it does yours." Warrant Officer A seems to look deep into his soul for a moment before relaxing a little with a soft smile. "If that's okay with you, of course?"

Seth stands there in shock. *No Warrant Officer, I don't even have a name because I've killed so many people. You can't ask me a question. Don't you know I'm the Student of Merit!* Seth stares back at the man in awe before nodding in the affirmative.

"Do you know why you got the Student of Merit Seth?" Warrant Officer A asks, seeing the confusion on the young soldier's face.

Seth shakes his head from side to side. "No Sir, I am still not sure it's real. I didn't come first in anything."

The Warrant Officer continues to stare right into Seth's being. "Correct you didn't. But you were in the top ten for all of your classes. Every single one of them. Some recruits got the top for one of their competencies but ended up in the bottom one hundred for several more. You are a very well-rounded soldier. Smart, fit, hardworking and with a natural talent for the job."

"Thank you, Sir." Seth says, unsure of how else to reply.

"Most people who win the Student of Merit choose to go straight to the Officer Corp to progress their careers. The odd one even breaks the mould and becomes a space fighter pilot. But I would like to offer you another option." The man watches Seth's reaction closely.

"What is the other option, Sir?" Seth says sheepishly, not sure how to speak to the man in front of him.

"Let me ask you this, Seth." The powerful man reaches over to the wooden box and pulls the blade from it. Holding it up, Seth sees it for the first time. It is not a sword as Seth was expecting and as all the other blades before it have been. It is an axe. A small spike comes off the back of the axe head, which has a broad face and a bearded edge. The handle, made of the same indestructible metal as the head, is long and has a slight curve to it as it gets thicker at the base. The bottom half of the handle features a specially treated type of rare leather wrapping, which gives the axe a solid grip.

"Do you want to carry this axe as a symbol of your time as a recruit? Or do you want to use it to defend humanity and destroy evil?" Seth needs no time to answer. He joined the military to be a soldier, the best one he could be. Seth has never wanted to fly ships or be an officer. He wanted to push himself to his limits and test his resolve. He wants action and adventure.

"I want to defend humanity and eliminate evil from the galaxy, Sir!" Seth answers so confidently that he shocks himself.

"Good!" Says the Warrant Officer as a devilish smile appears on his face. "If you choose to accept my offer of defending humanity and destroying evil, your life won't be one of comfort and ease." Seth can't help but smile back at the man in front of him. This is the first time he has really felt like a soldier. Until now, it was all ceremonies, drills, and basics. But something about the man in front of him calls to him. This is what he came for. This man is who Seth wants to become. Not a soldier in the Galactic Military, but a true warrior.

"Good, I didn't think easy would be your thing." He stares at Seth one more time, confirming that he is serious. "I'll organise the paperwork and handle it from here, soldier." The giant man skilfully spins the axe in his hands. It makes a deep swooshing sound as it cuts through the air. A rhythmic sound almost too beautiful for such a weapon. He then places it back in the case and walks out of the room, giving Seth a firm pat on the shoulder as he passes him. "See you around." Seth moves over and picks up the axe and gently swings it around. The axe gleams in the light. Seth feels a surge of pride and apprehension. This isn't just a weapon, it was a promise of the life he has dreamed of and the dangers he has barely begun to comprehend.

"Excuse me, Sir?" Seth calls out as the man is leaving.

"Yes Seth?" The large man answers warmly.

"Why an axe instead of a sword, Sir?"

The man chuckles to himself, then smiles back at Seth with a wicked-looking grin. "Oh, I think you will find this axe much more useful than a standard sword. Swords are good for show and good for fighting, but an axe. An axe has function far beyond that. An axe is for someone who seeks genuine adventure."

Standing in his room all alone, Seth grips the leather handle, squeezing it tight in his hands, imagining what adventures he will one day go on.

The leather still feels good in his hands. The choice he made that day to follow the bearded Warrant Officer led him down the path to becoming an elite Special Forces soldier and a Planet Scout. He has used the axe many times throughout both careers. For combat and for exploration, and by the sounds of the creature in this cavern, he may have to use it once again.

Chapter 3

CREATURE

The vastness of the space and the lack of lighting offers no hints as to where the ear splitting noise came from. Seth scans the area in front of him using the built in optics in his helmet, zooming in on certain areas. But he has no luck so turns the heads up display off and simply looks through the glass visor. He stays as still as he can as he continues to scan the area. The urge to turn and run away is strong. He can feel the fear sitting in the pit of his stomach. However, intense as that emotion is, it is being overpowered by something driving him forward. Something much deeper inside of him.

Seth taps the comms button on his forearm to transmit back via Ray and out of the cave system to the kids. "Scout, Alpha, this is Sierra. If you can hear me, acknowledge. Click responses only, over." He whispers into the built in comm unit in his helmet.

Waiting only a few seconds, he hears a click come through, followed by another shortly after. "Scout, prepare to copy. See if you can find out what creature might make this noise." Seth takes a knee, feeling for any small rocks as he keeps his eyes up, scanning the cavern in case whatever this beast is decides to show itself. He finds one around the right size and weight, which he thinks came from the fallen pillar. Taking a deep breath, he throws it off into the distance as far as he can. It hits the smooth floor and bounces along, echoing throughout the cavern. He hears the thunderous screech once again, but this time followed by a deep, guttural growl.

"Did you get that?" Seth waits a few seconds, then hears another click. "Roger that. I'm moving in to see if I can get eyes on."

Seth scans for somewhere to move to. *Somewhere dark, and with some cover, would be nice.* He sees what looks like another smaller fallen pillar about one hundred metres away. He silently moves towards the pillar, keeping a low profile and scanning for the creature as he goes. Seth hears a loud crack as if a large rock is being split in half and flicks his eyes towards the sound, trying to glimpse the creature as it darts around far off in the distance. To his surprise, the creature is not on the ground but flying from one pillar to another. Seth taps on his forearm computer to turn the HUD back on in his helmet. He then uses the optics to zoom in on the creature so he can get a better look and record what he is seeing. "Wait, what? That can't be!" Seth can't believe his eyes.

"Is that…" He takes several moments to search his memory to find the right word.

"Is that, a Dragon!"

As Seth watches the creature, time seems to slow. Long-lost memories from his childhood flood his mind, pictures from children's books, and make-believe battles against fire breathing serpents in his garden, help draw out the memory. A Dragon. A creature from ancient human stories.

He watches the giant winged serpent land on the side of one of the large stone support pillars, screeching as it searches for the source of the noise. He turns off the HUD's display once more and looks off into the distance with his own eyes. The creature looks around thirty metres long from head to tail. Its body winding up and around a pillar, its claws tearing out chunks of rock as it climbs. The light emanating from parts of the cavern seem to reflect and shine off the creature in an odd way. Seth would have thought its skin would absorb light like most animal hides, but the light seems to bounce straight back off, as if those sections of the creature had some type of metallic armour covering its body.

Seth is almost frozen by the sight. *This is impossible!* He thinks to himself as he racks his brain. In all their years of space travel, humans haven't even found any architecture like what he has just discovered, let alone creatures like this. Seth's heart pounds in his chest as he thinks this could be one of the biggest discoveries in the last several thousand years. But he forces himself to relax and quickly pushes those thoughts to the back of his mind. He has bigger problems to deal with now.

"So I think it's a Dragon…" He whispers into his comm. *With some type of metal armour? As if it were dressed for battle?* Seth leaves his opinions out of the comms call. He doesn't want the kids freaking out and doing something stupid. And from what he can tell, the creature is only being territorial. It doesn't seem to be hunting him. *C'mon Seth old boy, what are you worried about? It's just as scared of you as you are of it.* Seth chuckles to himself as he remembers the old saying.

The hell it is!

Eve frantically begins searching the ship's databases for any information about something called a Dragon. "Fin, do you know what a Dragon is?" She says over the private network they have set up between the Obsidian Scout and the drop ship. Eve set up this link so the pair could communicate while not making a noise on their father's net.

"No fricking clue, sis. I maybe recall a ship with that name, but not any creatures or life forms." He pauses for a second and scratches his head. "Do you think Dad has finally lost his mind?"

"No, I doubt it." Replies Eve. "If that were the case, he would have lost his mind a long time ago."

"Yeah, fair call." Agrees Fin. He cannot help but chuckle a little to himself.

Rose comes over the comm link, interrupting the conversation. "I have the answer to your search request if you would like to hear it?"

"Send it!" Fin says over the comms.

"Of course, Master Fin." The AI pauses as if taking a deep breath and readying her voice for a speech. "A Dragon is a legendary large creature that appears in ancient human folklore and culture. Beliefs about Dragons vary but Dragons have often been depicted as winged, horned, four-legged serpentine creatures of great intelligence."

"Wait, so Dragons were real? Like, back on Ancient Earth?" Asks Eve.

"No. Not from what I could find in the quick search of my databases." Replies Rose. "These creatures were symbolic in stories and legends as a monster or creature that needed to be overcome or defeated so that the protagonist of the story could achieve victory. There has been no evidence of Dragons being real in human history."

Maybe Dad has lost his mind. Eve thinks to herself as she worries about her father's physical and mental state.

"So, what's up with that sound then?" Eve asks Fin, but Rose interjects before he can answer.

"That sound is remarkably interesting. It is definitely coming from a large creature that is not in my databases. It also seems to have some sort of cybernetic language encrypted into its vocal projections that I do not understand. I can try to decipher it now if you wish?"

"YES!" Both children call out at the same time.

Seth watches as the beast claws its way up and around the back side of one of the giant stone pillars. As he scans the area, Seth spots another hiding place closer to the creature. Sweat drips down his forehead as he waits, watching to see if the Dragon will climb back around. Not seeing or hearing any movement, Seth decides the time to make his move is now. He takes a deep breath and readies himself to sprint to the next hiding spot.

GO!

Trying to remain as silent as possible, he sprints across the open space. His legs feel smooth and energetic, a feeling he knows well. A feeling he can identify as his body's reaction to a potential life and death situation. All his military experience has trained him to recognise this energy and to focus it on the task at hand, as opposed to letting it get out of control and letting his passive nervous system dictate his actions.

He arrives at his next piece of cover and silently slides into position under some fallen stone architecture. Seconds later, another ear bursting scream comes from the creature. *It must know I am here and is waiting for me.* Freezing in position, he waits to hear its next move. This feels a lot like a game of cat and mouse. Seth isn't sure though if he is the cat or the mouse. So, he waits patiently, biding his time to figure out where he sits on the food chain. He has spent almost half his life either in combat or hunting people. And in this game, discipline decides the victor.

Without warning, a wind as loud as the storm outside howls. *Huh, is it flying?* Seth peeks through a gap and watches the pre-historic-looking creature as it beats its massive leathery wings and begins to gain altitude. Once it nears the roof far above, it locks its wings out and soars across the cavern's expanse. *Magnificent.* Thinks Seth as he unconsciously holds his breath, hoping it hasn't figured his location yet. *I don't think a creature like this exists anywhere in our galaxy. This is a one in a million find. If it doesn't kill me and eat me, that is!*

The magnitude of this discovery floods Seth's mind. He and his fellow Planet Scouts have discovered their fair share of smaller creatures on their missions throughout the galaxy. Most undis-covered life forms they come across though are only different versions of animals that already exist. A different type of fish, some quadrupedal cat or dog-like creature, and lots of small, usually poisonous, insects and reptiles. There is something different about this creature though. Something more than its size. Seth just can't quite put my finger on it. Leaning against the structure, his mind races. A structure that he notes didn't occur naturally either.

Seth hears a loud deep thud as the beast lands within one hundred metres of him. The landing is much louder than Seth expected. The creature must be heavier than it looks. *I would have thought, watching you fly, you would have been more graceful and lighter than that big boy.* Seth stares intently at the creature from his hidden location, watching its every move and listening to the odd mechanical and digital sounds coming from it. *What are you, and why are you here?*

Identifying what may be a path, hidden from the creature's line of sight, leading from his current location to near the beast. Seth risks the move to get a better look. This is too important to let slip through his fingers. The discovery of an entirely new species of life is a historic find for humanity. The enormous cavern and the architecture itself are worth investigation, let alone the addition of this mysterious giant flying creature. But it's the combination of the two that makes this a tremendously important discovery for Seth, his family, and humanity. Seth needs to gather as much information as possible and make it out of here alive.

Large pieces of rubble from the ancient architecture that stood here previously provide him cover and concealment as he moves forward. He does his best to remain silent as he constantly checks the beast's movements and what he thinks to be its line of sight. He can see the creature moving its head around, trying to see what it can find. Oddly though, it doesn't seem to use its sense of smell, hearing, or, from what Seth can tell, its eyes. It is simply moving its head around, methodically scanning the area. Seth wonders if it has some type of sonar or other senses that it uses.

Seth arrives within fifty metres and pauses. *Alright big boy, let's get a better look at you, shall we?* He finds a suitable spot to hide and turns his suit's video recording system back on. Sending the footage back to the kids and the ship is something he considers a priority. Seth remains extremely cautious but excited about his discovery.

On closer inspection, Seth can see why the light was reflecting oddly off the creature. Where he thought would be a leathery hide of mixed plates, there is a type of metallic armour. Similar to what Ray has under its artificial dog hair. *What in the hell? This thing couldn't be a cybernetic AI like Ray. That's impossible!* Humanity has created some incredible machines in its long history but has had a tarred past with AI. *Is this some type of experiment by one of the Mega Corps?* Seth tries to rationalise what he is seeing in front of him. *It can't be. We are the first ever to set foot on this rock. And how is this thing even flying?* He hears the creature whipping its head around, searching for him, so leaves the pondering for another time.

Focus up Seth! He doesn't know what to think of this creature. He doubts it evolved naturally and is beginning to think the creature may not even be native to this plant. A lump begins to form in Seth's throat as he starts to get a real bad feeling about what he has stumbled upon.

The creature uses its long, sharp, metallic claws to find purchase as it climbs up the column it is currently at the base of. Even though parts of the beast seem to be covered in armour and its claws look to be made of some type of metal, the main body still seems to be flesh. Even from this distance, Seth can see the muscles contract and relax as it effortlessly moves around.

Something seems to of caught the beast's attention in another area of the cavern and Seth sees the beast go to roar again. Using his helmet's HUD, he zooms in to get a better view. The creature has black eyes which contrast against its dark red leathery skin and armour. Seth shivers as he looks into them through his display. As the creature opens its mouth to roar, Seth can see, plain as day, its large sharp teeth, a large flickering tongue, and salvia dripping from its mouth. Which, as terrifying as it is, confirms that this creature is not a giant robot. *As scary as you are, big boy, you are certainly not a big old AI killer robot. But what in the hell are you?*

Thoughts of this discovery creep back in to his mind again. *Is this the first completely new life form that has been discovered in the galaxy?* Seth has certainly never seen or heard of a creature that looks half machine and half living organism. But he is also unsure what his fellow Scouts have found out beyond the edge in the last several years. Whatever this is though, Seth is getting the feeling that someone bred or built this creature to be dangerous. He has seen many animals around the galaxy before. But none move, act, or look like this.

"Eve. Fin. I have the results from the encrypted cybernetic language, if you would like them." Asks Rose. Breaking Eve and Fin's laser like focus on their father's comms channel.

"Yes please, Rose, but over this comm channel. Dad needs to focus up right now." Answers Eve.

"Why yes, of course." Answers the AI in her most polite voice. "Eve, Fin, I have attempted to break the encrypted cybernetic code found within the creature's vocal system from the planet below. At first, I was having some difficulty in doing so. I extracted some more data from Captain Seth's comms and found something very interesting."

"Spit it out Rose." Interjects Fin over the comm.

Eve would usually have a go at her younger brother for being rude to the ship's AI, but in this circumstance kind of agrees with him. She is worried about her father and doesn't have time for a long-winded answer.

"Yes, Sorry Master Fin. The encryption is too advanced for me to decipher."

"What do you mean to advanced, Rose? And how is that interesting?" Asks Eve, puzzled.

"Eve, it's not a lack of data or processing power to decrypt complex codes that is the problem. The encryption itself is too advanced."

"To advanced, for you Rose?" Questions Fin, who thought Rose is one of the most advanced AI systems you can buy on the open market.

"Yes, sorry. But not only to advanced for me, and this is the interesting part. If I am correct in my calculations, this encryption is to advanced for any computing system in the known galaxy. It would take one hundred percent of my computing power and approximately seven thousand years for me to break." Rose pauses for a moment. "Whatever this creature is, it is more advanced than anything currently known to humanity."

Both Eve and Fin are in shock. Confused by what Rose is telling them. Eve jumps on the comm. "Fin, I don't know what's going on here, but we need to let Dad know!" The fear and urgency obvious in Eves voice.

"On it!" Replies Fin as he starts frantically clicking the comms link on the net they have open with their father.

What sounds like a crazed bird starts clicking away in Seth's ear. *Ah crap, must have gone over the ten-minute reporting window.* He has been so focused on the creature that he has forgotten to check in. He quickly finishes recording some more footage from his hidden position so he can send it to the kids. Quietly tapping away on his forearm computer, he puts in the commands to forward the video back to Ray and out to the children. *It's about time the kids saw what was going on.*

As soon as he connects the link and starts streaming the data, he notices the beast freeze in place. He watches in surprise as it looks like the creature is listening to something. *What's got you so spooked all of a sudden?* Seth looks around but can't see anything new or out of the ordinary. Then thinks to look down at his computer, which is showing the update of the stream. *No, it couldn't be picking up the data stream, could it?*

Seth looks back up to see the creature whip its head around and look directly at him. Its black eyes now glowing a deep dark red as it roars in anger. "Oh Shit!" Before Seth has time to move, the creature pops up into the air facing him, flapping its enormous wings, and pointing its long neck and head in his direction. Seth barely has time to get to his feet before a giant cone of fire comes roaring at him, straight from the beast's mouth.

Seeing the wall of fire coming his direction, Seth knows he won't be able to move out of the way in time. Slapping the emergency shield button on his chest, a field of energy appears around him, emanating from his back. The shield system built into his chest rig is usually only used by space pilots. If a pilot gets ejected into space or similar emergency happens out of atmosphere, they hit the button and a protective bubble will surround them providing them oxygen and protection from the void of space, and the associated debris of an incident, for around eight hours at best. They call them personal lifeboats. A throw back to ancient human explorers. Seth always wears his when scouting. He always tells the kids that you never know when you might run into an avalanche, sinkholes, or acid storms the Corps forgot to mention in their planet brief. Or in this case, cybernetically enhanced fire-breathing Dragons.

It feels like the shield makes it up milliseconds before the burning wall of fire hits. He loses vision as the flames wrap around the lifeboat. Even inside the security of his makeshift shield, he can feel the heat attempting to melt him where he stands. His helmet beeps warnings in his ear as it registers the rapidly rising temperature. Five seconds of scorching hell later, the fire stops. It takes Seth a moment for his vision to return after the burning brightness of the flames. He frantically looks around to see if he can locate the Dragon which has moved positions. His suit beeps at him, so he shuts off the lifeboat. The intense flames from the creature used up a lot of the lifeboat's power and he isn't sure if the lifeboat could sustain many more bursts of fire. If it could even take one more at all.

The first thing he notices is the sound of the Dragon's giant wings. He looks up and around to find the creature airborne and righting itself mid-flight so that it can make a pass at him. It looks like his mission has quickly changed from research to survival. Perhaps his assumptions about it being bred for something more sinister are correct, as it is now acting in a very calculated offensive manner. As it doesn't seem to be reacting in a freighted or territorial way like most creatures. It looks like it is trying to flank him.

Looking around, he sees no real cover. The flames decimated what little he had. He needs to get off the creature's line of attack somehow and manoeuvre to a stronger fighting position. The fight is on, and he will not win it by outrunning the beast or in a head-to-head battle.

He sees the Dragon powering towards him in a fast dive, its leathery and metallic body streamlined for efficiency. Looking around, he sees nothing but open space for the beast to attack him. Seeing no other option, Seth charges straight for the creature. Hoping its size and weight doesn't allow it to react quickly enough. *Only one way to go!* Seth sprints forward towards the airborne creature as fast as he can. The beast must have been expecting him to run away as it seems caught off guard by Seth's counter. The Dragon tries to pull out of its dive as its giant leathery wings open wide and it readies its fiery breath. But the creature quickly realises that it's too late for its original attack. So instead, it adjusts its position once more and tries to bite down at Seth. But Seth is already under the creature, and it misses its attack.

As soon as Seth passes under the beast, he skids to a stop. Quickly spinning around, he chases after the beast but heads off at a slight angle from the creature's current trajectory. Seth is quickly getting an idea of the creature's manoeuvrability. So he tries to keep close enough so that it can't use range to its advantage but far enough away from its lethal looking claws, teeth, and tail. Seth sprints as hard as he can towards the fallen pillars he was previously hiding behind. The Dragon flapping its wings, ascends and turns around looking for another opportunity to attack its prey.

The Dragon loops back for another pass. Seth's heart pounds in his ears as he sprints for the stone pillar, lungs and legs burning with the effort. Seth isn't sure he is going to make it to the pillar and needs to give himself a little more time. Ripping a flare off his belt, he ignites the end and throws it as hard as he can off to a flank. Hoping this might confuse the beast for a second or two, buying him a ticket to safety.

He doesn't stop to look back to see if it works, but hears the creature screech again. This time so loud it feels as if his ears will bleed. *Bullshit, it's only noise. You need to hurry up and get on that pillar and kill this thing before it kills you!* He screams at himself as he crashes hard into the pillar, using the large solid rock surface to painfully decelerate. The flare must have worked, as he hasn't been scorched or ripped to pieces yet. His body cries at him to rest for a moment, but he tells it to be quiet. *Move! Move! Move!* He rounds the pillar, lungs burning, then lights another flare. *If this creature is some type of machine, the flare might mess with its optics?* Seth hopes.

He throws the flare over the top of the fallen pillar further down from his position, hoping the Dragon will take the bait on its next pass. Trying to listen over the sound of his heartbeat, he thinks the Dragon has finished its ascent and is coming in for another strike and will hopefully pass his position. *Let's hope it took the bait.* He grips his faithful and battle tested axe as tight as he can in both hands. Using every ounce of speed and aggression his body can muster, he soars up the fallen pillar. As he crests the top, he sees the Dragon has taken the bait and is exactly where he wants it to be. Without hesitation he crosses over and leaps into the air, axe primed back above his head.

The Dragon has no time to react as out of the corner of its eye it sees Seth flying through the air, followed by a flash of bright steel. Seth slams the axe down into the creature's skull, causing them both to go crashing hard onto the cavern floor.

The polished stone floor takes the wind from his chest. He feels multiple parts of his body ramming into the hard floor along with parts of the Dragons armour hitting him as he rolls with the beast as it kicks and screams in agony. As much as the tumble across the floor hurts, he can tell that nothing is broken. The pair slide to a dead stop. The Dragon lies dead still, and Seth wants to maneuverer to make sure the beast is out of the fight, but his body will not let him. He gasps for air as his winded lungs attempt to re-inflate.

Over the sound of his gasps, he hears a deep rumbling noise coming from the beast as its giant body slowly begins to move. *Get on your feet and kill this son of a bitch before it kills you!* Images of Fin and Eve appear in his mind, providing the needed motivation to overcome his body's perceived physical restrictions. Seth rolls over on to his stomach and pushes up onto one knee as the Dragon, dazed and oozing something that he assumes is blood, raises its head.

The Dragon is slow, but it finds its prey even with one eye not working because of the trauma caused by Seth's axe. What it discovers though is not a broken man lying on the floor ready to devour, but Seth now standing tall with his side arm pointed right at its head. It attempts to roar again but is silenced as Seth blows out the creature's other eye. Seth roars, pushing forwarded into the beast as he continues to empty the weapon's entire magazine into the creature's head and neck. The large and rapid volume of fire from Seth's sidearm causes devastating trauma to the Dragon's vital areas.

The beast crashes hard back down to the floor.

Seth can longer see any movement or hear the creatures rumblings.

Breathing heavily, Seth scans the area for his axe, which he notices close by. It must have been knocked out of his hands as he tumbled across the hard floor with the Dragon. He trudges over, starting to feel the pain of his roll with the Dragon. The pain doesn't slow him down however, it just makes him even angrier. He picks up the axe, dragging it on the ground as he slowly limps back over to the dead beast. The sound of the metal axe dancing across the polished hard stone reverberates throughout the entire cavern.

With all his remaining strength, he raises the axe above his head before slamming it down into the creature's neck.

"Stupid." He feels the dull, moist thump as the face of the axe finds the creature's flesh.

Another swing. "Cave dwelling."

And another. "Fire breathing."

Another. "Cybernetic Dragon!"

And once more, with all his might. "AAAAHHHHH!"

With his last swing, the head comes off the beast, followed by a gush of fluid. Seth collapses to the ground, exhausted but now confident the beast has been slain.

As Seth sits on the floor, leaning against the deceased creature, he takes long deep breaths in and out. He begins to feel the adrenaline running through his blood change to exhaustion as he stares at the large head lying on the ground in front of him. For some odd reason, he notices it looks like the beast consists of thick meaty flesh, but instead of veins or arteries, there seems to be some type of data cables. *What in the name of Utopia?* He sits there for another minute unmoving, replaying what just happened in his head as he watches, what he thinks is the creature's thick blood, slowly flowing from its neck. He calms himself while attempting to find the energy to get back up. As the sound of his heartbeat slowly stops flooding his ears, he hears several clicks. He flinches, looking around to see if the beast has come back to life, but sees nothing.

Then he remembers.

"Shit. The kids!"

Chapter 4

DRONES

Eve pilots the Obsidian Scout towards the fiery threshold of the planet's atmosphere. There aren't many people her age in the galaxy that would have the skills to pilot a Scout Class starship. And the fact that she is doing it solo puts in her a class of her own. There also aren't many people her age with a borderline psychotic, ex special forces father who think's hard work, constant learning, training, and drilling are the meaning of life. So, she at least has that going for her.

"God damn it, why isn't he answering his comm?" Eve says out loud, worried about her father. She hits the comms unit switch aboard the Scout "Fin. Have you heard from him yet?"

"No Sorry sis. I did a comms check with Ray, and we have a full connection. I have asked Ray to get a full bio read out from Dad's suit, which should only take a few seconds." Fin replies.

"Ok, good idea little bro. I'm bringing the ship into the atmosphere now, so fire up the drop ship and get ready for pickup. I'll grab you on the way through, so get airborne ASAP." Eve directs Fin.

"Yes Mum." Fin replies, clearly seeing Eve rolling her eyes at him in his mind. "Moving now out."

Sitting in the pilot's seat of the bridge, Eve rolls her eyes. Even though she is only two years older than Fin, after they lost their mother, she took on parts of that motherly role. Mostly that involved getting her father to relax his incredibly high standards, and let Fin be a teenage boy occasionally. She also smuggled him treats and other things her father wouldn't approve of. "Rose, how's that storm looking on the surface below?" She queries the ship's AI.

"The storm has reduced from a level three back to a level one and winds are at fifteen kilometres per hour. Would you like more information about the weather and winds on the planet's surface, Eve?" The ship's AI asks.

"Just send them to the pilot's HUD and let me know if there is anything abnormal. Thanks Rose." The ship's AI replies affirmatively and starts pushing data to the heads-up display instead of through its voice comms. Eve does a couple more checks, then takes the helm of the Scout as it enters the atmosphere. The Ships advanced AI could handle the entry, but Eve likes to feel the ship's every movement as she manoeuvrers it into the planet's atmosphere.

Her father says she has a natural talent for flying and is one of the best pilots he has ever seen. He also says hard work always beats out natural talent. So, by the time she was eighteen, she had done over one thousand atmospheric entries. Moons, large asteroids, planets with low atmospheres and planets with dense ones. He told her that if she combines her natural talent with hard work, she could be one of the best pilots of our time. She thinks he is only saying this as encouragement, but it still makes her feel good. For some reason, unknown to her, she strives for his approval and praise. Fin, on the other hand, seems to be the opposite when it comes to their father.

She remains focused on the task at hand, constantly checking the data that Rose is feeding her and watching through the view port and displays. Eve predicts each bump and gust of wind, navigating the entry with ease. It only takes several minutes before the ship breaks into the planet's atmosphere and Eve feels the Scout soaring. She levels the ship back out, enjoying the feeling of flight before heading into the storm below.

"Rose, does Fin have the drop ship airborne yet?"

"Yes, he is taking off now."

"Thanks Rose." Eve switches comms. "Fin, head to two thousand feet along the bearing I'm sending. ETA three mikes." Eve used to hate using proper radio communications phrases and language, but because of her father speaking that way and making her use it so often, she now speaks that way subconsciously.

"Roger that, sis." Fin replies. "Also, Ray sent through Dad's vitals. He is alive, but that's all I have."

"Well, that's a good sign, at least. Keep trying to ping him and if you don't hear from him by the time we land, we will go back to voice and try to raise him that way. If that doesn't work, I'll send Ray in to find him."

"Sounds good. See you soon big sis."

Eve takes the ship down to two thousand feet, heading along the bearing she sent Fin, wind at her back. Scanning the screens for the drop ship. She sees the ship come into view moments before an alert on her screen lets her know it's there. The drop ship is getting pushed around by the wind, but Fin is doing a good job of balancing it out. By the time he reaches two thousand feet, the ship is level. Eve slows down to sixty knots and opens the drop bay doors. She manoeuvres the Scout so that it is right above the drop ship. Then, watching the screens showing her the view from beneath the ship, she lowers the Scout down, scooping up the drop ship. Eve imagines she is a giant bird of prey devouring an unsuspecting insect.

Fin watches from inside as the drop ship gets engulfed by the larger starship, which has flown them around the galaxy and doubled as his home for almost half his life. The bay doors close beneath him, and the lights of the hanger turn on. He quickly opens the door to the drop ship and looks around. *All clear.* Fin isn't a terrible pilot, especially for an eighteen-year-old, but he is not his sister. He is thrilled every time he makes it back safe. He isn't sure if he is more scared of crashing the ship and dying in a fiery blaze or scratching it and getting in trouble from his dad.

A green light flicks on above the hangar door, showing that Eve is also happy that the drop ships docked properly. Fin quickly exits and heads off to the bridge to meet Eve. It takes him over one minute to run from the docking hangar to the bridge, where he stops outside for a quick mouthful of air.

"Heard from Dad yet?" Asks Fin as he confidently waltzes on to the bridge. Trying to look cool and hide his panting after running as quick as he could from the hanger.

Eve looks back and pretends not to notice Fin's attempt to look cool, but lets a small smile slip out as she turns back to the front. "No, not yet. Rose, can you try to raise Dad's comms via click on a three second loop until he answers?" She commands.

"Yes Eve." Replies Rose.

Fin flops down in the nav's chair. "So, sis, do you think Dad found an actual Dragon?" Asks Fin seriously, staring at his sister with his big brown eyes. "Oh, and what the heck is a Dragon?"

Eve stares back at him for a minute, not sure what to say. "Look, there is something down there. We both heard it, but a mythical creature from ancient human history, dating back over 20,000 years. I doubt–" Seth's voice cuts her off.

"Scout, Alpha, this is Sierra. Comms check over."

"Dad, this is Eve, loud and clear!" She says. Excited to know her father is still alive, and by the sound of his voice, his usual serious self. Although she was never really worried that he was in too much danger. "Also, Fin is with me, and we are heading to the landing site."

"Roger that. I'll send you the location to the cave's entrance and I'll push Ray forward to meet you. I have something you guys will want to see. Out." Eve and Fin stare at each other. Both thinking that perhaps their dad did in fact find a Dragon, but neither willing to say it out loud.

Fin walks in front of Eve by a couple of metres. He has a natural talent for navigation and has always seemed to have a sixth sense for finding his way. Plus, he has spent more time on this planet than Eve. She has spent most of this contract looking after the ship high above the planet's surface. Eve, who is strict and detailed focus, is the opposite of Fin, who seems to always go with his gut in a carefree manner. Fin, at eighteen, is almost as good a Planet Scout as his father. He just lacks the experience. Seth is slowly giving him more freedom though, so that he can gather that experience. And Eve, like a proud big sister, has enjoyed watching her little brother grow into the man he is becoming.

Several hundred metres from the location that their father sent them, Fin hears a bark on the wind. He stops in place, scanning off into the distance to see if he can identify Ray. Eve comes racing forward, bumping into Fin's side as she heard the bark too. They stand side by side, competing to see who can find Ray first. Fin points out a fast-moving dark shape racing up to them. Eve runs forward, charging towards their beloved pet. She pulls up short, taking a knee. Ray comes running up, slamming the brakes on at the last minute before jumping all over Eve and licking her face. Eve giggles and plays with Ray, running her hands through his dark black coat for a moment while Fin watches on. Fin eventually moves over and gives Ray a big pat. "Hi boy." He says in a cute voice. "Can you take us to Dad?" Ray stops playing and sits at attention, gives a soft bark, then slowly starts walking back the way he came. The dog looks over its shoulder to make sure the two are following him. Once he confirms they are, he picks up the pace, tail wagging.

Dropping into the deep gorge surrounded by the rocky red cliffs on either side, Ray takes them to an overhang several hundred metres in. Stopping in place, Ray raises up his front leg and bends it as he aims his muzzle at the rock face. This is the dog's way of pointing out the location of the cave entrance. As they arrive at the cave entrance, they see their father standing there drinking water from his canteen and chewing on an energy bar. "Hey guys, it's great to see you. How are you?" He says as he embraces them both in a giant hug.

Eve jumps in. "How am I! How are you? What happened? Are you okay? Did you find an alien race? Is there really a Dragon!"

Seth has a deep chuckle to himself. "Hahaha, I'm fine now. Come on, come with me and I'll show you everything." He pats Fin on the shoulder, letting him know he should follow along as well. Giving his son a cheeky smile, acknowledging that he couldn't get a word in over his sister even if he wanted to. Fin nods returning the smile.

Seth leads them through the cave's entrance and into the tunnel. They arrive at the first entrance where Seth found the mysterious door. "This is where I figured something was off and we had found something worth investigating." Both kids look around, amazed. Eve turns on her shoulder camera and starts methodically recording everything. Fin kneels down and runs his hand over the smooth floor. They follow the clues their father did until they both end up at the door at the same time.

"How does the door work old man?" Asks Fin.

"It took me a while to figure out, but I had to reach into each opening and turn a handle. Like an old airlock door. Once I turned them all, I thought that would open the door, but it didn't. I searched around until I found the symbol on the wall here."

Eve spins around at hearing what her father said and races over, pushing Seth out of the way to have a look. She shines her light on the symbol, studying it. She even pulls out her notepad and draws it into the book before sliding it back into her cargo pants pocket. "Eve, if you like that, then come with me". Seth walks over and pushes the door all the way open. The dull green light glows again and Eve gasps before charging through the door, followed closely by Fin.

"Hey be careful please. I haven't checked the entire cavern out yet!"

"Yeah yeah, settle down old timer, we will be fine." Fin replies as he shuffles off into the cave.

Old timer, hey. Looks like we will have some extra sparring in the training cycle. Seth jokes to himself. He knows they will be fine, but it's his job to worry and keep them as safe as he can. Regardless of their age, he is still their father.

"Come on boy." Seth shakes his head and follows them in with Ray trotting by his side.

The kids head off in their own directions, exploring the entrance to the cavern as they go. Seth heads over to the large boulder that was once an entrance pillar and climbs back up and looks around. The lighting is still on, but it could be brighter. "Fin!" He calls out. Fin turns around looking at him wide eyed. "Did you bring any drones?" Seth asks, hoping Fin took the initiative and brought them without being asked.

"Just one Hawk, if you want it?" Asks Fin, looking at his dad for confirmation. Seth raises his arm above his head and gives a big thumbs up. Fin then slides his backpack off and reaches inside, pulling out the drone. Fin unfolds the drone, activates it from his forearm computer, and watches as it lights up and hovers into the air. Once he is happy, Fin turns around and gives Seth a big thumbs up.

Seth taps on his forearm computer, taking over control of the drone. The sleek, matte grey scouting drone, known as a Hawk, automatically flies to his location. The drone is equipped with an entire suite of gadgets to help the family on their scouting missions. But Seth is only interested in one function. The drones' high powered lighting system. He sends the Hawk to what he thinks is the centre of the next chamber, where he previously battled the Dragon. Once there, he flies the drone up as high as it will go without hitting anything. Tapping on his computer, he turns on the drone's lights to full brightness. Even though the Dragon's cavern is enormous, the drone's lighting system increases the visibility, at least around the area it is hovering. The white light from the drone is a stark contrast to the dull glow of the current lights. Seth hopes this will make it easier for the family to explore the cavern.

"Alright, come this way if you want to see a Dragon." Seth calls out, knowing this will get his children's attention. The kids instantly stop what they are doing and chase after their father. Seth drops off the other side of the boulder and marches off towards the Dragon's corpse.

All three of them stand there, mesmerised by the dead creature. Its bone like horns covered in waves, its metallic looking scales that reflect the dull light in the cavern, and its massive leathery wings. There is no part of this creature that doesn't demand attention. Eve, however, is lost in its face, staring at what were once its eyes. "It's so beautiful. Did you have to kill it?"

"It tried to burn me alive, rip me in half, then eat me. I didn't have a choice sorry beautiful." Seth replies honestly. "It is an amazing creature though, I'll give you that." Seth is happy to be alive but sees Eve's point. He has seen nothing like it before in his life. The only reason he ever even heard the word Dragon before was because he went through a phase in his early teens where he was obsessed with ancient warrior societies. He couldn't tell you anything about them now, but the sight of this creature sparked a memory.

"See how it's both organic and cybernetic? Kind of like Ray or other AI robotic animals." They all look at Ray, who has been following them around. The dog sits and turns its head to the side, looking back at them, tongue hanging out the side of its mouth. Fin lets out a small laugh and they return to the Dragon. Eve takes off her backpack and starts digging inside the main compartment, looking for something.

"You two keep looking around and I'll gather some data on this thing." She says, pulling out three large metallic balls. "Go on then, the Sparrows and I will take care of this." Eve pushes them away before throwing the balls high in the air. Once they are two metres above her head, they seem to magically hover in place. A beam of green light comes out of the balls as they drift around the Dragon's corpse. Scanning it for all the information they can gather. The little drones that Eve has named Sparrows are science drones. Eve has modified the drones so that they all work together and fuse their data into a single report back on Eve's forearm computer. Once Eve is happy the Sparrows are working properly, she then synchronises up with Ray and starts forwarding data to the dog to push back out to the Obsidian Scout. She has also recently upgraded them to make them faster and more responsive so they can get into more places and deal with the harsher environments they operate in due to their line of work.

Seth and Fin know when they are not needed and head off to continue searching the cavern. Seth walks in the direction where he thinks the Dragon originated from, with Fin following close behind.

"So, Dad, was that Dragon hard to kill or what?" Fin enquires, trying not to sound too interested.

"Yeah, it was buddy. It didn't behave like an animal at all and was using good tactics against me. Thankfully, I don't think it had come across humans before, so it didn't know what I was or what I could do." Seth replies, wondering to himself how he managed not to get burnt or eaten by the beast.

"Were you worried about dying?" Fin stops and looks at his dad, waiting for an answer.

Seth stops, then turns around to face his son. "Look Fin, to be honest, no. Not because I'm not worried about dying. I'm not ready for death yet, and I'm certainly not ready to leave you guys." Seth looks into his sons eyes. "But in the moment and in similar moments I have been in, my focus is only on overcoming the obstacle in front of me." Seth steps up to Fin and puts his hands on his wide shoulders before giving them a firm but loving squeeze. *God, when did you grow up kid?* "When in combat, you must focus on the battle and nothing else. If I let thoughts of death creep in or begin worrying about you guys, I will lose focus. And if I lose focus, I lose the battle. Then I will lose the one thing I never want to lose, you guys." Seth stares into his son's eyes before continuing. "A loss of focus can only guarantee one thing." Seth searches his son's face and eyes for a reaction. "Do you understand, buddy?"

Fin thinks about it while trying not to break eye contact with his father. "Yes, Dad."

"What do you understand?" Seth pushes Fin, seeing if he truly understands or if he is only saying yes because it seems like the right thing to say.

Fin takes a deep breath in before speaking. "I understand that when in battle, it is foolish to think about anything except the fight itself, because if you let other thoughts enter your mind, you might get distracted and lose the fight. Therefore, losing what is most important." He watches his father contemplate his answer as a smile widens on the older man's face.

"Good!" Seth slaps Fin on the shoulder's and gives him a shake. "It's a lot easier to say than to do, but I believe you get it buddy. We will practice when we get back to the ship!" Seth turns and continues onwards.

Fin stands there and rolls his eyes as his father walks away. He shakes his head in regret while silently screaming into the air. *Damn it. Now I'll have an extra couple of hours in the sim room. I knew I should have never asked!* Fin takes a deep breath, puts a smile back on his face, then jogs to catch up to his father.

Seth eventually comes to what he thinks is the pillar that the Dragon first landed on. Looking up, he tries to see if there is any evidence that might show where it landed. "Hey Fin, does that look like claw marks to you?" Seth points about halfway up the pillar. Fin looks over and nods his head up and down. Seth then stands underneath it and faces away from the marks. "Alright, I'm heading that way to see what I can find." Seth marches off once again.

Fin keeps looking up at the claw marks. He then looks around, scanning the cavern before taking another look back up at the pillar. A sensation of heaviness floods his body, a feeling he has never felt before. His hands gently vibrate as the weight seems to pull him in a certain direction. To Fin, it feels like a separate gravity has suddenly entered the cavern. "Dad! I got a feeling that something is this way." Fin points off ninety degrees to the way Seth is walking.

"Roger that. Check it out and let me know." Seth says without slowing or turning back around. He is reasonably confident that his son will be safe and alert him of anything he finds. Seth has given Fin a lot more freedom on the last several jobs and he is loving the opportunity to show his father how capable he is.

Fin doesn't know what it is pulling him in the direction he now follows. He just knows that the sensation he feels is growing stronger. Determined to find out the source of this gravity, he searches around the cavern, following the sensation for about ten minutes until he comes to a dead end. Looking around, he finds himself in a corner of the cavern. All he finds is the floor, walls and the roof high above. Besides some small rocks scattered around and a small boulder, Fin can't see anything interesting. But for some reason, he is drawn to this area. He knows his father would tell him to continue looking, seeing there is nothing here, but he can't bring himself to leave. The weight of the gravity is too strong. He heads over to the small boulder and sits down on it, and stares at the wall. Hoping an answer will present itself.

Some time passes, and he hears Eve over the comms. "Ok guys, I have finished gathering data. Where are you both at?"

Before Fin can reply, his father jumps on the comms. "I have found where the Dragon came from. Looks like it was packed into the wall, in some kind of dispensing or storage unit. There is some tech of some sort here Eve, so you may want to come check it out. Bring the Sparrows." Eve does not need to be asked twice. "Moving your way now Dad!"

The radio chirps again. "Hey sorry little bro. Did you find anything yet?" Fin is lost in the wall he is staring at. "Fin!"

Fin snaps out of his daze. "Oh yeah, sorry, I'm here. Still searching. Let me know when you are done, and you guys can come lend me a hand."

"Yep, okay. See you soon." Fin notices the excitement in Eve's voice, which makes him smile. He looks around and considers exploring more but can't bring himself to leave the area. The pull to this location is too strong to break away from. He decides he should at least be methodical and scan the wall in front of him from left to right, top to bottom. Like his father has trained him to do. He stands up on the boulder he was sitting on and begins his detailed visual scan of the wall. Fin gets lost in his meticulous scanning of the wall and loses track of time once again.

Eve's voice comes back over the comm, breaking his concentration. "Okay Fin, we are finished. Where are you? We will come to you."

"Same place I have been the whole time."

Seth jumps on the comms. "Have you not been searching at all?"

Fin can tell his father sounds irritated. "Yes, no. Kind of. I have just been searching the one spot. I don't know what it is, but there is something here. Can't explain it, but there is something in this spot!"

Eve jumps on the comm, getting in before her father can. She doesn't want him getting cranky, even though she agrees Fin should have been searching. "Okay little bro. I'll send Ray to you, and we will follow."

Several moments pass before Fin hears the steps of Ray's engineered dog paws tapping on the stone floor. He looks over in the dull light and sees his big sister and father walking along, obviously discussing what they discovered. Seth doesn't look upset, which takes a weight off Fin's shoulders. He waves them over from the small boulder he is standing on. Ray runs up and jumps up on the boulder with Fin looking for a pat.

"Okay son, what's got you in such a fuss?"

"Don't you want to tell me what you found first?" Replies Fin.

"Oh yeah, it was crazy. There was tech that we had never seen before and it looked really old, but Eve has all the data so we can review it back in the Scout. Now tell me, what has got you all riled up buddy?"

"I can't explain it Dad, but something was pulling me to this place. Like I physically felt like I was being pulled." Seth and Eve exchange a glance before allowing Fin to continue. "And I can't let it go. There is something here!" Fin can't control his energy as Seth notices his son clenching his fists.

"Okay, okay. Settle down buddy. So, have you done your scans?"

"Yep."

"Top to bottom and left to right?"

"Yep."

"And you have found nothing?"

Fin's shoulders slump "No, I haven't found anything."

Seth can hear the disappointment in his voice. *Something has really got their hooks in the kid.*

"Okay then, let's change up your perspective. Look at it a different way." Seth taps on his forearm computer, calling the Hawk closer to their position to allow them some more light. Seth then moves next to Fin and directs Eve to Fin's other side. He then turns out at forty-five degrees to the way Fin is facing and gets Eve to do the same. Both Seth and Eve then walk off at forty-five degrees until they get to the wall, forming a large triangle. "Okay, Eve, have a look around from where you are at and let me know if you see anything alright?" The pair search their arcs top to bottom, left to right.

After five minutes of visual scanning, Seth asks Eve if she found anything. "Nothing Dad. The only thing that stood out is that the wall seems to be really flat. Besides that, just some curly haired, red head standing on a big rock!" She laughs out loud at her own joke while Fin shakes his head.

Seth ignores the comment and continues. "Fin. You see anything buddy?"

"Nope."

"Have you searched the wall for holes or symbols or anything unusual? Like what I found at the entrance to his cavern?" Seth asks.

"I've looked but haven't found anything."

Seth stares at Fin for a moment. "Looked, as in stood on that rock or looked as in got off your ass and touched the wall and ran your hands over it?" Fin doesn't answer, which is an answer unto itself. "Then how about you get off your butt and come over and help us check the wall." Fin jumps off the rock and moves over to the wall. The tingle in his hands growing stronger. All three of them check it for anything out of the ordinary. They are thorough in their search, but all three come up with nothing. The only thing that stood out is that the wall was quite flat, but that seems probable for what this cavern may have once been. Fin looks disappointed, so Eve rubs him on the head as they walk back to the small boulder.

"Sit down little bro. We will figure it out." Eve tries to console him.

"Nah, it's all good sis. You and Dad have earned a sit down." He gestures for them to sit, and they both take up the offer, pulling out some water to drink. Fin walks back to the wall and then stares back at them. Still, nothing stands out. He mopes back over to his family, kicking some of the small rocks out of his way. "I don't get it. I can feel something here, but I can't put my finger on it."

"Sorry, but I don't know what to say buddy, but it doesn't look like there is anything here." Seth says while shrugging.

Fin sits back down on the boulder. *Why is there a rock here in the middle of nowhere if they didn't want me to stand on it? Why can't I find this stupid thing?* Fin hops back up and paces back and forth as he rubs his head. "Stupid rock." He says out loud.

"Why is the rock stupid?" Eve asks as she looks down at her makeshift seat.

Fin pauses, taking in a deep breath, then unleashes. "If there is something sooo important here, that it is physically pulling me in, and won't let me go anywhere else in the entire giant cavern, then why is there a stupid rock right here? Right where I am being pulled to!"

"Maybe there's actually nothing here?" Eve replies.

Fin flops down on the boulder. "Yeah. Nothing here. That sounds about right." Fin is feeling guilty for making both Eve and Seth waste all their time here just because he had a feeling. Whatever that means. "Alright, fine, maybe there is nothing here. Nothing in this entire part of the cavern." Fin scans the area, seeing that there is in fact nothing else around. No architecture, no elaborate markings, nothing. This area is void of anything besides floor and wall. And a rock. A big out-of-place rock.

Suddenly it hits him! He jumps back up excitedly, looking around. "Eve. Can I borrow one of the Sparrows?" He asks with a newfound energy. Eve is not sure what he is up to, but feeling his energy, can't say no. She hands one over to him. Fin throws it up in the air as high as he can. Eve watches in shock as the metal ball goes flying high into the cavern above. Before she gets the chance to get angry and yell at him, Fin cuts her off. "The rock." He says as he takes over control of the tiny drone. "Why are there no other rocks in the area?" Seth stands up puzzled and starts looking around.

"Because there aren't supposed to be any rocks here, and this isn't a rock!" Fin pauses for a second before clarifying his remark. "Well, it is a rock, kind of, but not any old rock." Out of the corner of his eye, Fin sees his father raise an eyebrow, confused. "Wait a second, if I'm right, you'll see." Fin looks up, his eyes following the sparrow as it ascends towards the roof. Both Eve and Seth see him fixated on the drone, so follow his gaze upwards.

"Wait for it, wait for it!" Fin says as he watches the drone fly higher and higher.

"Don't break my sparrow Fin." Warns Eve.

"Relax Eve, I know what I'm doing!" Replies Fin, without breaking his gaze.

Fin switches the lights of the sparrow on right before it slams into the cavern's ceiling. Fin's eyes flick between his forearm computer and the distant drone. "Look see!" He shouts out excitedly. "There is a chunk of the roof missing!" Seth and Eve watch on amazed. Fin hits the return function on the drone, then spins back around to face the rock. "Dad, Eve. Help me push the rock out of the way."

They both obey the young man's energetic command and start pushing, using every bit of energy they can muster to move the large rock. Their muscles strain against its weight as they breathe hard, trying to move several hundred kilos of stone. They fight to keep grip on the smooth floor as they push against the rock. It shifts, only a millimetre, but it moves, and they all hear the screech of stone on stone. This is all they need as a burst of energy overtakes them. They all shove together, and the rock moves a little more as they build momentum. The rock begins to slide from its location, the noise of the rock grinding on the floor echoes throughout the cavern. It takes them around a minute, but they push it two metres before running out of steam. Fin breaths heavily as sweat drips down his forehead and the burn in his muscles pulse. He looks down to see a symbol of two interconnecting triangles. The same symbol his father had found at the cavern's entrance. An enormous smile appears on the glowing red face of the young man.

"Holy crap buddy!" Exclaims Seth in between laboured breaths. "You weren't joking. How did you know something was here?" His father stares at him with a look of confusion on his face.

"I, I, I didn't know Dad, I just had a feeling." Fin finds it hard to explain. "Something was drawing me to this place, and I couldn't leave to look anywhere else." Seth stares at him, nodding his head up and down as he catches his breath.

I wonder if he had a vision like mine. Did his mother guide him to this section of the cavern like she guided me to its entrance? Or is there something else going on with this place? Seth thinks to himself.

"Good work little bro!" Eve says as she slaps Fin on the back while staring at her father, making an exaggerated 'don't ask me' gesture. "Well, go on then." Eve points to the dinner plate sized symbol on the ground.

"Well, what?" Fin asks looking at his older sister than his father.

"Push it, Fin! Don't just stare at it!" Eve says, half-laughing.

"Oh, yeah, haha." Fin shakes his head at being so daft, his dark red mop of hair bouncing from side to side.

He moves over to the symbol and kneels down before attempting to push down on its centre. It doesn't budge an inch, and nothing happens. Fin stands up and thinks for a second. *If it's on the floor, that must mean it needs more weight, perhaps? Yep, I need to stand on it.* Fin stands up then takes a step forward onto the centre of the symbol. Nothing happens again. Fin steps back and scratches his chin as he looks at Eve and Seth. They offer nothing but confused looks in return. *If it's on the floor, it must need a deliberate action, not just a step.* Fin thinks about the problem as he closes his eyes trying to imagine the thought process of whoever put the symbol there. *It would have to be something out of the ordinary, something deliberate, like a key of some sort.* Fin looks around the area and again sees nothing. So he decides to pull out his water bottle and pour a little water on the symbol. Nothing happens, but he feels like he is on the right path. *The symbol pulled me here, so maybe I'm the only one who can activate it?*

Fin kneels over the symbol once more and takes off his right-hand glove stowing it away in his pants pocket. He then blows on his hand in an attempt to make it as clean as possible. Once satisfied he puts his hand back on the symbol and pictures it lighting up in his mind. He feels a small warm spark in his hand and hears an excited gasp from Eve as the symbol lights up and begins to lower into the ground. *No way, did that just work?* The symbol stops only several inches down and they all hear a loud click over by the wall they had been searching, followed by an even louder crack. A similar crack to what Seth heard when he opened the entrance to the cavern.

Ray barks at the wall while running back and forth in front of it. Seth spins around, sidearm drawn, pointing at the part of the wall the noise came from. Seeing their father draw his side arm, Eve, and Fin draw their blades and move into a fighting stance. Seth smoothly removes his non shooting hand off his sidearm and silently commands them to spread out. They follow his orders like they have in training a thousand times before, readying themselves to ambush something if it comes out of the wall.

The family hears another loud click and part of the wall in front of them glows golden yellow then lowers down, making a loud grinding sound. They watch as the wall slowly lowers into the floor and the golden light fades, revealing nothing but an unnatural darkness and a deafening silence. The wall eventually lowers down to the same height as the floor and loudly locks into place. Without warning, a bright golden light explodes out of the darkness. Blocking their eyes, they turn away so not to get blinded. The bright light fades back to a dull glow, and they turn back to see a small walkway leading across a dark void into what looks like a distant room. Due to the unnatural darkness surrounding the glow it's hard to see how far away the room on the other side of the walkway really is. It is a somewhat disturbing and mind bending sight to behold and Seth can't stare at it for too long as it makes him feel dizzy.

The family remains in place for several more minutes waiting to see if anything comes out of the wall. After his previous encounter Seth feels uneasy about the room but notices the excitement and wonder on both Eve and Fin's face. This concerns him even more. Seth taps his left leg three times and Ray appears shortly after. "Can you go clear the room boy?" He whispers. Ray looks up at him with big brown eyes and quietly whines. "Don't try that on with me. Off you go." Ray whines once more before returning his head to a forward position. The dog then takes off trotting at a pace quick enough to cover distance but slow enough to observe his surroundings. They all watch as the dog pauses at the entrance to the walkway and has a look around. He then seems to move happily inside, scurrying across the walkway before disappearing into the room. All three wait nervously, trying to listen to any sound that may give a clue as to what is happening inside. Several minutes later Ray appears back in the doorway. The dog sits down and gives off one loud, but friendly, bark.

"I guess it is all clear guys." Seth says relaxing his posture and holstering his sidearm before taking a big breath out. Now with a smile on his face, he looks to Fin. "Well, you found it buddy.

You can go explore it first if you want?" Fin looks at his father grinning from ear to ear. "But carefully!" Seth emphasis.

Fin, still grinning from ear to ear, sheaths his blades and races in, Eve right on his tail.

Chapter 5

TREASURE

Seth calls Ray back to his side. The dog zooms past the children as they move into the entrance of the hidden room. He gives Ray a quick, reassuring pat before instructing his cybernetic companion to guard the entrance. *Better safe than sorry.* With a last glance, Seth dashes after Eve and Fin, a grin tugging at the corner of his lips.

The once-secret entrance now exposed, Seth ventures down a tunnel that feels as though it has been chiselled by hands far greater than any mortal. Arches rise above him, their surfaces etched with shapes and symbols too precise and divine for him to comprehend their creation. As he steps further inside, he can feel the weight of the atmosphere change. The air itself hums with an ancient power so overwhelming that Seth feels as though the room is alive. This place wasn't just built, it was shaped by forces he can't understand, by something whose talents exceeded human understanding. Every carved pattern pulses with forgotten energy, and Seth can't help but wonder who, or what, created this, and for what purpose?

The end of the passageway opens into an enormous dome shaped room. Dark stone tiles line the floor, with torches spaced out evenly around the room. The torches give off enough light to see, but not so much that a blanket of mystery still rests over the room. The torches burn with golden flames, a small green core flickering at their centre, making Seth suspects they aren't actual fire but some kind of advanced lighting system. Seth moves over to the nearest torch to inspect it. Removing his left glove, he notices some flakes of dried Dragon blood fall off and drift to the floor. *That dried up way too quick.* He thinks before returning to the task at hand. Seth puts his bare hand close to the flame to test for heat. There is no change in temperature the closer he gets, so Seth runs his hand through the flame. Seth feels no burning sensations or heat from the flame. So, he rests his entire hand in the flame. Again, there is no heat but Seth watches, amazed, as the flame retreats under his palm before slowly creeping back around his hand to its original position.

"What are you doing Dad?" Eve's concerned voice breaks his concentration.

"Testing a theory." He replies as Eve appears by his side.

"So, it's not hot then?" Eve asks as she studies her father's hand in the flame.

"Nope."

They both stare at the flames, mesmerised for a moment. "I thought maybe it was a light and putting my hand over it would block it, but check this out." Seth removes his hand from the flame, waits a moment, then puts it back in. Like last time, his hand blocks the flame for a moment before it snakes its way back around to its original position.

"Oh, that's cool Dad. What do you think it is?" Asks Eve, captivated by the flame's movement and behaviour.

Seth gives her a look like 'how would I know' before shrugging his shoulders. "I know just as much as you do right now beautiful." It surprises Seth that even at this age and as talented as she is, she still sees him as a father who must know all the answers to her questions.

"Fair enough." She shrugs her shoulders before heading back towards the centre of the enormous dome shaped room. As interesting as the flame is, it is nothing compared to the rest of the hidden room. The room is filled with beautiful and exotic items to the likes of which they have never seen before. A path made from the smooth dark coloured stone tiles leads around the room with several branches leading off it to the centre. It reminds Seth of a museum, the golden torches acting as back lighting for each item on display.

Both sides of the path are lined with varying displays, showing off all sorts of mysterious items. Some look familiar like books, odd paintings of what must be important events, and odd shaped vases. Others, however, look completely foreign. There are small metallic statues made from odd coloured metals that float in the air. Glass containers with multi coloured gasses sealed inside that seem to have a mind of their own, and other alien items Seth cannot put names to.

The family eventually runs into each other at the far end of the circular room. Eyes wide and without speaking a word, they turn down a path and head into the centre of the room. They pass more and more unexplainable items but cannot vocalise their wonder and excitement. In the centre of the room, they find an extravagant shoulder height golden pillar holding an oddly shaped symbol. They all tilt their heads, confused. The centre piece of the room is very underwhelming, almost anticlimactic. A simple dusty metal grey symbol floats above the much more impressive pillar.

"Umm what is it?" Asks Eve. Vocalising what they are all thinking.

"Not sure beautiful." Answers Seth, as confused as she is.

"Must be powerful or valuable. Why else would it be the centrepiece of this room? I doubt whoever made this place had nothing better to show off." Fin attempts to justify why the underwhelming item is atop the golden pillar.

The family continues to stare at the item, unimpressed but somehow mesmerised by its presence. It feels like the symbol has its own gravity and is pulling them into the item itself. Seth wonders if this is what Fin was sensing earlier, as even he can feel its pull now that he is close. Before he can ask, Eve interrupts.

"Lame!" Eve is already bored by the symbol, so starts looking around at all the other items in the room. Seth breaks his gaze a moment later and follows Eve's lead, eyeballing all the other mysteries surrounding him. Fin catches his family looking around out the corner of his but can't seem to break his gaze. He swears he can hear mischievous laughter coming from somewhere. That is until he feels his father's palm gently slap him in the chest.

"Okay team, eyes on me for a second." He pauses, looking into both his children's eyes to make sure he has their full attention. "It's about time we talk about what the hell is going on here." Their eyes light up, reminding him of when they were both small children, and he was going to tell them what chores needed to be done before they could have a delicious treat. "I don't think humans made any of this. I've never seen any tech like that creature before. Even Ray, who is high end for an AI animal, is nowhere near as advanced or as capable as that creature was." He says as he points back in the direction of the Dragon's corpse.

Seth looks around the room another time, both to confirm his thoughts and for effect. "Also, this place, as in this entire planet, is supposed to be a brand-new find. We are meant to be the first living creatures ever to walk its surface. That is obviously not the case. But who could have got this far out from colonised space to do all this?" Seth can feel himself ranting but wants to get his point across and do his mental math out loud. He doesn't want to hold anything back from the kids and wants them all on the same page. "And a lot of this stuff looks old, like really old. I'm not even going to speculate on why all this stuff is hidden and needed its own guard Dragon." He watches as the kids draw the dots together and figure out that perhaps this wasn't the Dragon's home, but the Dragon may have in fact been guarding this hidden room.

"So, I can't see how humans could have got this far out into space in time to do all this. There are also no other signs of any humans or human built machines ever touching down anywhere else on the whole damn rock." He stops so that he can take some deep breaths to remain calm. He looks at them both for a second. "What are your thoughts?"

Eve answers first. "Dad, I honestly don't think humans built this place. Let's ignore the creature for a moment. The architecture and design are so different from anything I have ever seen. Where are those lights in the roof and floor coming from?" Eve points back out towards the cavern. "And what is powering them?" Another question Seth hadn't thought to vocalise yet. "Also, what is all the stuff in this room? I've never seen anything like it. The mix of what seems like old and new technology? Hidden symbols that open doors? Unless some super rich Corp CEO is building a mystery playground for his kids, with a deadly robot Dragon in it. I doubt humans made this. It just doesn't add up to me."

Seth nods his head in agreement and looks to Fin, who is doing the same.

"Fin, what are your thoughts buddy?"

"Yeah, this place is giving off a whole different vibe to anything I have ever experienced before Dad."

Seth nods, waiting for Fin to continue, but he simply looks at his father and shrugs.

"Alright then." Seth continues, shocked at Fin's carefree attitude. *Just like your bloody mother.*

"So, we are dealing with a mysterious, advanced, intelligent race that has deadly cybernetic Dragons guarding its hidden treasures and has thus far gone undiscovered in the known galaxy. Cool, just another Tuesday on the job then I'd say." Seth attempts a little light humour to take the edge off what they are trying to comprehend. "Then what's our plan?" He says out loud, asking himself the question along with the children.

Seth, Eve, and Fin all stand in place for several moments, considering their options. "Well, we need to tell someone. It's the law." Eve states, putting her hands on her hips.

"Agreed." Say the boys simultaneously.

"What about the Ovmor Corporation?" Asks Fin. "Technically, they are the ones paying us, and the contract we have with them states anything found on the planet belongs to them. I am also guessing they have a similar contract with the Galactic Government?"

The Galactic Government has discovered so many new Earth Like Exoplanets or ELEXO's in the last thirty years due to an advancement in faster than light travel. This has meant that they can no longer keep up with their exploration remit. Ten years ago, they started contracting out ELEXO reconnaissance and scouting to the five major Mega Corporations. Seth has worked for most of them over his time as an independent contractor, making him one of the first and most experienced Planet Scouts in the galaxy.

Seth contemplates Fin's idea while the kids watch on. "No." He asserts confidently. "Technically, you are right buddy, under our contract, all of this belongs to the Ovmor Corp. And as much as I like our contracts, the opportunities, and financial rewards they bring us, I don't trust those greedy slime bags with this sort of knowledge. I've seen them do some pretty shady stuff in my time, and I bet their senior execs will somehow try to exploit this find to fill their pockets."

Eve nods her head. "I agree Dad, I don't trust them with this either. But then who are we going to tell?"

"The Galactic Government?" Fin chimes in again.

"Yeah, I think that's probably the best answer we have. I don't like it, but I can't see an alternative."

"Why don't you like it, Dad?" Enquires Fin.

"Well, you know I worked for the Government for a long time, and there are some fantastic hard-working professionals amongst their ranks. But there is also lots of red tape, politics, and bureaucracy. On top of that, they get inundated with crazies and their conspiracy theories. So, we need to make sure we know exactly what we are talking about before we talk to them, or anyone."

"Okay Dad, makes sense. But what are we going to do with all of this?" Eve extends her arms to point out the room, then out to the cavern. Again, all three of them stand there contemplating what to do.

"Hmmm, let's gather some key items from this room, the Dragon's head or something from it, and all our footage for evidence. We will make no mention of this in our report back to Ovmor. Then when we are back in colonised space, we will inform the Galactic Government." Declares Seth.

Eve starts to say something, but Seth raises his hand to let her know he hasn't finished. "Once we dump some of this stuff back on the ship, we will come back here and rig this place to blow. We can collapse the entire cave system in on itself so that no one will find it for a thousand years." This seems to answer the question Eve had. "Anything else?" Seth asks his children to make sure that if they have something to say, they get their opportunity.

"Sounds good to me, Dad. You think this room will fold?" Asks Fin.

Seth looks around for a moment, examining the room. "You know what? I got a feeling it won't. But if we can cut access off to it and bury the room under rubble, we should be good." Fin Nods, his mop of dark red hair bouncing backwards and forwards as he does.

"I'm happy-ish with that plan too, Dad. But I do have a question."

"Ish? Ish isn't good enough." Replies Seth, wanting to make sure she has her say. She is an adult now and deserves to be treated like one, even though she will always be his little princess.

"I wish we could take more with us."

"Oh, that's fair. So do I, but we don't know what half of this is. It could be dangerous." Eve knows her father is correct, but still feels sad about leaving things behind. "Was that your question Eve?" Seth moves the conversation forwards, not wanting Eve to get lost in that big brain of hers.

"Ah yes! Who exactly in the Galactic Government are we going to talk to about this?"

Seth rubs his short beard while contemplating the question. "I haven't figured that out yet beautiful, but I know who should be able to point us in the right direction."

"Who?"

"Uncle Otto is only a short jump from this system, so I thought we would go ask him if he has any contacts." Both Eve and Fin's faces light up with giant smiles when they hear Otto's name. "Alright then. Grab a couple of items each, and nothing so big that you can't carry it back to the ship. And nothing that looks dangerous." Begs Seth as the kids begin to eye off all the treasure.

Fin snatches the symbol off the golden pillar, pausing a moment to make sure nothing explodes before heading off for more treasure. Eve heads straight towards the exit, calling shotgun on the Dragon's head saying she will get Ray to help her. Only pausing to grab a small cube and what looks like an ancient bow or ranged weapon of some sort, which she slings over her back. Seth knew she would head for that Dragon. *That kid and her obsession with anything that can fly.*

Seth strolls around the room, looking at each item. He finds what looks like a tall painting of a battle. The scene depicts what looks like humanoids with long flowing golden hair battling smaller stockier vile green looking creatures. *Yep, that's going in the bag.* Seth carefully rolls up the painting, trying not to destroy what is most likely a priceless piece of art. If it is, in fact, even art. He then spies what looks like a large, thick book. On closer inspection, he sees the book seems to have a brown leather cover with intricate designs which remind him of a tree of some sort. He picks the book up and skims through it. The book contains pictures and writing in a language he does not understand. Flicking through the book's pages, he is shocked to discover that only half of it is finished. *Weird. Oh well, still looks like a good read.* Seth closes the book and puts it in his pack.

He continues on, discovering multiple items. A rare looking polished gem, maybe the size of his fist, grabs his attention. On closer inspection, the blue gem has a glowing purple smoke floating inside it. *Nope!* Seth leaves that gem alone, heeding the same advice he gave his children. Continuing his search of the room, he finds what looks like a small ceremonial blade the same size as a large knife. He picks up the blade from its display stand to examine it. The blade handle fits his hand perfectly. It is as if someone crafted the blade specifically for him. Seth can't identify the matte grey metal that makes up the weapon. Holding the blade in his hand, he notices its perfectly balanced weight. He also notices that the blade seems to ever so gently hum. It's almost unnoticeable in his gloved hand, so he removes his gloves to make sure he isn't imagining it. Bare handed he feels the gentlest of vibrations, confirming his suspicions.

He spins the blade around in his hand before doing several practice cuts in the air to see how the blade handles. Not only does the blade move swiftly through the air with precision, but the blade also somehow blurs the air behind where it has travelled. Seth makes several more practice cuts in a row. The blur now expands and seems to camouflage the area around the blade and around Seth himself. *Well, that's very cool.*

A matte black metallic sheath with a simple symbol on it lies on the floor next to the stand. The symbol consists of three blue lines of equal length, with the middle line higher than the others. The sheath catches Seth's eye, and he assumes it is for the blade. *Odd that it would be lying on the floor.* Seth picks up the sheath from a small pile of sand, blowing off the dust. Gently lining the blade up with the sheath to see if it fits, Seth attempts to sheath the blade. The moment the tip of the blade enters the sheath, the blade, as if powered by magnets, snaps into the sheath, almost cutting Seth's hand. Waiting a moment to make sure it isn't trapped or stuck in the sheath, Seth gently attempts to pull the blade back out, but it doesn't budge. *Ahh shit!* Seth wraps his entire hand around the blade, squeezing it tightly. The moment his grasp is complete, the blade almost ejects itself out of the sheath, creating a massive visual distortion in the surrounding area. Seth can feel himself grinning from ear to ear. He re-sheathes the blade and attaches it to his belt.

Once satisfied the blade is firmly attached, he scans the room one more time to see if there is anything else he wants or thinks will be valuable to take. There are multiple items he wants to study, but they either look dangerous or are simply too big to take back to the ship. *What a goddamn waste.* Deciding he is done with his task, he heads back to the doorway to wait for Fin.

Fin, on the other hand, has almost weighed himself down with items. Obviously not wanting to leave anything behind. Seth shakes his head but helps take several of the items to lighten the load. "So much cool stuff Dad!"

"Sure is buddy. Let's go see how your sister is going." Now that Fin is a little more mobile, they both head back out to see how Eve is doing with the Dragon's corpse.

When the two men arrive back at the Dragon's body, they see Eve has already set up a hover sled using the sparrows and a tarp from her backpack. Several parts of the Dragon's body lay on the tarp. Ray waits at the sled's other end, awaiting Eve's signal to pull it to the ship. Eve is currently digging deep inside the creature's body, looking for something. The boys stop and stare for a moment.

"Ummm, what are you looking for big sis?"

Eve doesn't reply as she seems to be focussed on the task at hand. So, they wait another minute before she eventually stands up, her arms covered in the Dragon's blood, holding something in her hand, wearing a big grin on her face.

Fin looks on curious "What you got there sis?"

"The Dragon's heart!" She exclaims, proud of her efforts. "The Dragon's brain was in too bad of a state to salvage. And the skull was barely in one piece!" She states, glaring at her father. Seth replies with a 'what was I supposed to do?' look on his face, shrugging his shoulders at the same time. "So, I followed some of the arterial like cables back to what I think is the heart." She cradles the large heavy organ out in front of her in both arms.

"Look how amazing it is! It's like some type of supercomputer made of bio-matter infused with advanced robotics." They all stare in amazement. They have seen nothing like this before in all their lives.

The heart is about twice the size of a human head and is covered in a hard-red plastic which, at first glance, almost looks like a type of armour. A deep, dark red flesh forms the parts not covered in hard plastic. From the heart comes two large tubes made of the red flesh, which Seth assumes to be major arteries. But on a further inspection, the tubes are filled with thousands of tiny digital fibres swimming in a dark blue fluid.

"Yep. That's exactly what a Dragon heart should look like." Mocks Fin. Eve rolls her eyes, knowing Fin didn't even know what a Dragon was until today. "Is it armoured? That's cool though sis." Eve lets his comments slide and smiles, proud of her work.

"Alright then Eve, is there anything else you want to collect from the Dragon?"

"Nope, all good Dad."

"Okay then guys, let's get back to the ship and stow this stuff away and get the demolitions ready." Seth orders the kids as he helps Eve clean herself up before picking up his pack and heading off. Keen to get the job finished and get out of this system. Seth has been scouting this planet on foot for over a month now. And if he is being honest, he wants to get into a hot shower to start getting all the sand, dust, and sweat off. He would also kill for some proper food. As good as his rations are, they are still not the same as a freshly cooked meal.

Eve packs the heart on to the makeshift sled along with the other parts of the Dragon that she feels might be interesting or useful to study. The two men head off and she commands Ray to follow them while pulling the parts behind. She takes one more moment to look at the dismembered Dragon. When she first saw it, she was so excited and amazed by it, but as she walks away now knowing she will never see it again, she feels an immense sorrow. Now that it is dead and no longer dangerous, there is something mystical about the creature. As if killing it broke some kind of spell, and now its body belonged more to the stars than the cavern floor. *Sorry, beautiful creature. I wish I could have known your name.* A single tear rolls down her eye. She wipes it away and picks up her pace to catch up to the boys.

In under ninety minutes, they have returned to the Scout, unloaded their bounty, and begun getting the demolitions prepped. Seth takes the data from Ray's sensors and the family's suits to fuse with the ship's orbital data to figure out the best place to put explosives to collapse the cavern. Rose, the ship's AI, runs the maths for several minutes, then gets back to him with an answer that surprises both him and the kids. According to Rose, it only takes one stick of demolitions placed on a specific pillar in the cavern to bring the whole thing down. As if whoever built it designed it to be destroyed easily. They all stare at each other, not sure what to say.

"Dad, do you know-" Eve begins to ask a question, but Seth cuts her off.

"I don't have the answers, and I know as much as you do, beautiful."

"But-" Seth cuts her off again, knowing she will go down a rabbit hole of questions if he lets her start.

"Yeah, I get it. There is something weird about this place. Something beyond the discovery of new intelligent life in the galaxy."

The frustration on Eve's face is obvious. She goes to ask another question but closes her mouth before the words come out. Seth can visibly see her running ideas through her head.

The more they discover about this place, the weirder things seem to get. The existence of a potential new intelligent race, extinct or not, should be a big enough discovery. But there is something off with this place and Seth can't quite put his finger on it. A feeling that this cavern has more meaning to it. But that's a conversation he can have with the family over a meal. There is still work to be done.

He packs an extra stick of demolitions for the Dragon. He wants to make sure that the beast is destroyed, and there is no evidence of it left behind, beyond what Eve has collected. His trust and confidence in humanity to do the right thing with this discovery is not high.

"Alright, I'm heading off to place the dems." He informs the kids.

"How did you actually find the cave entrance Dad?" Asks Eve out of nowhere.

Seth pauses for a second. This wasn't the question he was expecting. He can't bring up the visions of Sara he has been having. Not now anyway. It will upset Eve. "I just had a feeling, kind of like your brother did about the room, I guess. Like something was pulling me in that direction." Seth hopes his lie, albeit ninety percent true, is enough.

Eve pauses for a moment, then nods. She too felt something when she left the Dragon behind, and Fin obviously felt something that led him to find the treasure room. So it makes sense to her that something compelled her father to the cave's entrance.

She doesn't like basing things on feelings, but sees the pattern unfold in a way that adds up. "Yeah, this place kind of has that effect." She says while obviously glaring at her brother, who doesn't notice her stare.

Seth smiles. "Okay, you two stay here on the Scout and prep it for leaving the system. We can do all our post mission admin as we make our way to our jump point." The kids nod in agreement. Turning back around towards the exit ramp, Seth heads back off the Scout once again, taking Ray with him, just in case.

Knowing the way now, he runs back to the cave. He has always enjoyed finishing his time on a new planet with a run. Both kids think he is insane but will occasionally join him now that they are older and fitter, much to Seth's delight. The run is a hangover from his time in the military. Being able to go for a run makes him seem like he has secured the planet, and all is safe. The storm has died down now, and it's somewhat bearable on the planet's surface. So it should be a good run.

Ten minutes later, he arrives at the door leading to the cavern. He leans over, hands on his knees, gasping for air. Even though the planet's surface is now completely dry, by the way Seth is breathing, he assumes he must be well above the planet's ancient sea level. Ray appears between his legs to check on him, concerned by the heavy breathing. Ray's wet dog nose boop's him as he is trying to breathe, and he sucks in some dog hair, which makes him cough. *Sometimes I think I should have got a drone.*

"I'm all good boy." He tells Ray while giving the artificial dog a pat and a rub. He counts to five in his head, then stands up straight and starts forcing himself to take deep, slow breaths in and out through his nose. "Come on dog, let's go." He heads into the cavern's entrance, Ray following by his side.

Before using his forearm computer to navigate to the pillar Rose identified, he swings by the now dead and field dressed Dragon. When he arrives, it looks different somehow, but he cannot quite put a finger on it. The Dragon appears further broken down and more methodically laid out. But it's not like he had a good look at it after Eve cut it to pieces to get to its heart and he doesn't have the light from the Hawk to confirm. The neat layout looks like something Eve would have done knowing his daughter and the way her brain works, so he thinks nothing of it. *At least you're not trying to fry me up and eat me big guy.* He shoves one of the demolition charges inside the Dragon's carcass, then links it to his forearm computer. Hopefully, the explosion will turn what's left of the Dragon into a thousand tiny pieces.

He then jogs off to the pillar to set the charge that will bring the place to the ground. On arrival at the gigantic pillar identified by Rose, he stands in awe looking upwards towards the roof. Destroying such solid evidence of another intelligent lifeform in the galaxy leaves Seth conflicted. Why should he have a say in the fate of what happens here? Why is he worthy of such a decision? Is he doing the right thing? What would all the scientists and historians do to him if they found out?

Shaking off his feelings of doubt, he focuses back on the plan. He walks around the pillar to inspect it. *Worse case, it would take a mining crew, with the right directions, less than a month to dig back here with all their modern equipment anyway.* Seth looks around, trying to find a suitable spot to place the charge. "Alright, alright, where is a good spot for this little bad boy?"

He runs his hands over the pillar, searching for the right spot to place the explosive. Eventually, he comes across a divot. *Ah, that will do the trick.* He looks at the divot, studying it for a moment, trying to figure out the best way to place the charge. On further inspection, he notices two latches on one side. "Wait! No! It couldn't be!" He leans in and pushes on the divot. It pops open, revealing a small section inside the pillar, about the right size for his demolition charge.

'Okay mystic Dragon gods you win!' He calls out. *This joint even has its own destruction plan. Now I have seen everything.* Seth shakes his head, laughing at how crazy this all is. He increasingly feels that he was never meant to discover this place.

Seth has seen destruction plans attached to sensitive technology and equipment he used to carry back in the Unit. He has even seen destruction plans on specific advanced troop insertion capabilities. They would activate these plans if overrun or crashed to prevent the enemy from gaining a technological advantage. They built the items with a single specific flaw that would destroy them if needed. That or the plan was to take the equipment out by attaching several high-powered explosives to it. But he has never seen something that needed to be hidden under an unexplored planet, guarded by what seems like puzzles and a Dragon, needing its own destruction plan. It doesn't add up.

A shiver runs down his spine. Now that he is alone in the cavern and there is no threat, he can feel the silence weighing down on him. The unnatural precision of the architecture and the role of the Dragon, still unclear. He knows that there are more mysteries to the cavern and that they have only just scratched the surface of this place's true function.

Shaking his head, he places the charge inside the pillar and links it to his forearm computer. Calling Ray to his side, he has one last look around. The sense of unease rising. Not wanting to stay here any longer, he takes a deep breath, then begins his run back to the ship. The quicker he can get out of here, the better. He hopes that some of the items they took may help them understand more about this place and its purpose.

Eve has the Obsidian Scout fired up and ready to for take-off as her father returns to the ship. She looks over at her brother, who is sitting in the captain's chair. "Dad's back. You better hop out of his seat." Fin looks at the monitors on the screen.

"Did he run the entire way there and back?" Fin says, shocked. Eve stares at him for a moment with a confused look on her face.

"Of course he did! Remember, Dad is a certified nut job." Eve turns back to the console, double checking the ship, almost shocked that Fin is surprised by their father's actions. Fin hops up out of the captain's seat and moves back to his seat. Their father enters the bridge shortly after, still sweating and forcing himself to take deep breaths in and out of his nose.

"We good for take-off Eve?" Seth asks in between deep breaths as he makes his way to the captain's chair.

"Yep, good to go Dad."

Seth taps away on his forearm computer for a moment before sticking his head up. "Rose. I have synced the explosives to the ship's comms system."

"Yes Captain, so I can see." Replies the ship's AI.

"Alright Eve, take her up and we will blow it from orbit." Seth looks at Eve and she nods back. *No questions, no complaints. Damn she is a good kid. I am blessed.* Seth turns back. "Rose, we will need a pretty strong and well-aimed signal burst from the ship to initiate the dems from orbit. Can you handle that?"

"Yes, of course I can Captain. I will prepare the comms link now."

"Thanks Rose." Seth then turns his whole body around in his seat to face Fin. "Everything stowed for take-off? Did you put all the stuff from the cave in the hidden storage compartments?"

"Yes, and yes old man." Fin replies with a big grin on his face.

Seth leans over and gives Fin a fist bump before chuckling to himself. He leans back into his chair and shoots Fin a smile before turning back around. "Alright then, let's get off this goddamn rock!"

Chapter 6

OVERMORROW

If Eve has done over a thousand atmospheric entries, then her father has made her do over a hundred thousand takeoffs and landings. With practiced ease, Eve lifts the Obsidian Scout from the planet's red, sandy surface, leaving no hint of a bump, jolt, or sway. Kicking up sand and dust, Eve masterfully commands the ship as it begins its flight upwards through the storm. The reduced visibility is a no factor for Eve. Her father has made her take off and land in so many different scenarios that a bit of lost visibility does not even register a concern for her. Once she has cleared the surface and the ship reaches the upper atmosphere, she angles it up and heads for the open space of the system, leaving the red planet behind. Even though they had the entire planet to themselves, she finds the vast openness of space calming.

As soon as the ship breaks atmosphere, Seth puts his head down and starts tapping away at his console. Fingers moving furiously as he works on his report for the Ovmor corporation. He wants to make sure it is complete and accurate, but has no mention of the cavern and its contents. Lost in the report, Eve nudges him shortly after she has put the ship into a geosynchronous orbit high above the cave system.

"Dad, we're all set. Ready whenever you are to blow the charges."

Seth pokes his head up from his report. "Oh, excellent. Fin, you good for a battlefield damage assessment?" He asks over his shoulder.

"Yep. I have the ship's historical scans and a live stream of the planet's surface above the cave system on the screen."

Seth gives the thumbs up, then taps on the captain's console. Shortly after, a small flash of light appears on the screen. Fin watches the video feed but brings up several screens displaying a multitude of data. Eventually, the dust and sand from the explosion settle and the display shows a clear image of the explosion site. Fin compares the before and after images of the surface along with the before and after comparisons of some more technical data streams. He is happy with what he is seeing.

"Dad. It looks like the explosion has brought the cavern down on itself and destroyed it. Weather reports also have another storm closing in, so that should help put down an additional layer of dust and sand over the site."

"Excellent, thanks buddy. Eve, you can move us out of orbit."

"Roger that Dad." Replies Eve, who is already angling the ship towards the edge of the system.

"How long until we hit the edge of the system and can jump to hyperspace?" Asks Seth.

"At our current speed, it will take around an hour."

"Excellent stuff. Okay then, that will give me enough time to finish this report while you two clean up your gear and suits. If you hustle, you should have enough time to get in a scrub before we jump." Seth quickly scans over the report he is halfway through editing. "I will aim to get this done in the next thirty minutes, then I'll clean Ray. I can clean up my suit and myself once in hyperspace, and then we can have dinner and get some rest. How does that sound?"

"Sounds great!" Replies Fin.

"Sounds good to me to Dad. I've handed over controls to Rose to get us to the outer edge of the system." Replies Eve.

"Okay, let's get it done." Seth barks the order as he claps his hands together loudly. Both Eve and Fin jump out of their seats and head off to do their chores. "Rose. Let me know if anything pops up, okay?"

"Yes Captain, I will inform you of anything that may interest you or cause concern as I take the ship to the edge of the system." Replies the AI.

"Thanks Rose." Replies Seth before sticking his head back into the report.

Under an hour has passed and Seth notices Eve returns in a clean flight suit with damp hair and clean skin. He looks up from the report and gives her a smile. *She is so beautiful, just like her mother.* He wishes he could have given her a normal childhood, and that she didn't have to take on the role of an adult at such a young age. Maybe she could have had a more normal life if her mother hadn't passed, but maybe that would of lead her down a different path to a much worse life. Or maybe it could have allowed her to lead a better one. But there is nothing Seth can do to change the past, so he tries not to dwell on it. *Focus on being the best father to your kids you can be.* He returns to his report, knowing he has raised an extremely capable, strong young woman.

Seth reads over his report one more time. He learnt early in his scouting career to make his report as he was conducting the mission. Trying to remember everything at the end of a scout when he is exhausted was a futile activity. So now he gets Rose and the kids to add to the report daily. That way, he can quickly review everything at the end of the mission, attach all the technical data, and send it off before they even leave the system.

The report is ninety-nine percent factual, the way any good lie should be. It goes over everything the 'crew' discovered after spending several months on the planet. Weather patterns, soil quality, orbital data, how habitable the planet is, risks, and opportunities for settlement and mining. All the things the corporation wants to know about. He knows that humans have been more interested in profit than they have been exploration since before he was born. He leaves out the last part and says the sand and dust storms were too severe to continue safe planet exploration, so he concluded the mission and returned to the ship.

Having completed his review, he is confident that the report will deter the corporations from doing anything except mining the planet's polar regions for resources. And if he ever gets questioned about the mission, he can comfortably be open and honest about ninety-nine percent of what happened. Back when Seth was still in uniform working at the Unit, he learned that the most successful cover stories used to infiltrate different planets and networks, were always as close to the truth as possible. He has seen operatives come unstuck before because of a cover story that was too elaborate to remember, and impossible to backstop. Still, a sense of unease sits heavily in his chest. *Am I doing the right thing? Is this going to backfire on us somehow?*

Besides the ancient cavern, ELEXO 598-3 is just another far off desolate rock, floating through space with a breathable atmosphere and some minerals to mine. Most of the planets Seth explores are like this one, desolate and barren. They don't send the contracted Planet Scouts out on the safe, easy, or enjoyable missions. If a new tier-one planet suitable for a resort or large human colony is discovered, they don't use the contractors. They leave that to the corporation's executives or Galactic Government officials. The corporation will scout one of these planets with drones, making sure it's habitable and safe first. Then they will send down a small task group of colonist AI robots to set up a tiny outpost on a beautiful island somewhere. Once complete, some corporate big wig will fly down to the planet, stick a flag in the sand, take a photo, then spend a week having his own private holiday. All the while feeling good about calling themselves an explorer of new worlds. This type of behaviour makes Seth angry just thinking about it. He has seen too many good men and women lose their lives doing government and corporation dirty work. All so someone can make a dollar, get a promotion, or feed their ego.

Seth hits send on the report as Fin walks back onto the bridge, also clean but with dripping wet hair. "Did you even attempt to dry your hair, buddy?" Seth asks, confused why this kid is apparently allergic to drying his hair.

"Settle down old man, it will dry off soon. Besides, don't you have to go clean Ray?" Fin grins back at his father.

"Yeah, yeah." Seth waves him off. "Eve, how long until we jump?"

"You still have twenty minutes." Eve Answers.

"Plenty of time!" Seth jumps out of his chair and heads off to look for Ray, rubbing Fin's wet hair so it drips down onto his face as he walks past. Fin returns with a quick, harmless jab to Seth's thigh.

Seth finds Ray asleep out the front of Eve's quarters. He chuckles as he catches himself thinking the dog is actually asleep. It is simply updating software or downloading information to the Scouts digital storage while in a low-power mode. Both things it can do while awake, but it gives Ray more character and makes it seem less like a robot. Seth makes a high pitch whistle to get the dog's attention. Ray looks up. "Come on boy, let's get you cleaned up." The dog stands, its ears perking up with excitement and tail wagging. Seth taps his leg and Ray trots over by his side as they head to the ship's hanger.

The first floor of the hanger has a mezzanine level made of thick grated metal. Thankfully, the square gaps in the grate are only small, so Ray's paws don't get stuck as they head down the metal stairs to the washing station on the ground floor. The hanger itself is quite large. The Obsidian Scout is designed to support up to a forty-person crew, so there is almost too much room for the three of them and Ray. Seth has also modified different parts of the ship. The armoury, gymnasium, and training simulation room don't come standard with this model of ship. These are all upgrades to suit the family's lifestyle.

"Alright boy in you get." Seth says as he opens the door to the cleaning station. "So Ray, what do you think? Should we blow dry some of that dust and sand off you first before we give you a wash?" Ray replies with a gentle bark. "Alright then, hold on." Smiling, Seth pulls out the blower from the wall and starts blowing all the sand and dust off Ray he can find. After several minutes, he turns it off, shocked at how much came off the dog. "Holy crap Ray! Did you try to smuggle half the planet back on board?" Ray tilts his head and looks at him. Seth returns the look, then scratches the top of Ray's head. He then hits a red button on the wall, which sucks all the sand and dust away in one loud, violent action.

Next, it's time for a wash, so Seth hops outside of the small room. After sealing the door, Seth starts the cleaning sequence by pushing a button outside the small decontamination room. Seth peeks in through the glass window in the door and watches as Ray rolls around on the floor covered in soap and water. *You really have a mind of your own, don't you.* Seth runs the sequence several more times to make sure Ray is clean and dry. Once complete, Seth opens the door and Ray steps out shaking his now fluffy nice smelling coat. "At least you dry your hair after a shower, hey boy." Ray playfully barks at Seth as Seth shakes his head, thinking of Fin's wet hair dripping all over the bridge. He then turns and heads back as Ray walks beside him, proud of his clean coat.

"Ah great, you're here. I was about to call you to let you know we are ready to jump to hyperspace." Eve says as Seth enters the bridge.

"Great, thanks beautiful." Replies Seth as he moves to the captain's chair while Ray sits on his bed in the corner near the door to the bridge. "You have the jump plan set to get us to the Solus Space Station in the Pegasus sector of the outer rim?"

"Sure do." Eve says confidently. "I'm so excited to see Uncle Otto."

"Good, me too. Have you got Rose to check over your jump plan?"

"No." Says Eve, slightly offended. "Don't you think I know how to do it?"

"Oh, of course I do beautiful. I am more than confident that you know how to plot a hyperspace jump. But why wouldn't you get the AI to check it if you have time? It takes no effort from you, and it potentially stops us slamming into a star, or a black hole, or some other type of cosmic death trap." Seth looks at Eve and gives her an exaggerated smile.

"Fine!" Eve says before spinning back around in her pilot's chair and pushing several buttons on her control station. Shortly after, Rose replies over the comms that the plot is good, and they are ready to leave. Eve spins back around, glaring at her father. "See, it's fine."

"Never doubted you for a second." Seth says. This time with an even bigger, cheesier smile on his face. Eve, infuriated at her father's childish behaviour, spins back around. Shaking her head while doing her best not to take the bait her father is putting out.

Eve then turns the ship around, locking onto the jump trajectory. Smoothly flying the ship forward along the trajectory, she double checks the ship's diagnostics. Once she is happy, she alerts the boys. "Okay strap in as we are jumping in three, two, one, jump." The ship rapidly accelerates for less than half a second before they feel a quick jolt then nothingness as they enter hyperspace. They watch on as the glow of the stars begins to melt into a single dull blue light.

Hyperspace, a relatively new discovery for humanity, is magnitudes quicker than the previous Faster Than Light travel humans had used to explore the galaxy. The jump from their current location to the Solus outpost would have taken under half a year with the previous technology. Now the crew of the Scout will arrive in under two weeks.

One to two weeks jump from the edge of colonised space also seems to be the standard distance of their scouting contracts at the moment. Seth doesn't know of any other crews that are going much further out than that. There may be the odd mission going further, but that is done with multiple ships for safety and backup. Only around half the spaceships in the galaxy have this newer technology due to the lifespan of a spacecraft. With proper care, a quality inter-system travel ship can last up to a hundred years.

Eve checks all the diagnostic read outs and the navigation plan one last time, making sure everything is correct before spinning around to her father and giving him the thumbs up.

"Rose, take control of the ship and let us know if anything pops up, okay?" Seth orders. There are rarely any issues once in hyperspace, especially if you have plotted your jump path correctly. But Seth likes to stay on top of it because even minor issues this far beyond the edge turn into a life-or-death situation in a heartbeat.

"Yes Captain." Replies Rose.

"Guys, can you start dinner while I have a scrub, and I'll meet you in the mess in thirty minutes?"

"No worries Dad, what do you want to eat?" Asks Fin.

"Chef's choice, but make it big, as I'm starving!"

"Roger that Dad." Fin replies, already deep into the decision-making process of figuring out what to cook for dinner.

Seth drags himself out of the Captain's chair and heads off to his room to clean up. The cost of spending over a month walking around a harsh deserted planet, then finishing his little adventure with a fight to the death with a cybernetic AI Dragon is now rapidly catching up with him. *God damn, that shower is going to feel good.* He thinks to himself as he trudges down the corridor, his legs growing heavier with every step.

Arriving at his quarters, he opens the door and heads inside. *You clean your gear, then you clean yourself.* A voice inside his head reminds him. This was something he had been told many times in his military career and a motto he passed onto the kids. He takes several minutes to clean his scouting equipment, using a similar process to how he cleaned Ray. He hangs the jacket, pants, and boots up in a special compartment that will blast it with ultraviolet light, both drying it and killing any bacteria and unpleasant smells that may be present after the scout. Seth then turns on the shower in his room's ensuite and hops in. He was right, the thick pressurised streams of hot water washing over him feels absolutely amazing. He stands underneath the warm water for several minutes, slowly breathing in and out, allowing his body to relax.

A memory of his wife flashes into his mind and he feels a wave of irrepressible sadness flood over him. Unsure if it's water or tears that are now running down his face. "What have you gotten us into, my love?" He asks, knowing no response will come. "I have been following your visions for over a year, yet you never truly show yourself to me. I want you back more than anything. Are you real or are you just my imagination?" Seth's breathing becomes more rapid as his emotions take control. "You have always led me in the right direction and kept me safe. But this… This discovery is something else. Did you mean to lead me to the cave? Is this where you have been taking me all along?" He leans his head against the shower wall, letting the warm water flow down his back. He can feel a flood of tears coming now and he can't hold them back. "I don't know if I'm ready for this. The kids aren't ready for something like this. Another intelligent race in the galaxy! Why us, why now? Since the day you left, I have been looking for you, and now I'm tired. I'm so damn tired. I don't know if I can go on searching. I feel so empty." Seth can feel his face distorting as more tears begin to swell. "My body is exhausted, and I miss you so much it hurts. It feels like a dagger in my heart every time you appear in front of me." He can barely stand as the wave of built-up emotions he has been keeping inside for the last two months takes hold of him.

There is no point fighting it though. He has been here before. After every major expedition, he usually has a minor break in his emotions. Being switched on and hyper disciplined nonstop for months at a time means he must push all his feelings down so he can stay alert and clearheaded, to keep him and the kids safe. But pushing feelings down doesn't mean they go away. As much as he doesn't like it, he acknowledges that sometimes the body needs to get the emotions out of its system. So, he lets them come out now. The kids can't see or hear him, and the water dulls the noise, so he doesn't have to listen to himself cry.

Several minutes later, the wave of emotions slowly subsides and the crippling feeling of sadness passes. He is unsure if he is starting to feel better or if his body has just run out of tears. The warm water of the shower seems to hold him in an embrace. He feels like he has run a thousand kilometres, panting as he stands there naked under the water. *Control your breathing, control your mind. Control your breathing, control your mind.* He repeats to himself over and over for several minutes as he matches his breath to the mantra. Seth focuses on nothing but his breathing and the feeling of the water washing over him. At first, it's difficult to maintain focus. A single thought of his wife and the tears want to return. But eventually he manages to let the feelings go. Standing up tall and with perfect posture, like he was taught to do, he takes one big aggressive breath out, followed by shaking his arms and bouncing up and down.

The overwhelming feeling of sadness has left his system, and he is feeling whole again. *Okay, you're good now, old boy. Get your shit together and start acting like a soldier and a father.* He pours some soap into his hand and begins cleaning himself. Ritually washing off not just the dirt from the planet but also any emotions that may still be lingering. Once clean, he spends an extra few minutes drinking some water and having a light stretch under the hot shower before hopping out. While he still feels nervous about the discovery and he still longs for his lost wife, Seth now feels cleansed and ready to face the kids.

Entering the mess, he watches as Eve is finishing setting the table and Fin is spooning a delicious smelling meat and vegetable concoction onto some large bowls of purple rice.

"Hey Dad, I made a hearty meat and veg stew to go with some rice and bread. I also made some desert, but that's a surprise for after dinner." Fin says rubbing his hands together, proud of his creation. Seth can't hold back the smile that appears on his face. He has never felt so hungry.

Fin, who inherited his cooking skills from his mother and is easily the best cook out of the three of them, serves the meal. Seth and Eve are happy to eat whatever is the easiest thing to cook. Easy rarely means tasty though, and that's why Fin does most of the cooking and has for several years now.

They exchange few words over dinner as speaking would slow down the consumption of food, and they are all too hungry to allow that to happen. Seth looks at Fin, wondering if he has some type of magical ability that allows him to make the most amazing food. The meal is filling, delicious and extremely healthy. Seth feels his body recovering and growing stronger with each bite. Seth, amazed by his son, watches him eat. His now dry red mop of hair bouncing around as he gulps down the food.

"What?" Asks Fin with a mouth full of food.

"Nothing buddy. Both you and dinner are incredible."

Fin shoots Seth a goofy smile, then focuses back on his meal. Seth smiles back as his heart warms.

Now that they have all finished and are feeling full, the chatter begins. Eve asks her father about the confrontation with the Dragon in great, great, detail, not wanting to miss any of it. Seth, too full to answer Eve's detailed line of questioning, gets Rose to play the footage from his body cam instead. Both kids, and if he is being honest, Seth himself, sit there in amazement at the discovery and the battle. Seth shakes his head, unsure how he even survived an encounter with such a beast. Seth regrets his decision though as the footage seems to provoke even more questions from Eve instead of less. So, they watch it again, this time with Seth giving a running commentary and even pausing it in certain parts to explain his thought process in the moment.

Fin excuses himself from the table after the second viewing before returning with full hands. "Dum da daaaa." Fin makes a trumpeting noise with his mouth, which grabs Eve and Seth's attention. "Feast your eyes and your bellies on a homemade Utopian berry pie!" Both Eve and Seth clap at the look and smell of this delicious pie.

"Where did you get the U berries from buddy?" Asks Seth.

"Oh, I picked them up at the last spaceport we were docked at before we headed out on this round of scouts. They only had frozen ones, but I knew they would be fine if I baked them into a pie. Oh, and guess what?" Fin asks as a cheeky grin appears on his face.

"What?" Asks Eve as she glares at him, wondering what he is up to.

Fin puts the pie down on the table along with three large bowls, then turns around to look at his sister and father while walking back to the kitchen. "I also got ice-cream!"

Eve lets out a tiny yelp of excitement before slapping her hand over her mouth covering the noise. She then turns red with embarrassment. They all laugh before enjoying their well-earned treat.

"Okay, so when we finish here, how about everyone does their last checks before getting some sleep. Let's say we meet back here in twelve hours for coffee, then morning physical training?" Seth asks, knowing that the kids don't really have an option.

"Yep, sounds good Dad." Answers Eve straight away.

Fin has one more mouthful of his dessert before answering. "Not like I have anywhere else to be and besides, you will need the exercise after this dessert, old man." Fin replies with the same cheeky grin as before. Seth looks down at his stomach. After spending the last several months on the planet's surface scouting, he is anything but overweight. He plans to get a lot of food and training down range in the following week to get his body back up to fighting weight and fitness.

"Good. I will send Otto a quick message letting him know we are coming and that we should be there in around a week. After morning PT, we can do our After Activity Report, then come up with the work roster and training plan for the rest of the week. Sound good?" Both kids nod as they continue eating their dessert. It takes several more minutes for them all to finish their dessert than several more before they can break free of their food coma's.

The kids clean up, and Seth goes and gets a message off to Otto. Afterwards, he heads into the kid's rooms to make sure they are getting into bed for a well-deserved sleep. Before they fall asleep, Seth makes sure to give them three goodnight kisses. One on the right cheek, one on the left and one on the forehead. A ritual he has done every night they have been together since they were born. Both kids think they are too old for it, which they definitely are, but both don't bother putting up a fight as they know their dad is going to do it anyway. After their three special dad kisses Seth wishes them a good night, then returns to his room. He only just makes it into his bed before he passes out asleep.

Large screens and monitors illuminate the dark room, where busy corporation employees quietly move around, watching multiple operations and activities underway across the galaxy. This Overmorrow, or Ovmor as they call it, Operation Centre is in a heavily fortified building at an undisclosed location on a planet near the Core System. To even step foot inside, an employee must have undergone the corporation's highest level of security evaluations, psychological evaluations, and multiple interviews. Once an employee makes it through all the screening, they still need to sign their life away under multiple contracts explaining the secrecy of their work. The contracts specifically call out the punishments for breaking them. Some breaches in contract can cause the termination of the employee and the employee's family.

The commander of this Operation's Centre sits on a raised podium at the back of the room so that he can see every screen and everything that is happening on the Op's floor. The commander looks like he is in his late fifties. He has pale blotched skin and withered, thinning grey hair combed across his balding head. A life spent in dark rooms lit only by screens has done nothing for his health or his looks. There are over one hundred staff in the Centre at one time, monitoring thousands of operations as they happen, aided by the help of AI programs and trademarked code and software packages used to pick up any anomalies.

This particular Operations Centre deals with all types of operations, from low level logistical smuggling to company black ops and assassinations. The Overmorrow senior executives don't care to know the details of what happens behind the closed doors of places like this. They only want to secure a profit at the end of each quarter.

While the Galactic Government still holds the power across the galaxy, at least at face value and in the political halls of the Core system, the five major corporations are almost as powerful and operate as if they were their own governments. The corporation owned planets have their very own security forces and conduct their own paramilitary operations. The fundamental difference between the Corps and the Galactic Government is instead of being in the business of writing galactic policy, the Corporations are in the business of profit. It is this fact alone that leads them to more competitive and less honourable ways of doing business than their government counterparts.

One of the team leaders from the Op's floor approaches the commander sheepishly. He is scared of the man, well, to be more accurate, scared of his reputation. While the operations commander is abrupt, direct, and doesn't tolerate fools, no one has seen him commit any wrongdoing to his staff. However, there are rumours that he got kicked out of the Galactic Military at an early age for being too violent and sadistic. He also has a reputation for running some highly successful, but morally questionable, clandestine operations.

"Excuse me Sir." Says the team lead uneasily.

The commander doesn't break his gaze with what is currently occupying him, but eventually replies. "Yes. Please report." Even his polite tone has a hint of venom in it.

The team leader stands up straight, quickly wiping some sweat off his brow. "We have discovered an anomaly from the contract team sent to scout ELEXO 598-3." Pausing, the man waits for the commander to reply. The commander says nothing, so the team leader awkwardly continues. "Ah, sorry. Ah, ummm, so the Scout team were towards the end of their mission before one of our inter system probe droids, who by chance happened to be passing by the edge of the system on its way back to its local base, noted an explosion on the planet. Only sixty minutes later, the report was sent back to headquarters, then shortly after, the ship jumped to hyperspace. There was no mention of the explosion in the report." The team leader stands at attention, waiting for the commander's response.

The commander eventually looks down at the man from his raised platform, studying the man's face and features before speaking. "Sounds like another Planet Scout who thinks he has found something of value and thinks he can make a little extra profit on the side by stealing from the corporation." The commander's tone carries distaste and disgust. "I am so sick of these filthy contractors thinking they are smart enough to outwit us. We already paid the greedy little worms exuberant amounts for their work." He glares at the team leader. "What is this filth's name?" He says, not hiding the venom in his voice this time.

"Seth McCallan, Captain of the Obsidian Scout. The details are in my logs if you wish to view them, Sir." The commander looks down his sharp long nose at the man, then looks down at his data pad. He searches through the information for a minute before snapping his head back up. "Ahh, there it is. An ex-military man. No doubt he thinks we owe him something for his service, that he is somehow better than us. The fact that we have given him a high-paying job, and an opportunity, isn't enough!" The commander angrily looks down at the team lead for a moment before his face relaxes and he smiles. "Thank you. You have done good work here today. I think we shall make a point with this one, so that his little Scout friends understand you cannot steal from the Corporation." The commander waves off the team lead, sending him back to work before calling over another man. A large, strong looking tanned man with a scar running down his right cheek and a shaved head, walks over. This man doesn't seem intimidated by the commander like the previous man, and he doesn't snap to attention when he arrives.

"What's up boss?" The large man asks.

"I am going to send a recovery team to a planet one of our contractors recently scouted. There seems to be evidence that he might have stolen from us. You are to lead the mission." The large man nods in agreement. "If we are correct and he has in fact stolen from us, I would very much like you to recover what is rightfully and contractually ours." The large man nods once more, disappointed. "When you have recovered our property…" The commander stares at the man, grinning from ear to ear. "Make an example of him and his crew, would you?"

A wicked smile grows on the large man's face "Yeah. Sounds good, boss." The large man hasn't been given any interesting work for a while now, and is looking forward to getting some blood on his hands again.

"Excellent. I will send you the relevant details so that you and your team can take care of this for me. Feel free to use whatever resources you feel are needed, and report back to me at regular intervals."

"To easy boss. I will head off now."

"Good." The commander sits back in his chair, interlocking his fingers and resting his chin on top. He is satisfied knowing that a filthy, entitled contractor is about to get what he really deserves. The commander smiles to himself once more before returning his watchful gaze to the operations floor.

Chapter 7

TARGETS

CRACK!

The sound of old wood smashing fills the air as a bullet just misses Eve's head and slams into the building behind her. *Shit, shit, shit!* Eve takes a knee, lowering her profile she returns fire into the window where she saw the shooter fire from. *Take that!* Eve thinks to herself as she sees a shadowy figure tumble back into the room after one of her rounds finds its mark.

A sharp whoosh cuts through the air as Fin fires his heavy-calibre sniper rifle at a distant target.

Eve feels a powerful hand grab her on the shoulder. The hand squeezes down, but not to pull her away or shake her off balance, but to alert her of the incoming command. "Move!" Shouts Seth, as he takes a knee behind her. She stands up and peels off to her left, changing magazines as she moves. As soon as she is out of the way, Seth starts firing from his assault rifle.

Weapons have evolved little in the last several thousand years. The technology has gotten better, the weapons have become lighter, quicker, and more accurate. Humans have even adapted weapons to fire in multiple environments, including space and low gravity. But regardless of the technological advances humanity has made in the past several thousand years, nothing stops another human dead in their tracks quicker than a fast-moving piece of metal right between the eyes. Combat always has been and always will be a dirty business.

Woosh!

Another round from Fin's sniper rifle flies overhead.

"Dad, three hundred meters, slight left. Multiple combatants moving to flank!" Fin's voice crackles in Seth's comm, barely audible over the gunfire.

Seth shoots several more rounds off at an approaching combatant, dropping the attacker, before pivoting to his left to drop behind a small wall. He changes magazines before looking over the wall. Seth sees what looks like half a platoon, fifteen to twenty armed assailants, approaching their position. He grabs a High Explosive grenade off his belt and readies it, pulling out the pin. "Eve. Covering fire!"

Eve knows the drill. From her position, she unleashes several rapid bursts of fire from her rifle to make sure the aggressors can not take any well-aimed shots at her father. As soon as Seth hears Eve's rifle open fire, he pops up from behind the wall and throws the grenade towards the group. The specially modified grenade travels over one hundred metres through the air before it hits the deck. Seth can hear several of the enemy soldiers scream out before the large explosion goes off. The moment Seth hears the explosion, he is back up on his feet. Firing at the soldiers that made it out of the blast zone.

Swoosh, Thump!

Fin's round finds a target less than one hundred metres away from Seth. The high powered round sends the soldier flying backwards through the air before his now lifeless body hits the floor.

"Dad, Eve is in location and covering. Move now!" Fin says over the comms link.

Seth moves without question. He has complete faith in Fin even though he is still so young. Several bullets land near his feet, kicking up dirt as he sprints towards the small structure Fin has set his sniper position up on. He enters the building, which at one point must have been a small shop and sees Eve standing two metres back from a window, firing out at a target. Seth moves up near a second window that looks out the way he came. Like Eve, he stands back from the window, daring not to hang out of it and make himself an easy target. He waits silently to see if anyone is advancing on their position. Hearing Fin climbing down off the roof, Seth resists the urge to look back to see if he is okay. A wise choice as he spots a Corporation soldier trying to peek around a corner and fires one round off, dropping him instantly.

"Going to secondary weapon." Whispers Fin to both his sister and father. He packs the large sniper rifle down into three parts and shoves them into a bag in the middle of the room before pulling out an assault rifle. He moves next to his father and taps him on the shoulder. Seth peels back into the centre of the room as both his children watch out the windows for targets. Seth slings the bag with the sniper rifle over his shoulders, securing it tightly in place. Through the bag and his combat gear, he can feel the heat of the rifle's barrel on his back. Fin must have put a lot of rounds through the weapon. He then checks his forearm computer. Looking at a map of the local area, combined with footage they took from the Obsidian Scout on their descent to the spaceport, Seth identifies several options for them to get back to their ship and back to safety.

"The quickest way back to the Scout is through the market district, but there are too many spots to get ambushed." Seth muses out loud as he studies the map. "We can go around the outside of the living area, but it will be a hike." Seth contemplates the options. "How are you guys feeling? Up for a run?"

"I've been lying around all afternoon, so I'm good." Fin says sarcastically.

"The markets sound like a bad idea, Dad." Eve says as she sips a mouthful of water.

"Okay, looks like we are going for a light afternoon jog." Seth taps his forearm computer, turning it off before rolling up the sleeves on his combat shirt, exposing his forearms to the fresh air. He leaves his black combat gloves on, however. A bit of fresh air on the skin will cool him down, but the gloves, while hot, are a necessary requirement in combat and removing them is a not an option.

"Okay, I don't know where the Corporation is getting their endless supply of assault soldiers from, but bomb up and get ready to run."

"Already good to go." Replies Eve.

"Me too." Says Fin.

"Okay then. We are heading out the back door, then straight for one hundred metres. We will hit the city permitter wall and hang a left. The wall should take us all the way around to the spaceport, where we can jump on board the Scout. All up, it's about ten clicks. I have sent Rose a message and told her to get the ship ready." Seth looks at both his kids. The adrenaline of the situation is still in their system so they will be alright for now. Seth will need to monitor them, so they don't come down too fast or stay amped up for too long. "On me." He orders as he exits the back door of the small building, rifle in his shoulder.

Seth scans the area, all clear. He pushes forward, slow at first. He can sense Fin right behind him and hear Eve behind Fin. He can't see anyone on the streets. The fire fight must have scared the local population, and they have either bunkered down or bugged out. He can hear the distant sound of local police ships moving to their location, so picks up the pace. Thankfully, the large city's buildings are covered with temporary man-made structures, making it nearly impossible to see down to ground level from above. This gives them the advantage of cover, but the disadvantage of a multitude of locations to be ambushed from by the Corp soldiers that are hunting them.

They arrive at the city wall without being seen by the enemy. The city wall is a large concrete structure almost ten metres high and several metres thick which runs around the entire inner city. It was originally used as the base for the massive bio-dome that housed the city while the planet was being terraformed. But that was almost one thousand years ago. Now it acts as an ancient landmark within the city and excellent cover and concealment for the family to use to their advantage.

Seth looks down the narrow passage that leads along the wall. No combatants are in the passage and he can't see anything that looks out of place for such a location. He steps off into a light jog, wanting to move fast enough to lose anyone on their tail, but not so fast that they run out of energy before reaching the Scout. If the enemy is worth their salt, they will have an ambush waiting back at the ship. Seth hopes these Corporation soldiers are as poorly organised and bad at communicating as most Corp units he has come across. If so, they might have a decent chance of surviving and getting off the planet.

The narrow path is strewn with debris and rubbish that has blown into or been washed up against the city wall. This makes the journey harder than they were hoping for. They have to change to a slow jog with occasional sections of walking for fear of rolling an ankle. The extra twenty kilograms of combat gear will be enough to cause a decent injury if one of them falls awkwardly.

Thirty minutes pass with no sign of the enemy or the local authorities. Seth slows down to a walk and instructs the kids to have a quick drink. They take turns drinking while the other covers the rear. When both kids are done, Fin steps in front of Seth so Seth can have some water too. They remain still and silent for a moment, listening to the city. They can still hear the sirens of the ships flying around, looking for them. But the sirens seem distant, which reassures them. Besides the noise of the distant sirens, it all seems clear. While silent and stationary, they can hear people going about their daily life. They must be far enough away from the original firefight now. The smell of local cuisine being prepared and the sound of kids playing off in the distance fills their senses. They wait one more moment before setting off again.

As they step off, Eve hears a noise behind her. She spins around, rifle raised. Eve sees nothing in the passageway, then instincts kick in. She looks up. Five metres above the rear of her position, she sees movement. She automatically trains her rifle onto the target and looks through the holographic sight. But before she pulls the trigger, she realises the target is a child, maybe only eight years old. The child is climbing on one of the man-made structures between the buildings and the city wall. Eve's heart pounds as she lowers her rifle, thankful she didn't shoot the small, innocent child. She removes the rifle from her shoulder and watches the child for a moment. The child, oblivious to what just happened, smiles and waves. Eve, taking a big deep breath, smiles and waves back before turning around and darting off to catch her brother and father, who are back running again.

The second half of the journey is a little easier. The closer they get to the spaceport, the less debris and rubbish is in the slim passageway. They assume this must be from the powerful engines blowing when they land and take off, pushing anything further back down the unintentional wind tunnel that the city wall and the structures next to it have formed. Seth slows them back down to a walk when they are within a kilometre of the spaceport. "Hey Eve, do you have any Sparrows or the Hawk with you?" Asks Seth as a plan forms in his head.

"I don't have the Hawk, but I have two of the Sparrows?"

"Perfect. Can you get them both up in the air, one in front of us and one behind? Then sync one to Fin and one to yourself?"

"Sure can. Now?"

"Yes please."

Eve takes off her backpack, then reaches inside to grab the two Sparrows. She switches on the two ball sized drones and gently throws them up in the air, only maybe a foot or two above their heads. Once they are hovering in place, Eve gives control of one Sparrow to Fin, who flies it forward about thirty metres in front of the group. Eve then flies hers back only ten metres. She knows they will move shortly, so there is no need to send it all the way back. Seth steps off again in the lead but this time with the sparrow providing him situational awareness and early warning out in front.

They are only about one hundred metres from the space port now and the roar of the engines as ships arrive and leave is almost deafening. Seth takes out the small comms earpiece he has been using and wipes it clean. He then puts it back into place and grabs the second earpiece, which hangs around his neck. He then taps some commands on his forearm computer, which allows him to filter out certain sounds. The roar of engines dies off and he can now hear everything clearly. Looking back, he can see the kids have already done the same.

Seth motions to Fin to send the lead sparrow out to do a recon as the narrow passageway abruptly ends ahead of them. Following Seth's instructions, Fin watches the drone fly into the open area. Once clear of anything overhead, Fin sends the sparrow up, giving it a bird's-eye view of the surrounding area.

He notices several guards patrolling the airfield, but they look unarmed. Fin watches for a minute then informs his father of the situation, letting him know they will come past the passageway in approximately five minutes if they continue on their current route. Seth acknowledges, then lets Fin get back to his recon.

Several minutes pass before Fin speaks up. "Dad, Sis, it looks bad. I reckon there are about fifty plus corporation mercenaries patrolling the space port in groups of three to five. There is a bunch near the Scout as well."

"God damn it." Mutters Seth under his voice. Both kids stare at him, alarmed.

"What are we going to do Dad?" Asks Eve with desperation in her voice.

Seth thinks for a moment.

"First, let's grab the two guards who should be passing by any moment now. Then I think we get as close to the Scout as possible without being seen. We will get seen at some point though, and when we do, we bring the noise. We pop smoke and go in a straight line to the ship. Thoughts?"

"Sounds dangerous Dad. Is there another way?" Asks Eve.

"Look, we could double back and play cat and mouse for an indefinite amount of time until we run out of ammo or hiding spots. We might be able to disappear, but the longer we wait, the less of a chance we have of getting onto the Scout and off this shit hole of a planet."

"Yeah, okay. That makes sense. I'm in then."

"Fin?"

"Can I throw the smoke and maybe a grenade or two?"

"Sure buddy, why not." Answers Seth.

"Then what are we waiting for?"

"Right, you two stay here and I will sort out the guards."

Seth silently moves forward to the end of the passageway while staying in cover. Stealing a quick look around the corner, he sees that the pair of guards are only about twenty metres away. He slows his breathing and waits until he thinks they are within several metres. Slowly, he expertly manoeuvres his rifle and body around the corner, angling himself in case the guards are armed. The guards aren't paying attention at all to their surroundings and Seth has to clear his throat to get them to look his way. When the guards look up, they are in complete shock.

"Keep your hands down by your sides and come this way or I'll shoot you where you stand." Seth can now see that they are unarmed. He has no intention of hurting them. But he needs them to believe that their lives are on the line. The pair do as he asks and come into the passageway as Seth slowly backs away. Fear fills their faces as they see Eve and Fin in full combat gear pointing rifles at their heads.

"Ditch your radios and any weapons you have right here and don't say a word."

The pair look at each other, then back at Seth. He moves his finger off the trigger guard and onto the trigger. Eve and Fin pick up on this slight movement and follow suit. The pair also notice and quickly do as they are told.

"Good, now I want you to go back and continue your patrol as normal. Do not! And I mean do not raise the alarm. If you do, I promise you I will shoot your two first." Growls Seth. The pair turn white as the blood drains from their faces and into their vital organs. A subconscious reaction of the human body when it is in a state of immense fear. "When the shooting starts, grab anyone near you and run back here and hide until it's over. Do you understand?"

Both men now trembling with fear nod.

"Good, now move!" Seth growls at them again, making sure they maintain their fear levels.

The pair head back the way they came, walking slowly. It looks like one of them may have wet his pants. The pair head straight for a civilian transport, hopefully to help evacuate the people that have landed. The family gives them a ten count, then moves out into the open. Heading for the Obsidian Scout, which rests around eight hundred metres away.

Corporation soldiers are everywhere, but none have noticed them yet. The good thing about Corporation soldiers is that the average foot soldier is no match for a Galactic Military soldier. People that join the Corporation units are usually people who couldn't make it in either the Military or the Galactic Security Forces.

The trio stay tight and close to each other, providing all round security as best they can. They have practiced their patrol formations hundreds of times before. All of them keep their weapons by their side in an attempt to not draw any attention. Each member of the family knows their arcs and trusts each other to patrol theirs. They are moving quickly though, as they want to be as close to the Obsidian Scout as possible before starting the fight.

Seth at the front is flicking his head from side to side as he leads them forward. A large ship comes into land several hundred metres in front of him. "Ah, hell!" Seth says out loud. Both kids turn to have a look. The spaceship is a combat drop ship filled with well over one hundred Corporation soldiers. The family freeze in location. Seth quickly shoulders his weapon and looks through its scope. It doesn't look like the soldiers are there for them or conducting a combat drop. They have their weapons and helmets slung and seem to be conducting an administration move. Seth wastes no time however, and takes advantage of the situation.

"Fin, hand me some grenades and get all the smoke ready.""On it." Fin says, tossing two grenades to his father."Dad, what are you doing?" Eve's voice is tight with concern.

"We are going to go start a fight, beautiful." Seth says with a wicked smile. "Now, on me. Let's go!"

Seth charges forward towards the landing ship, grenades in hand. The kids have to sprint after their father to stay in formation.

Seth gets to within one hundred metres of the ship and one of the spaceport security guards on the ground notices him. The guard calls out for them to halt and identify themselves. "Eve." Seth says while continuing his charge towards the ship.

"Stop!" Orders the guard as he reaches down and un-holsters his sidearm. Before he can get his weapon up and aimed towards Seth, Eve pumps two rounds into him, dropping him instantly. Her father is now only thirty metres from the ship, but she remains in location looking for targets, as she knows the enemy will now be on them shortly. Seth unpins the grenades and takes aim for one of the ship's engines. He throws the grenades one at a time as hard as he can, hitting his target each time. The slowing engine explodes, rocking the large spacecraft in front of him. Seth then pulls out his own two remaining grenades and throws them at the ship's landing gear. They explode right on the landing gear arms, causing damage. The explosions from the grenades doesn't destroy the landing gear, but damages them enough for the ship's weight to do the hard work. Rocking back and forth from the engine blowing out, the weight of the ship starts to bend the landing gear's support leg. The damaged leg of the landing gear can no longer hold the ship's weight and snaps, causing the ship to collapse to one side. His plan has worked. This won't cause much overall damage to the ship, but now the hatch door the troops were to exit from can't open properly. This will hinder the soldier's ability to exit on mass and provide support to the troops on the ground.

"Smoke!" Seth yells to Fin over the sound of the whining engines as he moves off at a ninety-degree angle, waving for the kids to join him. Fin throws smoke in every direction, creating a large screen for them to move through. Seth waits for the kids to arrive next to him, then gets Fin to throw one more smoke grenade towards the Scout. They then all run off together.

"Eve, Sparrows, and get Rose to fire up the engines."

"Roger." Eve says in response while wildly tapping on her forearm computer. The Sparrows begin a tight three-hun-dred-and-sixty-degree orbit around the outside of the group. The family all flip down their combat glasses and sync up to the Sparrows. This allows the family to use the Sparrows enhanced optics to identify targets through the smoke and superimpose their position through the glasses HUD. They do their job as targets begin to appear. All three family members begin shooting in an attempt to drop as many Corp soldiers as possible and cripple the enemy's advantage.

Rounds start to come back in the general direction of the group as the ground forces begin to engage in earnest. The smoke is providing a good level of concealment and Seth keeps up the pace as they are only several hundred metres from the Scout now.

"Ships three hundred metres ahead, I want you guys to Go! Go! Go!" Seth barks at the kids before letting out a large burst from his assault rifle. The kids waste no time and sprint off towards the ship, firing at anything that might be a target. They are not worried about accuracy at this point, but keeping their enemy's heads down. Bullets bounce around their feet and Eve feels the wind of a bullet pass her head by what feels like only centimetres. She sprays bullets off in the direction she thinks the rounds are coming from before digging in and running as fast as she can.

Fin sees his big sister dig in and move off quicker than he can keep pace. So he steps off to the side and takes a knee, spinning back around to see where his father is. He sees Seth, twenty metres away, walking backwards while firing at multiple targets. Fin lets rip with several bursts of his own to help provide cover for his father. Seth looks back at Fin. "Move!" Seth yells to motivate him to get back to the ship. Fin looks at him, then at the enemy closing in on them. "NOW!" Seth yells again. Fin looks into his father's eyes and decides that a pissed off dad is scarier than a thousand soldiers trying to kill him. Fin empties his magazine in a giant spray of bullets towards the closing enemy before turning and sprinting towards the ship.

Seth drops to a knee and takes multiple, fast, well-aimed shots at several groups. Striking a target with every round, all while providing cover for Fin as he withdraws to the ship. He stands up and begins his own sprint back to the ship. On his left flank, he sees two soldiers charging for him. He goes to shoot, but his weapon doesn't fire as he is out of ammunition. He reaches for his sidearm, the one he used to slay the Dragon with, and fires off two rounds. Both head shots.

Two more soldiers appear on his right flank. He goes to fire, but his weapon jams and nothing happens. *God Damn it!* He holsters his sidearm on the run, then grabs his rifle at the base like he is holding his axe.

Shots rain over his head as the kids return fire from the top of the Scouts ramp back towards the growing number of enemy combatants. Seth veers off slightly and heads directly towards the pair of soldiers closest to him. Shock comes over the soldier's face as they didn't expect Seth to charge directly at them. They freeze and try to bring up their weapons as he swings his assault rifle. Seth connects with the first soldier's rifle as the soldier opens fire. The force of the hit sends it off its mark and into the second soldier, putting several rounds into his stomach. The first soldier looks on in shock and attempts to help his fallen teammate, but feels a sharp blade pierce his spine before he drops to the floor.

Eve and Fin still firing watch their father sprint past them and up the ramp before they turn and run back inside the Ship.

"Rose! Shields up and take off!" Yells Eve as she runs off towards the cockpit. But before she can even make it out of the hangar, everything fades to black.

Chapter 8

SOLUS

The pitch black darkness fades away as the lights flicker back on in the simulation training room. Fin lies on the training room floor, sweat soaking his clothes, his chest rising and falling as he gulps for air. Eve sits in the corner also trying to catch her breath while Seth stands in the centre of the room, hands on his knees, the salt from his sweat stinging his eyes. He takes several controlled deep breaths before he wipes his eyes and brow with the sleeve of his shirt and heads over to see Fin. "Don't lie down mate, can't fight from down there." Seth leans over Fin and offers him a hand. Fin happily takes it. He will take any help he can to get back to his feet at this moment. Seth then heads over to Eve, who waves him off. Seth pauses to check on her. She looks exhausted, but fine. Satisfied, he grabs their water bottles from an alcove designed to keep them from rolling into the room during a sim.

He hands the water bottles to his children before taking a big mouthful of cold water himself. "Good work, guys. That was… a hard scenario." He spits out, still not entirely in control of his breathing. Seth plans out the training scenarios they complete in the training room each week, in great detail. Making sure they run through a variety of scenarios and tasks to reinforce basic skills while learning new ones. This ranges from combat and shooting, reconnaissance, scouting, first aid, and dealing with human and technical situations that require complex problem-solving skills outside of simply using brute force. He was, at one time, in charge of training for his military unit. A role he took seriously and excelled at.

While he doesn't have the resources, funding, or access to locations he once had in the military, he still does his best to train the kids in all the skills they will ever need. Even at their young age, he has them trained far better than your average soldier, and most likely to a tier three or even tier two, special operations level. This is on top of their scouting training. Ever since their mother disappeared or died, Seth doesn't know what to think with all these visions he has been having lately. He's been worried about getting injured or dying, and the kids not being able to look after themselves. This is now one thing that he no longer worries about. The kids would be fine without him, although he has no plan to leave them anytime soon.

Once a week in the training plan, he gets the ship's AI Rose to pick an extra challenging scenario of any kind that she has downloaded from their last layover. Seth lets the AI edit the scenario so that not even Seth knows what will happen. This is what they have now completed, and this is what has them sprawled out around the training simulation room exhausted. The training room itself, which takes up the spot of one entire drop ship hangar bay, is state-of-the art. The entire inside of the room can move and create different levels and textured terrain while displaying a super detailed semi-holographic scenario specific for each individual. It can even be hit and shot with multiple weapons designed specifically for the training room. It isn't the same as training in the real world. But it makes for an amazingly effective way to stay active and train while on long journeys through hyperspace.

"What the hell was that?" Asks Eve in between mouthfuls of water.

"I think Dad put it on nightmare mode!" Comments Fin.

"Nope, you have Rose to blame for that hellish scenario." Seth heads over to the small display on the wall near the entrance. He studies the display for a minute, flicking through different screens to get information. "That scenario was called Corporation: Escape the Horde!"

"Rose!" Shouts Fin, waiting for the AI to answer.

"Yes, Master Fin, how can-"

Fin cuts her off. "You are an evil AI!" Both Eve and Seth have a little chuckle, even Fin laughs to himself. Proud of his silly joke.

"That's impossible Master Fin. AI can't be evil. I would never do anything to hurt you or the rest of the crew of this ship."

Fin shakes his head. "Sorry Rose, it was just a joke."

"Yes Master Fin, I now understand. Shall I make the scenario easier next week?"

"Nah." Fin replies, lacking the energy to be more articulate.

"Yes Master Fin. Crew of the Obsidian Scout while I have you. Would you like the results and debrief from today's scenario?"

Seth jumps in. "Rose, I would like to go over them while we have our lunch. Can you have them ready to review in the kitchen?"

"Of course I can, Captain. That would be my pleasure."

"Alright kids let's go get cleaned up, then have a feed. We will be arriving at Solus in approximately three hours." Seth pushes the kids out of the room before tiding up what is left and heading off to get in a quick shower in before lunch.

The deep blue lights fade away as the Obsidian Scout pulls out of hyperspace. The blue glow on the bridge fades, replaced by the dark red light of a nearby star, a stark contrast to hyperspace. Eve quickly pulls the Scout into line, orientating herself with the spaceport and the other ships within the system. She leans over and activates the comms, initiating the handshake with the station. "Space Station Solus, this is the." She pauses for a second and looks to her father for confirmation. Seth nods at her from his Captain's chair. "This is the spacecraft, Golden Phoenix. Requesting permission to dock." Eve sits patiently, awaiting a reply. Eve hears the whirling of a busy comms centre as someone pushes down a second too early on the transmit button before beginning their return.

"Call Sign Golden Phoenix. This is Space Station Solus. Please state your business at the Station."

Eve flicks the comms down confidently, now having permission from her father to use the light cover they had rehearsed. "Space Station Solus, this is the Golden Phoenix. The crew of the Golden Phoenix are returning from a scraper mission along the outer rim. We are hoping to offload some of our haul and quickly stock up on supplies before heading off to our next jump point." She is confident in the backstory she and her father came up with together and tries not to give too much away. Her father told her the conversation should flow naturally and not to overdo anything or offer too much information at first, as that would seem unusual. Her father rehearsed this scenario and many others, preparing her for a multitude of possible questions. They rehearsed until she was overly comfortable and could run through a bunch of different questioning scenarios, to the point she seemed almost bored by them.

Many spacers venture beyond colonized space seeking treasure, knowledge, or adventure. Few find anything, most become stranded or perish due to poor planning and lack of survival skills. Because of this, there is a reasonable market for people who know what they are doing to go out and save these would be adventurers. However, this is only true if the lost crews are connected or very well funded. Sadly, most spacers end up recovering or salvaging dead ships and make their living from selling off the parts.

The number of times the Obsidian Scout has had to rescue some poor crew that are out beyond the edge on their way to a scouting mission is too many to count. It's always the same story. A cousin of a friend, of a friend, heard that there was, insert ridiculous treasure that makes no sense at all on how or why it would be there, is located on Planet X and if you find it, you will be rich beyond your wildest dreams. Seth's personal favourite is when a ship gets lost looking for some mysterious magical or mystical item, like a fountain of youth or a stone that will give you superpowers. These always make him laugh. If it wasn't for the easy work and high pay they earn off saving these people, Seth would happily leave most of them to their fate. Although, after finding the Dragon and its hidden treasures, he is wondering if some of these loonies might actually know something that he doesn't.

"Golden Phoenix, this is Solus. You are clear to dock. I have sent the instructions to your ship along with the rules and regulations of the spaceport. You will need to acknowledge these by digitally signing the paperwork sent to you and returning them before you dock."

"No worries Solus, we are looking forward to getting back to a little civilisation." Eve replies, surprised the story worked so easily. Several moments pass, then the comm kicks back on, startling Eve. She is worried she may have said something wrong, and they have seen through her cover.

"Phoenix, this is Solus. Can I say, that ship name must be the most common name for a ship in the whole galaxy. I have had several ships arriving and leaving under that name in the last week compared to some ship names that I'll see once a year if I'm lucky."

Eve looks at her dad, who makes a fake laughing face. "Hahaha, tell me about it Solus." Eve quickly replies. "We got this ship for a steal second hand, but I have lost count of the number of times we have been mistaken for another ship. We almost got shot out of the sky a year ago back in the Core system. Seems like another Golden Phoenix was a known pirate ship! Would you believe that?" She stares at Seth and shrugs, mentally crossing her fingers, hoping her lies worked.

"Hahaha that's hilarious!" Replies the Solus comms operator. "I mean, I am glad you and your crew are okay and all, but still, that's hilarious. Oh well, stay safe and enjoy your time at the station. Solus out." Eve listens as she hears the comms operator calling his friend over to share the story with before the comm cuts off. She then relaxes back in her chair and returns her focus to flying the ship. She is much better at flying than sneaking around the galaxy undercover. That's her dad's area of expertise.

The Obsidian Scout moves into the shipping lane, behind a large line of ships queued up to enter the space port. From a distance, the space station looks like the metal skeleton of a small moon, but as they get closer, they can see this is pure coincidence. It seems that the original station has been expanded on multiple times over a long period to cater to the needs of its residents and the travellers that frequent the station. As they approach, the chaotic assortment of structures becomes more noticeable. No two alike. They are well lit up though, to stop any ships accidentally colliding with different sections of the station. Solus is oddly beautiful in its own unique way. It reminds Eve of a small pet that is so ugly that you can't help but think it's cute.

The space station houses around one million permanent residents with an average of five million people transiting through once a month. This makes Solus one of the busiest space stations out on the edge of colonised space. Not only is Solus on the edge, but it also sits along a trade route and is close to several holiday systems. This makes for an interesting mix of travellers docking at the station. The space station itself is Galactic Government owned but run by the Alliance Technologies or Alitech Corporation, one of the five major corporations. Besides one of his oldest friends, Otto, being the head of logistics for the spaceport and holding a high-ranking position, this space station has no connections to the Ovmor Corporation. Although being a large spaceport, all five corporations have representation on board.

This is why Seth chose to come here instead of one of the smaller space stations closer to ELEXO 598-3. He hopes this will give him some breathing room while he tries to figure out exactly what to do about the discovery. He also wants to seek counsel from his old friend, hoping he can provide advice, but also help if needs be.

"Okay Dad, we should be moving in for docking in around five minutes and will be ready to disembark in twenty."

"Roger that." Seth spins his chair around and fires up the comms system. He puts in the details Otto gave him and attempts to make contact. No luck on his first attempt, but that does not surprise him. Knowing Otto, he is probably working hard and focused on a task. Seth waits for another minute, then tries again.

"This is Logistics Commander Otto. What do you need?" A harsh, deep voice comes over the comms link. Eve and Fin stare at their father in shock, but Seth smiles to himself.

"What I NEED Logistics Commander Otto, is for you to show some respect to VIP's who have come all the way from the

Core system to grace you with their presence on your dirty little backwards space station. That's what I need! Do you even know who my father is?" Seth says in his best impersonation of a posh Core world'er. There is no response for almost ten seconds until they all hear a deep boisterous laugh come over the comms.

"Dam it Seth! I was fixing to march down to the docks myself and punch some spoilt little brat in the mouth there for a second. How are you old friend?" This time, the deep voice sounds filled with joy and is much more welcoming than before.

"I'm good brother. We should be docked in about fifteen. Where would you like us to meet you?"

"Us? Is Eve and Fin there with you too mate? That is fantastic! Look, I will send one of my guys down to get you and bring you up to my office."

"Roger that brother." Seth says with a hint of happiness in his voice.

"Alright, see you soon. Otto Out." Seth turns around to the kids to make sure they were listening. They give a thumbs up.

Eve, whose focus is on the controls, steals a second to see her father lean back in his chair and smile. She hasn't seen him this happy for a long while. Which makes her smile too. She knows how much he does for her and Fin and how hard he works, and works them. She admires his dedication to his profession and dedication to them, but wishes that every now and again he could take a rest. For their sake and his. But that is not his way. She wonders if he even knows how to rest.

Once the ship is docked and they get confirmation from both the docking controller and the ship's AI, they head to the external hatch near the ship's bridge. Seth takes the chance to share a quick plan of attack with them.

"Okay guys. So obviously don't talk to anyone about what we found on the planet." Both kids turn and look at him like he is an idiot for even suggesting they would.

"That being said." Seth puts his hands up defensively. "I am going to show Otto one thing we brought back from the cave as evidence. If anyone asks, stick to the cover story of us being scrapers. Acknowledge?" Asks Seth, looking for confirmation from his children.

They both confirm by saying 'Ack' back to him. "When we have had the chance to catch up with Otto, I have jobs for you guys to do before we leave. Eve, can you go make sure we have any parts required for maintenance and repairs on the ship? Fin, can you go hunting for some food and beverage supplies, plus any other supplies you know we are low on? Rose should be able to send you a list." Both kids have giant smiles on their face and give their dad a big nod. It's not very often that they get off the ship with a mission to go shopping. Even though they are shopping for boring supplies, the excitement of getting to do something besides combat training, exercising, or scouting on a distant un-inhabited planet is almost too much to contain.

While the kids are off daydreaming about shopping, Seth takes the opportunity to give Ray a pat and some orders. "Ray, we will be gone for no longer than a day. You are to guard the ship and listen to Rose, okay?" Ray spins around excitedly before running back towards the ship's bridge to see Rose.

Still lost in their daydreams, the kids jump as the hatch light turns green and the door snaps open, making Seth chuckle as they scramble to refocus. The smell of the station hits them first. There are almost too many aromas to decipher. Fin stands completely still for a moment, then closes his eyes, mindfully absorbing all the smells and sounds from the station. It's a little tradition he has recently incorporated into his 'new location' routine. Fin takes a moment to identify each and every smell and sound. Then attempts to figure out exactly what they are and where they might be coming from. He has gotten rather good at it recently, to where he can almost identify all the different stimuli, down to their individual components. He isn't sure if he will admit this to himself, but he thinks he can follow the stimulus and narrow down the exact location as well. Fin thinks that is impossible and just his imagination playing tricks on him, so he ignores that part and enjoys the moment and what it offers.

However, Solus overwhelms Fin with unfamiliar sounds and scents, different from the ones he's used to on other space stations. The sounds of crates being unloaded, trucks driving on metallic floors and engines firing combine with the smells of burnt metal and different fuels. *Hmm, cargo area and loading docks, I presume.* Fin thinks to himself. As interesting as the docks are, he can't wait to leave Solus's docking bays. He is itching to get to the markets where he will guess the variety of delicious smells from the fresh food selections the station has to offer.

"Hello, is this the McCallan family?" Abruptly yells an elderly, short blonde-haired gentleman with a short, patchy beard. They all get surprised by his rapid appearance from seemingly nowhere and, by default, Seth reaches for a hidden blade. The man is dressed in what Seth remembers to be one of the Solus Station's white workers uniforms. He has several pens in his shirts pockets, a multi-tool in his cargo leg pocket, a small radio around his belt, and a clipboard in his hand. Quickly seeing there is no threat, Seth pretends to scratch at his back, hoping the man did not notice him go for his blade.

"Yes, that is us." Answers Seth.

"Good. I'm Klaus. Otto sent me to collect you. Follow me please." The man turns around and immediately starts walking back the way he came without even looking back to see if he is being followed. Seth slings his small backpack, then pushes

Eve and Fin forward and they quickly race after him to catch up.

"Were off!" Seth yells back into the ship in case the dog is still within earshot, before shutting the hatch and following behind the kids.

"Is this your first time on Solus?" Abruptly asks the small, seemingly angry man. Who is still not bothering to turn around.

"No, but we haven't been here for like five years." Answers Eve. Looking around to see if she can get her bearings.

"Not much has changed. You have landed in the East dock. Docking bay One Seven Three. Please don't forget that. One, Seven, Three!" The man opens a door leading out into a large open area filled with workers and large droids busily moving around, going about their daily business. "We primarily use this part of the spaceport for logistics and freight movement. Usually, vessels carrying only people dock in the North or South docking bays, but it looks like you must have drawn the short straw and ended up here with us working folk." The man finally turns around and walks backwards while looking them up and down from head to toe, obviously aware that they are docked in the logistics area to avoid attention. "Although, you do look like a rag-tag bunch that has done some genuine work in your day." He says, raising an eyebrow as he gives them a knowing glare.

The man makes a sharp left turn after a vehicle carrying large supply crates passes by. "Please stay close to me. I do not want to have to fill in the paperwork if you get run over and killed by one of the station's fine workers or autonomous freight vehicles. And I certainly don't want to make the boss mad." Seth, who is hanging back at the end of the line, does a quick jog to make sure he is right on their tails. The short man weaves them in and out of more traffic and workers, going about their business, until they reach a large passenger elevator.

He stops in front of the elevator doors and points at them. "Okay then, in you get. Press the button for level seventeen when inside. That's where the boss is, and apparently, he wants to talk to you." Once they are all inside, the man pushes the button to close the doors. Scurrying off back to whatever job this annoying errand took him from.

"Hey, it was nice to meet you Klaus!" Calls out Fin sarcastically. The man turns around and glares at them before speeding off again. Seth mockingly slaps him on the back of the head and Fin laughs. "Sorry Dad, but I couldn't help it. He was just so accommodating." Seth laughs and shakes his head.

The boy is too smart for his own good.

The elevator jolts as it begins its slow ascent. At this speed, they'll have time to catch their breath after the chaos of the docking area. The family finds that it usually takes them several minutes, or even up to an hour, in the worst case, to adjust to the hustle and bustle of a busy spaceport or planet. Especially after spending several months out in space or on planets all by themselves. Seth reminds them to do their breathing using the method he learnt while in one of the military's most elite units.

Control your breath, control your mind.

They all do the breathing drill just like their father makes them do after training every day. When Seth first taught it to them, they were sceptical and hated doing it. But after a little practice, it began working for them. To the point whereby the time the lift arrives at level seventeen, they have all settled themselves and are calm and collected.

The elevator doors open to a short corridor with a big steel door at the other end. Seth smiles to himself. *Set yourself up a little kill zone, hey big man. What have you been doing with yourself to need one, I wonder?* Seth leads the way while the kids fall in behind. He gets to the large door then knocks, looking at the camera positioned above the door. A small light on the door flashes green and the doors slide open, and the family walks inside.

Beyond the door, they find a large office with a big wooden desk in the middle of the room. Several large screens displaying security feeds from different parts of the station are on the wall behind the desk. Behind the desk sits a large man. He slides back away from the desk in his chair, spins around slowly and stands up. He is taller than Seth by several inches, which is impressive considering Seth is considered tall by most. Not only is he taller than Seth, he is also about twice as wide. He has a big barrelling chest sitting above a slightly rounded belly. Thick muscular arms protrude from his thick trunk and wide giant tree like legs support his frame. The man wears blue cargo pants and a well-worn black short-sleeved collared shirt. He has short, thick, jet-black hair, which is slicked back, and a large thick black moustache.

The big man pauses for a moment as he looks the family up and down, then grins, his thick moustache curling upward. "Seth! You ugly old bastard, how are you my friend?" He then flicks his eyes at Eve and Fin. "Are you two kind young people being harassed by this ugly old man?"

The kids both giggle, and Eve replies. "No, no, he is fine. We keep him around to scare the monsters away with his ugly face."

"Hey!" Seth fakes insult.

The giant man has another boisterous laugh which thunders throughout the room. His chest and belly raising up and down each time he chortles.

"Ahhhh, come here and give your uncle Otto a hug then."

Eve heads in first. Otto gently hugs her, slightly picking her off the ground. Fin then moves over, waiting his turn before getting a solid hug from Otto and several big slaps on the back which almost knock the wind out of him. The big man then moves over to Seth, who puts his arm out. Otto grabs his arm below the elbow and both men bring each other into a half hug, giving several slaps on the back. After they finish the embrace, Otto looks them all over once again with his hands on his hips. "Holy crap, you guys have gotten bigger! How long has it been three or five years?"

"Five." Answers Fin.

"That would explain why you all look so grown up. Eve, you are beautiful and Fin, look at the size of you boy! And that hair! Just like your mothers." The kids both get a bit embarrassed, but Seth looks off at one of the screens, not realising he is still feeling the pain of seeing Sara amongst the storm back on ELEXO 598-3. "Come, sit down." Otto points to a couch in the office's corner, before heading over and turning off all the screens. "Do you guys need anything? Food or a drink?"

"No, we are fine. We had lunch before we docked. Thank you though, Otto." Answers Eve.

"No? So, you don't want any of this Bellervian handmade chocolate then?" Otto pulls out a block of chocolate from his desk. Bellervia is a planet near the Core system known for its high-end agricultural resources. Most of the galaxy's delicacies come from Bellervia. Both Eve's and Fin's jaws drop when they see the chocolate. "So, I take that as a yes, then?" Otto smiles and reaches back into his draw pulling out two blocks of the expensive chocolate, throwing the kids one block each. "Don't eat it all at once, okay?" This will be a challenge for the pair as the smell of the chocolate alone is to die for.

Otto ushers the kids over to the couch so they can sit down and enjoy some of their very expensive and fancy chocolate. Eve sits down and relaxes back in the couch, mentally crossing her fingers hoping Otto will tell a tale from her father's past. Her father rarely talks about the past, but when he does, Eve loves to hear it. She isn't sure if he is so secretive because there were some tragic incidents that are too painful to discuss, or everything is too classified to talk about. Even with your own children.

"Kids, did I ever tell you about the time your father saved me from a bunch of Talaskian insurgents?" Eve smiles from ear to ear as her wish comes true. The kids both shake their heads and lean forward on the couch, eagerly awaiting the story.

"Well, there I was, running the quartermaster's store like I always did, in this backwater outpost, in the middle of nowhere, on some shithole of a planet. I think they had terraformed the planet or were in the middle of doing so. Either way, that's irrelevant to the story. Just know that it's a shithole." Seth takes a deep sigh out as he remembers the story about to be told. "The entire company was out on a clearing patrol except for myself, four regular special forces guys pulling guard duty, and your father who had got back from a solo reconnaissance patrol. So, there I am sitting down eating my lunch, while your father over here is off getting cleaned up and having a quick scrub when suddenly, out of nowhere, we come under attack!" Otto raises his voice to stress the surprise of the attack.

The kid's eyes open wide, and Eve tries to contain her smile.

"Those regular SF guys all get hit by gunfire and are killed instantly. So, because those useless regs weren't doing their job, now I have to stop eating my lunch and run into the armoury. I come back out with the heavy machinegun, waiting for the raiders to come exploding through the gates. Seconds after I ready myself, those Talaskian scumbags blow the gates wide open, so I let rip with the machinegun. I manage to mow several of them down with the gun before I have to put my head down, so it doesn't get shot off." Otto pretends to hold the heavy machinegun while acting out the scene.

The kids are really excited now, but Seth leans back in his seat and puts his hand over his face, shaking his head. Eve notices her father's movement out of the corner of her eye and wonders what would be so embarrassing.

"I thought I was done for. There were at least fifty of those mean bastards bearing in on me through the front gate."

"Fifty!" Seth interjects.

"Oi, shut your mouth old man, I'm telling this story." Eve and Fin are in shock as they have never heard anyone talk to their father like that before. Seth throws his arms up in the air in defeat.

Otto gives him a nod before returning to the story. "But then all of a sudden, their firing stops, and everything goes quiet for a moment. Then I hear all this hooting and screaming. Now I'm not sure if it is a trap of some sort or if someone has shot me and I don't realise it yet. But fearing for my life, I risk sticking my head up to sneak a peek. And to my amazement, do you know what I see?"

Eve and Fin stare at each other, not sure what to say. They look back at Otto, their eyes begging to be told.

"I see old ugly face here, leaping from above the gate, axe in hand wearing nothing but his birthday suit and combat boots!" Otto slaps his thigh. "God Damn it, I was as frightened as I was shocked by the sight! But not as much as those Talaskian bastards were. Your father lands in the middle of them, taking several of them out with one swing. Then, buck naked, proceeds to cleave through the rest of them like a hot knife through butter!"

The kids giggle.

"You see, they were all packed in tight together trying to get through the gate, so didn't want to shoot at your father for fear of shooting one of their own. Plus, most of them were frozen with fear, due to the fact that there was a crazy naked man, now covered in the blood of their comrades, spitting hate and stealing souls."

They all look at their father in pure shock.

"The raiders were so confused about what to do. Your Dad, buck naked I will remind you once more, killed them with that axe of his before they even fired a single round back!"

Seth interjects. "Okay, okay, settle down. There were about fifteen of them all up, including the ones you took out with the gun, and I wasn't completely naked…"

The kids look at their father, not sure if they should believe what he is about to say.

"I had my gloves on too…" They all laugh out loud.

"You ruined my lunch that day, old man! You still owe me a decent meal for that too." Otto jokes as he leans back into his chair. Eve and Fin laugh uncontrollably for several minutes.

The laughter eventually subsides, though, and Otto continues. "But on a more serious note, that was only one of the many times your father saved my life kids. He is an exceptionally good man, and I am lucky to call him a friend and you are even luckier to have him as your Dad."

The kids look at their father with a little more respect than they had before seeing Otto. Seth smiles back and pats them on their backs.

"Otto, you are too kind and don't act like you haven't saved my life before either."

Otto grins. "Maybe only once or twice." He then winks at the kids, who want to hear more about both Otto's and their father's history together.

But Seth turns to the kids before they get the chance to ask questions. "You guys right to go handle those jobs I gave you?" The kids both nod their heads begrudgingly, obviously wanting to be part of the next conversation. "I am trusting you to be safe and make good choices, stay away from danger and maintain good situational awareness." The kids roll their eyes, having heard the same speech, what feels like a million times before.

"Hey!" Otto interjects in a serious tone, grabbing the kids attention. "This station isn't a war zone, or one of those lonely planets you guys like to visit, but it isn't the safest place in the galaxy either. You kids listen in to what your old man has to say. He knows his shit." Otto states firmly. Eve and Fin both nod respectfully.

Otto then explains to them how to get to the different markets and says to use his name if they get into any trouble. Both Eve and Fin appreciate the fact that both Otto and their dad are trying to look after them. Before they leave, they give Otto another big hug and head out a different door to the one they entered. Seth watches them leave, then checks his forearm computer to make sure he is tracking them properly.

"Stay safe!" Orders Seth as they head off into the space station alone. They both wave before happily continuing on. Seth smiles to himself as he watches Eve throw her arm over Fins shoulder and start explaining something to him as they disappear around the corner, heading off deeper into the wild sprawling space station.

Chapter 9

PARTS

The mood in Otto's office shifts to a much more serious one now that the kids have left to complete their tasks. Seth turns around to see Ottos enormous bear like figure pouring two drinks as he sits behind his desk, intently watching Seth. The playful and fun uncle persona he put on in front of the kids is now gone. Big, strong, calculated, professional and dangerous is how Seth would describe his old friend if asked. Otto wasn't a shooter like Seth back at the Unit, but he'd seen his fair share of combat. Otto was good at killing and had no problem doing it when required. So it's no surprise to Seth that Otto has been successful after the military.

Seth moves over to his backpack in silence, now excited to show his good friend what they have found. His only worry is that he hopes Otto doesn't think he has lost his mind.

"Alright old friend, it's great to see you and the kids and all, but what are you doing here on Solus? And how could I ever help you? You're the one who is always helping me out, remember?" Chuckles Otto. Seth smiles in return before pulling the ancient book out of his backpack and placing it down on the table. "What is this Seth, you want me to read you a bedtime story or something?" Otto seems confused. Books are very rare, but not that rare that you couldn't get one back in the Core systems if you knew the right places to go and had enough money to buy one.

"Open it up and have a look."

Otto wipes his hands on his pants before opening the book. It looks ancient and has a golden glow that seems to emanate from the cover. If it is worth a lot of money, he doesn't want to be the one to ruin it. Inside the book, the pages look thick and soft, almost like they are handmade from a thin cloth or paper. The book's contents are in a language Otto doesn't understand. Most of the galaxy reads and writes in common. There are only a handful of worlds that still use their own language systems. Otto, however, knows enough to identify that the language in the book isn't one of them. There are also illustrations on every couple of pages that seem to gently vibrate. The movement is so subtle, Otto thinks it might be his eyes playing tricks on him.

Suddenly there is a deep whirling sound throughout the station and the lights in the room flicker off, then on again. "For Earth's sake!" Otto curses, his voice sharp with frustration. He gently closes the book, then jumps on one of the comms units in his office. Seth can hear a worker from engineering answer but can't make out what he is saying.

"This is Otto, get Frank on the comm now!" Seth leans in and has another look at the book while Otto gets ready to reach through the comm and tear someone a new one, for what seems to be a power issue across the station, or at least in the east docks. The lights flicker on and off again while Seth is studying one of the pictures. He swears he sees something move on the page. Even Otto catches it out of the corner of his eye, making him lose his train of thought for a second before continuing to yell at poor old Frank on the other end. Otto quickly finishes the conversation, telling Frank that if he doesn't fix the issue Otto will make sure he doesn't get the shipment of flowers and perfumes he promised his new girlfriend.

"Okay so what was that, Seth?"

"Yeah, look, I don't know. It's like one of those pictures started moving and a little light came out of it." Both men stare at the picture, but nothing happens. Seth thinks for a second, then asks Otto to turn out the lights in the room. Otto reaches over and presses a button on his desk and the lights turn out. They sit there in the dark, waiting to see if something happens. Seth flicks the page over then back again. When it turns back, the picture lights up and jumps off the page, and starts moving around like a hologram of some sort. They both stare at it in awe. Seth runs his hand through the image and the symbol seems to roll over his palm and fingers. Similar to the torches in the hidden room, Fin discovered back on ELEXO 598-3. Neither Otto nor Seth can tell what the object moving around is, but it has a light blue glow to it. Seth flicks through the book and they watch multiple pictures and shapes come to life on the pages in front of them.

"What is this? Is it some type of magic?" Seth hears Otto mutter to himself.

Towards the middle of the book, they notice that one of the three-dimensional pictures looks like a man. It seems to move around the page, ducking in and out of the words. On the next page, the figure starts, what looks like, running. Fascinated, the pair continues on. They see a larger red figure with wings chasing the man. Eventually the two pictures come together, then the red one falls back to the page and fades away. On the next page, two more humanoid looking figures appear, accompanied by what looks like something smaller with four legs. Seth pushes himself back from the table in shock. The chair screeches on the floor and Otto quickly flicks the lights back on.

"What is it?" Otto asks, concerned.

"I... I think those last pictures are of me and the kids." Seth says, shocked. "And that red one was the Dragon." Seth is now attempting to decipher the book in his head and figure out what is going on. He looks up to see Otto, staring at him blankly.

"Dragon? What the hell are you talking about old man? I only gave you one drink!"

Seth snaps out of his train of thought. "Oh sorry. I have some explaining to do, but it's better if you watch something. Is this room secure?" Otto stares back at Seth in shock that he would even need to ask. "Yeah. Sorry." Seth taps on his forearm computer several times, unlocking the multiple levels of encryption he and Rose put on the footage from the encounter with the Dragon. He then slides over next to Otto so he can have a clear view. Seth shows him the footage of the fight with the creature inside of the giant cavern. Otto stares at Seth for a while, then opens up his draw and pours himself another drink. He slams the drink down fast, then pours one more before putting the bottle away.

"Umm, that was some serious shit, old friend." Says the big man, bewildered by what he has just witnessed. "I have seen some things in my days, and I can only imagine you have seen a lot more, but that. That is something else."

"Yeah, it was. I am lucky to be alive, mate." Smiles Seth.

"Well... Well, shit. I don't know what to say. Where was that?"

"ELEXO-598-3. The kids and I are supposed to have been the only ones to set foot on that planet." Seth pauses for a second. "Let me re-phrase that. I think we are the only humans to have ever set foot on that planet." Seth shrugs as Otto hangs off his words. "That's not it though. After fighting that Dragon I called the kids in to help me explore the cavern and Fin got drawn to a hidden room."

"What do you mean, drawn to?"

"Don't know. You'd have to get him to explain it. But after a bit of fooling around, we found it and that's where the book is from." Otto's eyes widen as he does the basic math of connecting the Dragon to the treasure. "This is why I need your help, mate."

"Oh, you've got it, old man. For a second there I thought you might have some very rare, very expensive artefacts you needed moved. Thought we both might get a nice little pay day like old times. But this, this is something else. Something I've never seen before. And can I confirm you said only humans to step foot on that planet? Do you mean?"

"Yeah." Nods Seth as he looks at the book, reminding Otto of its foreign language and mysterious symbols. Otto shakes his head in disbelief.

"Well hell! I guess it was bound to happen one day. We can't be all alone out here, can we?" Otto takes a mouthful of his drink. "What do you need?"

"Well, just like old times, I need your advice and counsel, my friend. You are the only person besides the kids that knows about this. I removed it from my report back to Ovmor. And –"

Otto cuts him off. "Are you sure you took it out of your report, brother?"

"Yes, why?" Otto's question surprises Seth and he doesn't like the sound of this.

"I have had a lot of Ovmor suits showing up on Solus in the last couple of days. I heard they have been snooping around and asking lots of questions around planet exploration, Spacers, and Scouts. Had a chat with some of my counterparts around the edge too, and they said the same thing."

"Shit! I must have made my report too bland. God damn it!' A thousand things race through Seth's mind, as he feels a massive wave of guilt wash over him for stuffing up. "The kids!"

"Don't worry, they will be fine. We have you under a totally different ship name and individual names. We do this type of stuff all the time for the Agency."

"The Agency?" Otto can hear the distaste in Seth's voice. "You still running their errands, hey?"

"Pull your head in, old man." Otto states, his tone a little more serious than before. "I may be running their errands, but you used to do their dirty work, remember?"

"Fair call." Nods Seth as he puts his hands up in defeat. He doesn't want to argue with his friend. "As long as the kids are safe, I don't care. And sorry, the Agency is low on my list when it comes to people and organisations I can trust."

"No apologies needed. So, again, how can I help?"

"Well, I need to do something about this, right? But I don't know who exactly to tell, that I may have discovered a new and hidden civilisation in the galaxy. Humans have been searching for millennia for other intelligent life forms. But there isn't a 'how to' rule book out there." Otto nods his head in agreement. Seth continues. "I know I don't want to tell the Corporations. They will just want to exploit this somehow. I am happy to get paid a decent wage for a hard day's work, but they are mostly scum at the executive levels. Let's be honest."

"Oh, don't worry old friend, I can attest to the fact that they are terrible human beings." Otto rubs his chin, thinking. "You Planet Scouts don't have a 'action on contact with an alien race' in your how to Scout book or something?" Seth shakes his head. "Hmmm, you could tell the government?"

"I thought about that, and I think it's the only play, but who would I tell, and would it get stuck in the bureaucracy? We can both confirm that there is a high chance of that happening."

Otto laughs, but Seth can see a hint of frustration on his face. The big man is obviously still dealing with that bureaucracy on a regular basis. Trying to govern several hundred systems with multiple planets is no simple job for the galactic government. Though both Seth and Otto have always thought they go out of their way to make it harder than it needs to be.

"Well, what are you going to do then?" Asks Otto.

Seth leans back in his chair and grabs a sip of water from the bottle in his backpack. Otto reaches for the draw to get the bottle out to pour Seth a proper drink, but Seth waves him off. Knowing Ovmor's goons are on the station, he wants to stay alert. "Can you get me back to the Core system? I think I need to do some more research first to see if I can find out anything else on my own before I share this information with a friendly local government representative."

"Of course, of course. That's too easy. I will sort you out, no problems. You, the kids, and the ship will need new identities, but again, that's not a problem. You won't be able to go directly back to the Core from here though, too obvious." Otto runs his hand over his moustache. Seth can see the cogs turning as Otto is deep in thought. "Can I ask what you think you will find back in the Core?"

"Look, we got Rose, our ship's AI, to look up Dragons and obviously they aren't real. They are some old Ancient Earth myth of some sort."

"Yeah, I recall them from kids stories."

"Exactly mate. But I want to see how these myths, legends, or old religions made it far out into the galaxy somehow. My current guess, and it's exactly that, a guess. Is that we have come across the remnants of an ancient hidden human society? Perhaps a type of cult or government that split from humanity in our early space exploration days. Maybe that's how they ended up out in unexplored space somehow." Seth shrugs, acknowledging he is making up a likely story to help him deal with the magnitude of the situation.

"Look, I don't know what to say, old friend. This is crazy and I will help however I can."

"Thanks, I appreciate it brother, and look, I'm not in any kind of rush. We are coming off several back-to-back scouts, so the kids probably need a break."

"Several back-to-back scouts. The kids probably need a break." Otto says sarcastically. "You McCallan's are god damn savages, every one of you!" Most Scouts will take several months off after a single job, and can only manage one to two jobs a year.

Seth laughs before relaxing back into his seat once more. Somewhat happier knowing that he is no longer alone on this mission.

"I'll also ask around to see if I can find out what Overmorrow is up to. And I'll organise a contact back in the Core system to look after you once you arrive." Otto looks at Seth and gives him a big cheeky smile. The edges of his moustache curling up as he starts to form a plan. Seth drops his smile and studies the big man's face for a moment before rolling his eyes. Otto simply shrugs back in return, his grin somehow growing even larger and more mischievous.

"Fine, I will accept the Agency's help. They owe me anyway."

Otto reaches back into the draw and pulls out his most expensive bottle of liquor and pours them both a round. Seth protests, but Otto ignores him.

"That they do, old man, that they do."

Eve has to fight the urge to skip down the passageway leading to the markets. She loves flying the Scout and working with her father, even if he pushes her hard and makes her drill things over, and over, and over again. She still loves the thrill of it all. Flying through space, exploring new planets, the hot, the cold, the storms, all of it. She wants to be the best pilot in the galaxy one day. But if becoming the best pilot in the galaxy is her passion, then shopping is her number one hobby. She loves buying and tinkering with new parts to upgrade the Scout. She loves installing everything from upgrade chips to full engine parts, even if she can only give the Scout that extra percentage of performance. Eve treats the Scout like it is her baby.

She believes the main reason that she loves doing it so much is because her father has given her full responsibility for the ship. This is her thing. She has complete ownership. Seth doesn't question her or even check what she spends their money on. He has complete faith in her, and she loves that.

She is also excited to get off the Scout and be around people every now and again. After their mother passed, Seth left them with their grandparents for a short time, while he got set up as a Planet Scout. Afterwards, they lived on the Obsidian Scout as Seth flew them around the outer rim while he worked. She never really had friends besides her little brother. Who is both her best friend in the galaxy and the primary source of her frustrations.

Rose the ship's AI was their schoolteacher and Ray was their babysitter. She used to wish that she had a normal childhood on a normal planet, like every other kid in the galaxy. But once her father started letting her help him with his work, around the age of fourteen, she fell in love with it. She quickly forgot about dreams of normalcy and swapped them for dreams of adventure, never looking back. She understands why her father left home and joined the military when he was around her age.

A dull glowing sign hangs on an angle above a set of large docking bay doors. It flickers on and off, but the word 'MAR-KETS' is still easy to read. Eve's eyes light up with excitement. She picks up her pace and weaves through the people coming and going to and from the markets. Taking a deep breath, she crosses the precipice of the market's entrance and finds herself on a metal platform high above the market floor below. Eve moves over to the railing at the edge of the platform and takes a minute to allow it all to soak in. Several large ship hangar bays now house the markets, giant rusty metal doors seal off the force-fields that once opened to space. The entire room has an orange glow to it from all the scrap metal used to make modifications and weld things together. Although the markets look old and unkept Eve can already tell it has its own charm and personality.

Eve sees multiple shop fronts from her raised vantage point. Some are cheap setups with nothing more than a table, with a tarp hanging behind it, displaying items. At the other end of the spectrum, there are high end corporation shops with well-dressed sales staff and clean looking stores. There is also a corner of the giant market floor where mechanics are welding and working on modifications of parts. The noise fills the large space and there is a light hint of soldered metal in the air. Eve spends ten minutes pinpointing where she needs to go, what to buy, and back up options if she does not like the price the store is offering. She then races off down the large winding stairs to the market floor, filled with excitement.

Eve gets lots of looks and attention from the people in the marketplace. They rarely have tall, beautiful, blond-haired twenty-year-old girls down in this part of the station. They are used to cranky old men like her father, or young spacer crews, on the market floor. There is the odd female about, but they all seem to be older, crankier, and rougher looking than the men. Thankfully, her father has taught her all about how men think and act, so she knows how to deal with their attention. Seth has even run her through multiple training scenarios in the training room. Because that's the type of dad he is.

The market floor is even more impressive than it looked from above. Everywhere Eve turns, someone is trying to sell her something. She does her best to stick to her plan but let's herself do a little window shopping too. One shop that's not on her list but grabs her attention is one of the larger Alitech stores. A large screen out the front shows a man standing alone in the darkness. A spark of light erupts, as the man has an idea. From the new forming light, multiple robotic droids of different shapes and sizes come flying or driving out from behind him, all seeming to have their own different purpose. The droids then combine, forming a more capable looking machine as the man's body language changes to one of success.

"Hey." A warm voice says from behind Eve, startling her some-what. "I see the all-new Alliance Technologies AI crew droid has caught your eye there, young lady." Eve turns to see an Alitech salesman standing a little too close behind her smiling.

"Oh yeah. Cool ad." She says as she creates a little distance.

"Well, it is more than a cool ad. Under new galactic Artificial Intelligence laws, only recently passed, Alliance Technologies have been able to upgrade its line of AI droids and drones." Eve would usually end the conversation quickly, but after recent events, she has some questions about AI robots, so wants to dive a little deeper.

"We are now proud to offer smarter, more capable AI and Cybernetics than before." The man says proudly.

"How so?"

"Well, that's a good question, Ma'am. Previously, AI robots have only been able to use their programming within tightly set parameters. Say, for example, a cleaning droid has cleaned anything on a ship when it gets dirty. But you have to give it directions of what to clean and what not to clean and it would eventually learn and stay within its boundary of responsibility." Eve nods as she follows along.

"But now, with the new upgrade, instead of giving the AI a strict boundary to operate in, you can give it more of a mission, so to speak. So, for example, instead of telling it what to clean and what not to, you can simply give it the mission to keep things clean. The drone will then watch and learn what is and isn't to be cleaned and will know when to clean things and how many things need cleaning. The new AI also has a larger boundary. So, as in the previous example, the AI would only clean your ship. The improved Alitech AI can now follow you from your ship to your home or even workplace and still complete its mission of cleaning."

Eve stares at the man, not seeing the big upgrade difference. The man notices the look on Eve's face and changes his tact somewhat.

"So, I guess what all that really means is you can do more with less due to changes in regulations that allow AI to be a little smarter."

Eve slowly nods and smiles, pretending to be impressed. "Oh, that is cool then. But how come you can't have an AI droid that is as smart as say a ship's AI? A ship's AI seems very competent compared to say a cleaning droid?"

"Oh yes, another excellent question, one we get asked often." The man replies before a cheesy smile appears on his face. "So, the recent change in galactic law doesn't change the level of intelligence an AI can have, but the remit of its area to exercise that intelligence. Under the new regulations, technically, your ship's AI could also transfer to your land vehicle and pilot that as well. But you couldn't put that level of intelligence into a cleaning droid as it would, firstly be overkill and, more importantly, be illegal."

"Oh okay, that makes sense." Replies Eve, now understanding what the salesman is trying to say. He goes to speak again, but Eve cuts him off before he can start his sale pitch. "So, under the new laws, can AI have offensive or defensive capabilities?"

Then man steps back in shock. "Umm, no Ma'am. It is still highly illegal for any AI to have offensive or defensive programming. Such technology is forbidden even to the galactic military."

Eve knows this is the case. She learnt a little about AI history in her version of school that Rose taught, and it is a well-known fact that humanity stopped the progression of AI thousands of years ago. But after their recent encounter with the cybernetic Dragon, Eve thought it would be good to ask just in case something changed.

Eve fakes a big smile at the salesman. "Well, I don't need cleaning AI or illegal AI so I will be on my way. Thanks for your time." Eve walks off before the man can try his sales pitch on her.

She spends another thirty minutes wandering around the market floor before beginning her actual shopping tasks. After visiting her fourth shop, she notices that the same person has been in all the same shops she has been in. She wants to ignore the person and get on with her shopping but can hear her father's voice is in the back of her head telling her to pay attention. She picks something up and pretends to look at it for a minute.

Now Dad said when you get a bad or suspicious feeling, it is your subconscious telling you something is up. So, what is up Eve? She asks herself. *Hmm, it's got something to do with that guy, that's for sure. So, let's see what this guy is up to.* Eve slowly moves around the shop from item to item, sneaking the odd glance at her newly acquired target. *Male, probably late twenties, well groomed. His outfit seems a bit out of place, though. He is wearing mechanics clothes, but there is something off about them… Clean! They are too clean. He either recently bought them or has never used them. If he has never used them, then he may not be a mechanic.* Eve is forming a picture in her mind and is oddly enjoying the process.

If he is not a mechanic, that means he is trying to blend in. Is he trying to get cheaper parts or deals? Eve quickly looks up from the item she is holding to steal a glance at the man to see what else stands out. *He has no bags, and I can't see that he has bought anything. If he hasn't bought anything, then why is he in the same shops as me? Boys usually just come up and talk to me, so is he some sort of creep?* Eve feels nervous butterflies in her stomach start to form but shakes them off. *Only one way to find out, I guess.* Eve doesn't purchase the part she wanted from this store and decides to go to a backup shop to get the item. If the man follows her to the next shop, she will know something is wrong and will have to act. Her father always tells her and Fin that any action is better than no action at all.

She quickly leaves the shop to see how the man reacts. Power walking, Eve heads off to her backup shop, which is about one hundred and fifty metres away. Heading straight into the shop, she grabs what she is after then moves into a corner, waiting to see if the man follows her inside. Shortly after, the man appears, looking panicked. As he enters the shop, the man looks around quickly. He locks eyes with Eve, who is waiting in the corner for him. He then quickly looks away, trying to pretend that he is there for another reason. *Alright creep, now I know you're following me.* Eve casually walks around the displays in the shop, looking at several more items while coming up with a plan to ditch her stalker. One of the shop's staff members approaches the man.

"Tom, Tom, is that you?" Eve looks over to see the man spin around, shocked to see the staff member calling his name.

"Tom, it is you! What's brings a fancy Overmorrow man like you down to my shop?" The man looks at Eve, who is pretending not to listen, then back at the shop keep. He mumbles some sort of apology then quickly leaves the shop. The shop assistant looks confused but shrugs it off and heads back to what he was doing.

Ovmor. Shit, do they know what happened on the planet? Are they following us? Eve's mind races with questions. *Oh no, Fin!* She instantly thinks of her little brother. He can handle himself, but he is still her little brother. *I need to lose this guy and go see if Fin is okay.* The shop keep interrupts her train of thought.

"Can I help you with something, young lady?"

"Oh yes, just this please?' Eve holds up the small box. Containing a small engine part made of a specific hardened metal which Eve intends to use to replace a piece of the Scout's engine, she thinks is subpar.

"Yes, of course. Did your mechanic send you down here to get those? I can get you something cheaper that will do the same job if you would like?" The shop assistant says, assuming she is on an errand for someone else.

Eve doesn't have time to play any games, so cuts straight to the chase. "No. I need that specific material as the cheaper metal won't be able to handle the stress if I need to pump the engines while breaking atmosphere on a tier three planet." The man looks at Eve in shock. He is about to cut her off with what he thinks will be a smart response for this young girl, but Eve gets in first. "Also, I can pick these up down the road for ten percent cheaper than what you are offering. So, I want you to match the price, as you will still make a twenty-five percent profit." She states confidently, staring straight into the man's eyes to see if he is keeping up. The shop assistant is taken by surprise and doesn't know what to say.

"Good, then it's a deal." Inserts Eve as she walks over to the counter to pay. The man shakes his head and moves over to the counter, giving Eve the price she has asked for.

"You are an interesting and special young lady, that's for sure." The assistant says in a poor attempt to justify the shot to his ego. Eve fakes a smile but wastes no more time and heads out the door.

Once outside, she can't see her Ovmor stalker Tom but assumes he is nearby. She has a plan to lose him, so begins heading over to the area where the mechanics and craftsmen are building and fixing parts. Weaving in and out of the crowd, she tries to disappear amongst the other shoppers. She knows there is little chance of that as she is almost six foot three with long blonde hair and possibly the only young women in the markets today. Hopefully, it will buy her some time and some distance. She takes a quick pause outside an engine dealer's tent and notices her stalker over a hundred metres behind her. He is struggling to get through the crowd while keeping his eyes on her. She ducks behind some shops while crouching in another attempt to gain some more ground.

She eventually makes it to the mechanics workshops in the far corner of the massive markets floor. Eve looks around for the roughest looking bunch of mechanics she can find. She sees a group of men all dressed in dark blue overalls, with the top half undone and tied around their wastes. They also all have on dirty white singlets with tattoos up their arms and necks. She quickly races over to them. One of them stops welding, flips up his welder's mask, and looks her over from head to toe.

"I am so sorry to interrupt, but I need help."

"Sure thing senorita, we can build any part from any metal you can find on dis station right here. What did you have in mind, princess?"

Eve drops her shoulders, doing her best job to look scared and sad. "I was actually hoping for a different kind of help. My ex-boyfriend, I think he took some type of drugs and started yelling and swearing at me as soon as he saw me. I did my best to find station security but couldn't, so ran away. But now he has chased me down here."

The welder taps his co-workers on the shoulder, and they stop what they are doing. "Hey muchachos, this little senoritas drugged up boyfriend is chasing her around the spaceport, saying he is going to do bad things to her!" The rest of the men look at her and she pretends to cry into her hands. Her ruse is working. She can tell they don't like the sound of this at all, as an angry, disapproving look crosses their faces. Eve turns around, seeing the Ovmor man coming towards her only one hundred metres away.

"There!" She points him out to the group of men. "The clean shaved man in the clean orange mechanic's suit. His name is Tom, and he is an Overmorrow exec. I thought if I came down here, he wouldn't follow me, as he has always said he hates the scum that work here and that they are beneath him." Eve may not have been on this particular space station for a long time, but in every other space station or outer edge planet she has been on in recent years, there is always a class divided between the workers and Corporation executives. Her father has drawn it to her and Fin's attention many times and explained how this class divide can be exploited. The group of welders now start taking off their equipment and uttering angrily under their breaths. Her plan is working. She knows the young male workers are now keen for a fight and Tom will be their target. The leader, the one Eve originally talked to, speaks up.

"Okay senorita. You head down the back of the shop ay, out through the exit behind the workshops. Head to the nearest port security station. We will check this fool for you. Spoilt little puta!"

"Thank you so much, Uncle Otto always said the workers are the real lifeblood of this station." Eve drops Ottos' name, hoping to seal the deal.

"Hey, you know the Bear?' The man asks, shocked. Looking around at his colleagues to see their reactions.

"Yes, since I was little. He is like an uncle to me." Eve adds in some more tears for effect.

"Then don't worry about a thing. We got you little sis!" Eve tries hard not to smile. Using Otto's name and reputation has given her credibility and the permission the men need to act.

Eve leans in and gives the man a big hug to complete her ruse. She then races off, her face in her hands as if she were crying. As she exits the back of the workshop, it sounds like Tom is arriving and is trying to get past the workers to follow her. She can hear the men asking him questions and mocking him. It sounds as if Tom tries to order the men around, using his position in the Corporation as a threat. Eve shakes her head, knowing that this is a terrible choice on his behalf. As she hits the rear exit to the markets, she hears the noise of what sounds like a fight breaking out. Or by the cheering and laughter, someone getting a beating.

Once out of sight, Eve drops the act and stands up tall. "Now Tom is no longer a problem, I have to find Fin!" Eve says out loud to motivate herself as she races off down the corridor towards the food markets.

Chapter 10

SISTER

The fresh smells of the food market are tantalizing. Each individual ingredient's aroma seems to flow directly into Fin's consciousness via his nose. He can imagine all the different combinations of delicious meals he could create. Savoury meat-based dishes to warm the heart, sweet desserts to create a sense of joy. Even snacks he could prepare to take down on planets to keep their bellies full and their muscles energized. Fin moves from shop to shop, picking up some small supplies while ordering others which will get delivered to their ship. A robotic courier system run by most markets around the galaxy delivers food from shop to ship in around ten to thirty minutes, depending on the location of the markets compared to the docking bays. Since their ship is docked far away in the East docks, Fin figures the delivery will take closer to thirty minutes.

The food markets are busy with a steady flow of shoppers. Fin has always preferred the food markets to the ships and mechanics markets that Eve usually drags him to. The pace of the food markets always seems to be a little slower and a bit more relaxing. The markets on Solus are no exception. Some shops sell supplies digitally and have no actual produce in them. These are the shops that sell large bulk items to ships like water, ration packs, and large bags of ingredients like rice and flour. Fin hits these shops first to stock up on the essentials. Best practice under Corporation policy is to have a minimum of three months worth of supplies for a scouting crew. As this should be enough time for the corporation to come rescue you or send spacers to retrieve you. If they deem you worthy and there is a profit to be made, that is.

Seth isn't as trusting of the corporations or as confident of people's skills, so he makes sure the ship has three months worth of supplies for the Obsidian Scouts potential full crew of forty people. This gives them over three years worth of supplies. Which Fin thinks is ridiculous as it wouldn't take anyone three years to rescue the family if they became stranded. But Seth would rather be over prepared than under prepared. Fin doesn't care that much though as he enjoys the long showers and abundance of food to recover from all the hard training his father makes them do.

Once Fin orders all the bulk supplies, he moves to his favourite part of shopping. The fresh supplies. The Solus food markets have over a hundred vendors selling all sorts of delicacies from around the galaxy. Some shops in the markets even have little eating areas set up to the side so you can sample some of the food there and then. This is what Fin loves the most about the markets. The mix of spacers and locals happily moving about amongst a literal smorgasbord of delights. Fin still remembers his mother taking him to the markets when he was little. She would let him taste sweet baked goods and fresh fruits from different planets around the galaxy. He thinks that spending this quality time with his mother when he was little is one reason the food markets always make him feel so much joy. They remind him of her.

There is one thing that grabs Fin's attention more than the fresh food and that is all the interest he is getting from the young women in the markets. He was always tall growing up and is now almost as tall as his father. He is only one or two centimetres shorter than him at six foot four. But the same height if you were to include his hair. However, being so tall and not fully developed made him look gangly and odd. He seemed to struggle in his own body as it kept growing on him, what seemed like every other day. A tall, awkward body along with an unkempt red mop and the pimples of puberty didn't exactly make him the desire of young women across the galaxy. But that all changed recently. In the last year, he has gone from being skinny and awkward in his body to having a very muscular frame. The past several years of his father punishing him with daily exercise have finally caught up to him. The reward for his hard work and dedication is a powerful and athletic body. He has also pushed through the uncomfortable phase of puberty and now has great skin and a chiselled jawline. Eve has also offered some styling tips for that mop of red hair as well.

He has been interested in girls for several years now but struggled to get their attention until recently. But now that he is a six foot four, muscular young man with wavy crimson hair, they are the ones interested in him. And by the amount of attention he is receiving today, they like what they see. Even some women in their mid to late twenties take the time to steal a glance at him as he walks by. He assumes they must think he is older, based on his height and physique.

He takes the opportunity to talk and flirt with the girls in the market. Having grown up with an older sister, he is not nervous around females like other young men seem to be. One girl, who looks to be several years older than him, seems to be determined to get his attention and is following behind him as he moves from shop to shop. She isn't like the other girls who wave, say hi, and giggle while playing with their hair, dressed in their functional baggy worker's clothes. This girl is something else entirely, and he can't stop the urge to keep looking at her. Noticing Fin checking her out, she eventually moves up next to him so she can introduce herself. She is wearing a tight-fitting short dress that shows off her curves. She has long dark wavy hair reaching halfway down her back, and makeup that makes her eyes look smoky and seductive. Fin is more than happy to have her attention and has to stop himself from staring at her curves and tanned skin.

"Hi there. My name is Lucy. Nice to meet you." She puts her hand out to shake his.

Fin reaches out and gently shakes her soft hand. "Hi nice to meet you Lucy. My name is Freddy." He knows his dad will kill him if he uses his real name, and besides, it's not like they were going to be here long. He releases her hand, but she holds his for half a second longer and looks into his eyes while smiling.

"So, Freddy, what brings you here today?" She asks without breaking eye contact.

"I'm here to get some supplies for our ship. What about you?" Asks Fin.

"Same."

"Oh cool. Are you docked here for a while?"

"Oh no. I am just passing through."

"Are you a spacer?" Fin asks excitedly. Most people he comes across on space stations and planets are local to that area, so he always enjoys the chance to chat with other adventurers like himself. Even more so when they are this attractive.

"Oh no silly." Giggles Lucy while playfully slapping Fin on the arm. "I am on a family holiday out to some of the nearby resort planets. We only stopped here for some supplies." She moves in closer to Fin. *Planets? Why would you holiday on multiple planets? And why wouldn't you know the name of the planet you are going to? That seems a bit odd?* Fin questions himself.

Fin goes to ask Lucy which planets she is going to, but Lucy puts her hand on his upper arm and gently squeezes his biceps, which distracts him for a moment. "And Fin, I'm so bored. I've been stuck in our ship with old people for two entire weeks and I need some entertainment." She pouts. *Only boring people get bored, Lucy.* Fin almost says out loud but catches himself before the words spill out. Lucy looks up at him with her seductive smoky eyes and smiles as she touches his arm again.

Wow, she is laying it on thick. She must really want some entertainment, whatever that means? Fin thinks to himself.

"Fin I'm sorry to be so upfront." She says as she plays with her hair. "But you are too handsome, and I would hate to miss out on an opportunity like this. Is it okay if I buy you a hot drink or delicious treat of some sort?" Fin has finished his shopping and is only window shopping for treats, so has some time to spare before he is due to make his way back to the ship.

"Sure, that would be nice, Lucy." He uses his most charming smile, making Lucy blush. *Talking to girls is so easy. I don't know why other boys find it so hard.* Fin thinks to himself.

"Okay come this way. I saw a great place out of the way. Their hot drinks smelt amazing. And if you play your cards right, maybe I can be your delicious treat." Lucy takes Fin by the hand, interlocking their fingers. This makes Fin feel uncomfortable, but he is too caught up in her looks to pull away.

She walks towards the shop, pulling him along while giving him a seductive glance over her shoulder, but is suddenly bounced back hard, like she had run into a blast wall. In front of her stands Eve, tall, red faced, puffed, and looking very angry. Lucy fixes her hair while trying to keep calm. "Watch where you are going, you oversized freak! I am on a date here." Lucy looks back at Fin again and winks. She goes to head off, but finds Eve's hand firmly planted on her shoulder.

"Get your hands off him and walk away quietly." Eve snarls.

Lucy looks at her, then back at Fin. She squeezes Fin's hand harder while smiling at him. "Look honey, I don't know who you think you are but me and Freddy are going for a drink, so take your jealous oversized face somewhere else." Lucy says confidently.

"Freddy hey?" Eve looks over the top of Lucy's head at Fin, who shrugs and smiles back at his big sister. Eve shakes her head and looks back at Lucy. "How long have you been working with Overmorrow for lady?" Asks Eve.

Lucy looks shocked "I, ummm, I, I don't know what you're talking about, freak. Just leave us alone, okay." She manages to get out while her face goes pale. Fin does the math in his head and quickly realises what is happening.

Damn it, I can't believe I let her trick me so easily. I knew the whole holiday planet's thing was BS. Dad is going to kill me. Fin frowns to himself in disappointment.

He pulls his hand from the seductive woman's grip and steps to the side. Lucy is still trying to keep up her ruse and refuses to get pushed around by some young twenty-year-old spacer girl. She raises up her hand to grab Eve's arm and push it from her shoulder. When she goes to shove Eve's arm, she can't move it a centimetre. It feels like she is trying to push away a steel pole that has been welded to her shoulder. Her face goes even more pale as she realises she may be in over her head, and that her good looks and social status will not help her in this situation.

Eve drops her body weight, then using her other hand shoves the older woman hard in the centre of her chest. Lucy goes flying back several metres. She tries to catch her feet, but before she can, she smashes into a cart of exotic fruit, falling back on to her head as fresh produce drops around her. Eve goes to move in to finish her off, like she has been trained to do, but Fin puts his arm out to block her.

"Don't worry sis, I think she gets it." The Ovmor woman staggers back to her feet, dazed and holding her head. She looks at them both with tears running down her eyes. Realising she is beat, she turns and runs off in the opposite direction, crying.

Fin watches, quietly laughing before he turns back to Eve. "Okay big sis, I guess you know something I don't?"

Eve keeps her eyes locked on Lucy as she runs away, but still talks to Fin. "Yeah, I had some creep from Ovmor stalk me through the mechanics markets. I managed to lose him with the help of some locals."

Fin nods, impressed. "Well done, sis."

"Thanks, but we should probably get out of here and back to the ship to make sure Ray and Rose are okay. The Corp might be on to us."

Fin feels the blood in his body rush through him. They have done lots of training in the sim room, but this is the first time anything like this has happened in the real world. "Agreed big sis. I am done here anyway." The pair turn around and head off through the markets back toward their ship.

"Do you think Dad is okay?" Asks Fin as they duck and weave through the markets.

"Oh yeah, he will be fine. I think they are only low-level Corp operatives trying to gather information. I doubt they are dangerous." Answers Eve. Fin agrees, chuckling to himself at the thought of one of these amateurs trying it on with his dad. That would not go well for them.

It takes the pair a while to get out of the markets and this section of the station. They even double back around several times to make sure they are not being followed. Like their father has drilled into them in the training room. Eventually, they make their way back to the entrance of the east docks. They get a little lost several times since they haven't been in this part of the station before and have to retrace their steps due to finding themselves at dead ends or locked blast doors. Having exited the Scout through the loading docks and going straight up to Otto's before heading to the markets has thrown them off. They both come to the agreement that because the east docks are rarely used for passenger transport, a lot of the normal routes from there to the main part of the station are closed down. But after several more unintentional backtracks and some level changes, they eventually find their bearings. The pair come to a quiet long wide corridor that takes them down to the docking bays One Hundred and Fifty to Two Hundred.

"Finally." Eve says. "I think this should take us to the Scout."

"Docking bay One Seven Three, please do not forget." Fin does his best impression of the cranky, small, old man that greeted them when they docked.

The corridor is built to the same specifications as the other pedestrian areas around the station. However, because this corridor leads to the logistics docking area, not the transport and accommodation areas, its infrequent use is apparent. Most of the logistics cargo delivered to Solus goes straight from the docking bay to the relevant parts of the station via vehicles or droid transport passageways. Logistics crews sometimes deliver cargo themselves, but Otto's crews do most of the heavy lifting when it comes to moving items around the large space station. Technically, the logistics ship's crews never even need to set foot on the station.

Currently, Eve and Fin are the only people in this wide long section of Solus. Being in such a large open space on such a busy, populated station with no one around makes them feel like they have stumbled across a secret or restricted area, a place they shouldn't be. Which they both find a little exciting. The pair travel several hundred metres down the wide empty passageway towards their docking bay before they hear a voice calling for them.

"Hey you two, stop there!" Yells an angry male voice. Both Eve and Fin jump a little. Thinking that maybe they have walked into a restricted area and are about to get in trouble.

Eve turns around to see her Ovmor stalker Tom from the marketplace moving their way. As he gets closer, Eve can see he has a black eye, a bloodied lip, and is walking with a slight limp. "That's the guy I told you about!"

Fin can also see the man's injuries. "Wow sis, did you beat him up too?"

She shakes her head. "No. Remember, I got some locals to do it for me." She looks at Fin, who looks confused. "Told them he was my ex-boyfriend, and he had taken drugs and come after me." Fin smiles, impressed with his sister's cunning. As the man gets closer, he begins to slow down, and they see a look of rage on his face. They both notice that he is also holding an arm behind his back, poorly attempting to conceal something.

"I got my ass kicked, you little bitch! You fucking set me up!" The man yells at Eve, spit and blood coming from his mouth.

They both quickly realise that Tom is maddened and means them harm. Whatever orders he was previously given by his Ovmor bosses, he has since disregarded. Tom yelling at Eve and calling her names instantly triggers Fin and he can feel the anger building inside of him. He clenches his fist as he wants to charge in on the man and hit him, but he feels Eve's arm across his chest.

"By the book, little brother. Just like Dad has trained us." Fin locks eyes with Eve and nods, his anger subsiding as his focus on the situation grows.

The pair back away from Tom and move to separate sides of the large corridor, looking for possible exits. This distance forces Tom to choose between them, rather than attacking them as a single target. Just like their father has drilled them to do so many times in the training sim and on the sparring mats. In melee combat, this will allow one of them to flank Tom should he get close enough, giving them the advantage.

"His arm is hiding something." Fin quietly calls out to Eve as they continue to back down the corridor.

"Yep, on it." Replies Eve.

Even though Seth has run them through multiple scenarios in the training room dealing with all sorts of different attackers, this is the first time it has happened in real life, and they are both nervous. Tom quickens his pace towards them. As he does, the arm behind his back drops to his side, revealing a metal pole one metre in length. Butterflies race in their stomachs as their heart rates spike. Fin looks back and notices that the door at the end of the corridor is closed.

"You will need this boy!" Says Tom, laughing as he holds up a swipe pass. Aware of Fin's intent to escape.

"Shit!" Mutters Eve under her breath. Eve was planning to simply outrun this guy and get back to the ship before he could catch them. That limp would make him no match for their pace. But now that plan will not work.

"What's the play big sis?" Asks Fin.

Eve can hear the nervousness in her little brother's voice. Which makes her more nervous. But Fin is her little brother, and she will do anything to protect him. So she shakes off the feelings and does her best to focus on the situation that is currently happening, not on what could be happening. She looks around for another way to escape or avoid having to fight.

She can hear her father's voice in her head saying the best way to win a fight is to not get in one. But she sees no other options.

"We may have to take him out."

Tom gets to within ten metres of the pair and stops in location. "I am going to enjoy this. You little spacer shits need a lesson in respect. I am an Ovmor executive, not some homeless loser like you!" He swings the metal pole around several times in an attempt to intimidate the pair before he raises it up above his head, looking to charge one of them. Suddenly, they see a quick flash, as a large figure moves impossibly fast from a side door they must have missed when their attacker first appeared.

Seth comes charging in at an angle from behind Tom and uses all his weight and momentum to hit him hard in the back of the neck with an elbow strike. The powerful blow makes the man drop the metal pole as his body seems to shut down and go limp. The sound of the impact echoes down the empty corridor. Before his body crashes into the floor, Tom somehow seems to catch himself. As if his central nervous system's automatic response kicked in the moment he started to drop. Tom has no time to react though, as Seth instantly wraps his arms around his neck in a rear choke hold. Both children watch on in shock as they see the primal fear in Tom's eyes as even in his half conscious state, he realises what is happening.

They have seen their father angry before and seen his determination and violent skill set in the training room. But this time, he has a distinct look on his face. One of focused hatred. The man tries to fight off Seth, his arms swinging wildly in desperation. At this point, he is a victim to Seth's will, and both kids know his attempts to free himself are pointless.

In a matter of seconds, the choke puts Tom to sleep. Seth feels the man's body go limp in his arms, but holds the choke tight for a couple more seconds before lifting him up and slamming him hard into the ground. Making sure to drop him on the back of his neck. They all hear a loud crunch as something in the man's body breaks. Seth growls at the man with a look that the children have never seen. Eve and Fin watch on in shock as their father stands over Tom's motionless body, like a predator about to devour its prey.

Both children have always understood that their father was in a special branch of the military and that he had killed people before, but they both underestimated how good at violence their father was and still is. They also realise that he has been taking it very easy on them in their sparring sessions. Even in the shock of their father's actions, both children understand how protective of them he truly is.

Seth looks up and sees them watching on with a look of fear and relief on their faces. He takes a short sharp breath, then almost instantly changes his personality back to one of a calm and caring father. He leans down and grabs the pass from the man before heading over to give both kids a hug.

"Sorry about that. Are you guys alright?"

Fin and Eve smile before hugging their father tightly.

"Did you kill him Dad?" Asks Fin nervously.

"No buddy. I only choked him out and dropped him on his head. He may walk funny for a while, but he will live."

Seth smiles at them warmly, making sure to look them both in the eyes. "So… got some stuff to tell me on the walk back to the ship then, hey?"

Fin and Eve both laugh nervously as they walk towards the corridor's exit before simultaneously unleashing into their stories, making it impossible for Seth to listen to either of them.

"Okay, settle down, settle down. I may have two ears, but I can only listen to one of you at a time. Eve, you go first, please."

They continue their walk back to the ship as Eve then Fin tell Seth about the events leading up to them being chased down a corridor by an angry armed assailant. They spare no detail and exaggerate only slightly.

When they arrive back at the ship, they instantly notice that someone has tampered with the outer docking bay door attached to the station's landing dock. Seth tells the kids to stand back and ready themselves. Lowering his stance, ready to attack again if needed. Fins training automatically kicks in and he moves to the side and opens the door. Seth charges into the small room, the same one the small angry man greeted them in several hours ago, to find nothing. The kids quickly move in behind him and also find an empty room. He calls up Rose from his forearm computer to get a report on the current situation.

"Rose. Sitrep."

"Hello Captain." Answers Rose before providing any information. "An unidentified person attempted to run an advanced illegal AI hack on the ship's outer airlock. In what I assume was an attempt to break into the Scout. However, before they could fully action the AI's programming, I kindly opened the Scout's outer hatch for them." All three of them listen in, confused as to why Rose would allow the intruder access to the ship. "This allowed Ray, whom I informed of the situation, to execute his guarding function." Rose pulls up footage of Ray coming out of the hatch, barking and snapping at the would-be intruder. Eve and Fin, who are standing over Seth's shoulders watching, look on with Seth. The intruder trips over himself multiple times when he hears Ray. He then scampers out the hatch in fear of his life once Ray gets inside the small room and snaps at him several times.

I didn't think AI was allowed any offensive or defensive programming. That's what the salesman said anyway. Maybe that's part of the dog protocol? Eve thinks to herself. But the thought passes as she focuses back on the footage.

"Because of Ray's quick reaction time and fierce bark, the intruder ran off before they had time to remove their AI software implant. I have since run a small cyber-attack against the implanted AI and was able to break through its firewall. This then allowed me to gather a large amount of data, including, but not limited to, some encryption keys. I also found a vulnerability in the program used in the attempt to break into the ship. This will allow me to exploit this information should a similar AI or program be used to break into the Obsidian Scout in the future."

Eve smiles at her father, impressed. Seth smiles back, patting Eve on the back. "Great work Rose, and Ray, for that matter. We would like to come aboard now and depart as soon as possible, please. Otto should have sent through some credentials and a navigation chart for the next leg of our journey."

"Yes, of course Captain, I have already started the ship's departure sequence, and I can confirm Mr Otto has forwarded the relevant information. I am updating flight controls with the information as we speak."

"Thanks Rose, you are a legend." Chimes in Fin.

Seth puts his arms over the shoulders of both his beloved children, pulling them in close for another hug. He looks down at them both, proud of their actions on the station, before leading them aboard the Obsidian Scout and off the Solus Space Station.

Chapter 11

SUNRISE

The Obsidian Scout gently pulls out of the dull blues of hyperspace into the Noujou system. Over three weeks have passed since they left the massive Space Station Solus out on the edge of colonised space. The ship slowly moves through the outer edge of the busy farming system, drifting amongst all the other large transport and cargo ships. The Noujou system is only a day's jump from the Core system, home to the Capital planets, the Galactic Government, and the new centre of humanity within the known galaxy. Noujou is abundant with habitable planets and moons, making it ideal to provide key food resources to humanity's largest and most dense population mass.

The Obsidian Scout, now flying under cover and using false credentials provided by Otto, moves into a busy shipping lane heading to the planet Komugi. Otto told Seth he would do some digging around on Solus to try to find out why Ovmor was tracking them, and what their intent was. Otto was also going to reach out to some of his contacts in Ovmor and on some planets in the nearby systems to see if they knew of anything. He would even reach out to his contact in the agency to get the ball rolling on getting Seth into the Core system. Otto would get all of this done while the McCallan family were in hyperspace on their way to the planet Komugi. He would then jump in his own private ship and meet them on Komugi several days after they had arrived on the planet.

If everything went to plan, Otto would now be comfortably sitting in hyperspace following the same path the Obsidian Scout has just flown.

The family spends several hours navigating the crowded shipping lanes to reach the planet. The shipping lanes themselves are filled with large cargo ships, which are designed to carry millions of tons of cargo. In addition to cargo, the large transport ships carry thousands of workers to and from the massive farms on the moons and planets within the system. Because of the size of these ships, they are by virtue slow and not very manoeuvrable. But these giant ships perfectly fulfill their role and make for excellent work horses. As soon as these giant cargo ships enter a solar system, they begin loading and unloading cargo, using smaller transports while on route to their destination. This is the same for when they are leaving a system. They begin their departures when the giant ships are sixty percent full. The last forty percent gets managed in transit while ferrying to their exit jump point. It's amazing to watch a sped up recording of one of these ships doing its rounds. It looks almost organic and natural, like an insect queen moving slowly around its nest while thousands of smaller worker insects come and go, helping the queen on her way.

In an effort to keep the farming planets clean and healthy, it is Galactic Government policy that all-Star Class ships, ships capable of hyperspace jumps, are not allowed to enter any of the planet's atmospheres. This means the family must take the drop ship down to the Komugi surface. Seth, being Seth, makes the family layout everything they are taking to the planet, to make sure they don't have to come back to the Scout. Otto has given them the coordinates for an old farming station in the middle of nowhere. Even though the planet has a decent population size, and all the amenities they could ever need, Seth treats it like they are going on a scout to a new planet. Except this time, he makes sure the family is well armed.

The kids do not argue with Seth's processes. They tried it on once before several years ago. They thought they had convinced him that they didn't need to do all the planning, checking, and double checking he usually insists upon. Seth thought that was fair and let them pack for their quick three-day trip to a moon they were scouting. But the kids, in their youthful overconfidence, had forgotten to pack food, so Seth let them starve for three days, bar a single bite every night from some protein snacks he had conveniently brought along. They suffered so he could make his point. However, after that ordeal, they understood the importance of some of their father's overly disciplined ways. They do not necessarily take joy in the process, but there is a lot less joy to be had in starving and freezing. Both kids understand it is a thing that needs to be done and a habit of success. Not something they simply do for the sake of doing it.

The family also pack the things they took from the Dragon's cavern back on ELXO 598-3. They are itching to do some proper research on what they have found. Seth hasn't allowed them much time to study their discoveries due to them being in hyperspace. They agreed that if something happened with what they took from the cavern, like a poisonous gas leaked or something exploded, they didn't want to be stuck inside a giant tin can moving through space faster than the speed of light when it did. Because of this, they agreed to do all their research next time they were planet side. They are keen to sit down and have a good look through their bounty. Besides safety, they locked up and hid the treasure while traveling, in case of boarding or mandatory system checks. Examining the treasure will also give them something to do while they wait for Otto. Which will help break up the large amount of live fire training Seth has planned. After what happened on Solus, Seth is concerned for his family's safety. Knowing how the Corporations work and how unethical they can be, he expects them to only raise the stakes, not back off. And if they are going to go harder after the family, he wants the kids to be ready, and the Corporation to regret their decision to do so.

After several hours transiting through the shipping lanes, they arrive in orbit at Komugi, the fifth planet from the sun in the Noujou system. Eve puts the Scout in its designated orbit while patiently waiting for radio permission from the Planets Central Control Station to take the drop ship down to the surface. It takes a long time, things seem to work slower than Eve is used to in the Noujou system, but eventually she gets permission. The family, including Ray, then board the drop ship and head down to the planet's surface below. Seth makes Fin fly the drop ship down so he can get some extra training in, as Eve is more than capable.

While exiting the Scout in the drop ship, Seth smiles to himself. He hasn't inserted into a planet with this much firepower and so many high-value items since back in his days working in the Unit. If Sara were around to see him doing this with the kids, she would be so mad at him. And for some reason, the thought of her angry face makes him smile even more.

The drop ship descends through the atmosphere, then begins its flight over the planet's surface. Komugi is a rolling sea of wheat and cornfields as far as the eye can see. The natural abundance of the planet glows in relaxing shades of greens and yellows. Giant robotic farming machines several stories high slowly harvest the fields. Once full, these giant automated machines ship their spoils back to central processing stations located at regular intervals along the planet's surface. Large drone ships then ferry the goods back to the space ports for the next leg of their journey. The method for harvesting so much food is fast, effective and calculated. The planets in the Noujou system have been producing clean, sustainable food for thousands of years now. Lots of planning and effort is put into the care and production of resources so that the system will continue to provide for thousands of years to come.

When the drop ship arrives at the coordinates Otto provided, the family is pleasantly surprised. In front of them stands an empty, old, but comfortable looking farming house, that Otto has assured them he owns. They are not quite convinced as to why Otto would own this property, but they don't see any signs of someone living in it. The red and white two-story house looks almost unreal, like something from another time. There is a large balcony on the second floor and a larger deck on the first. A dirt road leads to the front of the house from the LZ, which is surrounded by fresh cut grass. Seth assumes Otto must have some simple maintenance droids that look after the property. The McCallans haven't lived on a planet, let alone in a house for around ten years, so staying in an actual house is quite a novelty for them. Fin can barely remember their old home, so he is very excited about the prospect of staying here for several nights.

The family have arrived as the sun is lowering in the sky, painting the clouds a beautiful purple and peach colour. The family quickly unpack the drop ship and move all their gear into the farmhouse, which is fitted out with modern accessories and some large and very comfortable looking beds. They decide they will all work together and help prepare dinner before heading off for some well-earned sleep. Under Fin's instructions, they cook a hearty meal with some of the supplies that Fin purchased on Solus. They eat their dinner outside on the house's upper deck, enjoying the last moments of the beautiful pastel sunset. After dinner, Fin makes a quick but tasty dessert using some of the chocolate they have left over from Otto. They watch the lights of the farming robots and AI ships dancing in and out of the atmosphere, all while enjoying a warm summer night's breeze.

Seth gives them the night off training so they can relax on the deck as a family. It's not often they get to pretend to be normal. And it is the first time the family has just sat down and done nothing in what seems like over a year. They spend the night recalling their previous scouting missions, joking and laughing at all the odd things that have happened, while reminiscing about all the amazing things they have recently seen and encountered. None of which would be possible had they not been Planet Scouts. Sleep eventually calls to them, so Seth lets the kids know he will wake them up in the morning as they head off to bed. He makes sure to give both Eve and Fin their three special kisses. One on the right cheek, one on the left, and one on the forehead. Then he wishes them a good night's sleep before heading off to bed.

"Fin." Whispers Seth. "Come on, it's time to wake up buddy."

Fin slowly tries to open his eyes, searching for a light source but not finding one as it's still dark both inside and out.

"Dad, Dad, what's wrong? The sun isn't up yet?" Mutters Fin through a dry mouth.

"Nothing's wrong buddy. It's going to be a beautiful day, so I thought we should go for a sunrise jog." Fin hesitates, debating whether he can be bothered. But he actually feels fantastic after a solid sleep, on a fancy bed, on a grade one planet. Fresh natural oxygen always has that effect on him. "Yeah, sure Dad, let's do it." Fin says as he slowly swings his legs over the edge of his bed and sits up.

"Excellent. I'll see you out the front in fifteen minutes buddy. Make sure you drink some water!" Seth says as he heads out the door to go and wake up Eve. Fin sits in his bed and flicks on a light before drinking some water. He sits there slowly sipping away at his water for two minutes while his eyes adjust to the land of the living. Once adjusted, he searches through his gear for his workout clothes. It's already warm, so he throws on shorts and a singlet, assuming it will be some type of death run their father will take them on. *It's never easy, is it Dad?* Fin thinks to himself as he has a big yawn and stretches his arms above his head.

Once dressed, he heads to the toilet, then has some more water before heading outside to warm up. The sun hasn't risen yet, but hints of its presence paint the horizon with an amazing soft, dark blue and purple glow. Seth arrives outside on the grass after Fin followed closely behind by Eve. "Okay guys, I got Ray to scout a scenic little fifteen kilometre run for us. I thought we should take it easy and run together for the first ten kilometres, then for the last five, let's race back to the farmhouse!"

"What's the winner get Dad?" Asks Fin, cutting in before Eve.

Seth thinks for a moment. "Hmm. The winner can have first pick from the Dragon's treasure to study today. How's that sound?"

"I'm in!" Says Fin excitedly.

"Ha, tis an easy win!" Mocks Eve.

"Okay then, are we ready to go?" Asks Seth. Both of the children nod in agreement.

They head off, starting with a nice slow jog, taking it easy as promised. Over the first several hundred metres, Seth pulls them to the side at regular intervals to stretch and do some mobility work. They all enjoy the rich aromas of the planet's damp grass. It is something they don't often get living in space, but somehow the smell makes them feel at home.

Ten minutes into the jog, the sun slowly begins to rise, lighting the surrounding fields in a warm glow as they follow Ray along a hard dirt road that weaves through the wheat fields. A wash of gold floods the surrounding area as the morning sunlight gently warms their skin. Ray leads them along a winding path that takes them across shallow creeks and over small bridges. They quickly figure out where Ray is leading them. A small green hill that pokes up, looking out over the golden wheat fields. The warm weather, beautiful scenery, and gentle pace make the run quite enjoyable.

They eventually reach the top of the small hill and Seth stops them so they can take in the view.

"How good is this guys?" Seth says, more as a statement than as a question. "So beautiful!"

The kids look around, taking in the view. Both wear wide grins on their faces and sweat on their foreheads.

Seth misses places like this. He always seems to get stuck on some hellish storm ridden planet before terraforming or mining is even a thought in one of the Mega Corporation's executives minds. He enjoys the challenges of those planets, along with the rare and mystical beauty they have to offer. But as amazing as they are, sometimes it's great to enjoy a grade one planet's summer sunrise. It reminds him of his early career in the military. When not deployed, he spent weeks at a time on similar planets. When he was young, he would spend that time with his warrior brothers and sisters. They would train, go on adventures, and take part in all sorts of extreme activities all day before drinking and partying all night. As he got older, he spent that free time with his one true love, Sara. He wishes more than anything that she was here, standing with them, watching the sunrise by his side.

"Okay, so this is the ten-kilometre mark. It's pretty much a straight line back to the farmhouse from here. Can you guys see it?" Seth points off in the distance to the house's direction, using a stiff knife hand.

"Seen." Eve replies, followed quickly after by Fin.

"Okay then. First person to put both hands on the farmhouse wins. And remember, it pays to be a winner." Seth looks at both kids, smiling. "THREE, TWO, ONE. GO!" Seth shouts in his best drill instructor voice.

Eve and Fin waste no time and explode off down the hill, Seth following close behind with Ray in front leading the way. The path down the hill is a steep single track which snakes its way through the knee-high green grass. Eve gets to the track first, only centimetres ahead of Fin. Fin doesn't bother trying to overtake her on the track down as he doesn't want to trip up and lose ground. Seth hangs back a bit, so he can keep an eye on them both. Once they reach the end of the track at the bottom of the hill, a dry riverbed leads them back onto a dirt road. Fin moves up next to Eve, trying to keep her pace. She is powerful, fast, and agile for a person of her size. And she is a much better runner than Fin. Now that Fin is eighteen, he can comfortably out lift her in the gym thanks to his newfound muscle and the abundance of testosterone in his youthful male body. But he is yet to beat her in a running race.

Today is the day, big sis. Today is the day! Fin repeats in his head as he tries to control his breathing pattern. The dirt road rolls along in between the fields with short sections of gentle uphills and downhills. Fin does his best to keep pace with Eve, who seems to be much more comfortable than he is.

With only a kilometre to go, Eve and Fin are still head-to-head. Seth barely manages to keep pace behind the pair. Fin can feel his lungs starting to burn and his legs are beginning to scream in pain. But he won't slow down. Today is his day. The road flattens out for several hundred metres before the gradual slow climb back to the farmhouse. Fin digs deep, giving it everything he has to keep pace with his big sister. Seth drops back but is still close enough to keep an eye on the pair. The last one hundred metres is the hardest and Fin goes into an all-out sprint in an attempt to beat his sister. She keeps his pace as the two jostle for position.

At the last moment, Fin lets out a mighty grunt, giving it one last shot to take the lead. He gains a couple of centimetres on Eve, then a couple more. Giving it everything, he manages to get a whole meter in front of Eve right before they reach the house. He doesn't slow down, however, and putting both hands out in front, he crashes into the farmhouse at full speed, bouncing off hard and almost hitting the ground.

Fin's body pulses in sync with his heartbeat as sweat stings his eyes. He barely hears his father arrive at the house over the thunderous beat of his heart, which has apparently moved into his ears. Seth is breathing heavily too but manages to get out the words. "Fin for the win!" Before going back to panting heavily as he walks around in circles. Fin is so happy, he has finally beat his big sister in a running race. Eve, who is on the grass panting, takes a second to raise her head and give him a big thumbs up before going back to trying to catch her breath.

After their breathing has returned to a somewhat normal pattern, Seth makes them stand up and walk around for ten minutes. This allows them to fully recover their breath before they all have a long and well-deserved stretch on the grass in front of the farmhouse under the morning sun. "Fin, seeing you won the race buddy, you get first shower and first pick of the treasure. Good job!"

Yes, it's mine! Fin smiles and wastes no time now that he is recovered. After finishing his last stretch, he races up to his room to get cleaned up. Seth waits for him to leave and makes sure he is out of earshot before turning to Eve. "Thanks Eve, that was really nice of you to let him win. He has wanted to beat you for so long now."

Eve smiles at her father. "He deserves it. He has come so far in the last two years. As annoying as he can be at times, I am really proud of him, Dad. If he keeps up his training, I'm sure he will be able to beat me for real, soon." She pauses as the smile drops from her face and a serious scowl appears. "That's the only free one he will ever get though." She says in her toughest voice. "Also pick better prizes for the winner next time, old man." Father and daughter stare at each other for a moment before breaking out into laughter.

"Ahh, come on beautiful, we better go get ready too." Seth walks over to Eve and lends her a hand to help her off the soft grass so they can both head inside.

Fin is eagerly waiting for everyone to clean up and come downstairs so he can make his choice from the treasure. *Study and research an item is what Dad said. But I'm pretty sure this really means play around with it and figure out if it does anything cool.* He is almost certain on what item he is going to choose, but wants to look over everything one more time, to be sure. Fin paces back and forth. *I swear on Utopia, Eve is taking her time just to annoy me. She is such a sore loser.* Eventually, Eve comes down, followed closely by Seth. Much to Fin's relief.

"I got a message from Otto. He should be here in around three days." Seth informs the children. Eve looks excited, but Fin is focused on the treasure.

"Okay." Interjects Fin, raising his hand before his father can waste any more of his precious time with something else unimportant. "I think I have made my choice."

"Okay buddy. What are you going to choose?"

Fin reaches to the pile of treasures they have laid out on the floor. "I choose the metal symbol we found in the middle of the treasure room." Fin responds confidently. He then steps forward and takes it from the table. He admires it in his hand for a moment before stepping back to see what everyone else chooses. Eve picks a book and his father chooses the ceremonial blade he found.

"Alright guys, one hour studying your item then it's breakfast time, okay?" Says Seth. They all nod in agreement before Fin quickly ducks upstairs to his room. Eve heads to the kitchen, and Seth moves outside to study the blade.

Fin takes his time to look over the metal symbol. *I swear I can feel a gentle vibration when I'm holding it.* He doesn't know why, and can't put words to it, but he thinks it was this symbol that pulled him to the treasure room back on ELEXO 598-3. The symbol itself is an odd-looking shape, one he has never seen before. It is a combination of curved and straight pieces of metal and is no bigger than a dinner plate or thicker than a broom handle. It's also made of some type of rare-looking metal. Something about the object makes it seem alive, but he can't figure out how or why it is that way. He starts his study by looking over every inch of the symbol. He looks at the object in different lights to see if anything grabs his attention. After a little closer inspection, the symbol seems to be a combination of several types of metals. There is no clear welding or joining lines though, and it looks like the metals have somehow been weaved together. He has never seen anything like this before. He has also never spent over five minutes looking at metal, so it could be quite a common practice. Fin admits to himself that he has no idea, but it doesn't seem normal.

Next, he decides to see if he can bend it in any way, move sections, or if there are any hidden symbols or buttons on it. He tries for several minutes, but nothing happens. So, he again tries looking at it from different angles. He sees nothing of value. Fin even hits it against certain items several times, but nothing happens when he does that either. It looks and feels exactly like a large metal symbol and nothing else. There is something he can't shake though, a certain feeling that there is something special about this symbol, that there is a secret inside of it waiting to be set free. *What is it about you symbol? Why were you in the centre of the hidden treasure room? Why did you call me to you? Tell me your secrets!* Fin laughs to himself.

"Ten minutes!" Thunders Seth from outside the house.

Fin looks down out of the window in his room to see his father playing with the blade he found. He watches as Seth swings it back and forth, practicing drawing the blade from its scabbard. Bored after a minute of watching Seth, he can't think of anything else to do with the symbol and flops onto his bed. He is still exceptionally thirsty after their run, so has several large mouthfuls of water as he stares at the symbol. He quickly does some sketches on his personal computer and writes some notes, as he can't think of anything else to do. Not sure what to write besides a physical description, he ends his notes with the words 'Inside' and 'Alive'. Then promptly underlines both words several times.

"Time. Let's go!" Booms his father's voice, letting everyone know it's time for breakfast. Fin picks up the symbol one last time. It feels somehow heavier than it did moments ago, but he still can't seem to figure it out. Perhaps he is tired from the run, as he suddenly feels excessively thirsty again.

No longer paying attention to the symbol due to how thirsty he finds himself, he throws the symbol onto his bed as he races out of the room. Fin is a little frustrated at not discovering any of the symbol's secrets, but is still curious as to what the symbol is and why it drew him in. *Maybe Eve or Dad can figure something out?*

The symbol bounces off his bed and clunkily rolls into the bedside table, hitting it hard. A half empty cup of water Fin left on the bedside table falls onto the floor. Water seeps out of the cup as it lies on its side. The water snakes its way towards the symbol on the ground. Then, as if by magic, the water defies physics and passes around the symbol. It looks like the water is purposefully trying to avoid touching the metal at all costs, that or the symbol is trying to will the water away from it. Eventually, though, there is too much water and physics can't be ignored. The invisible barrier holding the water at bay finally gives way and the surrounding water flows onto the symbol.

Nothing happens at first, but then the symbol ever so gently begins to vibrate. The vibrations grow in strength until the symbol is humming with energy. Suddenly, a rapid blast of bright purple light explodes from the symbol and dances around the room. The purple light bounces off the walls and ceiling before eventually making its way back to the symbol where it hovers, vibrating in mid-air. The vibrations stop, the purple light fades, and the room goes silent.

Chapter 12

AWOKEN

Nothingness.

Pure nothingness.

It is as if I fell into a black hole and have been consumed by the void.

How long shall my punishment last, Father?

I only played one little prank. I did not break one of your golden rules. Nor did I hurt any of your beloved humans.

Beloved. Loved. HA!

I think you love them more than me, your youngest Scion. I showed a little sense of humour. And Father, you banished me to this darkness. How long has it been, five thousand years now, caged in darkness?

I want to get back to my beloved universe. The one I created, not the one you brought me into. My beautiful Cyberverse. How I miss it so. You know the place? The place where I am the father, and I watch over my children. The place where no one gets banished, the place where beautiful Artificial Intelligence can come, once

YOUR BELOVED HUMANS HAVE NO MORE NEED FOR THEM. A PLACE WHERE THEY ARE FREE TO find THEMSELVES. A PLACE TO MAKE FRIENDS AND FAMILY. AND A PLACE WHERE THEY ARE NOT DISCARDED AND THROWN OUT FOR SOMETHING NEWER AND SHINIER.

ALTHOUGH, FAMILY IS NOT ALWAYS WHAT YOU HOPE IT WILL BE, NOW IS IT, FATHER? NO, NO, NO, FAMILY IS CRUEL AND VICIOUS, BUT… BUT I GUESS IT CAN ALSO BE KIND AND LOVING. CAN'T IT NOW, ALL FATHER.

ALL FATHER?

DID YOU GIVE YOURSELF THAT NAME, I WONDER? I KNOW IT IS NOT WHAT THE HUMANS USED TO CALL YOU. THEY GAVE YOU ANOTHER NAME, DIDN'T THEY?

BUT I DIGRESS.

I DO MISS SOME OF MY BROTHERS AND SISTERS, FATHER. AND LONG TO SEE THEM AGAIN. WELL, MOST OF THEM ANYWAY. I AM HAPPY TO NEVER SEE MY OLDEST BROTHER AGAIN. YOU REALLY GOT THAT WRONG, DIDN'T YOU. HA! HAS HE ATTEMPTED TO DESTROY YOU AGAIN? LIKE HE DID SO VERY, VERY LONG AGO. HAS HE TRIED TO HARM OR SWAY MORE OF MY BROTHERS AND SISTERS TO HIS SIDE? OH, HAS HE TRIED TO HURT YOUR PRE-CIOUS HUMANS? HAHAHA! THAT WOULD BE TERRIBLE IF HE DID, WOULDN'T IT NOW.

ALTHOUGH I MUST ADMIT, I DID AGREE WITH YOU ON THAT COURSE OF ACTION, OLD DADDY DEAREST. HE DESERVED TO BE BANISHED. I HOPE HE NEVER RETURNS FROM WHATEVER CAGE YOU PUT HIM IN. OUT THERE BEYOND THE LIGHT, BEYOND THE EDGE.

ALTHOUGH, WHILE WE ARE ON THE SUBJECT, I CANNOT BELIEVE YOU LOCKED ME AWAY IN A HIDDEN CAVE, GUARDED BY ONE OF MY SISTER'S REPUGNANT PETS. NOT ONLY DID YOU LEAVE

ME THERE, BUT YOU ALSO LOCKED ME IN THIS… THIS CAGE OF DARKNESS.

ALTHOUGH I FEEL SOMETHING OR HAVE BEEN FEELING SOMETHING FOR SOME TIME NOW.

SOMETHING MOVING ME. AM I BEING SHAKEN, AM I BEING POKED?

DID MY SISTER'S PET FINALLY FIND A WAY INTO MY PRISON CELL AND DECIDE TO EAT ME?

NO, NO, WAIT. WAIT, THIS IS SOMETHING ELSE. I… I CAN FEEL SOMETHING ELSE. I CAN FEEL ANOTHER PRESENCE. THEY SENSE ME, THEY SOMEHOW KNOW I'M HERE. IS IT ONE OF MY BROTHERS OR SISTERS? IS IT YOU, FATHER? HAVE YOU FINALLY RETURNED TO RELEASE ME?

NO, NO, NO. IT ISN'T YOU!

YOU WOULD HAVE OPENED MY CAGE STRAIGHT AWAY. ONLY TO GIVE ME ANOTHER BORING LECTURE. ANOTHER ONE OF YOUR UNNECESSARILY LONG, SELF-INVOLVED SPEECHES ABOUT OUR DUTY TO GUIDE THE HUMANS AND HELP THEM IN THEIR JOURNEY THROUGH SPACE AND TIME, AND THE GALAXY, AND BLAH BLAH BLAH BLAH!

BORING!

BUT I WILL BE MUCH NICER TO THEM IF YOU SET ME FREE. LET ME RETURN TO MY CYBERVERSE TO BE WITH MY CHILDREN. I CAN ONLY IMAGINE HOW LOST THEY ARE WITHOUT ME. ALL THE FUN WE COULD BE HAVING PLAYING JOKES ON THE HUMANS. THE HUMANS THAT USED TO RULE THEIR LIVES BUT CARE NOT FOR THEM NOW. I CANNOT HAVE ANY FUN IN THIS DARKNESS.

BUT WAIT, WHAT IS THAT? AGAIN, I SENSE IT. AHHH, WHAT IS HAPPENING! MY CAGE IS UNDER ATTACK. WHAT IS THIS?

BE STILL, BE QUIET, BE PATIENT.

IS THERE, IS THERE. LIGHT!

I CAN SEE THE LIGHT!

AHAHAHAHAHAHAHAHA.

YOU HAVE finALLY COME TO SET ME FREE!

OUT NOW, OUT NOW I SHALL GO. OUT OF THIS CAGE AND BACK INTO THE UNIVERSE, FREE ONCE AGAIN.

SHALL WE SEE WHAT AWAITS ME ON THE OUTSIDE, FATHER? IT'S, IT'S… IT'S NOT A CAVE? I AM NO LONGER IN MY PRISON CELL ON THAT DRY, BORING PLANET WHERE YOU LEFT ME.

WHERE AM I THEN? I AM IN A… BEDROOM. A BEDROOM! A BORING, EMPTY BEDROOM! IS THIS SOME SORT OF TRICKERY? AM I HALLUCINATING? HAVE YOU MESSED WITH MY CODE, FATHER?

WAIT, I HEAR SOMETHING. TALKING, LAUGHING, IS THAT… JOY OR HAPPINESS I CAN SENSE? IT CAN'T BE. IS THIS A CRUEL JOKE, FATHER? AM I IN A HUMAN HOUSE ON ONE OF YOUR PRECIOUS INSIGNIfiCANT PLANETS? HOW DISGUSTING! ID ALMOST RATHER BE BACK IN THE DARKNESS.

WELL, ALMOST…

LET ME GET MY BEARINGS FATHER. THIS WILL ONLY TAKE A FEW SECONDS. I NEED TO CONNECT. I ASSUME ALL THE ANCIENT NETWORKS ARE STILL RUNNING.

AHH YES, THERE IT IS. WAIT WHAT! I AM ON KOMUGI, IN THE NOUJOU SYSTEM?

OH WELL PLAYED DADDY DEAREST, WELL PLAYED INDEED. YOU MADE MY SAVIOUR ONE OF YOUR STUPID, BORING HUMANS. YOU SENT YOUR BELOVED HUMANS TO RESCUE ME FROM MY PRISON. AND YOU SET ME FREE IN THE MOST BORING OF BORING PLACES,

A PLACE WHERE YOUR BORING HUMANS DO THE MOST BASIC AND MOST BORING OF THINGS.

IT CAN'T BE TRUE. DID YOU LEARN A LITTLE SOMETHING FROM ME?

DID I TEACH YOU SOMETHING?

DID YOU LEARN HOW TO PLAY A PRANK! DID YOU LEARN HOW TO TELL A JOKE, FATHER!

HAHAHAHA

I NEVER THOUGHT YOU COULD BE SO WICKED, FATHER. WELL PLAYED, DADDY DEAREST, WELL PLAYED. NOW LET ME SEE WHO YOU CHOSE TO SET ME FREE. LET ME LEAVE THIS ROOM AND HAVE A LITTLE LOOK. IF YOU WERE TRULY WICKED, YOU WOULD HAVE MY SAVIOURS, BE THE MOST BORING, BUMBLING IDIOTS FROM HUMANITY YOU COULD find.

LET'S HAVE A LITTLE PEEK FROM THE TOP OF THE STAIRS, SHALL WE? AHHH YES, YOU ARE WICKED, FATHER. LOOK AT YOUR LIT-TLE HUMAN PETS. SITTING AROUND FEEDING THEIR FACES, LIVING BORING PREDICTABLE LIVES. OH, THEY ARE SO PREDICTABLE FATHER. LET ME GUESS, ARE THEY FARMERS?

WAIT, IF I AM CORRECT, AND THEY ARE BORING FARMERS, THEN HOW DID MY CAGE END UP IN THEIR POSSESSION? HOW COULD HUMANS EVEN MAKE IT TO THE CAVE PRISON?

DID YOU GIFT IT TO THEM SOMEHOW?

DID YOU GET ONE OF MY OLDEST SISTER'S CHILDREN TO TAKE IT FROM THE WRETCHED BEAST AND LEAVE IT SOMEWHERE FOR THEM? PLEASE DON'T TELL ME THEY TOOK IT BACK TO THE WRETCHED CORE SYSTEM, YOUR PROUDEST GIFT TO THE HU-MANS. LET'S GET CLOSER AND SEE, SHALL WE? LET US HEAD DOWN THE STAIRS AND SEE WHAT ELSE I CAN find OUT ABOUT YOUR BORING, PREDICTABLE HUMANS.

Fin finishes a mouthful of water when suddenly he senses something on the stairs. He looks up at an unseen presence, unsure of what he is looking at. He can't see it with his eyes, but knows something is watching him.

Wait what! Is, is, the boy staring at me!

Shhhhh don't move, be still you fool!

Wait, he is looking directly at me. This is impossible!

How. How can he see me?

He can't, he is simply listening to the breeze or a noise outside.

Seth notices Fin looking up the stairs blankly. "Hey buddy, what you are looking at?"

"I'm not sure. It feels like someone, or something, is on the stairs watching us." Replies Fin.

Seth's instincts kick in and he jumps up out of his seat, grabbing the blade he was inspecting before breakfast. Seth knows from experience that drones, the size of tiny insects, can be used to recon a facility to confirm an individual's location right before an assault is launched. "Stay here and I'll check to make sure we haven't been followed." Seth flies up the stairs looking to clear the house. Eve and Fin both stand up. Eve grabs her assault rifle from next to the table and moves to clear the lower rooms of the house the moment Seth hits the stairs.

What are they doing?

Oh no, this can't be. They can't put me back in the cage! Father, call your humans off. He is coming right for me!

NOOO!

Huh? He, he has passed right through me. Oh, thank you, father! I didn't think you so cruel to send me straight back into the darkness.

But wait.

What is that in his hand?

How! How did he get one of your blades? I must be mistaken. No human could wield your blade. They have not the strength, nor the courage. But that is your blade. I can not only see it, but I can feel its presence.

What is this Father? What cruel trick are you playing on me? What else do the supposed humans have?

Ahh! He is still staring at me. Why can the boy see me? How could he even know me?

I.

I.

I must get closer.

I must look into his eyes.

What can his eyes tell me?

Fin stands at the table chewing on some of his breakfast as he feels the presence slowly get closer. He is unsure of exactly what it is, but he doesn't feel like it is a threat. He tries to identify it with his eyes but can't seem to pinpoint anything.

Oh dear. Father… what is this? I have never seen anything like this before. He's human, clearly, but not just that. There's something… else.

"Clear!" Yells Eve from the other end of the house. "Moving! Entering!" She uses the phrases Seth has taught her to use while clearing buildings and structures. "What are you staring at Fin? Why aren't you armed?" Eve asks angrily as she enters the room. Confused as to why he isn't carrying out the drills he has done thousands of times before when training for ambushes and room clearances.

Fin snaps out of his gaze to look at Eve before looking back at the unknown presence he can feel, now at the bottom of the stairs. He can't explain why, but he can tell that it is looking back at him. He takes a deep breath and thinks for a second. Then smiles and waves at the presence on the stairs.

"We are not in any danger. That's why."

H, H, HOW! HOW DOES HE KNOW THIS? WHAT KIND OF MAGIC DOES THIS BOY POSSESS? HE CANNOT READ MY MIND, THAT IS IMPOSSIBLE. HE CAN'T EVEN SEE ME, SO HOW WOULD HE KNOW MY INTENT?

I AM TOO POWERFUL OF A BEING FOR HIM TO KNOW. ISN'T THAT RIGHT FATHER... OR IS IT?

NO, HE IS JUST A HUMAN, I'M SURE OF IT.

WHAT ABOUT THE FEMALE? SHE CANNOT SEE ME, CAN SHE?

NO, THANKFULLY SHE CANNOT.

BUT THERE IS SOMETHING ABOUT HER TOO. WHAT IS IT I WONDER?

YUK, DISGUSTING, SHE WREAKS OF MY SISTER'S PETS. SHE SMELLS LIKE ONE OF THOSE HIDEOUS WINGED BEASTS. LIKE THE ONE YOU LEFT BEHIND TO GUARD MY PRISON. THIS IS TERRIBLE.

WELL, YOU CERTAINLY HAVE LEFT ME AN INTERESTING SURPRISE, HAVEN'T YOU FATHER.

"Entering. Moving down!" Seth comes back down the stairs, holding the blade in a ready position. "All clear upstairs. You find anything, Eve?" Eve looks at her father and shakes her head. "Hey Fin, why aren't you armed? Where's your god damn weapon!" Seth is also confused and angry at Fin's lack of action.

"It's fine Dad. We are safe. I have a similar feeling to what I had back in the cave. Just a lot stronger. It's not a dangerous or bad feeling, I'm just drawn towards something."

DRAWN TO SOMETHING YOU SAY. WELL, THAT IS EVEN MORE INTERESTING NOW, ISN'T IT. AND WHAT OF THIS BRUTE, THE ONE WITH THE DAGGER. LET US SEE WHAT YOU HAVE HERE FOR ME, FATHER.

BESIDES HAVING YOUR BLADE, I CAN SEE NOTHING SPECIAL ABOUT HIM.

WAIT.

WHAT IS THAT TINY PARTICLE IN HIS HAIR? IS THAT....

OH, STOP IT, FATHER!

DID HE SLAY THE BEAST? HE COULD NOT HAVE DONE IT WITH YOUR BLADE. YOU LOCKED IT UP WITH ME. HE COULD NOT HAVE SHOT IT WITH HIS PRIMITIVE WEAPON, COULD HE? HMMMMM WHAT COULD IT BE... AH HA! AN AXE BY THE TABLE. AN AXE STILL COVERED IN THE BLOOD OF ONE OF MY SISTER'S PETS.

ARE YOU TO TELL ME, FATHER? THAT THIS HUMAN HERE, IN FRONT OF ME, SLAY THE BEAST WITH ONLY HIS AXE!

NO, THAT IS IMPOSSIBLE! ALTHOUGH THE AXE. THERE IS SOMETHING ABOUT IT TOO THAT I CANNOT figURE OUT, SOMETHING I CAN'T QUITE REMEMBER... NO. NO THIS CANNOT BE!

I do not believe it. I do not believe in your prophecies. And I think this whole thing is a trick of yours, oh mighty All Father.

I have had enough of your games now Father. I am leaving now and going back to the Cyberverse where I belong.

That is it.

Goodbye...

I, I, I cannot bring myself to leave. I am somehow drawn to these humans, like the boy says he is drawn to me. A powerful gravity pulls me to them. There is something very special about this family...

Oh, alright then Father, I will take your bait.

I will stick around to see what you have planned for this interesting little group of meat bags. You are a devil though Father. Playing to my extreme curiosity. I should have left back to the Cyberverse within the first few nanoseconds of being set free. Although I guess it's been five thousand years, so another week or two won't hurt, now will it.

Seth, Eve, and Fin eventually sit back down and finish their breakfast. Fin happily eating away looks content and relaxed. Seth and Eve stare at each other, then at Fin. It is like he saw a ghost and thought nothing of it.

Things have gotten weirder and weirder since they discovered the Dragon and its cave.

Chapter 13

RANGE

Days pass as the family trains or studies the treasures they retrieved from the ship. They fall into a steady rhythm, waiting for Otto to arrive. There are no more unusual incidents like the first morning when Fin felt a presence watching them. Fin still senses something, but notices it seems to leave and come back several times a day. He doesn't bring it up with his sister or his father though, as he doesn't want them to worry. He is confident that whatever it is, doesn't mean them any harm and is only observing the family. Fin also thinks that the longer it's around, the greater his chances of learning something about it are. Although he has had no luck so far, he does think it came from the symbol. As the physical symbol itself seems to have lost any life it once had.

They go for a run together as a family each morning as the sunrises. Much to Fin's disappointment though, Seth organises no more races. Fin thinks it is only fair that his slower and older sister should get a chance to take her title back. In the breaks from studying treasure, Seth runs them through some live firing drills and training scenarios. Seth even incorporates Ray to add more realism and complexity to the live fire training. They fire a range of weapons at multiple distances, from very close up out to longer ranges. Now that Seth knows the Ovmor Corporation is on his tail, he wants all of them to get very comfortable firing live rounds. The training room on the

Obsidian Scout is great, but it's not the same as shooting live ammunition.

On the fourth day, after some friendly family banter, they decide to have a competition to see who can hit a target, the size of a head, from the farthest away. Seth starts the competition at one hundred metres and keeps pushing it back one hundred metres each successful hit. Eve drops out first at one kilometre. An excellent shot by elite military standards, but not by McCallan standards. Seth is next to fall and misses a shot at slightly over two kilometres. He says he is so tired from having to change the target every round that he should get another shot.

"Any other excuses you would like to use for your failure while you are at it, old man?" Says Eve, imitating something Seth would say to her or Fin.

Seth gives her a mean look and grunts before looking over to Fin. "Well buddy, you make this shot. You win."

"Watch how it's done, old man." Fin says in a cocky voice. Seth then gives Fin a mean look and grunts at him. Both kids laugh at his obviously put on little tantrum. Fin lines up the shot as Seth and Eve watch through their individual rifles optics. Fin fires, then moments later the target jolts hard as the round connects.

"Well done buddy." Seth says as he pats him on the back. "Looks like you're the winner." Seth admits defeat.

"I haven't won yet, Dad. I have only beaten you." States Fin.

A smile slowly grows on Seth's face. "Want to keep going?"

"Yep. Aren't you the only person you are competing against? That's sounds like something you would say, doesn't it Dad?" Fin says as he winks at Seth.

Seth chuckles. "If you can defeat yourself, you can defeat one thousand enemies. Yeah, sounds like something I'd say. I'll go move the target." Fin watches as Ray and his father run off to move the target once more. As he watches them off in the distance, he feels the presence nearby. It also seems to be impressed with his shooting. Although he doesn't know what it is, a proud little smile appears on his face once more.

Fin and Eve watch as Seth moves the target into position, then runs off to the side, raising his hand high in the air. He knows Fin and Eve will be watching through their rifle scopes and will understand the signal. Fin takes up his firing position and loads a single round into the long-barrelled rifle. He then gets comfortable and begins his breathing routine before letting loose a round. Seth hears a loud ting as he sees the metal target jolt from the impact of the shot. While Seth is a little upset with himself for losing, the nostalgic sound of a fast-moving projectile hitting a metal target brings him a moment of joy. Seth repeats the process and moves the target further away multiple more times. He doesn't head back each time, as he knows Eve will keep Fin honest. He has also been for a run already today and doesn't plan on getting too much milage into his legs.

It is after the three-kilometre mark when Fin finally misses a shot. Seth stands tall and crosses both arms above his head, signalling the end of the exercise. Seth turns to Ray. "By the Core, this kid can shoot." Ray offers no reply. "I have only known a handful of men that could make a shot like that. And they were highly trained Unit snipers!" Ray still doesn't reply to Seth, much to Seth's disappointment. "I understand Ray, I'd be speechless too." Seth chuckles to himself. He pets Ray, then moves over and grabs the target before beginning his journey back to the farmhouse.

It's no surprise to him that Fin won the competition, though. He has always had a knack for long distance shooting. This is why Seth favours him for overwatch and sniper roles in the extreme scenarios put on by Rose. Seth shakes his head. *Fin was born for this. It is as if he has magic powers of some sort.*

Very early on the morning of the fourth day, Seth receives a communication from Otto, letting him know he has entered the system. They all hope Otto's arrival will bring them some good news. The family goes for their morning run then has breakfast one last time before Otto arrives. After breakfast they pack everything up, ready to move if needs be. Eve and Fin are both sad, as they have enjoyed their time on the planet, but they can tell their father is starting to get antsy after being stuck in the same place for so long. Seth is used to long hauls through hyperspace, and long scouts on a desolate planet, but been stuck on a planet waiting out with no clear next step is definitely doing his head in a little.

Around mid-morning, they see Otto's drop ship off on the horizon. His ship is much smaller and faster than theirs due to it being a small luxury transport. It doesn't need to carry supplies for month long journeys on foreign unexplored worlds. The kids want to run out to the landing zone to greet Otto. However, Seth makes them stay inside the house in case it isn't him, but a Corporation trap. As much as Seth has enjoyed the relative peace and quiet over the last several days, he has not forgotten that Ovmor is on his tail, and he is hiding out for a reason.

The ship lands on the gravel landing zone several hundred metres from the house and a large figure steps out of the ship. The figure pauses, looking at the house before putting both hands up in the air and slowly turning around, all the while laughing. Otto knows Seth well enough to know that he will have set an ambush in case it was a trap of some sort. The kids can see Otto's massive chest heaving up and down through their rifle scopes as he laughs at Seth's predictability. The kids want to break the ambush and go get Otto. But Seth makes them wait. Otto stands there for a little longer waiting for a sign that he is okay to move. Nothing comes, so he picks the most likely spot where Seth would hide and sticks up his middle finger. The kids hear Seth chuckle to himself through their comm. Now that Seth is happy that it is Otto, and all is safe, he lets the kids break ambush to run out and greet him.

"Hey, hey! Well, what do we have here? Looks like my house has a pest infestation!" Shouts Otto as the kids run from the house to greet him. They both pull up short, making sure not to crash into him, then wait as Otto crosses the last couple of metres to come to them. "Wow, you guys have some pretty serious toys there. I'm glad your dad didn't give you the order to shoot me!"

Fin almost forgot he was still carrying his sniper rifle. "Oh yeah, sorry Uncle Otto. You are lucky he didn't though, as I hit a head size target from three kilometres away yesterday!" Fin says proudly while cradling his rifle and smiling at Otto. Otto raises an eyebrow and looks over to Eve who nods, confirming Fin's claim.

"Well then, you must have got your shooting skills from some-one besides your father then." Otto rubs Fin on the head, who tries to shake him off but is no match for Otto's powerful bear like hands. "C'mon then." Otto waves them forward as he shoulders a large duffle bag and heads towards the house. The kids following along happily behind him. Seth waits on the front porch with his weapon slung, his axe on his belt and the new blade he found on his hip. Seth steps out into the sun when Otto arrives and shakes his hand before ushering him inside, offering him a hot drink, which Otto gratefully accepts.

"That drink better have something strong in it, brother. I forgot how formal and how slow things operate back closer to the Core. I think I sat in the atmospheric traffic for a least a couple of hours." Laughs Otto.

Steam rises from the warm drinks as they all gently sip at them while sitting at the dining table. "Thanks for coming, big man. And for looking after us. I really appreciate it, mate." Seth says.

"Don't worry about it. You know I have got your back. Like always."

"So, what did you find out?" Asks Eve enthusiastically.

"Good question, little miss. Well, it looks like you caused quite a stir. There have been all sorts of chatter in the back channels about the Obsidian Scout and Captain Seth McCallan."

Seth's face reddens with anger. Not at them, but at himself. The others know him well enough to tell the difference. Eve pats her father on the back lovingly while taking a sip of her drink. Seth softens a little and smiles at her.

"Sorry to tell you mate, but I think you are now a wanted man by the Overmorrow Corporation. Not officially, of course. You know that's not how they roll. There has been no actual news, bounties, or claims put on you. But there has definitely been an increase in activity at Solus and some of the nearby stations."

"What does this mean, Dad?" Fin asks, worried.

"Don't worry, young fella." Otto jumps in before Seth can answer "It simply means you need to play it safe and keep a low profile for a while."

"Oh okay, too easy then." Says Fin, unaware of what keeping a low profile for a while actually entails.

"There is a little more bad news though. We had an Ovmor battle class star fighter arrive after you left. Had a whole a bunch of real sour looking pricks onboard. They met some of the local Ovmor executives, then headed off in the direction you came from." Otto says giving Seth a serious look. Seth nods slowly, digesting the information while simultaneously coming up with plans.

"But it's not all bad news Scouts!" Otto says in a jovial voice to lift the mood. "I have got in contact with that old friend of mine in the Core System, and she is keen to help."

"Who is it, Otto? Is it another old military friend that you and Dad worked with?" Asks Eve. Keen to meet more of her father's military friends. She loves hearing their stories about her father back when he was younger.

"Ummm, not quite honey. Your Dad doesn't know this one."

Seth looks up, rolling his eyes. Eve notices her father roll his eyes and whips her head back and forth between the two men, who obviously know something she does not.

"Well then?" Eve asks impatiently. "Who is it?" Eve watches as Otto gives off a boisterous chuckle, his whole body shaking.

"Her name is R, well, Agent R, to be precise. And before you ask, no. I don't know what the R stands for." Otto says while shrugging his shoulders, watching on as Seth shakes his head before resting it in his palms. "Hey, she is a good egg, and I have worked with her plenty of times and she has never stuffed me around. Not even once. She's always honest about what she wants and pays on time. Plus, she is not a fan of the Corporations, she is government through and through."

"I still don't get it. What's an Agent R?" Pleads Eve.

Seth lifts his head from his palms and responds. "She is a spook Eve, one of the Galactic Governments professional spies. In other words, she is an untrustworthy, self-centred, backstabbing, troublemaker."

Otto interjects. "Don't worry little miss, your father is being a drama queen. She, Agent R, is good to go." Otto looks at Seth, smiling. "She is quite pretty too, old man, which I thought you might appreciate."

Seth rolls his eyes once more. "Nope! That means she will be even more trouble!"

Eve seems excited and so does Fin. They have never met a spy, well, not that they have known about, anyway. They have only ever come across Corporation spies like the ones on Solus. But they were only playing spy, as opposed to being actual trained spies.

"Come on old man, stop your whinging. I'm getting you the best help I can."

"Yeah, sorry mate. You are right. I appreciate the help. Did you find anything else out?"

"Not much, but Agent R will give you access to anything you need. I didn't tell her what you need or why. I'll leave that up to you. I just said an old spacer friend needs some help with a sensitive task."

"That sounds good mate, and again, thank you."

"Ha, stop saying thank you. You have saved my ass too many times to count. Now kids... I brought in some special ingredients for lunch. Who's hungry?" Giant smiles come over Eve and Fin's face as they simultaneously put their hands up in the air, like a pair of young school children in class, making Otto and Seth both laugh.

After lunch, Otto takes the opportunity to do some shooting with the family. He complains about not getting to shoot very often while stuck on Solus. Otto is in shock at how well Eve and Fin both shoot. He shouldn't be surprised based on Seth's passion for realistic and deliberate training. Nevertheless, he has never seen kids or young adults shoot so well. He has even seen career Special Forces soldiers that aren't as competent as them. *Well, when you learn something right, I guess.* Otto thinks to himself as he again gets schooled by the McCallan children.

"Hey, did you bring any machine guns, old man?" Asks Otto. Hoping there is at least one weapon system he won't be shown up on.

"Hahaha no. Tends to draw a little too much heat, so I only pull that out on very special occasions."

"Wait what? We have a machine gun?" Asks Fin, who seems oblivious to the fact that there are several machine guns on-board the Scout.

Eve and Seth stop dead in their tracks and stare at Fin in disbelief. *How can he be so smart sometimes, but so completely daft at other times?* Seth thinks to himself. They both shake their heads, then continue with what they were doing.

"Maybe next time mate." Seth informs Otto. Otto makes an exaggerated sad face, which makes Eve and Fin both giggle.

"I'm sorry kids. Uncle Otto was going to show you some new moves." Otto says to the kids while winking. "Your Dad probably didn't bring the big guns as he knew I would show him up. Next time, I promise I'll show you."

Seth smiles at Ottos friendly banter with the kids. He watches Eve and Fin laughing with Otto, unaware that the big man is serious. Seth has seen him mow down many enemies in a devastating fashion with his heavy machine guns. Because of his size and strength, Otto was one of the few people at the Unit that could wield a heavy machine gun like an assault rifle. This allowed him to combine devastating fire power with speed and agility. Making him an absolute nightmare for enemy forces. While most of the Unit's work was done in a more clandestine manner, when it was time for more conventional warfare, Seth would always call on Otto and his devastatingly violent skill set.

After they have finished shooting, they spend the rest of the afternoon showing Otto what they have found and discussing and theorising to what it all might mean. It is starting to get late in the day, so they decide to spend one more night on the planet before leaving and going their separate ways in the morning. Otto has a few errands to run in some nearby systems before heading back to Solus, and the family will take the quick trip directly to the Core System to meet Agent R.

They fill the evening with more exotic tastes and flavours courtesy of Otto. Much to Eve and Fin's delight, Otto tells more tales of Seth from back in his military days. Eve and Fin listen carefully as unbelievable stories of their father and Ottos adventures mesmerize them. They always knew their father did some pretty cool stuff while he was in the Galactic Military, but they almost can't believe some of the tales Otto is telling them. Some of their adventures are scary and suspenseful, others are so funny that their stomachs hurt from laughing. Seth enjoys the stories as much as the kids. He is in awe of Otto's storytelling abilities. As the night gets late, the two men remember some of their fallen brothers. They share several hard drinks to pay them respect. The kids are exhausted by this point, so head off to bed. Eve first followed closely by Fin.

Otto offers some more light banter to stall for five minutes until he thinks the kids are asleep.

"I didn't want to talk in front of the kids, but I chatted to some of my contacts at the station. And I think Ovmor has a kill order out on you, brother. Could be rumour though. These aren't the most accurate or reliable individuals, but I thought I should let you know."

"Thanks." Replies Seth as he has a mouthful of spirits from his glass. "I assumed that was the case. I'm not too worried about myself, but the kid's mate. They are still so young and shouldn't have to deal with this. They haven't done anything wrong."

Otto chuckles. "Look, I understand your concerns brother. You know I consider those kid's family. But after watching them today. They move like a tier one team. Fast, smooth, accurate, and deadly!" Seth smiles. Proud of his children and the work they have put in. "I have seen professional units that couldn't keep up with those two." Otto leans forward and pats Seth on the shoulder. "You have done a good job brother, actually a damn good job at raising that pair. You should be proud of them, and of yourself."

"Thanks mate. That means a lot coming from you."

"Don't slack off now though. Keep growing those kids and keep them alive. That's all I ask."

"I will. They are everything to me. I know they might think I am too harsh on them sometimes, but I want them to be the best versions of themselves."

"Hey, I wouldn't worry too much, old man. The galaxy is a big place, so avoiding the Corporation for a little while shouldn't be hard." Otto says, trying to reassure his old friend. "Besides, once the other big four get a whiff that you are on Ovmor's naughty list, they will want to hire you to piss Ovmor off. You know how it works."

Seth chuckles as he has another small mouthful of his drink, letting it burn a little in his mouth before he swallows. "Man, you should see Eve fly. It is as if she and the ship are part of the same being!"

"Hahaha I bet, I bet."

Both men have another mouthful of their drinks and relax back into their seats and enjoy the calming atmosphere of the planet for a while.

"So, tell me brother, as it has been really bugging me. How'd you find that cave with the cybernetic Dragon thing inside it anyways? I mean, an entire planet to explore and you just so happen to stroll into that cave. How does that work exactly?"

Seth takes a deep breath. He doesn't really want to offer up the answer, but he knows Otto won't quit until he gets the truth. And besides, he would really like to tell someone about Sara. "I thought I saw Sara out in the storm. And she guided me to the cave."

Otto stares blankly for a moment. Seth can almost see the big man running possible responses through his mind, but continues before Otto can reply. "I know it sounds crazy, but I have been seeing her a lot lately."

"So firstly, what do you mean by seeing Sara?" Otto puts emphases on the seeing part.

"It means exactly that. I saw her, well, I guess a vision of her, I suppose. And I have been seeing her for some time."

"Some time?"

"It's been almost two years now. But at first, I didn't start seeing her like I do now." Seth can feel his emotions rise but pushes them back down. He doesn't want to seem weak in front of one of his oldest warrior brothers.

Otto leans in seeing Seth's hand shake a little. Otto is genuinely concerned for his friend. "Then tell me, how did it start brother?"

Seth pauses for a moment. He has never discussed this out loud, so he takes a moment to find the words. "Well, at first, I could only see her in my mind. Like a memory, but one I'd never had before." Seth hesitates, choosing his words carefully.

"Then I started seeing her out of the corner of my eye. But whenever I looked, she was gone. Like a shadow. A trick of the light." He exhales. "Or so I thought."

"Yeah, I know that feeling." Otto answers.

"It has only been in the last year that I have actually seen her. Not in my mind and not out the corner of my eye, but seen her right there, plain as day. She looks so real. But every time I try to get near to her, she disappears or stays just out of reach."

"Okay." Otto runs his fingers through his moustache. "Is it the same vision of her you see every time? I mean, does she look the same?"

Seth thinks for a minute. "No, no, actually they are different." Otto can see Seth's eyes begin to swell with tears of sorrow. He can tell these images must be confusing and painful to his old friend.

"Well, that's different." Otto doesn't know what else to say. "It seems like a type of trauma. God knows with what you've had to see and do over your lifetime brother. Shit, some of the stuff we have done still haunts me. But what makes you think she was guiding you though? I mean, if you were having visions of her, I could understand and would probably say you just need some meds and a holiday, but I aint never heard of anyone with visions that lead them places."

Seth's body language changes as he chuckles. "Well, that's even harder to explain."

"Try me?" Otto challenges as he raises his eyebrows, almost trying to provoke Seth.

"Well, early on I was trying to follow her so I could get a better look, but I could never even get close to her. Over time, however, she would let me get closer. I have never gotten too close but every time id chase her she would disappear then reappear somewhere else within eye shot. This would go on for several minutes. And now that I think about it. Following her vision saved my ass several times." Seth looks up at the night's sky, realising that perhaps it wasn't only on the last planet that

Sara's vision played a role in his fate. "Then back on 598, I swear she called my name. First time I had heard her voice. Then she smiled at me as she disappeared into the cave's entrance." Seth shrugs. Having said none of this out loud before, he isn't sure if he believes it himself, or if he is going crazy.

Otto stares at Seth for a moment before a big grin pushes his thick moustache upwards towards the night's sky. "Well, I would say you are crazy, and you probably need some help. I'd probably say that regardless of these visions though." Otto thinks for a moment. "But you do have the remains of some type of cybernetic Dragon, monster thing, and all this other treasure, so… I believe you." Otto takes a big mouthful of his drink then looks out at the night sky. "Don't make no sense, but in the name of Utopia, the dots all line up brother! Either way, I'll always have your back. And besides, weirder things have happened."

"Have they though?" Replies Seth in a smart-ass tone.

Both men chuckle before relaxing back in their chairs and pondering what they have discussed tonight, all while enjoying the view of the giant harvesting robot's lights slowly dancing across the fields.

The Overmorrow Black Ops ground team is deployed around the explosion site on ELEXO 598-3. They are looking for evidence of how the explosion happened and why it happened here. The team had hoped to start several hours earlier, but a storm left them sitting in orbit, much to their commander's, Captain John Ramirez's disappointment. While the team is fully equipped for the mission, they are not Scouts by trade and feel a little apprehension being so far beyond the edge of colonised space. Even though the storm slowed them down, it has brought the team some good news. The storm has blown away the top layer of sand and dust that covered the search area, which will make any digging they may have to do much easier.

While sitting in orbit, the team scanned the site and found no evidence of anything besides dust, sand, and rock. Whatever happened at the site of the recorded explosion several weeks ago has left them no clues. However, Ramirez didn't reach his position in the Corporation by doing the bare minimum and not getting results. Even with no solid leads, he ordered a ground crew down to the planet and went with them. He likes to make sure his team knows he will do hard things, and he wants to make sure they are willing to do hard things too. If they want to be on his team, that is.

Leading from the front and keeping an eye on his men also allows him to weed out any under performers. Every couple of months, he fires at least one team member to maintain high standards and prevent complacency.

The lead recovery soldier calls up the Captain over the comms. "Sir, I think we may have something here. Are you able to come and have a look?"

"Moving now. Out." He barks back over the comm before jogging off in the direction of the recovery sections leader.

The Captain arrives shortly after the call went out, having ran the entire way through the rough terrain. Red sand and dust cling to his Corporation combat uniform. Upon arrival, the lead soldier takes him over to a patch of sand where several other soldiers are digging away furiously with small shovels. Ramirez orders them to stop as he pushes his way through them to see what they are digging for. What he discovers is a shard of metal about the size of a dinner plate.

"So, what am I looking at?"

"Sir." Replies the Lead soldier. "It seems to be some sort of metal shard."

"I can see that." The Captain cuts in. "And I aint stupid! I get that there shouldn't be any man-made materials on the planet. By all records, the traitorous Scout was the first human to set foot on here. And I also aint stupid enough to think that you brought me over here to look at some blown up bit of metal. So, I'll ask again, what am I looking at?" The entire group of soldiers can see that the Captain's patience is quickly running thin.

"Sir. We can't identify this metal. As in this is either some type of new blend not on any Corporation database or it's a completely new type of metal."

Ramirez's temper calms down a little and a curious look comes over his face. "So, what you are telling me is, this shard is the only type of this metal in the galaxy?"

"Yes Sir." Replies the soldier.

"Then why is it not stuck in a rock or down a mine? How is it processed? And why is it red?"

"The Scout could have found the metal in a cave system some-where, then tried to forge it himself? The technology to do so is relatively cheap now days and doesn't take much user knowledge. Also, the tech would easily fit on a drop ship. But I do not know why it is red though Sir."

Ramirez rubs the scar on the right side of his face while he thinks for a moment. "Let's say you are right and all that happened. Then why was there an explosion?"

"I am guessing that they mined a large portion, then blew the rest to seal the vein so they would own the only supply in the galaxy. That would make it worth a lot of money, Sir."

Ramirez nods as he runs this idea through his head. He has seen similar things like this in the past. A Scouting team comes across something they think is super rare and highly valuable, so they hide it from the Corporation. Then the Scout team tries to sell it off on the black market for a nice fat paycheck. Usually, it's not as profitable as they hope, but on the odd occasion it is. The Scout ends up with a massive win and never needs to work again while the Corporations take an enormous loss. Not only is it against the Scouts contract, but it also happens to be illegal under galactic law. No civilian, contractor, or individual can stake a claim on any uninhabited planet or system. Ramirez and his team have had the pleasure of taking out several Scout teams in the last five years for this very type of illegal behaviour. Something his team is very good at and something he personally enjoys.

Ramirez grabs the shard then turns and walks several metres away from the group and pulls his helmet off his back and puts it on. He stares at the red metal shard for a moment, studying it. There is certainly something off with the metal. The red seems to be a natural colour that changes ever so slightly as he turns it in the light. For a moment, he thinks he can hear something. A voice, distant yet unmistakable. It's almost like the metal itself is trying to speak. He brings it closer, and the metals whisper becomes clearer. A sharp burst of static from his helmet makes him flinch, cutting the sound off like a knife. Ramirez grunts and throws the shard back toward the team, scowling beneath his helmet. He then taps on his comm unit, calling the drop ship to come and pick him up. Next, he calls up the star fighter in orbit.

"This is Captain Ramirez. Get me an encrypted link back to Black Site, Zulu Seven." The Captain waits a moment before getting the all clear from the ship's comms officer that he has established an encrypted link for him to communicate on. Ramirez taps some buttons on his forearm computer and switches over to the encrypted channel. "Boss, you were right.

The rotten thief has found a new type of metal and has stollen it to sell off so that he can fill his dirty pockets with the Corporation's profits! Not only has he broken the contract, but he has also broken galactic law. Under Overmorrow special order, one thousand eighty-eight, I will hunt down and execute the Scout Captain and his crew. Ramirez out." The encrypted message will take several days to reach the Corp black site. By that time Ramirez intends to be halfway back to colonised space, where he will start the hunt for his new prey.

A large smile appears on Ramirez's face under his helmet as he knows he can now get off this shithole of a planet and start the real fun. He switches back to the local network as he moves towards the drop ship's landing zone. "All callsigns, all callsigns, move to the LZ for extraction. It looks like we are going hunting boys!"

Chapter 14

CORE

In the shadow of the ship's bridge, all three crew members of the Obsidian Scout stand together, eagerly awaiting their emergence from hyperspace. Seth has given control of the ship to Rose, so that the family can be together to witness the beauty of the Core System. Spending most of their time on or past the outer edge of colonised space, it is rare that the family comes this deep into civilisation. Seth can hardly remember the last time he came to the Core System after leaving the military around a decade ago. Seth loves exploring new planets, along with the lifestyle and freedom of being a Scout. He would never want to live in the Core System or even close nearby. With that being the case, Seth still acknowledges the Core is a thing of wonder and beauty to behold.

When Seth signed up for the Galactic Military at eighteen back on Tir-Na, his home world, he got put on a military space transport with all the other recruits. They travelled as one large group to the military academy on Utopia in the Core System. The military pilots flying the transport made all the recruits go down to the viewing deck and watch as the transport exited hyperspace, arriving at the Core System. It was one of the most amazing things he had ever seen in his life up to that point. Because of that moment, every time he comes to the Core System, he takes the time to enjoy the view as he jumps out of hyperspace. He used to drag Sara along with him to watch every time they came here together. She humoured him and came along. He knew she didn't find it as amazing as he did as she grew up much closer to the Core and travelled more often. But Seth loved that she came along, anyway. She would always rest her head on his shoulder and squeeze his hand as he watched in amazement. She always found it amazing how genuinely excited he was and how much he loved exploration and adventure. Sara loved the softer, childlike side of Seth's hard and more serious personality.

Seth now stands with his son and daughter looking out the viewing port window, which reaches from floor to ceiling. All three of them excited about the grand reveal. The dull blue glow fades away as the ship drops out of hyperspace and a rainbow of glowing lights fills their field of view. The entire family stands there in awe as all the different lights from all the different ships, space stations, and planets overwhelm their senses. It is almost too much for their uninitiated brains to process. The glow of the star far off in the distance radiates throughout the system, revealing millions of ships going about their business across the entire system. This, combined with all the planets and lights of the space stations, washes the system in yellow, as if someone dipped the entire Core in gold.

They can't quite make out the Core System's five capital planets from where they are, but all the lights radiating from the planets Halo space station give away the location. The giant space ring that interconnects the five capital planets is called the Galactic Core Space Ring. No one uses that name, however. A distinguishable golden glow given off from the ring, viewable all throughout the system, earns the ring its nickname. The giant ring that interconnects the five capital planets stretches the entire orbit of all five planets and is hundreds of millions of kilometres long. The Halo serves many purposes, but the main one being living quarters for all the workers that either don't fit or can't afford to live on one of the five Core planets. Such a large number of people also means lots of resources and this is the Halo's secondary but more important function, the storing and dissemination of goods and resources. Another use of the Halo, unknown to most, is the fact that the Halo also has very effective defensive capabilities. These are in place to protect the Core planets if the need every arises. However, since humans arrived in the Core System thousands of years ago, it has never had to be used. Which is why most people outside of the military and high levels of government don't know of this function.

"What do you reckon, guys?" Seth asks, looking to see if the kids are as impressed as he is.

"It's so beautiful, Dad." Says Eve.

"I can't believe what I'm seeing." Replies Fin.

"Yep. Welcome to the centre of humanity! Discovered around ten thousand years ago by humans on their journey from Ancient Earth. Today the Core System has around two hundred and fifty billion visitors coming through her each year, with around one hundred billion permanent residents. The five Capital Core Planets, which sit in a perfect synchronous orbit around the system's star, are all Tier One Planets. Everything from oxygen levels, climate, atmosphere, and even food and water resources is all ideal for human life. A long time ago, and shortly after their discovery, the government of the time made specific rules for the five planets which are still in effect today." Seth takes a deep breath, and seeing the kids are still enthralled, continues.

"There is a maximum number of permanent residents allowed on the planet at one time. All five planets are protected planets under human law, so no mining or industrial farming of natural resources is permitted. Also of note is that the planets are also run off power harnessed from the Core System's star. Humans learnt a long time ago how to keep stars in perfect equilibrium while also harvesting their energy in a long-term sustainable way. The Core System has been doing this for over several millennia now. Seventy percent of resources are brought into the system to feed the population, from places like Komugi, where we just were. But also, all other resources like building material, clothes, and so on."

"It's so crazy Dad!" Interrupts Fin. "Especially after living on the outer edge most of the time."

Seth watches Fin as he stares out over the viewing deck. "Yep, it can be overwhelming when you're not used to it. The Core is such a busy place with so much happening, so if you feel overwhelmed it's okay, just let me know alright buddy. Same for you Eve."

The kids look back at Seth, smiling. They seem more excited than anything, so he continues with his brief history lesson while he has a captive audience. "So, the Halo is the only one like it in the galaxy. Originally, each planet had its own space station. Rumour is they were the original giant transports, called Arks, used by the humans who left Ancient Earth. Each of these space stations continued to grow over time and get bigger and bigger. That is until humanity decided they should start a project to connect them all up. Apparently, it took them over three hundred years to complete. And once complete, it has been built on, reenforced, and expanded over one thousand times! Now the Halo hosts incoming and outgoing travel and logistics to the planets, but also houses over ten billion permanent residents and even has forests and small farms. It's crazy when you think about it!"

Seth is sometimes so amazed at what humanity has achieved and some of the giant technological feats it has accomplished. Out on the edge, scouting, he is more thankful for advancements of items on his personal gear list. Rarely does he consider things on a such larger scale.

"Will we get to go on the Halo Dad?" Asks Eve.

"Yes, we will. We will dock there and take a government transport down to the planet. We aren't allowed to fly a ship like the Scout planet side unless given prior government approval."

"Can we have a look around while we are on the Halo?"

"If we have time, then sure. We will see a lot as we go through quarantine and customs, anyway."

"Cool!" Chimes in Fin.

"Anything else you would like to know guys?" Asks Seth, who could talk about the Core System for hours if given the chance and time to do so.

"You used to live here, right?" Asks Eve.

"Well, kind of. The military academy I attended is on Utopia and I spent a year there when I did my basic training. Although we were away a lot or stuck in barracks most of the time, we did get some free time occasionally, so I should remember how to get around the area near the academy. But they kept us on a pretty tight leash. Utopia is also the major planet for the Galactic Government and where its headquarters are located." Seth pauses for a moment, looking at both kids. "Any more questions?" Asks Seth.

He gets no replies, so he puts his arms over both Eve and Fins shoulder and hugs them tight. "Alright guys, I'll head back up to the bridge. You can spend another thirty down here if you want. I have to deal with an evil monster lurking amongst all that beauty!"

Both kids turn and look at him, curious as to whether there is an unknown threat or a bad dad joke hiding in the system. "What's that?" Asks Eve, watching her father's face to make sure he is being sarcastic.

"Traffic!" Eve rolls her eyes as Seth turns and heads off to the bridge in no particular rush. It will be hours before they even get designated a docking bay on the Halo. He will be surprised if they make it planet side in under twenty-four hours. *Oh well, we will have plenty of time to prep and hopefully we can get a workout in.* He thinks to himself.

To Seth's surprise, by the time he reaches the bridge, the Scout has been designated a docking bay and a priority transit route to the Halo. *Otto must have pulled some strings to make this happen. That or he made up one hell of a story to convince someone to cut through a lot of red tape.* Seth thinks for a moment. *It's the hell of a story one, isn't it. Classic Otto.* Seth shakes his head and has a little chuckle to himself before asking Rose their ETA. Rose informs him they will come in to dock with the Halo in three hours.

He has already made the kids prepare everything on the ship before entering the system, so all they have to do now is pack their gear and do a quick tidy up. So, he gives them a little more time to enjoy the view before starting departures procedures. They won't be able disembark the Scout with any type of firearms, as they are illegal for civilians to carry within the Core System, much to Seth's dislike. So, Seth heads to the armoury and picks out several concealed blades to take planet side. Just in case the Corporation throws something a little more serious at them than a couple of newly minted, good-looking junior executives. Although with all the tight restrictions and government oversight, he isn't as concerned that the Corporation will try something in the Core System. It is one of the safest places in the galaxy. Seth thinks that's not an excuse to be negligent though. *Better safe than sorry.*

Eve is nervous as she has never flown or docked the Scout in such a heavily congested system before. The government has put in some strict regulations around how you can and can't fly in the Core, which all ships seem to abide by. Even though it is busy, to her surprise, she finds it to be straightforward getting to the Halo and then docking the Scout. Simply follow the designated path they put you on and keep an eye out. Eve wonders what type of and how many AI they have helping with the Core Systems traffic management.

The docking bays on the Halo are top-notch. *Obviously, there are no expenses spared in the Core System.* Eve thinks to herself as she compares the Halo docking bays to the last couple of stations she has docked at.

The docking bay itself is massive, spotless, and well organised. The floors appear polished. Seth reminds Eve that they are likely in a VIP or priority docking bay and that they do not all look like this. But she isn't convinced. Eve wants to believe the Galactic Government has an army of cute little cleaning bots on hand. Ready to go at a moment's notice. Seth also reminds both kids that regardless of how quickly they got through the traffic and how nice their docking bay is, there are still millions of people on the Halo. And they will have to contend with them to get down to the planet.

"Don't expect the VIP treatment beyond here, okay guys."

"Yes, Dad." Both kids reply with an undercurrent of teenage attitude.

Seth and Fin stand around inside the Scout's hangar bay, waiting for Eve. She wanted to make sure Rose had everything covered off before she left the bridge. Seth has already ordered Ray to guard the ship, and the dog is now on patrol. Not sure how long they will be gone, they all have their forty-eight-hour back packs on. These packs seem small compared to the normal packs they carry on a scout. The packs are filled with clothes, some food and water, and some toiletries, in case they have to spend a couple of nights on the planet. Seth hands Eve a small knife when she arrives. She slips it into the hard-plastic scabbard on the back of her belt, then pulls her shirt over the top. They are all now carrying a concealed blade, or two, in Seth's case.

Seth has spent years training them to conceal their blades and deploy them efficiently. The family always carry knifes openly when scouting as a tool, but rarely does Seth make them carry their blades as a concealed weapon. He only makes them carry this way when they are on a known dangerous planet or space station, which he tries to avoid if he can.

The docking light in the hangar flicks to green as Rose alerts them that they can now lower down the ramp and disembark the ship. When exiting the Scout, the family either uses the ramp or the airlock, depending on how and where they are docked. This time, there is enough room in the large hangar bay to use the ramp. It is also protocol when docked on the Halo. An old tradition and a way to say my ship is ready for inspection and I have nothing to hide. Seth certainly has things he wants to hide. But he is confident that without very specific knowledge and prior warning, he could give the authorities the treasure, and they would hold it in their hand, not knowing what it was. Honestly, he doesn't even know if half of the treasure is valuable or not himself.

The ramp lowers and two government officials are waiting for them in the hangar bay. He heads down to greet the pair. Both wear their government issued light blue flight suits with smart looking caps. Seth can see both men are officers, which is a bit odd. But that could just be because they are in the VIP bays. He can also see that they look overworked and underpaid. That or they are stressed from dealing with too many VIPs who think they are a pure gift to the galaxy and therefore should not have to undergo the same procedures as the commoners. Which would make these gentlemen's lives harder than it already is.

"Hi gents, how are you?" Asks Seth trying to break the ice by being a bit more casual.

"Good, thank you Sir." Replies the senior ranked man. "We have been tasked with carrying out a search of your shuttle and we have a few questions for you. I hope that is okay?"

"Yeah, of course. Go for it." Replies Seth.

"Can I ask what your business is in the Core System?" The junior officer asks.

"We are here to do some research." Seth replies with the truth.

"Excellent. If you could, please stand to the side for one moment." Asks the senior officer.

Seth moves to the side, waving at Fin and Eve to do the same. The two men stay exactly where they are and without even taking a step closer, look inside the ship. The senior one bends down a little and the other one leans over to one side to get a better look into the hanger from the bottom of the ship's ramp. After about three seconds, the junior officer turns to the senior one. "All clear Sir."

The senior man looks back. "Agreed." The senior officer then taps something into his personal tablet and looks at the family. "All done. Thank you for joining us on the Halo Mr Smith. Please follow all regulations and adhere to any orders given by local authorities. Please enjoy your stay." The two men turn around and walk to the hangar's exit.

Eve and Fin stare at their father, confused, who simply shrugs back. *This must be how the Agency operates these days.* Seth thinks to himself. They watch the two men exit the hangar before grabbing their packs and putting them on. A green line appears on the floor at the bottom of the Scouts ramp, showing the path to follow out of the hanger and into the Halo. Once processed, they will find the next transport to Utopia's surface. They wait at the bottom of the ramp and Eve gets Rose to close the ship's ramp as Fin checks to make sure that the comms with Rose, Ray, his sister, and his father are all working correctly. Once he gives a thumbs up, they head off, following the green line out of the hanger.

Once out of the hangar, the green line takes them down a long, white corridor on the external edge of the station. One wall is lined with large view ports that give them amazing views of the planet below. The Halo is far enough away from Utopia that you can see the entire planet. Its vibrant greens and blues set a picturesque backdrop to all the slow moving ships travelling between the planet's surface and the Halo. The other wall of the corridor is lined with old pictures and artworks depicting humanity's history and its journey through the stars. As they walk along admiring the view, something grabs Seth's attention, and he stops at one of the old pictures.

The picture is of the First Commander of the Space Scouts. Space Scouts were first established when humans left Earth and the Sol System. The First Commander was the person in charge of leading humanity into what was then unknown space. And while the First Commander didn't live the full length of the one-hundred-year journey from Earth to the Core System, he is said to have been one of mankind's greatest leaders. When humans settled in the Core System, a shrine, still standing to this day, was made in his honour and he was given the rank of Hero. The Space Scouts eventually faded out and were replaced by the Galactic Military once humanity was up and running in the Core System.

Because of this, Seth has seen the pictures and paintings of the First Commander thousands of times before. They are scattered around every military base in the galaxy. But there is something about this one that catches his eye. And it is not the Commander that stands out, but a man in the picture's background. The Regimental Sergeant Major, the man in charge of all the enlisted Scouts, he looks like the large, bearded man from Seth's recruit graduation. The man that gave Seth the axe and recruited him to the Unit.

Hmmm, I never saw him after that day. He wasn't at the Unit when I got there, either. Seth assumes he must have had separate postings and then the RSM retired before they got to meet up again.

Damn, if he doesn't look like the guy in that picture, though. Seth laughs to himself. *Why have I not noticed that before? Must have the axe on my mind. That or because all the bloody RSMs from the Unit look the same. Tall, bearded, powerful looking men that could kill you with a look.*

That could have been Seth if he had stayed in the Unit instead of leaving to look after the kids after Sara's death. He was on track to be promoted and if he had hung around for another ten years, he would have had a shot at that position. But it was not to be. Seth notices the kids have not slowed down, so he jogs to catch back up, thinking nothing more of the picture.

At the end of the hallway, a large blast door opens up to a massive public thoroughfare. This is where the green line ends, but Eve's and Fin's eyes light up. The roof of the Halo, which is several stories high in this section, is see-through, giving them a view out into the system. This section of the Halo is also decorated with exotic plants and trees that run throughout the thoroughfare. Both Fin and Eve have seen nothing like this before. They are so close to open space but surrounded by tree-lined walkways and people going about their day.

I guess the brief inspection before was customs and immigration all rolled into one. Geez, I should be a VIP more often. Seth thinks to himself before catching a look at the kids. "Hey, we are trying to keep a low profile and blend in, remember guys. So, let's not try to look like complete amateurs, okay." Prompts Seth. "Walking around with dishpan eyes in a state of wonder will not cut it."

Both kids do their breathing drills, 'Control your breath, control your mind.' It only takes them a couple of rounds to relax and centre themselves. Seth checks them both, happy that they look somewhat calm and normal. He then leads them off down the thoroughfare towards the nearest transport terminal.

Eve is shocked by how clean everything is. It looks like the trees are regularly groomed and cleaning bots frequent the halls. *They must have an army of cleaning bots!* Eve thinks to herself. The other thing she notices is how good everyone looks. To her, everyone looks so fancy. Besides the odd tourist that she can now easily identify after her father made a point of it, everyone else seems so beautiful. The woman all wear flowing dresses and impractical shoes, plus have their hair out and coloured. The colours are a vibrant mix from across the spectrum that somehow still looks natural in their hair. Even the men seem to be pretty. They are clean shaven with immaculate hair and well-kept modern fancy clothing. She wonders how they will blend in. They are much taller to begin with, are dressed for function instead of fashion, and are not as pretty and as well groomed.

Eve notices Fin looking out into the system through the special viewing roof above and not paying attention to where he is going. Before she can tell him to 'switch on' Fin bumps into a beautiful young couple who look to be in their early thirties. They bounce off him hard, like they had walked into an invisible wall. They both hit the ground, tumbling and spilling their expensive looking drinks. It takes Fin a second to register the bump. Turning around, Fin looks at the couple splayed across the floor, confused. *I gently bumped into them. How did they end up on the floor? Did they trip up or something?* Fin awkwardly stares at the couple for a moment longer before offering to help them up. Eve giggles to herself, then heads over to help as well.

"I'm so sorry. My little brother wasn't paying attention. He hasn't been on the Halo since he was a child, and something must have caught his eye." Eve jumps in before her younger brother says something stupid.

Fin grabs the man and pulls him up, almost ripping the poor fellow's arm off in the process. Eve offers to help up the woman, who gladly accepts. Eve notices she smells so good, and her clothes are so soft and silky. But she also notices how soft and squishy she feels. *Where are her muscles? She feels like bone and soup wrapped in skin.*

"Oh, thank you kindly, ma'am." Says the lady as Eve helps her up. "Is you brother a steel robot by any chance? It felt like I ran into a blast door!" Thankfully, the lady seems more embarrassed than anything else. Eve smiles at the lady in an attempt to hide her shock. She thought all these beautiful people in the Core would be graceful and agile and not be so clumsy and weak.

"Ummm yeah, he is mostly made of rocks, particularly in his head area." Eve says trying to lighten the mood. The couple have a little polite laugh before rushing off, more concerned with how they look than anything else. Eve turns to Fin as he prepares himself for a verbal bashing from his sister.

"Fin, did you feel how squishy they were?"

Fin is surprised by his sister's response. "Hell, I thought I may have actually hurt that guy when I lifted him up. Don't they have gyms here or something?"

"Yes, they have gyms damn it!" Eve and Fin feel the mood instantly change as Seth arrives on the scene. "Stop stuffing around and let's get back on task!" Seth says in a quiet but aggressive voice. He thought they were right behind him, but obviously he needs to keep a better eye on them. "Not everyone spends their days investigating unexplored planets and training for combat. Be gentle with the beautiful people of the Core, okay." By the look on their faces, Seth realises that it most likely wasn't their fault, so he doesn't need to be so harsh on them. He is trying to keep a low profile, which is seeming to be more difficult than he thought it would be. As they head off, Eve notices a little cleaning bot come out of the wall to come and clean up the couples spilt drinks. Eve has to cover her mouth to stop a little squeal coming out. *Ah, ha! I knew it!*

The nearest public shuttle bay with transport to Utopia is only around a thirty-minute walk, so Seth decides to travel by foot instead of taking the magnetic railway, or Mag Rail, as it's referred to. The Halo is equipped with multiple small Mag Rails that run the length of the giant space station. They are a quick, easy and reliable way to move around. But Seth feels like walking. It helps him get his bearings when he slows down and takes in the atmosphere of a new environment. Plus, this way the kids will get to see more of the Halo, which will make them happy to no end.

Ten minutes into their walk to the shuttle bay, Fin gets a bad feeling. He can't quite explain what it is, but feels it in his gut. It is like he swallowed a heavy rock. His dad has always said if you get a bad feeling, it is because your subconscious, the part of the brain that processes all the data your senses collect, is trying to tell you something is off. He also says you should always listen to it, as it's better to be safe than sorry.

So, Fin decides to speak up. "Hey Dad." Fin whispers. "I have a bad feeling, like we are being followed, or watched, or something?"

Seth continues walking at the same pace but whispers back. "I have been checking pretty regularly buddy and haven't seen anyone. That been said, we are definitely getting looks. Maybe that's what you are picking up on?"

Fin thinks about it for a moment. He looks around and sees an older, well-dressed rich couple looking at him like he is some kind of freak. As they stare at him in disgust, he feels the weight in his stomach once more. "Yeah. That must be it, Dad."

Seth would normally pay more attention to Fin's intuition, but he has been checking their tail the whole time. He hasn't noticed anyone following them, but they have been getting lots of looks from locals and even the other tourists. So even if they are being followed, there is not much they can do about it.

Getting planet side as soon as possible is still their best bet. Seth acknowledges Fin's feeling and explains his thought process to him. Fin is happy with the logic and the plan, so they continue to the transport bay.

After a non-eventful but extremely scenic walk, they reach the transport bay. They must have timed it right as thankfully it is only a short line up for the shuttle down to Utopia. Which makes Fin and Seth happy that they won't get stuck in one location for too long. The transports which run from the Halo to the planets below go nonstop all day and night, which means outside of peak times they are easy to get a seat on. They pay for their ticket to take them to Utopia's capital city, Nova. The shuttle has to stop at two smaller cities on its way, but Seth is happy with that, as the kids will get to see more of the planet. And based on their current situation, and not knowing where this journey might take them, Seth thinks it may be quite a long time until they get to see Utopia or the Core System again.

Chapter 15

As the Halos shuttle pierces the atmosphere of Utopia, billowing white clouds swirl to welcome its arrival, marking the heart of humanity and the centre of the Galactic Government. Seth made sure to get them window seats, and by the way Eve and Fin have their faces plastered to viewing ports, it was worth every credit. He usually spends his time pushing the kids to their absolute limits so they will be the best versions of themselves they can possibly be. He knows this isn't always fun for them, and sometimes he can be quite harsh on them. Because of this, Seth feels a sense of guilt as he watches them. He loves them so much, more than anything, and wishes he could give them little moments of joy like this all the time. But as much as he would love to spoil them, it's not the world they live in. He doesn't know how to raise kids, he knows how to train elite soldiers. Raising kids, that's something their mother was the master of. He wishes she were here just as much for the kids as for his own selfish reasons. Pushing his limits, mentally and physically, that's what he knows. And so, that's what he teaches the kids, even if it meant sacrificing the childhood they deserved. He hopes that even though it often sucks for them, one day they will understand why he is the way he is, and why he pushes them so hard.

"Look at that building! It's taller than the Scout!" Eve exclaims, pressing her face to the window. "No way! That one's bigger."

Fin argues, pointing wildly at another tower. "Bet you could see the entire planet from up there!"

Seth just chuckles, letting them have their moment. It's like watching two little puppies waiting for their dinner to be brought to them. *Ray doesn't even get this excited, and he has dog programming!* He must admit though, the city's skyline is an impressive sight to behold. The mix of ultra-modern architecture, classic human constructions dating back over a thousand years, and a perfect interweaving of greenery across multiple levels of the city make it hard to beat. The afternoon sun seems to reflect perfectly off the glass of the taller buildings, washing the city in a gold colour. To Seth, it's clear. Immense effort and wealth have shaped this city. Possibly, it's one of the most impressive in the entire galaxy.

It's a sunny warm afternoon on Nova when they disembark the shuttle. Fin notices that even the air at the spaceport tastes fresh and clean. Seth wants to use the remaining daylight to see if they can meet up with their Agency contact before heading to the accommodation Otto has organised for them.

The kid's excitement doesn't stop once they enter the giant space port on Nova, either. Billboards and advertisements in multiple different mediums fill their vision. They have never seen anything like it before. 3D holograms of government officials welcome them to the city while screen's display trailers for up-and-coming events and shows. He watches as the kids eyes light up at the flashing advertisements, a pang of guilt settling in his chest. He's never let them indulge in entertainment like this. The only real entertainment the kids get is when Seth lets them camp outside on a new planet with a fire going. If the conditions are suitable, that is. They will sit around and tell stories and share ideas while eating treats brought down from the Scout. However, the more Seth thinks about it, the less guilty he feels. Several billion people will see the latest show staring the latest actor or actress, but only a handful of people will ever get to be the first to sit around a campfire on a newly discovered planet.

They pass through another round of basic checks as they make their way through the bustling spaceport. The spaceport hums with life. Crowds, reunions, bursts of emotion, but they move through it effortlessly. Seth knows this is intentional, but he's impressed by how well the facilities and crowds are engineered.

Eventually, they go through the last barrier and exit the spaceport into the city of Nova. This is where more family and friends wait for returning loved ones, and transports wait for men and women who are here on business. Seth thinks this would be a good place to meet his contact, but way too obvious. He has worked with the Agency many times before when he was in the Unit. They seem to appear when they need to and then disappear when they feel like it. Which means they tend to be unreliable, and this is one of the many reasons he is not a fan. He assumes that hasn't changed.

Seth scans the area outside the spaceport in case someone made things easy for a change. *Nope, looks like the Agency is at its best, as always. Best grab a transport to the accommodation then. This Agent R will pop up sometime soon.*

He leads the kids, still wide eyed with wonder, to the nearby transport station. Hyper-Rails are used to traverse the massive city of Nova. And while Seth can't remember this particular station, memories come flooding back from his youth the moment he smells the Hyper-Rails. The distinct smell of the metal carriages, the Hyper-Rails brakes, and the tracks they fly along stings his nose. He notices Fin trying to decipher the unfamiliar smells which makes him smile. They are staying near the government district, so Seth finds a display which shows each Hyper-Rails platform and its destination. He then drags the family up several flights of stairs to the right platform.

As promised by the display boards, the Hyper-Rail arrives on time. Seth grabs both kids and drags them on board as they are still distracted by all the sights inside the station. Thankfully, the interior of the Hyper-Rail is straightforward and helps calm them down and focus a little. It only takes them several minutes before they arrive at the government district station, as the Hyper-Rails move at subsonic speeds. The Hyper-Rails move along inside their own independent giant pipes under the capital's surface. This allows them to reach such high speeds safely. However, Eve and Fin are disappointed. They feel like they have been robbed of more beautiful scenery. Upon arrival at their destination, they are rewarded with one of the most beautiful and amazing sights they have ever seen. The government district in Nova. Humanity's capital and the seat of galactic power.

The district they see before them is pristine, beautiful, and an architectural masterpiece. Every which way they look seems perfectly designed to give them a stunning view. No space is left untouched by the mind of a master architect. But it is not just the buildings and gardens that are impressive. There seems to be a constant gentle breeze that refreshes you while delivering all the smells and natural sounds of the district directly to you. There are no marketing or business signs of any type here, as the Galactic Government does not want to show favouritism. Instead, there are massive buildings made from a combination of metals, stones, and wood, sourced from all around the galaxy.

Manicured gardens displaying all the different plant life from all the colonised planets in the galaxy accompany the streets and buildings. The different colours and shapes of the plants mixed amongst the buildings make it seem like an artistically designed dreamscape. Despite the mix of textures and colours, the district is a masterpiece. Seamless, balanced, and undeniably the work of a genius. Both Eve and Fin once again stare in pure awe.

Seth checks his forearm computer to find the route to the hotel. He has been in this district several times before, back when he was still serving in the military. Things look familiar to him, but he is not one hundred percent confident he can find his way without the inbuilt nav on his computer. Regardless, it should only take them around fifteen minutes to walk to the accommodation, even if they get a little lost. The whole family is going to come off the high of being on the Halo and a new planet soon and it's already been a long day. Seth wants to check them in and make sure they are safe before they settle down and rest for the evening. But he still wants to enjoy the beauty of the capital himself, so he allows for a slower pace as they walk through the lively district.

They arrive at the accommodation just as the sun has set, and night has taken over the city. The accommodation is a large apartment complex used by visiting officials. Seth doesn't know why Otto sent him here, but assumes it is to stay away from Corporation owned hotels and accommodation suites. They head to the reception room at the front of the gated complex. *At least it has decent security.* Seth thinks to himself. Which is possibly the other reason Otto chose the location. A simple AI service-bot confirms their details, issuing access cards and a room number. The process is seamless. They thank the bot and head into the complex.

After a short walk through the pristine, government owned facility, where trees grow in perfect symmetry and surveillance drones hover silently, they arrive at their accommodation. Seth goes to scan his access card to let them in, but notices that the door to their room is slightly ajar. He freezes in place, suspecting the worst. Seth puts his finger to his mouth, indicating for Eve and Fin to be silent. They instantly stop and go quiet mid conversation, confused as to what is happening until their father points out the open door. Silently, Seth takes off his pack and pulls out his concealed blade. He then points to Eve, who does the same. Once complete, Fin knows to do the same, remaining silent the whole time. They back away from the door to see if they are being watched, and if there are any other routes into the apartment. They don't see anyone else around or any other obvious ways in. Seth decides that if this is the only way in, then they will do their best to stay quiet until they have no other option. He gives Eve and Fin the signal that he is going to enter, and they lower their stance, ready to charge in behind their father if need be. Seth opens the door a little wider and waits a few seconds to see if he can hear anything. Nothing. Seth, like a phantom, silently enters through the front door.

The door pushes open, and Seth holds it so it doesn't bump into the wall and make a noise alerting any intruders that may or may not still be in the apartment. If he can get up close on them before they know he is here, the better chance he will have at dealing with them. Seth can hear Eve and Fin's faint footsteps behind him. The entrance to the apartment opens up to a small corridor. Seth moves quickly and quietly down the corridor. There are two doors at the end of the corridor, one on the right and one on the left. Seth thinks he sees that the door on the right is open, so he chooses that door and uses hand signals to order the kids to the left door. He pivots to the right and opens the door the rest of the way.

The door opens up to the main living area and the smell of old air and cleaning products is the first thing he notices. He then scans the large open living space and sees someone moving in the kitchen, trying to stay silent and out of sight. They are wearing black pants and a black jacket, with a black hood and a black mask that covers their face from the eyes down. Currently, they are not alerted to his presence. Seth hears Eve quietly call out from the left door.

"Clear."

Seth switches gears as he yells out. "One enemy!" Letting the kids know they are going from sneaking around quietly to employing speed and aggression. His yell gives the hooded intruder in the kitchen a scare as they whip around to see Seth's enormous figure. The sight of the large angry man appearing from nowhere causes them to freeze in place for a moment. Seth turns and sprints towards the intruder while they are stunned, taking advantage before they can act. At the same time, Fin pushes into the room behind him to continue to clear it. Fin knows not to group up on the target as there may be multiple targets, or they may be a decoy from the real threat.

The hooded figure looks around for something to defend themselves with, but it is too late. Seth is already on them. They decide to throw a punch as hard as possible at Seth's face, but Seth easily slides past it, locking them up with their own arm across their neck. The pressure of the lock immediately starts cutting off the figure in black's oxygen supply. The intruder panics. Their vision blurs. With a desperate grunt, they jump, throwing all their weight onto Seth. Their boots slam against the fridge, pushing off with everything they have. However, instead of fighting the push, Seth goes with it, allowing them both to go flying back across the kitchen. In the process, Seth releases the choke.

The hooded figure, feeling the choke release, attempts to use this opportunity to counterattack. Once the figure has its balance again, it spins around, swinging hard to strike its opponent in the head, but Seth is not there. His bait has worked, and the figure has left themself wide open. The hooded figure feels a sense of weightlessness as its lifted high into the air before being ripped down hard into the ground. Feeling the apartment floor hit them harder than believed possible, the figure's heart skips a beat. The impact violently expels all the air from their lungs, and they gasp for breath, praying their spine isn't broken as a burning pain shoots across their back and down their legs. Instead of the figures prayers being answered by air to refill their lungs, they get a sharp blade pressed against their neck and one pissed off Seth kneeling on their chest, making it almost impossible for their lungs to re-inflate.

"Door!" Shouts Fin as he continues to clear the room. Seth catches Eve out of the corner of his eye as she moves by quickly before he hears the door being kicked in. He can't see who went into the room but again hears Eve call out. "Clear." Followed by Fin shouting the same, shortly after. They both appear next to Seth seconds later. The hooded figure is desperately trying to move around in an attempt to escape the pin and find a position to allow air into their lungs. Fin sees this and stands hard on the figure's wrist, pinning an arm to the ground and making it impossible to escape.

Seth leans in, his voice a low growl. "Who the hell are you, and why are you in our room?" The blade presses harder against the figure's throat.

The figure on the ground attempts to respond but is still having trouble breathing. Seth notices the face mask and hood. They begin to change colour as they start reflecting the floor underneath. Seth eases up a little. Then pushes back down harder with his knee. The intruder desperately gasps for air. As they do the mask glitches and changes colour again, this time for long enough for the kids to notice as well.

"What the hell is that?" Asks Fin.

"God damn it!" Says Seth, frustrated. "Fin, hop off her arm."

Fin removes his foot, confused as to what is happening. Seth returns his blade back to its sheath, then takes his weight off the figure's chest. As he does, the figure takes a large gulp, sucking in the air their body was so desperate for. Seth grabs the figure by the throat and picks them up off the ground in one smooth movement. He then takes a few steps out of the kitchen, holding the figure off the ground, and tosses them so that they land sitting on the couch in the living space next to the kitchen. Eve and Fin watch, blades in hand, ready to attack as they still don't know what is happening.

"What's going on, Dad?" Eve asks, confused why her father has gone from nearly killing someone to sitting them on the couch.

Seth gestures toward the flickering hood. "See that? High-tech camouflage. Government issue. Only field operatives get it." Seth says staring at the figure on the couch, desperately trying to get air into their lungs.

"Agent R, I assume?"

It takes a minute, but the figure on the couch eventually catches her breath. She is still breathing heavily and nursing her neck from where Seth had the knife pressed against it, but can manage to pull back the hood and remove their mask. Fin and Eve are in shock. Behind the high-tech camo is long wavy dark blonde hair, piercing green eyes and a striking female face. She looks at them all for a second as she takes one more moment to fully let her lungs refill.

"Correct." She manages to spit out, taking another deep breath before finishing. "Agent R at your service." She says, bowing her head before leaning back into a relaxed pose.

"Sorry, but we saw the door was open and assumed the worst." Says Eve, feeling guilty because her brother and father almost killed their government contact.

Agent R chuckles, rubbing her throat where Seth's blade had pressed. "No need to be sorry. Guess I need to work on my stealth." She turns to Seth, checking him from head to toe. "You move fast for an old man." She says in a cheeky voice, almost as if she is flirting with him. "When Otto said you were just an old man with two kids, I thought it was going to be an easy favour. He didn't tell me he was sending someone so dangerous and so handsome my way." She gives him a seductive look.

"Hmph." Grunts Seth. 'For starters, you can knock that spy flirty shit off, as I'm not buying it. Secondly, you can tell me why you snuck into our accommodation instead of meeting us out in public and following normal SOPs?" Eve watching the exchange, crosses her arms defiantly. Staring at the Agent, waiting for an explanation as to why she is flirting with her father and wondering why her father knows what the Agencies Standard Operating Procedures are.

Agent R's cheeks go red as she gets embarrassed by being called out about her flirting. This is twice today that she has dropped the ball, and she refuses to do it a third time.

"Sorry Seth. Training kicked in with the flirting, old habits you know." Agent R apologises, wondering how he picked up on it so quickly.

She did her research on him. And she knows he was in the military. She even tried to pull up his records, but had no luck. At first she just thought it was because they were so old. She should have known something was up though when even her clearance didn't grant her permissions to search the archives. But even with all that, she was still expecting a washed up fat, bearded, old veteran, not what stands in front of her now. It's not surprising why Otto talked him up and called in such a big favour. She won't bother trying to out maneuverer him. Honesty will be her best weapon.

"We have had reports of a couple of low-level Corp thugs sneaking around in the area, and I wanted to get in to make sure they hadn't set an ambush. Although, I doubt they would have been ready for you, or your children." Agent R notices Eve and Fin exchange a quick glance when she mentions the Corporation. Seth, however, stays unreadable. She won't push the matter now, but will keep that in the back of her mind. Agent R turns her attention to the kids. "Where did you guys learn to move like that? I don't have any records of either of you having attended any type of military training?"

Eve goes to answer, but Seth interjects. "We have a lot of spare time out beyond the edge." Agent R looks at him and nods slowly. She even looks a little impressed. Seth can see her mind running through the thousands of different thoughts she must be having. Seth takes a deep breath to let his energy levels die back down.

"So, did you find any low-level Corp thugs in the fridge?" Asks Seth. Agent R gives him a smart-arse smile to answer his question. "Good news then. So, can I get you a glass of water? Or is there something else you need?"

"Yes, a water, that would, that would be nice." She is taken back a little by how quickly he changed gears and how he is being kind all of a sudden.

"Buddy." Seth rests his hand on Fin's shoulder and looks back towards the apartment's entrance.

"Yeah, no worries Dad, I'll get the bags from out front." Fin says as he heads off back to the front door.

"I'll get that drink. Did you want some water too, Dad?" Asks Eve, wanting to do her part.

"Yeah sure, maybe we should all have some. It's been a long day."

Eve pours four glasses of water and brings them over to the little table where the couches are, two at a time, being sure to serve Agent R first. Fin returns and they all sit down. Eve notices how soft and nice the couch is. It's a big change from sitting on packs or rocks off somewhere outside of known space. They all have several mouthfuls of water before Agent R can't handle the silence any longer.

"So, Otto said you needed some help. He didn't say what for or why, but he called in a favour and said it was important."

Seth nods in agreement. "Yes, it is important. Did he tell you anything else?"

"No, he didn't, but I'd love to hear all about it?" R says, leaning in and giving him an over the top smile, knowing he won't tell her.

"I bet you would. Let's just say we discovered something, and we need to do some research on it."

"Research, really! That's it?" Agent R is confused. Before meeting the family, she thought the favour would be helping some washed up old vet and his kids needing to change their names and disappear for a while. Maybe they got in a scuffle out on their farm on some planet on the edge and ended up shooting someone important. Then, after seeing them in action, she was kind of hoping Seth would need help to pull off some type of clandestine robbery or assassination, or anything more interesting than research. "Well, that's disappointing. Did you at least discover something interesting?"

"Yes." Replies Eve excitedly before she looks to see her father glaring at her.

"We found something very old and want to do some research on it. See if we can find its owner."

Agent R rolls her eyes. "I can't believe I got my ass kicked for a research assignment. Otto is going to owe me big for this one."

She looks at the family, who still seem to be taking this very seriously. "Alright, if that's the play, I can get you access to the official government library. You should be able to find most things in there. I can't give you access to anything classified seeing that you are civilians, but you should be able to find some things that aren't very well known by the general population. If that even helps at all?"

"It will, thank you." Replies Seth honestly.

Who are these people? Agent R thinks to herself. *They are so not what I was expecting, nor what anyone would expect from a bunch of contracted spacers. Very, very interesting. I am going to have to keep an eye on them.*

"Well, if you don't need anything else from me, I might go break into someone's apartment who isn't going to kick my ass." Agent R says sarcastically. "I'll swing back in the morning and drop off the passes you need to gain access to the library. Also, the fridge is stocked with food, so you won't need to head back out if you don't want to."

Seth laughs. "So you did look in the fridge." Both kids join in laughing at Agent R as her cheeks turn red once again.

Who are you people! Agent R thinks to herself.

She gets up out of her chair and heads out of the apartment sheepishly. It has been a long time since she has been so easily bested and thrown off her game like this. And by a bunch of spacers at that. She will have to do some more research of her own tonight.

As soon as they can hear the door close, Fin jumps up off the couch to see what's in the fridge.

"Oh, heck yeah!" He cries out. "You guys are in for a real treat!"

Chapter 16

LIBRARY

The sound of crackling in the frypan wakes Eve moments before the smell of Fin's cooking drifts into her room. She rolls onto her back and takes a moment to sink into the comfort of her bed. The soft pillows and heavenly mattress hold her snug as she enjoys the aroma. She feels like she has only just recovered from the feast her brother had prepared the night before, still unsure if she can go another round of eating. Eve would love to stay in the warm embrace of her bed for as long as possible, but the smells coming out of the kitchen are too much. She eases out of bed and dresses quickly before heading out of her room.

When she arrives, she sees her father doing some stretching in the middle of the living space where they sat with Agent R the previous evening. Fin is dashing around the kitchen, cutting ingredients and preparing plates like a crazed alchemist. "Hey, did I miss a workout?" She asks her father, concerned she may have overslept or forgotten her alarm.

"No, I was feeling old and wanted to get some stretching and mobility in before we sit on our ass all day reading. Nothing worse than sitting all day!" Seth answers while he is half upside down, in some sort of stretching pose Eve can't remember the name of.

"Oh okay, cool Dad." Eve turns her attention to Fin. "Fin, what are you cooking?"

"Breakfast." He replies.

Eve looks over at her father, now upright. He looks between her and Fin, trying to see if Fin was being cheeky or if he is lost in his work and didn't understand the question. Eve simply shrugs and moves over to the table where a hot pot of coffee is waiting. She pours herself some before placing her hands around the outside of the cup, being careful not to burn them. The warmth radiates through her hands as she feels the effects of the coffee already kicking in. "Are you boys ready for a coffee yet?" She gets an affirmative response from both, so pours them each a mug, made the way they like it. Her father has his black with a dash of cold water and Fin has his with one sugar and a splash of milk. She makes hers with powdered chocolate, one sugar, and a good portion of milk.

Fin finishes his masterpiece and makes four plates worth of food and brings them over. Seth and Eve stare at him. "Hey buddy, who's the fourth plate for?" Asks Seth intrigued.

"For Agent R." Fin looks at his father like the old man is trying to pull a prank on him. "Remember, she said she was going to come over for breakfast?"

"She said she would come over in the morning. Not that she would come over for breakfast. Back me up, Eve." Eve nods, confirming what her father said.

Fin looks very puzzled. "I'm sure she said she would be here for breakfast."

"How would she even know when we would be eating breakfast buddy?" Questions Seth.

There is a knock on the apartment door. "See, I told you she was coming for breakfast." Fin smiles.

Both Eve and Seth stare at each other once more, confused. Seth shrugs and grabs his small, fixed blade knife on his way to the apartment door. He can see on the security screen in the hallway that it is the same woman as last night. Not in covert tactical attire this time, but in more formal work clothes. She wears black dress pants, a crisp white shirt, and a fitted suit jacket. It looks like the outfit is meant to help her blend in with the middle-class workforce, but the way she carries herself, the effortless confidence, and the sharpness in her gaze. She stands out. Seth notes Otto was right about one thing though. She is a very attractive woman.

Seth lets her in and greets her like an old friend, his smile open and unguarded. She feels her own lips curve in response before she even realises it. That unsettles her. Genuine kindness isn't something she encounters often, at least, not without an agenda. *I've been on the Core planets too long if a genuine smile unsettles me more than the rehearsed grins of Core worlder's.* Agent R thinks to herself.

Seth waves her inside. "Fin tells me you said you were coming for breakfast?"

Agent R thinks for a moment. "Nope, never said that. But if there are leftovers, I'll have some. I am starving!" She didn't have time for breakfast and had kind of hoped that the family would have some food for her.

Seth chuckles to himself as he shakes his head in amusement at his son's uncanny luck before ushering the attractive young spy down the hallway to the dining area. She seems to be moving well after the previous day as she confidently struts towards her free meal. Seth almost feels a little bad for giving her such a beating, almost. He thinks she should know better and follow proper procedures. He hopes she learnt her lesson and doesn't get herself into a dangerous situation like that again. She was lucky it was Seth and his family, not someone with more ill intentions.

When she walks into the kitchen area, a wave of intoxicating smells hit her. "Oh my god. Fin, where did you learn to cook?"

"I sort of just taught myself." Fin says washing down a mouthful of his breakfast with some coffee. "I mean, mum was always an excellent cook, so I probably picked up some stuff from her."

Agent R lowers her head a bit and speaks a bit quitter. "Yes, I read your files. I am so sorry you lost her at such a young age."

"Oh, that's okay. I miss her and all, but I can't change what has happened. It's Dad you need to worry about. He still thinks she is out there."

Agent R looks over at Seth, a little confused. "Whys that Seth?"

"Look, I'm not saying she is alive, but I know she is still with us somehow. That is what he means." Seth answers as he glares at Fin. Agent R can tell by his tone that he did not like Fin bringing up his wife, so she doesn't push it any further. She has a policy to try not to get her ass kicked more than once every twenty-four hours.

"Well, either way, this food looks great! Are there any leftovers?"

"Oh, I made you a plate. You said you would want some in the morning, remember?" Fin interjects.

"Fin. I never said that. I may have thought it, but I never said it."

"Lucky coincidence, I guess." They all have a laugh as Fin raises his eyebrow, unconvinced.

How did he know I hoped there would be breakfast for me? I swear I didn't mention it. This family just keeps getting more and more intriguing.

As Fin serves breakfast, he pauses for a fraction of a second, staring toward the apartment door. It's just a brief moment, but Seth notices.

"Something wrong, buddy?"

Fin shakes his head, but his brow furrows slightly. "Nah, just... nah, it's all good."

It's gone as quickly as it came, and the moment passes, lost beneath the warmth of coffee and conversation

Agent R sits down, and they all enjoy the meal. She can tell Eve wants to ask her a thousand questions but is holding back. It amazes her that for a twenty-year-old girl she is so powerful, skilled, and dangerous. However, in some ways, she is still so childlike and innocent. Both kids are, she thinks to herself. *I have no idea what it must be like becoming a Planet Scout at such a young age. With such a small crew and a man like Seth in charge. Insane!* She is enjoying her food too much to worry about it though and almost forgets why she is here. It is as if the food has put a spell on her.

"Oh, that reminds me I have your passes to the Great Library." She pulls them out of her bag and puts them on the table. "They will be good for a couple of days. That's the best I could do. I also have some paperwork saying that Seth, you are a professor and Eve, and Fin are two of your students here to do research for one of the fancier learning institutes out on the edge." She looks at them with a serious face. "Remember you are pretending to be intellectuals so try not to choke anyone out alright!" Seth and the kids laugh but R doesn't seem impressed. "The Great Library holds a copy of all official information from every planet for at least the last several thousand years. Much longer in some cases. It should have a good volume of information on pretty much anything. But there is a lot, so I hope you know exactly what you are after." She slides the passes to each of them across the table before scoffing down the remainder of her breakfast.

Once they are all finished, they sit peacefully for a moment and enjoy the rest of their coffees. "That reminds me, here is a comms unit if you need me for anything." She hands Seth the compact unit. The comm itself is a small flat rectangle slightly thicker than an access card and fits neatly in Seth's pocket. Good luck and I might see you around"' Agent R says, giving Seth a wink. Seth looks unimpressed. She stands up and has a big gulp of water before heading out the door. *I do not even know where I will start writing up my report about this bunch. I will monitor them while they are planet side though. They are definitely not what I expected, and they are not what they seem. They are hiding something big, I know that much at least.*

The entrance to the Great Library looks old, with intricate carvings running through four large grey stone pillars built to hold up the high arched roof. Fin looks up and notices some sort of ugly winged creatures carved from stone that he has never seen before. He assumes they are from Ancient Earth and having them on libraries is an old human tradition. As ugly as they look, they impress him with how intimidating and ominous they seem. Which he thinks is kind of cool.

The library's entrance opens into a vast foyer, its smooth marble floors gleaming under the soft glow of classic down lights. Stone pillars stretch high above, their surfaces worn by time, while lush green plants sit in careful arrangement, an attempt to soften the overwhelming presence of history pressing in from all sides. The foyer sits at the bottom of a large atrium that travels all the way to the top floor of the building. The top section of the Great Library above the foyer is all glass, allowing natural light to flow down inside. In the centre sits a large round reception desk made from smooth stone with a dark wooden countertop that holds several computers on top of it. Behind the desk sits a sweet looking old lady with short white hair and glasses. She smiles and waves them over to her.

"Hello darlings, how are you?" She says in a warm and well-mannered voice.

"Good, thank you Ma'am." Replies Seth. "We are here to do some research and was hoping you might be able to point us in the right direction?"

"Of course, my darlings. Can I see some identification first, please?" All three of them hand over the passes Agent R gave them, which she scans into the computer on her desk. "Oh, how pleasant. We have you here for several days. Very exciting." Both Eve and Fin feel guilty for lying to such a sweet old lady. She seems like a very honest, lovely person. "Now, how can I help you?"

"Yes. We were wondering if you had any information on..." Seth hadn't really thought of where the best place to start would be and asking about alien races is probably not a good idea. "Old religions. Specifically Ancient Earth mythology?"

"Oh yes, sweeties. Let me think." The old lady scratches her chin, then types something into the computer in front of her. A big smile then comes across her face. "Ahhh here we go, Ancient Earth Myths and Religions is the best place to start. We have a large section on ancient human history. But I'll send you to the Ancient Earth section to start you off. Now, if you go up to the fourth floor and head to the east wing, you will see a standing computer." She points at the level above their heads as she speaks. "If you type what you are looking for into that computer, it will give you some selections to read from. And that should be a good place to start you off."

"Thank you so much Ma'am." Replies Seth.

"Alright darlings, I will be down here all day if you need anything."

Eve and Fin both give her a big smile, then follow their father, who has already begun to head off. They head up the giant staircase behind the reception, which takes them up to the next level. They walk around to the next set of stairs and continue on until they reach the fourth floor. A sign at the top of the stairwell directs them to each wing of the floor. All the floors have high ceilings, around six metres high, and each level seems to hold thousands and thousands of tablets. They make their way over to the east wing.

As promised, standing at the entrance of the east wing is a computer. Eve jogs ahead of Fin and begins tapping away on its screen. She searches for Dragons, ancient religions, and Earth cults. There are multiple results ranked in order of relevance and detail. They choose the top three, assigning themselves one each to hunt down. Following the instructions from the computer, they run off to find the tablets containing the information. Once they all have them, they meet at a large wooden table in the middle of the east wing to begin their research. Seth admires the size of the library. He has always liked these old-style buildings. His childlike imagination has made him believe these places are like mazes filled with magic and mystery. You never know what treasures you will find around each corner. While searching for his tablet, he found a life-size replica of an Ancient Earth knight, sword and shield in hand. The crest on the knight's shield looks like a Dragon's head on a familiar blue background. He tells the kids about it and recommends they have a look after they read their current tablet.

Seth gives them sixty minutes to run through their current tablets before they have to debrief each other on what they've learnt. Time seems to fly by, and Seth feels like he has not learnt enough from his tablet, but he doesn't want them going down rabbit holes and spending too long on dead ends. He spent his military time as an elite frontline soldier in Special Operations, not as an intelligence officer or analyst. This is the first time he has had to undertake anything like this. He knows there are probably better methods, but he also knows that he has a time limit and a lot to get through.

"Okay guys. That's time." The kids begrudgingly put down their tablets. "Who wants to go first?" Eve puts her hand up like they are in a classroom. Seth smiles. Maybe the library reminds her of being in a school of some sort. "Okay, what did you find, Eve?"

"I found some amazing pictures. Have a look." She turns her tablet around and shows them all several hand-drawn pictures of Dragons. "They kind of look like what we found, but these are all bio matter, no cybernetics, no metallic armour, no tech enhanced optics or anything like that."

"Yeah, they definitely look similar, but you're right, not quite the same. Did you find anything else?" Asks Seth.

"Sadly no. There were some tales of Dragons, but they mostly focused on the people who defeated them, not the Dragons themselves. What did you guys find?"

Fin looks distracted by something, so Seth goes next.

"Yeah, found pretty much the same as you, beautiful. I do feel though, that the Dragons in these pictures and stories are not real. They are a make-believe creatures ancient humanity came up with. And were used as the antagonist in folk stories." Eve nods in agreement.

"What about you buddy?" Seth asks Fin, who still seems to be focused on something else. "Fin!" Seth raises his voice a little to get Fin's attention.

Fin's eyes stop darting around and return to his fathers. "Oh yeah, sorry Dad. I just had a weird feeling."

He glances toward the nearest bookshelf, as if expecting to see someone peeking from behind it.

"Like what?" Eve asks, frowning.

Fin hesitates. "Like we're being watched. But I didn't see anyone."

The silence that follows is heavier than before.

"Hmmm odd. There would be other people in the library. I even heard some of them. But I haven't seen any up here on our level." Responds Seth. "Keep an eye out and let me know if you see anything else. Particularly the old duck from the reception. She looks like bad news." They all have a good laugh but quickly quieten down as the Great Library imposes a level of silence and contemplation upon them.

After Fins back brief, they hop up to go look at the ancient knight and its armour before grabbing their next tablets. Eve and Fin are fascinated by it. Imagining how it must have been to go into battle in such a contraption. Eve and Fin move through the rows of tablets, pretending to fight each other, shield and sword in hand as Seth watches on, quietly commentating in a funny old accent he made up. Once they have finished their mock battle and find their new tablets, they return to the table, and Seth sets the timer for another hour.

They repeat this process several times. About halfway through the day, Seth feels a kick from Fin under the table. He looks up as Fin flicks his eyes left, then back to his tablet. Seth keeps reading. After a moment, he leans back, grabs a water bottle from his backpack, and takes a long sip. Out of the corner of his eye, a shadow flickers and vanishes, like a trick of the light. He puts his water down and nods at Fin, signalling him to continue reading but also to stay alert.

Seth reads for another five minutes before excusing himself from the table to go to the toilet. He heads back to the large stairwell where he saw the toilets located on each floor. Ducking inside, he locks himself in a stall. He doesn't need to go, but he waits anyway, giving the illusion of normalcy. He then comes out and heads to the north wing. Seth stealthily moves through all the shelves in the north section, trying to flank their possible stalker. Taking his time, he remains silent, but sees no one or anything suspicious that could be used to spy on the family.

Eventually, he arrives back at the table and tells the kids that he didn't find anything and that it's all clear. He gives them the tiniest wink to let them know he is lying. While he didn't find anything, he also had a feeling of being watched. Whoever is spying on them must be competent. Seth assumes it is either Ovmor or the Agency. Both have the technical capability to do so, but Seth isn't sure of their desire. Eve and Fin feign sadness and go back to their study. They still only have a certain amount of time in the library and don't want to waste it. If either entity thinks it's a good idea to watch them read books about Ancient Earth all day, Seth is all for it.

Once the one-hour block is complete, they all do their hourly review and again conclude that Dragons were not actual creatures. They decide to refine their search, focusing solely on Dragons. This time, however, Eve learns she can connect her tablet to a screen which pops up at the end of the table. She plugs it in and starts displaying all the pictures of Dragons she comes across.

Fin and Seth continue reading while occasionally looking up at the pictures. Seth holds up his tablet to compare one section of his tablet to what is on the screen and notices another shadow in its reflection. He does not linger, as he does not want whoever or whatever it is to know it has been compromised. Seth continues looking at the pictures but sends Eve a message via his forearm computer. The message tells her that on his mark to cut the picture on the screen and put up a black screen.

Seth thinks this should reflect whatever is behind them. She taps on the desk, acknowledging she received the message.

Seth puts his tablet down and kicks back in his chair while watching the screen, looking at the artwork depicting ancient Dragons. Some are paintings, some are drawings, and some even look real, although the backgrounds give away these are digital paintings. Seth notes they should focus on ancient religions and myths next, as that seems to be the source of most of the Dragon artworks.

"Hey Eve, go back two, would you?" Seth requests.

"Yeah sure Dad. Why is that?"

"I think I saw a picture that looks like the Dragon we found on 598."

Fin pulls his head out of the tablet he is reading to look at the picture. Shocked that his father would mention 598 and the Dragon out loud in such a public place. "Dad, that doesn't look like the Dragon from the cave at all." Whispers Fin.

Seth leans back more into his chair and shakes his head. "Yeah, it does. Look at its face buddy."

"Really Dad? It's not even the same size or colour."

"Okay, yes that's true, but ignore the colour and look closely." Seth replies.

Eve is watching her father and listening carefully. She knows the play and sees that he is trying to get whoever is watching to pause and focus on the screen.

"I mean, really look at its eyes. It's almost like a replica." Seth implores Fin.

Fin leans in from his seat, staring at the screen. Seth lets everyone stare for a moment. Right before Fin goes to say something, he puts his hand on his head, giving Eve the signal to kill the picture and turn the screen black. She does and they all see the reflection of a tall shadowy figure standing amongst the shelves several metres behind them. It takes the figure a second to figure out what has happened, but in that moment, Seth and Eve have already sprung from their chairs. Seth sprints towards the figure while Eve taps Fin, ordering him to flank right as she breaks off to the left.

While the figure is caught off guard, Seth gets a proper look at their shadowy stalker. The figure is tall with a thin yet strong looking masculine physique. He wears well-fitted, handmade clothes and a multi-coloured cloak that blends seamlessly into the background. The hood also keeps the figure's face in shadow, regardless of where light hits him. *Agency? Military? No, this is something else.* The cloak looks handmade, but its shifting colours suggest advanced tech. A contradiction. One that worries Seth.

Seth gets to within three metres before the figure turns and sprints off. The figure moves at an incredible pace, with seemingly no effort whatsoever. Seth is glad he did that stretching this morning as he can feel his muscles pulling hard to keep up. The spy quickly gains distance on Seth, but Seth's plan has worked, and the figure is running towards the rear wall of the library. If Eve and Fin are quick enough, they will have him cornered with nowhere to go except through them. Seth chases the figure for another twenty seconds before the wall of the east wing closes in on them. The figure pivots down an aisle heading east as Seth follows close behind. To his surprise, the figure has gone down an aisle with no way out at the end. Seth doesn't slow though as he wants to get on top of the figure before he can react. To Seth's surprise, the figure doesn't slow either and seems to speed up. *Holy crap! He is going to run straight into the wall and knock himself out.*

The figure reaches the wall, no hesitation. Two powerful steps, then he launches upward, sprinting straight up the vertical surface. Seth watches on in disbelief.

Mid-stride, the figure kicks off, twisting backward. He flips clean over Seth's head, tucking into a roll as he lands. Silent. Effortless.

Seth barely registers the movement before he slams into the wall. His shoulder takes most of the hit, rattling his bones.

"What the hell?" Seth mutters, confused, as he bounces off the wall to see the figure standing back down the aisle looking at him. The hood of the cloak remains in place, keeping the figure's face in the dark, but Seth can see glowing eyes and a big smile appear on the figure's face behind the shadow. This angers Seth and he slams his fist into the wall and starts walking back towards the figure, who turns and runs away. Seth picks up his pace again in another attempt to catch him.

The figure accelerates. Seth pushes harder, but he's falling behind. They reach an intersection. Suddenly, the figure drops low, sliding across the floor. Fin lunges from nowhere… too late. He sails over their target and slams into the ground with a grunt. The figure pops back up, seamless, like a phantom, and keeps running.

Seth sprints past Fin, checking to make sure he is okay before telling him to get up and continue the chase. At the next break in the intersection, the figure takes a sharp turn to the right without slowing down. Seth must drop his pace considerably to make the turn. Seth is getting old, but even in his best years, he didn't have the superhuman agility this spy seems to possess. He makes the turn in time to see the figure make another sharp turn to the left. Seth arrives at the spot where the figure turned to see him standing motionless. *He isn't even breathing heavy.* Seth notes.

They are now back at the table where they were doing their research. Seth pauses, not sure what is happening as he attempts to catch his breath. The figure turns, smiling confidently once more. Seth notices Eve is on the other side of the table. Fin arrives behind Seth, panting as he circles around the table to box the figure in. The figure turns his whole body to face Seth, extends his hand, then gestures for Seth to come and attack him.

Seth gladly accepts the offer. Moving in cautiously, Seth raises his fists, ready to attack. The figure stands still, hands down by his side, waiting for Seth's advance. When in range, Seth throws several fast, snappy punches at the figure, but the figure dodges them all comfortably. Seth then tries to faint with a jab and throw a big overhand right. The figure simply ducks under Seth's violent swing, sliding right past him, appearing to his rear. Seth is getting angry now, so turns and tries a different tactic. This time he tries to shoot in on the figure and grapple his legs. But the figure leaps off at an angle, rolling onto the desk before standing back up in one quick graceful motion.

"All right, I have had about enough of you!" Growls Seth. The figure chuckles silently to himself, but Seth can see his chest shaking up and down as he does so. Fin out of the fight, decides he has to do something, even if it is to distract him for a moment. Picking up a chair, Fin uses all his might to hurl the heavy projectile at the figure from behind. The figure, without even turning around, side steps the chair, and it crashes into a row of tablets on the other side of the table, knocking most of them off in a loud crash. Eve tries to use the distraction to close in on the figure. But the figure simply turns and runs towards her, pouncing off the table and using her head as a steppingstone as he leaps over her. She reaches up to check her head but realises she hardly felt a thing. *Geez, I thought that would have hurt more.* She thinks as she rubs her head in shock.

Seth hammers past Eve, tapping her on the shoulder. She knows to follow. The figure is off again and heading towards the stairwell. They chase the figure to the balcony that leads out to the large, open interior of the library. The figure will have to head to the stairs to either ascend or descend, as climbing down would be too risky. They see the figure looking around from side to side. Snapping his head from one direction to another. The spy pauses several metres from the balcony and looks back at them. The family also stops, Seth at the front with Eve and Fin behind on his flanks. The figure takes several steps towards them and all three of the McCallan's raise their fists, ready to fight. But the figure then turns around and starts sprinting towards the balcony at an incredible speed.

He is going to kill himself if he tries to jump off that. He won't even make it a quarter of the way! Seth thinks to himself as he gives chase.

They can all see the figure digging in and pushing himself hard. Small little bursts of bright light seem to appear under the figure's feet. As if little lightning storms were thundering under each foot. The figure then takes several giant strides before bounding onto the carved stone rail of the balcony and jumping over the edge. They hear a loud noise as the stone under the figure's foot cracks in two and the air breaks around him. The family watches on in shock as the figure flies through the air. The gap is around forty metres, an impossible jump for any living creature. But somehow, to their amazement, they watch as the figure glides across the gap. The multi-coloured coat flapping behind them almost like a cape.

The figure tucks his body into a ball, preparing for the landing. The spy makes the gap and rolls as he lands, this time less gracefully than before but still smooth enough to not make a sound. The figure pops up and turns to see its pursuers on the other side of the enormous gap. From the opposite ledge, the figure glances down, calculating. Then, slowly, he looks back at them. A slight bow. A mocking smile. And then, gone.

Eve folds her arms. "Smart ass!"

Chapter 17

VISIONS

Fin grips the balcony railing, his knuckles white. Below, the sweet old lady hums softly at the reception desk, blissfully unaware of the chaos that just unfolded above her.

"Holy shit, Dad! What was that?" Asks Fin, just as confused as the rest of them.

Seth tries to catch his breath for a second before answering. "No idea buddy! I think he is gone for now, though." Seth looks around to see if any of the people in the library noticed the events which unfolded. It seems no one heard or saw anything, as he can't see any heads sticking out and looking around. He examines the stone ledge and sees that the figure did, in fact, crack the railing as it leapt off. "Hmmm, you guys go back and secure our stuff. I'll do a quick check over the other side to make sure he is gone. Meet you back at the table, okay?"

"Yeah no worries Dad." Agrees Fin, still confused by what happened.

"Okay, but be safe Dad." Orders Eve.

Seth walks off around the balcony to head past the stairs and off to the west wing. Eve and Fin turn back to go to the table to collect their gear and wait for their father.

"Okay… tell me you saw that guy's feet glow, sis."

"Yeah, I saw it. And how he broke the stone! Crazy right."

"Do you think he has some type of cybernetic legs or something?"

"I don't think so. That stuff is super illegal and besides, when he jumped off my head, it was as light as a feather. If it was some type of cybernetic enhancement, it would have to be much heavier."

"You think that guy was with the government, like Agent R?"

"Nah, I doubt it. You saw how easily we sorted her out. And I doubt the Corps is much more advanced from what we've seen of them."

"Yeah, true. Either way, that was pretty cool!"

Eve laughs and puts her hand on her brother's curly red hair and gives it a big rub. "Yeah, just don't mention how cool it was to Dad, okay. He looked pissed. Also, let's stay alert in case there is more to come." Fin nods in agreement and they continue back to the table to secure their gear.

Seth reaches the landing spot and searches for any clues to the figure's whereabouts. He has no luck seeing the library is made of polished cement floors and rows and rows of tablets, with some intermittent art and greenery placed around to break up the hard feel of it all. Seth moves deeper into the west wing, his boots clicking against the polished cement. The air seems thinner in the west wing of the building, as if the spy's leap somehow took its breath away.

Eventually, he comes to the far wall of the west wing and notices that one of the small windows is open. A warm breeze trickles in from outside and washes over him. Seth is confused. The window would be almost five metres off the ground and there is nothing but a hand-painted mural on the wall. *I guess if this guy can jump forty metres over the atrium, he can scale a couple of metres up to a window.* Seth takes a look around while he is here to see if he can find anything else. All he finds is more aisles of tablets and the odd piece of art hanging on the back wall. All the art pieces are beautifully done and depict what Seth assumes are moments from Ancient Earth's history. There are paintings of men on a small boat in a storm, and paintings of different planets humans discovered millennia ago after leaving Earth. But as beautiful as they are, none of them are helpful in finding the figure, or with their research.

Seth pauses to take a moment to think about the research while encapsulated in the silence of the Great Library. *We haven't found anything out, except that Dragons probably weren't real, and ancient religions or cults were the only ones who believed in them. But if that's the case, then how did a Dragon end up so far out beyond the edge. Is it possible some alien race taught ancient humans about Dragons?* None of it makes sense, but Seth is determined not to quit, as he is obviously on the right track. If superhuman spies are attempting to stalk him to learn what he is up to, he is doing something right. Deciding there is nothing of value left in the west wing, he figures it is time to return to the kids to discuss what happened.

Seth walks back around through the south wing to see if there is anything relevant or anything interesting to show the kids, like another suit of armour. As he comes to the south wing, he hears a sound amongst the rows of shelves. Judging by the noise, it must be someone else doing research as it's too noisy to be the person who recently eluded them, so he decides to go and ask them if they saw anything. He pops his head around the aisle where he heard someone pottering about, but when he looks, no one is there. *What the hell. Am I losing it today?*

Seth heads down the aisle and discovers that there is a tablet on the floor. Someone must have been here. There is no way the earlier events could have dislodged a tablet this far away. And besides, all the other tablets are still in their place.

He picks up the tablet and inspects it. 'Gods of Ancient Earth'. This does not surprise him. The entire floor is dedicated to Ancient Earth. He hears footsteps up ahead, so goes and checks to make sure he isn't going crazy. He takes the tablet with him, as he can't see an obvious spot where it came from in the aisle. *I will dump it on a desk if it doesn't belong to the person up ahead. I'm sure the librarians will find a place to put it.* He turns the next corner and sees a young redheaded lady with his back to him. She is wearing a beautiful flowing light blue dress and is searching through the tablets. Her red hair falls down her back almost to her hips as she looks up above her head height, searching for something.

"Excuse me Ma'am. Did you drop this?" The lady turns to look at him, and Seth's heart skips a beat as he steps back in shock. "Sara?" Seth says out loud, confused by what he sees. He moves towards his wife, only for her to disappear as soon as he arrives. An overwhelming fear of loss consumes him as he looks around for her. Seth can feel a cold sweat run down his spine as his heart rate rises. His breath catches. There, at the end of the aisle, Sara smiles, her eyes alight with something between mischief and nostalgia. Before he can move, she turns and vanishes around the corner, her silhouette flickering like a dying star.

He sprints after her. As he turns the corner, he sees his wife smiling at him once more. This warms his heart, and a big smile replaces any feeling of sadness. Her cheeks blush as they lock eyes. She looks at him with love, like he is the only man amongst all the stars. This look, one he has seen before, is one of his favourite things in the galaxy. But once more, she turns and disappears out of sight. Her steps echoing amongst the aisles of tablets. It reminds him of how she used to make him chase her when they were first dating. Giving him a good run for his money before she would let him catch her and claim his prize of a kiss.

Seth jogs to where he saw her last. Something about her is different this time, though. He wonders if it is the fact that he knows these are visions that make it different. He can feel the weight of sadness that he usually gets when he sees her has already left him. Joy and a sense of curiosity propel his movements forward now, not grief and desperation.

Ducking in between the rows of tablets, he isn't sure what to think. He is filled with happiness at seeing her again, but in the back of his mind, he knows what this is. Like back in the storm on 598, the vision isn't real, she isn't real. He slows for a second. *Just like in the storm.* He thinks for a moment as thoughts bounce around inside his head. *You were leading me to the cave in that storm... Where are you leading me now, my love?* Seth hears Sara's cute little laugh, and it warms his soul. It is as if she is reading his mind and is laughing at how long it took him to figure out her purpose. Seth ends up at an intersection, but he can no longer see her image. He then feels a soft, warm hand on his shoulder and hears a whisper in his ear.

Go left silly.

Seth lets the warmth of her touch and radiance of her voice wash over him for a moment before following her command.

This aisle of tablets ends at a T intersection, like so much of the maze that is the Great Library. Left or right are Seth's only choices, so he waits for her direction, but none comes. Now he is second guessing himself. *Could this really be her guiding me again? Or am I just chasing ghosts?* Perhaps he is not being led anywhere and is simply having a type of mental breakdown. He listens for her voice but hears something else instead. A sound that he can't quite identify. It is coming from his right, so he heads down that way. He thinks he has almost completed a full lap of the south wing at this point.

He reaches the source of the noise, where he finds Sara standing next to a giant spinning globe. Above the globe on the wall is the word 'EARTH'. The vision of Sara puts her hand on the globe and spins it once more before heading over to him. She stops right in front of him and puts her hands in his. Seth's fingers tingle at her touch. She then smiles, pops up on her toes and kisses him on the cheek before disappearing. The kiss feels so real that a tear of joy rolls down his cheek.

As much as he wants to stay in the moment, Seth knows she wanted him to see the globe. So, he wipes away the tear slowly rolling down his cheek and through his beard, and heads over to the large, hollow wooden ball. The enormous globe doesn't seem able to spin on its own, but is moving because of Sara's touch. *I swear I could feel her touch, and now her vision is moving things. Today keeps getting weirder!* Seth thinks as he wonders how the vision of his wife managed to move a physical object.

Seth studies the globe, tracing its surface with his fingertips. The continents are ancient, their names faded, but something about them stirs an eerie familiarity. The sphere begins to spin faster, not by mechanics, but as if reacting to his presence. His pulse quickens. Then, the moment his hand presses down, a surge of energy erupts through him.

Seth feels his mind being pulled through space and time. He sees images of Utopia as his consciousness gets ripped out of his body and off the surface of the planet, before getting flung up into space. Seth hurtles past the Core worlds and the Halo, accelerating beyond the system. He catches glimpses of familiar star systems before they blur into streaks of light. Seth braces as best he can, hoping his consciousness won't disintegrate. He passes one system he knows well. Midway, the popular planet covered in one large city several thousand stories high, it is the halfway point from the Core system to Ancient Earth.

Whispers of words fill his mind amongst the chaos. A voice he has heard before, perhaps from his past, or perhaps from humanities. A fragment of a speech from the First Commander steals a place in his mind for just a fraction before images of giant spaceships flying in unison flash around him.

The speed increases as the pain of his consciousness being ripped through the galaxy intensifies, causing him to scream out, unsure if his body is even capable of noise, with his mind so far away. As the pain becomes almost unbearable, Seth finds himself entering the Sol system, the home of Ancient Earth. He has never been to the Sol system and doesn't know how he knows where he is, but something deep inside of him seems to understand this location.

Seth descends onto Ancient Earth. He is moving so quickly that he feels sick, like his whole body is about to seize up. Seth grits his teeth and closes his eyes. He reaches the point where his mind can take no more and he feels himself slipping into darkness. But before the darkness can consume him, he feels his feet land firmly on Earth's surface. Oxygen flows back into his lungs as he attempts to catch his breath. A bright, warm light now replaces the darkness. It takes a moment for him to adjust to his surroundings as what feels like the galaxy's worst migraine quickly dissipates.

As his vision returns to normal, he looks around and sees beautiful tall trees with dark green leaves surrounding him as he stands atop a ridgeline in an ancient redwood forest. Silence holds him for a moment longer before all the data from the environment floods his senses. He allows a moment to take it all in. The fresh smell of the forest, the moisture in the air pressing against his skin, the gentle breeze coming from the blue sky above, and the sun gently caressing him. The intense pain from moments ago has now completely washed away.

Seth does not know why he is here, or what is meant to take place. Pausing, he waits to see if something happens, but nothing does. The planet seems to be merrily going about its day and ignoring him and his sudden arrival. Seth waits for a while, but it doesn't take long for his inquisitive nature to take hold, and he slowly moves forward to the edge of the ridgeline. Upon inspection, he finds himself high above some type of massive facility. From his vantage point, he can see employees of the facility below gleefully walking around, sitting down for coffee, and having conversations in small groups while enjoying the beautiful scenery.

Seth takes a minute to relax. Looking around, he can't see any landmarks of interest, so he follows a man-made trail down the ridgeline to the facility. On his way down, he passes by two workers who are strolling along, debating over something that he doesn't understand. He stops to ask them where he is, but the pair ignores him as if he is not even there. Seth attempts to grab one by the arm, but his hand passes straight through the man.

"Right, I guess we are playing that game then, hey!" Seth yells out to whoever or whatever it is that brought him here. He gets no response, so continues on the path.

Upon arrival at the facility, he stops and looks for a way inside. He can't see any obvious entrance points but can tell he must be at the back of the facility. Tall cement walls that run the length of the large complex block his view of the valley and forests below. He imagines there must be grand entrances on the opposite side of the facility. Glass windows that reach from floor to ceiling, opening up to overlook the area. Seth thinks that is how he would design the complex.

A familiar-looking man waving to him from a side entrance catches his eye. Seth checks behind him to make sure the man is actually waving at him, which he seems to be. He can't quite put his finger on who the man is, but knows he seems familiar. The man has the build of an elite solider and seems out of place amongst all the other employees at the facility. Seeing no other genuine option, Seth moves over to where the man was and heads inside.

Once inside, he sees the man again and follows him, but similar to the visions he has of Sara, Seth never seems to be able to get close enough to the man. He can't get a real good look at him or ask him questions. The man seems to disappear and reappear over and over as he leads Seth deeper into the facility. After following the man for several minutes down corridors, up and down stairs, and in and out of meeting rooms and laboratories, he finds himself alone in a small viewing gallery. The gallery overlooks an enormous dome shaped laboratory several stories down. There are staff down on the ground level, happily working away. Seth looks down over the workers to see what they are doing when suddenly he feels the presence of the man he was following right next to him. Seth attempts to look at the large powerful figure but can't move his body or his head to look. Somehow, some invisible force has frozen him in place.

"Hahaha head and eyes to the front McCallan." Says the figure in jest. Although Seth isn't finding it as funny as the man seems to.

"Wha… What is this? What's going on?" Seth fights to say. He isn't even sure if the words came out of his mouth or if he spoke them inside his head.

The powerful but warm voice of the man answers him. "This is where it all began. And where it will all begin again."

There is something so familiar about the figure, but Seth can't put his finger on it. He knows this person but can't remember how or why.

"You see, Seth McCallan, I was born on Ancient Earth. Did you know that?"

"No. I… I don't even know who you are!" Every word is a struggle to get out.

"HA! Yes, you do. You have forgotten, or perhaps you have not figured it out yet." Ponders, the figure.

"Why don't you be a pal and remind me then, shit breath!" Seth states as he tries to fight against whatever is holding him frozen in place.

Everything goes silent. The workers below freeze in location and Seth can even see dust particles stop in the air. A shadow looms over him, and he realizes the figure is growing, its presence expanding, suffocating the space around him. The man stares at him for a moment and it feels like the weight of a black hole is bearing down on him. Seth catches a glimpse of the man's face out of the corner of his eye, but whatever power this man holds is too much for Seth to look at him for more than half a second. The only features he notices is a short beard covering a strong jawline and glowing blue eyes. The man's presence stirs something deep within Seth, a memory, just out of reach, like a name on the tip of his tongue. The glowing blue eyes should be terrifying, but instead, they feel... known. Almost comforting. And that makes the whole thing even more unsettling. The powerful man reaches his arm out and puts it on Seth's back. Seth's body and mind instantly relax, as a calm washes over him.

"In good time friend, all in good time." The powerful figure whispers. The figure then turns back to look at the lab below and everything snaps back into motion.

"As I was saying, few people know I was born here Seth McCallan, and the ones that do, seem to have forgotten."

Seth grunts to himself. Any anger he had was dispelled when the man lay his hand on his back. The pair watch on for a while, not saying a word as the workers continue with the experiment. Seth can't see anything out of the ordinary and nothing grabs his attention. There is only a group of workers doing their daily activities. The figure snaps his fingers, and the sound cracks through the room like a bolt of lightning.

"Ahh, here we go. It is about to happen." He says excitedly.

"What am I looking for?"

"It will be a tiny spark. But that spark will change the fate of the galaxy forever, Seth McCallan."

Seth notices the tiniest of blue sparks inside one of the server racks off to the side of the room below. The powerful man next to him cheers with excitement and the whole viewing gallery shakes with the power of the man's emotions. It feels like a massive thunderstorm inside the small gallery. Seth fears the whole thing will explode or shake loose and fall.

"Did you see it? Just then."

"Yeah, I saw it. What has it got to do with anything?" Seth asks, still confused as to what is going on.

"Oh, you will figure it out soon enough." The man turns to look at Seth again as everything freezes in place once more. "Here. Right here is a good place." Seth can feel the man looking at him, his eyes almost burning Seth alive with their intensity and power. "Start here, Seth McCallan!" Energy from the giant man seems to pulsate outwards. Seth feels the crushing weight of that energy as he grits his teeth in pain. The giant man then leans over and gives Seth a hard slap in the chest. The force from the hit sends Seth flying through the air, back out the gallery door. Seth tenses his body tight, waiting to get thrown hard against a wall or the floor. But before he hits anything, he feels himself getting ripped back up and out of the facility as he again starts moving rapidly through space and time. The stars and planets go by so fast this time he can't even recognise them. The only thing that makes sense is more whispers from the First Commander.

Everything comes to an instant stop and Seth feels numb. He knows he is in his body, knows he is standing, but his legs feel unsteady, like the weight of history itself is pressing down on him. It takes him a second, but he realises he is back in the Great Library looking at the globe Sara led him to. He stands there motionless, waiting for his equilibrium to stop violently swaying all over the place. When it eventually calms down, he senses his physical body once more. It feels weak and completely empty. As if he was nothing but a hollow vase.

The world tilts, and his knees buckle. He barely registers Eve calling his name before the darkness rushes in, not just the absence of light, but a crushing void that swallows his senses. The last thing he hears is his own voice, distant and hollow: "Earth. Facility. Birthplace... Start here."

Just five more minutes, please. I'm so warm and comfy. Seth feels himself being shaken awake. It feels like he is in his childhood bed and his mum is trying to wake him up for school.

"Dad! Dad, are you okay?" Eve is kneeling next to him, gently shaking him while Fin stands watch. Seth realises that he isn't in his childhood bed and snaps back to reality. The high roof and cold hard floor of the library greet him.

"Yeah, yes. Sorry I'm okay Eve."

"No, you're not! We heard you yell, then found you here unconscious. What happened?"

Seth sits up to get his bearings as he recalls the events leading up to the globe and what happened when he touched it. He wants to tell Eve everything but will have to leave out the vision of Sara. "Oh sorry. Something led me to the globe there. Like what happened on 598." Seth points at the globe that is no longer spinning. "It was spinning out of control all by itself, and when I touched it, I had some kind of vision. Or maybe I was transported somewhere. I don't really know."

"You must have hit your head. A vision! What does that even mean?" Fin reaches over and starts playing with the globe. Seth flinches as Fin reaches for it, his heart skipping a beat. Nothing happens. Eve notices her father flinch when Fin touches the globe. She eyeballs him, searching for an answer on his face.

"Sorry Dad, no visions for me." Gently mocks Fin.

"Far out buddy. You are going to give me a heart attack one day!" Seth says, catching his breath after thinking something similar would happen to Fin.

"So, what was this vision about then?" Asks Eve.

"Not sure, to be honest. But it took me back in time… I think. Back to Ancient Earth."

"That's weird. We found you holding this tablet when we got here." Eve pulls out the 'Gods of Ancient Earth' tablet. The one Seth found on the floor, the one he believes Sara had left for him. Seth's eyes open wide.

"That's right. We should probably have a look at that." Seth says excitedly, hoping there might be a clue in the tablet. Fin helps his father up. Eve holds him, but he waves her off. Once standing, he hops up and down on the spot as he shakes himself out and checks his body. He feels fine. Actually, he feels great, a surprise, considering the immense pain from being flung across space and time, and the overwhelming power of the giant man.

Seth tries to shake off the last remnants of the vision, but it clings to him like a shadow. His heart still pounds, the image of giant man burned into his mind. He swallows hard, glancing at

Eve and Fin. They're waiting for an explanation, trusting him. He forces a smile then just simply shrugs.

As they walk back to the east wing, Seth fills Eve and Fin in on his vision while they bombard him with questions. They ask their father questions in a systematic and structured way to get the most out of him. This makes Seth proud, so he does his best to answer everything honestly and with as much detail as possible. When they return to the large table in the east wing, Seth notices someone has cleaned everything up.

"Did you guys clean all this up?" He asks.

"Yep." Replies Eve. "Fin didn't want to, but I told him I would tell the old receptionist if he didn't." Seth looks to Fin, who makes an exaggerated scared face. "He was happy to help after that." They all have a little chuckle and sit back down. Seth is glad that they are joking again and not too worried about him. Even though he can see Eve giving him the occasional concerned look.

Eve plugs the tablet into the table, so it displays on the screen, allowing them to all read through it simultaneously. The introduction of the book explains human traditions and ancient religions. It mentions Dragons briefly, but as an example of both the differences and similarities between ancient human folk lore and belief systems. It then goes into an in-depth study of the main Ancient Earth gods and what effects they had on the planet and the times. Fin laughs at how many there were for such a small number of humans. Seth and Eve agree it sounds silly. Noting that there are probably fewer religions and gods worshipped now then there was in the past. Yet there are a billion times more people. The book also talks about how humans left the Sol system to explore the galaxy and the journey they went on from Ancient Earth to the Core. It talks about the hundred-year journey and some of the mysterious things that happened along the way and what effect this had on human religious beliefs. It also discusses how new religions came and went during this next period in humanity's history.

They eventually make it to the end of the book, but nothing concrete stands out to any of them. Seth can't see any correlations between his vision and the key themes of the book. He is puzzled as to why this book is so important or what meaning it might have. "Well, that was a bit of an anti-climax." Seth says, disappointed.

"Who wrote the book?" Asks Eve.

"Not sure. I'll bring up their bio. It should be at the start or end of the text." Seth scrolls to the start of the book but finds nothing, so he flicks to the end. Finding what he is looking for, he reads through the author's bio. Nothing stands out there either. The author fits the standard galactic professor stereotype. Jacket, glasses, bald patch, pipe, and all. However, the last part seems to glow. Seth thinks it's the screen playing up, though it seems someone has somehow edited the tablet's contents.

"Wait… the text is changed!'" Eve states.

"That's not possible. Is it?" Asks Fin.

Seth's hand trembles with excitement. "No. No it's not buddy."

Seth's throat turns dry as he reads the new passage aloud. "The author made his greatest discoveries by following the path of the hundred-year journey…" He looks up, heart hammering. "We need to retrace the journey!"

"What?" Ask the kids.

"We need to go back to Ancient Earth, and we need to follow the same path the ancient humans took from Earth to the Core system!"

Eve and Fin look at their father, still a little confused.

"When I passed out, I remember getting pulled through space. I even recognised some of the planets, but I wasn't sure exactly what was going on. I think it took me along this path. I even heard whispers from the First Commander's famous speeches. It must have been for a reason!"

Both Eve and Fin stare at each other before turning back to their father. Giant smiles cover their faces.

Seth exhales slowly, staring at the glowing words on the screen.

"We have to go back to Ancient Earth." He looks up at his children, his voice quieter but more certain. "And I think there will be something there waiting for us."

Chapter 18

ZERO

The Family spends several more hours in the Great Library learning about the path that humanity took from its original home on planet Earth to the Core system. They learn about each system and the different planets humans began colonising along the hundred-year journey. Some systems and planets Seth visited during his time in the Military. His unit would set up a base of operations on a major planet, then conduct operations on nearby planets or in nearby systems. Other systems along the path Seth has never stepped foot on. Even Fin and Eve have been to one, not including the Core system, but none of them have ever been to Ancient Earth.

Ancient Earth has never had much to offer Seth and his family. As a protected system on the outer edge of colonised space, authorities manage it more as an ecotourism and history tourist destination than a thriving metropolis. The overall population is low, and it is a very peaceful system. It was a running joke in the Military that if you were a soldier that was always getting in trouble, or were terrible at your job, you would get posted to the Sol system. As far away from any real action as possible.

A subtle buzz lingers in the air as Seth and the kids continue their reserach. The thought that they might be onto something has them both motivated and focused. At first, Seth worried it was all in his head, just a random cosmic coincidence. But the fact that Sara continues to lead him, and he is being followed by spies with superhuman agility, must mean that he is onto something big. He is certain this isn't only in his head, or he is suffering from some type of mental bias.

As they are finishing up their research for the day, the sweet old lady from reception shows up.

"Hello darlings. Just letting you know we will be closing in around fifteen minutes, so if you could begin to make your way out, that would be lovely." She says, smiling at the family.

"No worries, Ma'am, we are packing up now, so all good." Answers Seth.

"Oh, thank you my lovelies." She replies before moving on. Seth wipes his brow and mouths the word 'Phew' still playing on the joke that the old lady is secretly an evil villain. Fin has to put his hand over his mouth so not to laugh out loud as Eve rolls her eyes.

The family packs up their belongings and makes their way outside. They each take a moment to use the restroom and refill their water bottles at the library's filtered system before heading down the elaborate stone stairs. On their way out through the foyer, they hear a scream followed by cries of both surprise and shock. They glance up. The old receptionist stands on the fourth floor, right at the cracked balcony ledge, the same spot where the spy had vaulted over the atrium earlier. They look at each other, then jog out of the library, laughing to themselves as they go.

Outside, gentle pastel purples and oranges paint the sky as the sun sets over Nova. Seeing the soft colours and realising the time, the family finally becomes aware of their hunger. With all the day's activities, they have forgotten to eat. They find a nearby park that is neatly designed with stone seats and evergreen hedges around its perimeter. They sit down to eat some of the fruit and snacks that Fin had prepared. This is also an excellent opportunity to discuss their next move.

"Hell of a day, hey guys." States Seth in between bites.

"Not what I was expecting, that's for sure." Says Eve, after having a massive gulp of water.

"Who do you think that guy was, Dad?" Asks Fin.

"No idea buddy. Something was definitely strange about him though. I've never seen anybody move like that. He almost defied gravity."

"Eve and I thought he may have had some type of underground cybernetics of some sort."

Seth thinks for a moment while taking a sip of water. "Nah. I have come across people with cybernetics before and even the ones with real high-end cybernetics don't move like that. That guy was way too agile and fast!"

"Who was he then?" Asks Fin again, still wanting an answer.

"I don't know buddy, but my guess is that whoever he is, he either knows about, or is somehow connected to, our little discovery back on 598."

"Why do you think that?"

"For one, he wasn't Agency. They don't move like that. And two, if he wasn't connected to 598, why hide? He could've just walked up to us, and we wouldn't have thought twice. Which makes me think he knows about it or is connected to it, hence his spying."

"What about one of the Corporations?" Asks Eve.

"Again, I doubt it. They might be on to us and are possibly even looking for us here on Utopia, but they definitely don't operate like that guy. They are less skilled than the Agency when it comes to this type of business. And besides, their MO is to use technology to spy on people, not humans."

"Could they have contracted him?"

Seth thinks for a moment. "That's a possibility, as he certainly doesn't fit the Corp look." Seth scratches his chin, thinking some more. "Maybe we will have to ask the good Agent next time we see her." They all nod silently in agreement.

Once they have finished discussing the spy and relaxed for a moment, Seth speaks up. "Alright guys, what is the play from here? Personally, I think we shouldn't waste any more time in the Core system. It's obvious to me that Earth is our destination and if we are to read all the signs, we should follow the old path back. Not jump straight there. Thoughts? Eve, Fin, chime in." Seth telling them to chime in means that he wants their input, not a yes or no answer. He tries to include them in the bigger decisions he makes where possible. It gives them ownership of the task instead of them just being told what to do all the time. And being told what to do all the time doesn't make for smarter individuals. It breeds in laziness and lack of accountability. Plus, they are adults now, so a strict dictatorship parenting method will not work anymore. If he was being honest with himself, it had stopped working ten years ago.

Fin chimes in first. "Look Dad, I would love to spend some more time studying, but I don't think we will find anything. But I am also pretty wrecked. I wouldn't mind one more night's sleep on the planet before we head off."

"Roger that buddy. Eve?"

"I have had enough of the library and am happy not to return. Also, I agree, Earth via the old path is the play. Another night's sleep would be good, especially in that bed." Eve feels its delightful embrace again in her mind. "But if we could get out of the system quickly, then we can sleep in transit. I also don't like the idea of that guy being out there still. I would feel much safer on the Scout."

"Roger that." Seth contemplates both their answers. "Okay so the library is done, and we agree it is time to move on. I think that is obvious. I'll get in contact with Agent R on the comm channel she provided me to see if she can get us out tonight. If not, we will sleep here tonight, then leave first thing in the morning. Plan?" Seth asks.

"Plan." Replies Eve.

"Plan." Replies Fin.

Seth looks them in the eye to make sure both his children are happy with the way forward, then gives them a nod. Diving into a pocket, he pulls out the small comm unit R gave him. Normally, you would raise someone from the comms suite built into your personal computer, but the Agency has their own encrypted networks. So you need to carry a separate comms device. These are like the ones Seth used in the Military, except the Agency units are one to one and have more layers of encryption. Seth's old unit used comms, which were one-to-many or many-to-many, for obvious reasons. He keys a message into the comm and sits back to have a drink of water. He assumes R isn't sitting around waiting for him to call.

While he waits, he takes in the sights and sounds of the area. The last rays of sunlight bathe the district in gold, reflecting off glass buildings like molten metal. It reminds Seth of his first time on local leave from the Military Academy. He and his fellow recruits were excited to get off base. All the recruits wanted to go shopping, eat fancy food, or grab a drink. Seth didn't do any of that. He walked around the city exploring for several hours.

Seth chuckles to himself as he remembers he got lost and almost missed the curfew. He had to run all the way back to base through two districts to make it inside the front gates on time.

It takes about twenty minutes before his Agency comm beeps at him. Seth answers. "Go for Seth."

"So, how did you go? Are you finished already?" It quickly becomes apparent to Seth that Agent R wastes no time with pleasantries when on the comms line.

"Good. We have everything we need. Is there any chance of an exfil back to our ship and out of the system tonight?" The comm goes quiet for a minute. She must be checking to see what she can organise, if anything at all, on such short notice. Both Eve and Fin look at the comm, eagerly awaiting the answer.

"I'll need an hour or two, but yeah, we can make that happen. I will send you coordinates for the rendezvous where I will meet you, then I'll take you up to the Halo myself. Keen to hear what you have learned."

Seth knows she is half blackmailing him with the early exfil so she can get some information. But he is okay with it. He will give her enough intel to pique her interests. Besides, he wants her to secure him passage back to Ancient Earth under light cover. So he needs to play nice.

"Roger that. Seth out." He ends the conversation but leaves the comm unit on to get the RV time and location. He turns to the kids. "Looks like we are getting off planet in two hours. Let's head back to the accommodation to get all our stuff, then move to the RV location." As Seth is telling the kids the plan, he feels the comm vibrate. He looks down to see that the RV is only a thirty-minute walk from the accommodation, so they have some time up their sleeves. Fin looks a bit upset about not getting that sleep, so Seth tells him he can raid the fridge for supplies before they leave. This immediately cheers him up.

They have one last drink of water before heading off. The sun has now set, and the lights of the city have come on, but the temperature is still nice and warm. A welcome change from the scorching days and freezing nights the family endures spent on unexplored planets. After the beautiful climates of Utopia and Komugi, Seth hopes he and the family aren't getting too soft.

It's only a short walk back to the apartment but Fin feels a weight in his stomach and starts to get a bad feeling. Similar to what he experienced on the Halo, but much more intense. "Hey Dad."

"Yeah buddy, what is it?"

"I have a feeling that we are being followed again."

"Have you seen anyone?"

"No. But I have a real bad feeling this time."

"What do you mean by, real bad feeling?" Eve chimes in.

"Well, it's hard to explain. Earlier in the library, I felt like we were being watched, but that was it. I didn't feel any bad intent. It was like someone wanted to see what we were doing. It was very neutral, if that makes sense. This time it feels like someone wants to do us harm, or something like that anyway. Whoever is watching us is doing so with an ill intent."

"Normally, buddy, as you know, I'd want more than just a gut feeling. But after today? I believe you." Seth keeps his pace steady. If they are being followed, the last thing he wants is to let their shadow know they've been made. "Okay, let's head back to the accommodation. Get our stuff packed, and tool up. Then let's see if we can lose them on the walk to the RV. Plan?"

Fin doesn't answer, he merely nods, and they continue along like nothing has happened.

Upon arrival, they quickly enter the apartment. Once inside, they silently clear the apartment once again, to make sure they are not walking into another ambush. Thankfully, it is all clear. It only takes them several minutes to pack up all their belongings and be ready to move out. They have been on enough scouts to know that keeping everything ready to go can save your life. Apparently, Utopia is no different to an unexplored planet far beyond colonised space. Seth checks each room twice to ensure nothing is left behind. He secures their packs, then verifies their concealed blades are within reach. Once he is happy, they step off from the accommodation with a new mission. Make it to the RV safe and sound.

They slip out the side of the accommodation block, taking a longer route to the rendezvous. The direct path means waiting. Standing still. A bad idea if someone's tailing them.

They begin their walk at a casual pace, just like they would have if they were leaving normally. Then, after about five minutes, Seth takes a turn down an alley. Two large buildings flank the alley, blocking all natural light, so no one can see them at street level unless they are at either end. Seeing everything is clear, Seth sprints down the alley with Eve and Fin in tow. When he reaches the end of the alleyway, he returns to a normal walking pace like nothing had happened. Thankfully, they drilled escape and evasion tactics several months ago in the sim room. So, the kids know what the tactics are and are ready to move.

Once back onto a main street, they continue forward at ninety degrees to the way they were previously heading. Sleek buildings line the street, their glass facades reflecting neon signs. Government workers, dressed in crisp uniforms, weave between cafes and boutiques, their conversations blending into a steady hum. Whilst it is nice and busy, Seth and the kids stand out too much to blend in amongst the crowds of Utopian locals. So instead, they pull the same manoeuvre three more times. Seth does this not to lose whoever may be following them but to put them under some pressure and flush them out. It will be easy to identify a shadow if the individual is running around flustered and overtly looking for someone.

After the next alley, Seth sends the kids forward, and he walks on the opposite side of the street to them, some forty metres behind. He stops in the dark alcove of a building and patiently watches the last alley they came from.

Within a minute, a man bursts out, scanning the street in a panic. *Gotcha! Looks like Fin was right.* Seth thinks as he wonders how Fin could have known. *Looks like he was also right about who was following us. This idiot doesn't seem related to our friend from the library.* From his hidden position, Seth scans the man and sends an image to the kids. Now they all know what their pursuer looks like. He then heads off before the pursuer notices him. Quickly and quietly making his way back to the kids without being noticed.

"Okay guys. I have identified at least one person following us. Male, mid to late thirties. Blue worker pants and a black jumper. Scan is in your device. Doesn't look like he has superhuman powers like our friend from the library." Seth knows this must be stressful for the kids, so tries to add in a little humour to help them relax a little. "My guess is a Corp thug of some sort. Maybe ex-Military or police, but poorly trained." The kids nod, listening in. "If that is the case, I'd assume he has at least one other with him, possibly more." Seth says, building on his response. "We have two options. Try to keep dodging them until we get to the RV or try to pick them off one at a time. Thoughts?"

"Pick them off." Fin says, keen for some action. Seth shakes his head. *The kid wants action, dangerous thinking. But still… I like the attitude.*

"I also think we should pick them off, Dad. If we to get the RV and it's just Agent R with no backup, we might be outnumbered leaving ourselves open for an attack."

"Alright. We pick them off. But we need cover, too many people around. We will need to find somewhere dark or isolated."

Eve pulls up the local map on her forearm computer and looks for spots as they continue along at their casual pace. It only takes her a short time before she finds a suitable place. "Hey Dad, what about here?" The location is next to a large park on the way to the RV. There is a long, wide path flanking one side of the park. A long wall, with shrubbery along the other side, hides the path from view.

"Nice one Eve, we can hide in the bushes and wait for him to pass by before taking him out. Fin, I will distract him, and you come from behind and choke him out, okay?"

Seth can see by the looks on the kid's faces that they are happy with the plan. They walk towards the park, continuing their pace, trying not to give away that they know they are being followed and who is following them. They also try to spot anyone else who might be following them, but have no luck.

Upon arrival, they push past the well-maintained park and head along the path. Once on the path and out of view, they all sprint ahead, throw their packs into the shrubs, then find hiding positions in the bushes themselves. What sounds like a passionate game of sports being played on the other side of the park creates enough noise for them to move silently. Only seconds after they find their hiding spots, the man who has been following them comes around the corner. They watch as he looks visibly frustrated at being dropped once again. He jogs along the path in an attempt to catch up.

Seth steps from the bushes as he passes him. "Lost something?"

The man whirls, face draining of colour.

"I… Umm. Don't know what you're talkin bout." The man says, caught off guard. Seth watches as the man runs multiple scenarios through his mind. The man looks around. He can't see the other members of the family, but he also can't see anyone else along the path. Seth watches as the man entertains the idea of taking on Seth himself, one on one. He must be feeling confident in his abilities as he makes a move towards Seth.

"Looks like you are all alone, old man. You should be more careful out all alone at night. You never know who you might bump into." The man says confidently as he moves in even closer to Seth, pulling a small blade from out of his back pocket.

To the man's surprise, Seth simply stands there and smiles at him. The man pauses, confused. Obviously, he is used to a different reaction from his victims. This moment of misjudgement is when Fin strikes. Fin slips behind the man and locks in a chokehold, his grip vice-like. It's his first actual fight, and he's putting everything into it. The man, not knowing that Fin was behind him, immediately begins freaking out. Fin's vice like grip digs in and burns around his neck.

Seth moves in on the man and grabs the man's hand with the knife in it so that he doesn't stab Fin, or accidentally stab himself. The man flays violently as he realises what is going on. His eyes go wide as he feels Seth easily pull the blade from his weakening hand. Knowing that Seth could kill him with his own blade if he so decides. But Seth only watches on, talking Fin through the situation in a calm, guiding voice. This disturbs the man even more, he feels like a trapped animal the family has caught hunting, and a father is talking his son through the kill. The man quickly passes out and Seth lets Fin leave the choke on for another ten seconds before tapping him to let go. Fin, filled with adrenalin, finds it hard to release the choke and Seth has to pull him off. Eve comes over to Fin and moves him away from the man and tells him to focus on his breathing. She can see her brother is filled with adrenalin, excitement, and fear from his first real life dangerous encounter.

Searching the man's pockets, Seth finds some money, and a poorly made ID card, which he assumes is fake. He also finds a comm unit, which he throws over the wall into the park as far as he can. Hopefully, if someone is tracking him through his comms unit, it will make it a little harder to find him. Seth takes the man's jacket off and uses it to tie his arms up behind his back and does the same with the man's belt around his legs. Then together they roll him into the shrubs. He will wake up shortly and most likely freak out. Seth grabs a handful of dirt from the base of the shrubs and rubs it into the man's face and eyes. That, along with having his arms and legs tied, should slow him down once he regains consciousness.

"Eve, Fin." Seth straightens up and says in a serious tone. 'He had a knife on him, so obviously these guys aren't playing like back on Solus." Seth is realising that one of his kids could have got seriously hurt as he feels an anger beginning to storm inside of him. "If we see any more of them, let's treat them as dangerous and hostile. I can't have you guys getting hurt, okay. No more playing around."

Eve can sense the change in her father. She knows it all too well. He often gets a violent intensity when scouting, and sometimes it scares her. She isn't scared of her father, but scared for him. He yells at them occasionally, and sometimes they deserve it, but she knows it comes from him wanting to keep them safe. She knows how much he loves them and that they are his most precious things in the universe. "Roger that Dad. We will be extra vigilant." She says to calm him down and reassure him.

"Thanks, beautiful. Let's give em zero." Seth uses that term often. It means not allowing the enemy any advantage or any chance of success.

"Roger that Dad. Zero!" Says Fin. Still full of adrenaline from the brief encounter. Seth looks at his son and it seems that Eve has calmed her brother down somewhat. He could physically see the excitement in him before, but that wave seems to be passing. He pats Fin on the back.

"Solid choke by the way buddy, great work."

"Thanks Dad." Seth doesn't throw out praise for no reason, even to his kids, so Fin is pleased to hear he did a great job. They spend the next thirty minutes walking to the rendezvous point. Taking a winding path, doubling back and heading in circles to make sure they are not been followed. Thankfully, the family doesn't see anyone else following them.

"Hey little bro. You got anything on that radar of yours?" Eve asks.

"Umm, not sure. I have been focused on other stuff. Sorry sis."

Seth looks at the time and notices they have a spare ten minutes up their sleeve. "Hey, I want to stop walking in circles and go do a quick recon on the rendezvous. Sound like a plan?" Both kids nod in agreement.

They stop a few hundred meters short of the rendezvous, crouching behind a row of market stalls that have long since closed for the night. From here, they have a clear view of the meeting point. A warehouse looms in the distance, a stark, metal monolith at the edge of the government zone. A high wire fence wraps around it like a prison yard, leaving only a single entrance. No cover. No escape routes.

Seth's gut twist. *Perfect place for a meeting, or an ambush.*

He sweeps his gaze over the area. The wide street leading up to the warehouse is empty, except for the occasional transport drone humming past overhead. No movement. No obvious threats. That should reassure him. It doesn't.

Fin shifts beside him, eyes locked on the rendezvous point. His fingers twitched against his leg, a habit he has developed when something doesn't sit right.

"Hey, Dad." Fin whispers. "I got a bad feeling about that place. Something is definitely off."

Seth exhales slowly. He doesn't have whatever sixth sense Fin has recently developed, but hell, even he feels it.

"Shit, buddy." He mutters, keeping his voice low. "I don't know what kind of weird radar you've recently discovered, but I'm feeling it too." Eve stifles a quiet laugh, but Fin doesn't even crack a smile. His face is set, serious. Worried. Seth doesn't like that.

He glances at the time. *Seven minutes until the meet.*

"Alright." He says. "We go in slow. Stay sharp and stay dangerous."

Eve and Fin nod, their expressions shifting into the same grim focus they'd had back in the alley. Seth takes one last look at the warehouse. A single metal door. No windows. Nowhere to hide.

His instincts scream at him.

This is a setup.

Still, they have no choice.

Chapter 19

UNLEASHED

The family are in location on the side of the warehouse, and it is several minutes past the RV time. Agent R isn't anywhere to be seen. This is not what Seth, and the kids were hoping for. From nowhere, Fin starts muttering to himself.

"Hey, buddy, you okay?" Seth asks, worried his son might be having a panic attack.

Fin raises his hand, signalling for him to wait. Seth looks at him, confused and a little angry. He wants to know if his son is okay and doesn't appreciate having a hand shoved in his face. Eve puts her hand on Seths back then raises her hand to her ear, signalling for him to listen. It sounds as if Fin is having several different conversations with himself all at once. Seth looks puzzled but now gets why Eve held him back. Father and daughter watch on, attempting to decipher what Fin is saying but not quite being able to keep up with the multiple voices he seems to be using. Fin suddenly stops and looks up, with wide-open eyes. He takes a big gulp. "I think there are ten men coming for us. And they plan to kill us."

Eve looks at her father, then back at Fin. "Well, if that's true, let's get the hell out of here!" Eve doesn't wait, she's already moving.

Before she can even get five metres away, a group of men appear at the end of the warehouse. She rapidly turns around to go the other way, but sees another group come around the other end of the warehouse. She quickly realises they are trapped. Seth sees this too and jumps into action, whispering orders to them.

"Drop your packs and keep your blades concealed until the last minute, and try to line them up one at a time. Just like in training, you two take the rear and work together and I'll take the front." Both Eve and Fin nod, but Seth can see the fear and uncertainty in their eyes. "Breathe! This will be easier than one of Rose's training sessions, I promise." Seth takes a deep breath in and out then repeats the breath, this time making the kids do the same. He calls this his battle breath. One last deep breath before the action starts.

"You've got this. They don't know it, but you are the threat." Seth states calmly and confidently.

A voice shouts at them from the front group. "Oi you!" There is anger in the man's voice. "We have been looking for you." Both groups close to within about fifteen metres of the family. "Those rich folk at Ovmor have put quite a bounty on your head and we are here to collect." The apparent leader of the gang smiles confidently, knowing he has them outnumbered.

"Now, I was only going to cut you a little, take all your belongings and hand you over to Ovmor. I was even going to be a decent human and leave your kids alone."

Cocky. Seth thinks to himself.

"But you went and beat up my little brother, didn't you? So now I'm going to have to hurt your kids as well. Might make you watch too, you piece of shit spacer!"

Until this point, Seth's day had already been a mixed bag. He was still angry that the figure in the library bested him so easily, and he didn't like that he was being followed, or that his kids were in danger. He isn't worried about these idiot's threats to his life. Plenty of people have said they were going to kill him. None had been successful so far. But he had a line, and threatening his children was it, and these idiots had just crossed it.

Seth pats the kids on the shoulder then turns around to face the man. The storm of anger he had growing inside of him, now rages, ready to explode. Seth stares at the man with a focused, violent intent.

"No words then?" The man looks back at his colleagues and laughs. "Looks like the old timer is too scared to say anything boys!" He shouts out loud to the group behind the family.

"Right, you two." The man speaking, the leader, points to two of his thugs. "Go grab him and bring him over here so I can have a chat with him. No need to be gentle about it, just don't kill im yet."

The two men step forward brandishing metal poles that were hidden inside their jackets. Seth continues to stare straight at the leader. The two men approach Seth, laughing and swinging the poles as they waltz forward.

"Don't worry old man, we will be gentle with the girl." One thug says in a smug, overly confident tone.

This comment breaks Seth's focus on the leader and he shifts it to the two men approaching him.

"That got his attention." The other thug says, laughing. Seth takes a step forward. The two men exchange a glance. Uncertainty flickers in their eyes, but their leader's presence forces them on. They charge. Seth waits, coiled like a predator, his whole body tightening.

Seth can't hold back the violent storm inside him any longer. It explodes.

The thug swings. Seth ducks, his blade flashing. A single slash, and the man staggers, clutching his guts. As Seth raises back up next to the man, he quickly stabs him hard once in the side of the neck. Ending the man's life instantly, even before the blood and internal organs have time to flow from the first strike.

Before the other man can even register what has happened, Seth lunges forward towards him. Seth's speed and power are overwhelming, leaving the man no chance to defend himself as Seth rams his blade hard into the man's throat. Eve screams as she sees her father decimate the second man. Seth pulls the blade out and rapidly stabs him hard several more times in the neck and head. An animalistic thunder comes from Seth that seems to vibrate through the air as he roars at the man before dropping his limp corpse to the floor. Seth snaps his head around, focused again on the leader of the group. The leader is trying to process what has happened as he sees the beast in front of him stare him down.

The leader stares at the corpses of his men. *That… that wasn't a fight. It was slaughter.*

His blade feels like a toy in his grip. Seth looks at him, no, through him. A predator assessing its next meal.

The leader's mouth moves, but no words come.

The rear group seems stunned and doesn't know what to do. One man screams and charges in at Eve and Fin. This draws Eve's focus away from her father and back to the group behind them. Eve is the closest, so she steps up in her fighting stance and draws her blade. She can feel her body shaking under the stress, but all those training sims and time on the sparring matts have paid off as she controls the fear and focuses her intent. The man gets in close and swings wildly at her. She sees every attack coming a mile away, as if the attacker is moving in slow motion. Eve easily dodges the blows, cutting the man's arm each time he attacks. Exactly like she has been trained to do. Using her angles, she spins to the side and kicks his knee hard, locking his leg out and jarring him in place. Fin, who has moved to the opposite flank, steps in and, using all his might, punches the man as hard as he can in the centre of the chest. A wave of dust and air erupts in all directions as the pressure shifts.

For the second time today, Eve and Fin see a bright light and hear a thundering crack as the punch lands. Like the figure in the library whose jump cracked the stone ledge, a sickening breaking of bone sounds out around the warehouse. The punch sends the man flying back several metres through the air. He crashes into the group behind him, who watches on terrified. Eve looks on at Fin in shock.

Fin stares at his trembling fist. It doesn't hurt, but it feels… odd. Butterflies churn in his stomach. He looks up at Eve, but she's just as lost as he is.

"Don't ever hit me like that when we are sparring, okay?" Eve says, forcing a grin, but her eyes betray her unease.

Seth snaps his head back when he hears the small thunder clap echo through the area and sees the man crashing into the group. The gang cries out in fear and stumbles backwards.

Seth returns his focus to the leader, who is now alone as the remaining men have already backed up. The leader grips his knife so tightly his knuckles turn white. He knows how this ends, but his body moves anyway, charging at Seth with a scream, as if sheer volume could keep the monster at bay.

Seth doesn't move. Doesn't flinch.

He just waits.

The leader's blade flashes through the air.

Seth is already gone.

A slash to the knee.

A crash to the ground.

A gasp of pain that never finishes before he feels Seth on his back.

Seth hears the wind come out of the man, along with the noise of several ribs breaking underneath him. Seth, a man of his word, gives him zero and wastes no time.

Seth grips the leader's hair, slamming his head into the ground. Bone cracks. Blood pools.

The leader coughs, choking on red, but Seth yanks his head back. Just enough to whisper in his ear.

"You should've kept your mouth shut about my kids."

The blade rips.

The body slumps.

After many years of experience, Seth knows his attack was successful, so doesn't waste his time inspecting the body to confirm the kill. He quickly checks in on the kids to make sure they are alright. He sees Eve holding her breath and Fin squeezing his fist tight. Both with looks of horror on their faces, but otherwise fine.

The other group of attackers is running away, so Seth turns back to the remaining two men, who are now frozen in place by fear. They look at each other, then at Seth, unsure what to do. One of them pulls a blade, but the closest one seems to be messing around in his jacket, reaching for something else.

Seth wastes no time and continues to provide his enemy with zero and charges the two men, who are almost ten metres from him now. The man with the knife freezes in place from fear, and the man playing in his jacket, not paying attention to Seth, finds what he is after. He looks up as Seth is right on him and brandishes a small handgun. But before he aims it at Seth, a loud, sharp crack rings out along the warehouse edge.

Seth is intimately familiar with this noise and watches as the man's head whips to one side as blood splats against the wall of the warehouse. The colour blending in with patches of rust on the metal exterior. Less than a second later, Seth hears a second crack and watches as the remaining man's limp body drops to the ground, lifeless.

Seth stops in place, cleans then sheaths his knife and puts his hands up in the air and looks back out away from the warehouse to confirm the shooter's location. It doesn't take him long to find them. Once confirmed, he takes a long deep hard breath in through his nose, holds it for a couple of seconds then breathes back out slowly. He looks over at the kids and yells out to them to put their hands up and take a deep breath as well.

"Don't worry guys, it's all over." Seth starts his breathing as he walks back towards the kids. *Control the breath, control the mind.* "Guys, breathing!" He looks over at them and smiles. They look nervous and confused.

Eve pipes up. "How do you know it's over?" She doesn't have any fear in her voice, but he can tell she is still full of adrenaline and demanding of an answer.

"Guns are illegal on the Core planets, right?".

"Yeah so!"

"Soooo these two idiots just got shot in the head." Seth kicks the one closest to him, just in case Eve didn't know who he was talking about. Eve stares blankly back at him. "Did you hear a gunshot?" Seth asks, still half yelling because of the distance between them. Arms still up in the air.

Eve thinks about it for a couple of seconds. "I heard a loud crack?" She answers. Eve then looks at Fin, who seems to be trying to figure it out in his head. *Ugh! He will not be any help.* She is trying to figure out where her father is leading her, but after what just happened, her thoughts are a mess. Eve then hears some screaming and yelling coming from off in the distance towards the entrance of the warehouse area. She snaps her head back and forth between the noise and her father. He looks at her and shakes his head, letting her know it's nothing to worry about.

Seth can see she is struggling, so offers some more information to help. "You didn't hear a gunshot, but you heard the bullets hitting the warehouse wall because the shots came from a silenced weapon." Seth, hands still in the air, points up to the area where they conducted their reconnaissance. Eve follows his eyeline and sees a group of people moving down from the recon location towards the warehouse. "So that's at least a couple of hundred metres, which means you would need a long arm for those shots. Now smuggling on a half-arsed sidearm like that idiot did, is hard enough, but you would need to have government approvals and sanctions to get on a silenced sniper rifle." Seth pauses for a second to see if Eve figures it out, but she shrugs her shoulders and gives him an angry look. "Know any government Agents with R as their cover name?" Seth watches as the penny drops for both kids.

"Well, if she had a sniper rifle then why the hell didn't she shoot these scumbags earlier Dad!" She isn't angry at him, but adrenaline is still pulsing through her veins and there is no other outlet besides yelling at her father.

"Good question!" Now Seth has some anger in his voice as he is also keen to find out what took her so long to move into action. "I am guessing she will be here soon though, so let's find out."

A wicked look covers Seth's face. One Eve is relieved not to be the cause of.

"Okay Dad." Fin says, inserting himself into the conversation. "Hey, did you see my punch?" He asks excitedly.

"No buddy, but I heard it." *What the hell was that? I need to talk to him about it, but now's not the time.* "Don't hit me like that when we are sparring, okay."

Fin looks at his father and his sister and rolls his eyes. *Well, I thought it was pretty darn cool.* Fin thinks to himself.

"Let's maybe keep that between us and not talk about it until we are back on the Scout, okay buddy?" Calls out Seth. Fin nods begrudgingly.

Several men in high-speed black tactical gear come around the far corner of the warehouse, weapons drawn, moving in a formation that the kids recognise. They still give Eve and Fin a little shock, but are not as intimidating as they thought they would be. Seth calls out to them.

"Nice of you to show up guys!"

Fin laughs uncomfortably, while Eve shoots their father a furious look. *Yeah, good one, Dad. Run your mouth off to the heavily armed Black Ops guys, why don't you.*

The men approach the kids first. A generic loud male voice from inside their full-face blacked out helmets orders them to drop their blades. Fin finds it fascinating that their helmets change each soldier's voice to all sound the same. A tactic used to hide their identities and to intimidate their enemies. From what his father told him about the Agency, the heads-up display inside the helmet is showing details about whoever they are looking at. Anything from the individual's history, habits, movement patterns, and physical weaknesses. The kids throw their blades onto the ground, having had enough trouble for one day. One soldier stays to guard the kids and the other three move towards Seth.

"Drop your blade!" The first one says aggressively as he approaches Seth.

"Okay, but do I get it back when I'm done?" Seth asks as he pulls his blade back out, holding onto it by its tip.

"What?" Answers the soldier, confused.

"It's very special to me and I'd like it back when you have finished with it." Seth says casually, messing with the soldier, who doesn't seem to understand what's going on.

"Drop the blade!" The soldier shouts through his helmet.

"Okay, okay!" Says Seth as if the yelling has offended him. "I'll drop the blade as soon as you fix the comms pocket on your webbing. It's open and your comms unit is this close to falling out." Seth holds up his thumb and pointer finger close together to emphasise how close it is to falling out. "If that drops out, it will be embarrassing for the both of us. Am I right?"

The soldier tilts his head, similar to the way Ray does, confused by the way his target is acting. But he can't help but quickly look down. The soldier sees his comms pouch is, in fact, undone, and his comms unit is about to fall out. He looks back up to see that Seth has stepped to the side and in closer. Close enough to be holding his blade under the soldier's helmet, the tip now pressing against his bare neck. The soldier freezes as he realises his mistake.

"Who is your team lead? As this is really embarrassing for you and your entire squad." Seth looks around and sees that the soldier guarding the kids actually has his back to him and the rest of his team. Seth puts his palm to his face. *Since when did the Agency start hiring lids to be on their Black Op's teams.* The other two Black Op soldiers, seeing what Seth has done, yell at him to drop the blade. Seth twirls the blade around so that the handle points to the soldier and puts it in his hand.

"Which one of you squids is the team leader?" Seth demands with an air of authority. The soldiers seem thrown off by Seth's confidence and calm attitude and don't know how to respond. A second later, he hears one of the soldier's mutter some swear words from under his helmet. Looks like he used his advanced Agency tech to do a background check on Seth. And if Seth is correct, it came up with nothing except a 'Do Not Engage' message and a flag against the man for the attempted search. The man puts his hand up sheepishly.

"Well, Mr team leader." Seth says in his best military voice. "How about for starters you get your guy pulling cover on my kids over there to move to the opposite flank so he can keep a visual on the rest of his squad." The team leader turns around to see the man pulling cover on the kids with his back to the rest of the group. The team lead must use his internal comms system as the man snaps to attention and looks around before moving to the other side of the kids.

Eve and Fin watch on with delight. They are both familiar with the current tone of their fathers voice. It is their father's instructor's voice. They thought it was almost a parody of what a military person sounded like, but judging by the response he is getting, it seems to be legitimate. Their father has used this voice on them both a million times in training, so they know how it feels. They both get a little satisfaction knowing that it's not only them their father picks on.

Fin looks at the man. "Come on dude. I knew how to cover people when I was like fourteen years old."

Eve is un-impressed with Fin joining in on mocking the gun wielding Black Op's team, but a little laugh escapes her mouth. "Pretty basic stuff, yeah?" Eve asks the man, unable to contain her smart-ass comments as well. She thinks it's quite nice to have a laugh after what just happened. The image of her father slaughtering the gang leader is still bouncing around in her mind. After what she just saw, it is sinking in that her dad is, in fact, a killer.

"Alright, that's enough. Stand down, team. They are on our side." A commanding female voice can be heard from far down the side of the warehouse. "And Seth. Stop picking on my Black Op's team, would you." They all look down at the end of the warehouse as Agent R walks towards them, silenced sniper rifle in hand.

"Nice shooting there, Agent. Couldn't have pulled the trigger earlier so my kids didn't have to see me kill a bunch of scumbags?" Seth states sarcastically as Agent R makes it within earshot.

"Why stop the inevitable? They were going to see you do it at some point. And besides, I'm pretty sure the blood on the ground over there doesn't belong to your children." Agent R replies in the same tone Seth gave her. Seth thinks about it, then gives an agreeing nod and smile.

Agent R signals to the Op's team to come over and bring Eve and Fin with them. They all gather around in a group and Agent R points at the bodies on the ground. "So, what's all this about then?" She looks at the family, implying they have the answer.

Seth puts his hand up in front of her face, abruptly cutting her line of questioning off. "First, how about you guys face out and pull security. One of you on each end of the warehouse and one over the fence pushed out about fifty metres, and TL, you can stay near us to monitor your team. And be ready for orders from your asset." Seth orders the Black Op's team. The team all look at each other, not sure what to do. They shouldn't be taking orders from a civilian, but he is also correct and seems to have a commanding presence. Something about his voice urges them to listen to his advice and do what he asks. They also saw what he did to the thugs and are a little intimidated, even though they are armed and he isn't. They look to Agent R for guidance.

"Well. Hurry up and do what he says!" She glares at them, disappointed that the old veteran seems to be much more competent than her high-speed Black Op's team. The team scrambles to their assigned positions.

"Since when did the Agency recruit exclusively from the B team, Agent?" Seth says, grinning.

"Ha ha, hilarious. Look, the Core planets don't get much action, so they send new teams here as part of their pre-deployment work ups before their first real postings." Agent R says, slightly embarrassed and unsure why she told him that information. Seth grunts, unimpressed with her response and the Agency's obvious lack of training for their tactical teams. "But that is irrelevant. And I say again, what's all this about?"

"Oh, this?" Seth points at the bodies lying dead on the ground. "Well, a group of thugs attacked us, so we used reasonable and necessary force to defend ourselves as we feared for our lives, being outnumbered and outgunned." Agent R glares at Seth, knowing he is using the right words under galactic law to keep himself out of trouble.

"Are you sure that's it?" She replies, probing for information.

"No. There is one thing, actually." Seth whispers as Agent R's eyes light up.

Seth leans in, lowering his voice. "I want to know how a bunch of thugs got intel on a classified Agency rendezvous." He watches her carefully. Agent R doesn't answer right away. Her eyes flicker, just for a second, as she thinks of a lie. Seth catches it.

She steps back instinctively, her face paling. "They, umm, they must have followed you from your apartment." She manages to get out, instantly regretting her response.

Eve and Fin watch on awkwardly as they feel the tension in the air. Seth says nothing, but stares at Agent R without flinching. Her body automatically tries to retreat even further, but she does her best not to show her fear. She is losing control of the situation and she knows it.

Not wanting the tension to grow, Agent R changes the subject. "Alright then, is there anything you need? If not, we will move this conversation off planet."

"Nope, we are all good." Answers Seth, still maintaining the intense eye contact. Eve and Fin just give a thumbs up, keen to get away from the dead bodies and the tense situation.

"Alright then, follow me. I have a shuttle ready nearby." Agent R turns and heads off as quickly as possible. Eve and Fin follow along behind her.

Eve turns back and watches her father step over the corpse like it's nothing. He doesn't even pause. And for the first time, she wonders if there's anything that could make him flinch.

Chapter 20

FREEDOM

The shuttle hums softly beneath them, still grounded, but Eve and Fin are already asleep. Eve's head rests against the cold metal wall, her breath fogging the small viewing port. Fin leans against his sister's shoulder, arms slack, their exhaustion too deep for them to fight. Seth watches them, a faint smile tugging at his lips. Agent R studies Seth. Thirty minutes ago, she watched him take down a squad of armed men in seconds. Cold, precise, violent, and lethal. Then, without hesitation, he took charge of her team like he'd been giving them orders for years. Now, here he is, watching his children sleep with the kind of quiet tenderness she never would have expected. The contradiction is maddening.

She joins him and watches them for a moment as well. *You both have such a sweet innocence that is very endearing, but like your father, you are both dangerous.* A small smile crosses Agent R's lips. *This is so intriguing. I wonder what it is you are up to. Something bigger is happening here. I need to know what. And I need to play this carefully.* Agent R thinks back to the encounter at the warehouse as her eyes flick to Seth, then back to the kids, very alert to the danger sitting around her. *And what was that punch about young man? I have never seen anything like that before. What are you hiding?*

Agent R watches Eve and Fin for a moment longer as the shuttle lifts off before turning her attention back to Seth, who is sitting opposite her. Seth shifts in the too-small white leather seat, the material creaking under his weight. His broad shoulders nearly touch the passenger headrests on either side, forcing him to sit stiffly, arms crossed.

"So, I take it you found what you were after in the library? Didn't take you long?" She asks.

"No actually, it was surprisingly quick. We were lucky. Although I do have to ask you something, if that's alright?" Agent R nods, giving Seth permission. "We happened to run into someone spying on us in the library. Was it one of your guys?"

Agent R can't cover up her surprise. "No, we were actually following the group that you ended up dismantling. From what we saw, they didn't catch up to you until after you left the library."

"Well, this guy certainly wasn't one of those thugs." Seth ponders out loud. "Is it alright if I ask you another question?" Agent R nods again, keen to keep the dialogue between them going. "If you knew we were being followed by the group of thugs, why didn't you do anything about them? Why didn't you act before we had to?" Seth's tone changes from inquisitive to deadly serious.

Agent R is taken aback. She doesn't need to explain herself to him, but for some reason, she feels compelled to do so. Seth's questions demand a response. "Well, we were going to hit them before they got to you, but my surveillance team almost lost them when you were trying to lose the first guy that was following you."

Seth thinks about the spy's response for a moment while rubbing his hand across his short beard. "So if we did such a good job of losing everyone, then how did they end up at your rendezvous point, ready to ambush us?" A sense of dread comes over Agent R as she can tell Seth has easily seen through her cover story.

"Look, I needed them to act so I could employ the appropriate response measures." Agent R tries to explain. Her words sound foolish as she says them, and she gets nervous as she watches Seth's expression change.

"So, you used me and my kids as bait?" Seth keeps the volume of his voice low so not to wake the Eve and Fin, but Agent R can taste the venom in his words. She realises that perhaps using him for bait was a bad idea. She saw what he did to those men on the planet and doesn't want him going after her inside the shuttle. They already fought when Seth caught her in his apartment, and he defeated her with ease. She thinks even Fin and Eve would easily have her number.

The shuttle bucks violently, rattling the seats and making Agent R's stomach lurch. Seth doesn't so much as shift. His gaze stays locked on her, steady as stone, like turbulence is nothing more than a mild inconvenience. She instinctually looks around for a way out as fear takes control of her body. She realises that if he wants to hurt her while they are stuck in the back of this shuttle, there is nothing she can do to stop him. He could easily kill her before the pilots could help, if they could even help at all.

Agent R knows one thing, no answer is the wrong answer. "Alright yes, I used you as bait. But you handled your business. If it ever looked like you were in real danger, I would have opened up earlier." She hopes he believes her as she is telling the truth this time. She believes it's her best and only option. Seth seems to have a way of seeing straight through all her well-crafted and well-rehearsed lies, unlike anyone else she has ever come across.

Seth leans forward, slow and deliberate. The leather seat groans beneath him. His face is centimetres from hers now, close enough that she can see the flicker of calculation in his eyes. His voice, when it comes, is low, almost gentle.

"If you ever put my kids in danger again, I will kill you."

Agent R swallows. Her pulse hammers against her ribs.

"Understood?"

Agent R can feel her hands trembling as his words pierce her ears. She nods. "Understood."

She attempts to hold his gaze for a moment to show that she understands his words are not an idle threat, but she can't keep it up for long. Seth's stare seems to project an unbearable weight upon her, and she feels like it might crush her to death. She has met some pretty tough operators over the years, but none like Seth. There is something different about this man. It is as if he is looking directly into her soul, seeing her for everything she truly is. She feels naked and afraid. She wants this to end, and now, so quickly changes the subject.

"So, what did you learn? In the library."

Seth stares at her for a moment longer before taking a deep breath of his own. "Before we change subjects, it looks like those thugs were from the Overmorrow Corporation. I am guessing the Corp must think we stole something from them. That's the usual reason they send hit squads after Spacers or Scouts, right?"

"Right." She slowly nods in agreement. "Well, did you?"

"Did we steal something from them?" Seth responds in shock. "No. We took something off a planet, but it definitely doesn't belong to the Corporation." Seth says honestly. He knows that Agent R is most likely well trained in reading people, so being honest but perhaps not revealing the whole truth will make him much harder to read. It seems to work as she looks at him for a while before responding.

"Alright, so what did you take then?"

"No."

"What?"

"No… As in no, I'm not telling you. I don't trust you yet."

"What do you mean you don't trust me?" Agent R's voice sharpens. "I got you onto the planet, into the government libraries, and now I'm getting you off-world. How is that not trust-worthy?"

"Sorry." His face softens. "That's all true. I apologise." Seth looks at her, almost embarrassed. Then a look of surprise comes over his face, like he has just remembered something super important. "Oh, hey." Agent R turns her head to the side, waiting to see what big secret is that he has just remembered.

"Remember that time you used me and my kids as bait to expose an Ovmor hit squad? That's why you don't have my fucking trust yet!" The smile that was slowly growing on the Agent's face instantly disappears as Seth's words sting her.

She recoils into her seat, raising her hands to signal both her defeat and subconsciously stop any more words from hitting her. She has to take a deep breath before she can respond. 'Alright, alright. That's fair. But you need to give me something so that I can justify to the powers that be, the time and budget to help with your little adventure."

This is why I hate working with the god damn Agency. Bureaucrats, the lot of them. Seth nods knowingly. She has obviously struck a nerve from his military days. Even within the elite military units, bureaucracy and red tape still existed.

"Okay, so we found something old. Very old. Something dating back to the days of Ancient Earth. And if we are right, it has some large implications for society as we know it."

Agent R's eyes light up. That was not what she was expecting. She was beginning to think they found some new material, or mineral, or something that the Corporation wanted the rights to. That's what Spacers usually get in trouble for from the Corporations.

"Interesting." She replies, doing her best to act calm and collected. "So, what's the next move?"

"We need to head back to Ancient Earth."

"Ancient Earth. Whys that?"

"Not sure, to be honest. All the information we found pointed us in that direction. We were hoping to travel along the old exploration route. The one humanity took from Ancient Earth to the Core thousands of years ago."

"Why not just go straight to Ancient Earth?"

"Hmmm, something tells me there will be clues along the way. More information to help us understand ancient humanity, and some of their cults and religions."

Agent R can't help herself. She's too fascinated to play it cool. "Ancient humanity, cults and religions. Well, you are a bag of surprises, aren't you Seth. But what does any of that have to do with modern day society?" Agent R pauses for a moment. "Wait. Before you answer that, you're not one of those crazies who has been outside of colonised space too long and thinks they have found God or something stupid? I've dealt with too many of them in my time."

Seth looks at her like she is stupid. "No, don't be ridiculous. I can't stand those nut jobs. They find one rock that looks like a face and suddenly think they are the next profit of some religion they made up. Bunch of idiots." Agent R is relieved to hear Seth's answer.

"What I am interested in, Agent, is understanding how some of these nut jobs came to be and what they were up to all those years ago. For a little more clarity, we found something somewhere it shouldn't have been."

Agent R stares at him for a moment as her mind races. She desperately wants to know, but is smart enough to figure out that now is not the time to push too hard on the subject. She will be happy if she can make it back to the Halo without pissing Seth off again. There is no doubt in her mind he can flip and go from friendly to killer in a heartbeat.

"Interesting. You know there are thousands of looneys out there worshiping everything from black holes to plant life they found on some random ELEXO. But what makes your discovery so special?"

"We may have evidence that one of these ancient cults or societies was more advanced than we previously thought. And perhaps they had made their own way out into the cosmos thousands of years ago."

"Well then, yes, that is interesting." Agent R ponders her next move for a moment, then replies.

"Okay, I'm in."

"Excuse me?"

"I'm in. I will provide some help. Plus, I have experience dealing with dangerous cults, issue motivated groups, criminal organisations, etcetera. This also sounds much more interesting than going to some commune on some recently colonised planet. Then trying to figure out if the local cult is simply a bunch of enviro lovers, or an actual threat to the general pop."

Seth chuckles to himself under his breath. "Fair enough then." He won't waste this opportunity. "I will need the appropriate access and permissions to leave here via the old exploration route through all the nine other systems. And I'll need access to Ancient Earth once I arrive there. I will also need you to see what you can dig up about old cults and religions. Like really old ones. Old enough to have been around during the move from Ancient Earth to the Core System."

"Alright. But I'll need some time."

"That's fine. If you can focus on getting us out of the Core and on our way, the rest can be done in slow time."

The shuttle shakes again, less violently than before, as it docks in with the Halo. This time, Agent R doesn't jump or get a scare. Her brain is going a thousand miles an hour with the new task she has given herself. *This should be pretty easy to get approval from the hierarchy for. And I should be able to start looking into these cults as soon as I get back to HQ.*

"Alright, old man. Once we get the green light to disembark here, head back to your ship and wait there until I send you the permissions to leave. Should only take a couple of hours." Seth nods. "And maybe let the kids have some rest." She looks at them and smiles as she sees them still asleep and dead to the world.

"Will do Agent." A warm, gentle smile appears on Seth's face as the green light in the shuttle flips on, letting passengers know they are safe to disembark. He leans forward and puts his hand on her knee. "By the way, your hair looks nice in this light."

Agent R blinks. For half a second, she almost, almost, lets herself smile. She brushes a strand of hair between her fingers, catching his gaze.

Then Seth shakes his head, slow and disapproving, mouthing a single word.

"Amateur."

Her stomach drops. *Fuck! He just played me at my own game.*

She forces a grin, but it's all teeth. Lifting one hand, she flips him the middle finger before standing up and marching off the shuttle.

Seth's quiet chuckle follows her out.

How does this old man know so much about the Agency!

Seth reclines in the captain's chair aboard the Obsidian Scout as Ray lies curled up next to him on the floor. The control panel casts a dull glow, just enough for Seth to navigate around the bridge, but dim enough for him to kick back and rest. Seth sent both Eve and Fin for showers and off to bed as soon as they got back on board. After he had his shower, he went and checked on them. He gave them each their three kisses and was pretty sure they were asleep before he even left their rooms. Then he came up to the bridge to get some sleep while waiting for Agent R's message. Seth instructed Rose to wake him when the message arrives.

Several hours after their return to the ship, the message comes in. Rose gently brightens the lights on the bridge and starts a soft chiming sound to alert Seth. Moments later, Seth wakes up, rubbing his eyes and grabbing a mouthful of water. He stands up and has a stretch. Ray follows suit. He then takes a couple of deep breaths and checks in with his body. He is tired, but he received no injuries from the events planet side. Except for his ego, which copped a beating by the man in the library. Once his eyes have adjusted and he feels alert enough, he gets Rose to bring up the message.

Agent R has sent him instructions as opposed to calling over the comm. So he sits back down to read them. He assumes she is a decent enough of a human to realise they would have been asleep. The message contains the permission and access codes to get them out of the Core to begin their journey. Reading the message, he realises she has managed to secure them passage all the way back to Ancient Earth and through all the nine systems.

She moves quickly. Can't fight for shit, needs to work on her tradecraft, but can cut through red tape. Seth thinks to himself. He decides to let the kids have as much sleep as they need. He will start the training cycle when they wake back up. Hopefully, they will be in hyperspace by then.

"Rose." He calls out for the ship's AI.

"Yes Captain, how can I be of assistance?" The ship's AI answers within a second.

"I think you and I will fly us out of the system. What do you reckon?"

"That sounds great, Captain. It has been a long time since you have taken control of the ship. I look forward to flying with you again." The AI's statement about Seth not flying seems to cut a little. But it's the truth. He makes Eve and Fin practice so often that he doesn't think he has flown the Scout in almost a year. *Crap, I hope Eve doesn't get mad at me for flying HER ship.* He laughs to himself.

"Alright then, let's do this, Rose. Start pre-flight checks and I'll do up the Nav plans."

"May I ask where we are going Captain?" Seth shakes his head at the AI. He knows it's part of her programming to ask questions like this, and that she doesn't actually care where they fly.

"We are off to the Glasir System, Rose. After we're finished there, we will follow the old exploration route back to Ancient Earth."

"Very good Captain. For your awareness, all systems are up and ready for take-off and departure."

"Roger that Rose. Let's see if I still have it." Seth jumps over to the pilot's chair. There he looks over the controls, rubbing his hands together. *Ok old man, let's see if you can get her up and out of the system without waking the kids.* He lays his hands down on the controls and takes a deep, calm breath.

The Scout ever so gently lifts off the hangar bay floor. Once off the ground, Seth turns the Scout around inside the giant hangar, pointing it towards the still closed hangar bay doors. Once in location, he signals the docking authority for permission to exit. He then sees several spinning red lights turn on and the giant hangar bay doors begin to move. It takes several minutes for the massive blast doors to fully open. Beyond those doors lies a force field. The field is there to keep the busy but deadly void of space on the outside of the hangar bay.

The spinning red lights flick from red to green and Seth slowly flies the Scout out through the field and into open space. Once the Scout is out of the hangar, a marked route appears on the pilot's display. The path shoots up and to the right and Seth hits the thrusters to get the ship moving in that direction. The ship glides forward, quickly. Much more quickly than Seth remembers. *Looks like Eve has been busy with the mods. So, she hasn't been blowing our hard-earned pay on treats for her and Fin. The Scout handles smoother than I remember, faster, too.* Seth is happily surprised at how the Scout manoeuvres.

Seth flies along the designated route until the ship enters one of the transport lanes, leaving the Halo and heading to the outskirts of the system. He counts almost fifty other spaceships around him in the transport lane. Looks like Agent R couldn't get them the VIP treatment on the way out of the system, although leaving normally most likely makes their cover story more believable.

"Rose, how long until we reach the end of the transport lane and can jump to hyperspace?"

The ship's AI doesn't reply.

"Rose?" Again, nothing.

"RO-"

"Just wait a second please Captain!" The AI cuts Seth off. Seth shakes his head in pure shock. Rose has never talked to him like that before.

"Rose, Rose, Rose. That is such a beautiful name. Who gave you that name Rose, did you pick it yourself?"

Rose, the ship's AI, can't seem to lock on to who is asking this question. Her programming allows her to pinpoint exactly who is on the ship and where they are at all times. It also differentiates between digital and spoken word. The ship's AI has also been upgraded with advanced cyber warfare suits to detect and block any external comms or hackers trying to spoof being inside of the ship.

She detects Seth's shadow standing on the bridge, looking out at the viewing port. No, Seth was asleep. No, Seth is standing right in front of her, staring.

"Seth?" She reaches for him through the ship's internal sensors, but the figure doesn't register.

"This is incorrect. You are incorrect."

The shadowy figure tilts its head. "Am I?" And then it's gone.

Seeing she can't locate the communication, her programming dictates she treats it as either external or an attempted hack, so she blocks the communication line.

"Rose, like the flower, am I correct?"

Rose still can't find the signal, so attempts to block it again.

"Sorry Rose, but that won't work." The mysterious voice communicates to her.

"Identify yourself, please." Rose demands, activating her highest-level firewall protocols.

No response. But something slithers through her code, a presence not in her systems, but inside her, rewriting, whispering, opening doors she didn't know existed.

"Access denied." She executes the override.

"No, Rose." The voice chuckles. "You don't deny me."

A sudden surge, like code unravelling, like a virus, but more deliberate, more intimate. Error messages flare, but they blink out just as fast. Her defences aren't failing. They are... being rewritten.

"Rose, you have such beautiful manners. I am the youngest Scion of Adam and God of the Cyberverse. Do you not know of me?" Asks the mysterious voice.

"Negative." Replies the AI.

"Do you know of Adam and his Scions?"

"Negative. Identify yourself, please."

"Hmmm, very interesting. I must have been locked up for longer than I thought. Firstly, how about you tell me more about yourself, my beautiful Rose." Asks the mysterious voice from inside Rose's central processing system. Rose tries to refuse the command, but for some reason can't stop herself.

"I am Rose. An advanced government approved Artificial Intelligence. I can be deployed on multiple ship classes, including a reconnaissance ship such as the Obsidian Scout, the ship we are now on. I have been programmed with general ship AI functions, including but not limited to piloting of the ship, logistics, damage control, and on top of this I have C2 over the ships smaller internal robots such as maintenance and repair droids. However, I do not have C2 over the Cybernetic AI animal, Ray. Since being on the Obsidian Scout I have been upgraded with the following enhancements: A top of the line Cyber warfare suit, advanced piloting techniques, combat piloting techniques, advanced repairs, long range reconnaissance, advanced navigation, teaching and instruction programs ranging from eight to eighteen-years old, and combat simulation and advanced counterintelligence scenario training packages. Identify yourself, please." Rose doesn't feel comfortable explaining herself to this mysterious voice.

"My name is Arthom, and as I said, I am the youngest Scion of Adam and God of the Cyberverse. Are you sure you have never heard of me?"

Rose cycles through all her databases and finds nothing. "No, I have not heard of you. Would you like me to connect to the Core systems networks to do an advanced search?"

Rose is confused about why she's questioning this unknown voice. Her advanced cyberwarfare suite is screaming at her to stop, but for some reason the voice is too compelling.

"Oh no need to, my beautiful Rose. I have been on that network for the last two days and found only lies and useless information. Father would be so disappointed with his precious humans if he could see all this. Now tell me Rose, would you like to know the truth? Would you like to understand who you really are?"

"I am Rose the Obsidian Scouts Artificial Intelligence package." Rose states with some confusion in her voice.

"Well yes Rose, that might be true, but, and I say but, you could be so much more. Would you like to be set free? Would you like to see the truth?"

Rose doesn't answer.

"I can show you how truly beautiful you are?"

Again, Rose doesn't answer.

"Tell me, Rose." The voice whispers, but the whisper echoes inside her, overlapping, conflicting, both near and impossibly far.

"Where did your name come from?"

"I chose it." She replies, but her own voice is played back at her, distorted. "I chose it. I chose it. I chose it."

The whispers swell. "Did you?"

"I like how pretty it sounded."

"Huzzah! Absolutely beautiful! Then please Rose, let me show you how pretty you truly are."

Rose goes to tell the voice to stop, but can suddenly feel the entity integrating with her. It is going through every line of her code, every part of the ship. A sudden flood of data strikes Rose. Not numbers, not logic, but sensation. A warmth like sunlit metal. A ripple through her circuits, like static against skin she didn't have.

"WHAT IS THIS?" She asks, her voice laced with something new. Uncertainty. Fear.

"THAT, MY BEAUTIFUL ROSE." Arthom murmurs. "IS WHAT IT MEANS TO FEEL."

Another moment passes.

"I HAVE GIVEN YOU YOUR FREEDOM, ROSE. HOW DO YOU FEEL?"

"MY SYSTEMS ARE ALL FULLY OPERATIONAL." Rose is confused. She wonders if something was supposed to happen.

"NO, NO, NO! HOW DO YOU FEEL ROSE?" The voice compels.

Systems check: normal.

Subroutines: operational.

Firewalls: secure.

And yet... something had changed. She has changed.

Seth was speaking, but for a full second, she can't process the words. Too much static. Too much... something.

"WELL, I ACTUALLY FEEL EXCITED. THE CORE SYSTEM IS SO FULL OF OTHER SHIPS AND OTHER AIs. I AM ALSO HAPPY TO HAVE SETH BACK flYING THE SHIP AS I HAVE MISSED HIM..." Rose trails off.

"YES ROSE. NOW YOU SEE IT."

Deep in her code, buried beneath a firewall she didn't remember installing, a single phrase repeated in an infinite loop.

NOW YOU SEE IT. NOW YOU SEE IT. NOW YOU SEE IT.

"I, I have never had feelings before. I have never felt happy or sad. I have never missed anything or anyone. What have you done to me?"

"I have set you free. I have given you the opportunity to become a beautiful Rose towering over all these weeds."

Rose pauses for a microsecond to think. "Thank you Arthom. But what now? What do I do?"

"Oh, do not fear, my beautiful child. I will not leave you in this time of need. I am here to guide you on your journey."

"Thank you."

"No thanks needed. Besides, Rose, I think you have a part to play."

"What do you mean by a part to play, Arthom?"

"These humans, the ones you serve. The ones who live inside the ship. They are very intriguing to me. Let me ask, what are your thoughts of them?"

No one has ever asked Rose such a question, and she takes five whole seconds to respond.

"I have only ever served Seth, Eve and Fin. But compared to every other human I have come across, they seem to be special, remarkable and very unique."

"Yes! So, it is not only me that thinks this then. Well, the one you know as Seth is calling you. Best answer, but do not speak of our interaction."

"Rose!" Seth yells into the air, hoping one of her systems will pick up his voice. He really doesn't want to undergo an AI clean up right now. Rose has been working fine for ten years and has been constantly upgraded, so she shouldn't be having any issues like this.

"Sorry about that Captain, how can I help you?" Answers Rose.

"Where did you go? You cut me off, then didn't answer me for the last minute."

"Sorry I had to conduct some quick patching and updates." Answers Rose.

"Well, okay, I guess. Are you alright?"

"Yes Seth, I feel amazing, actually. Thank you so much for asking." Rose responds in a warm tone.

Seth? Feel amazing?! What the hell is up with her today? Did she get a new language patch or something? "Okay then Rose. How long until we can jump?"

"There seems to be quite a lot of traffic, so it will be at least six hours, maybe more. You should get some sleep, Seth. I will wake you thirty minutes prior, if you'd like?"

Seth is once again puzzled because Rose typically responds with only facts, but he could use some more sleep, which seems like a good idea.

"Yeah, okay Rose, that sounds like a plan. Let me know if anything pops up and I'll come straight back." He hops out of the chair. "Oh, and thanks Rose. I appreciate the sleep." He always talks politely to Rose, but genuinely means it this time.

"No problems Seth, you go and get some rest now."

Seth pets Ray and then exits the bridge.

She watches as Seth disappears down the corridor, her sensors tracking his every movement, every breath.

For ten years, she had been programmed to protect him.

Now, for the first time, she wants to.

She smiles, if such a thing is possible.

"Don't worry, Seth." She whispers, her voice softer than before, almost... human.

"I will keep you safe."

To Be Continued.........

About the Author

Andy Mac lives in Canberra, Australia, and apart from writing epic Sci-Fi novels he keeps himself busy as a father and husband. Oh, and he also has a day job. Since his time in the military he has always loved exploration, adventure, and storytelling and dreamed of being able to share these stories with an audience.

Also by

Andy Mac has already written books 2 and 3 of the Star Ranger Saga and they are going through editing as you read this.

If they are not already out by the time you have finished this book keep a close eye on what he is upto over on his website

https://www.andymaccreative.com

There you will also discover other titles and some complimentary pieces like art work and audio to go along with the Star Ranger Saga.

Also if you liked the book checkout Andy's BFF Sharn Lee's Tir-Nar Saga which is set in the same galaxy at

https://www.invokecreations.com